THE DEVILS PUNCHBOWL

THE DEVILS PUNCHBOWL

M. Dalbec Mills

Copyright © 2001 by M. Dalbec Mills.

Library of Congress Number:		2001116316
ISBN #:	Hardcover	0-7388-6216-9
	Softcover	0-7388-6217-7

All rights reserved. No part of this book may be reproduced or transmitted in any form or by any means, electronic or mechanical, including photocopying, recording, or by any information storage and retrieval system, without permission in writing from the copyright owner.

This is a work of fiction. Names, characters, places and incidents either are the product of the author's imagination or are used fictitiously, and any resemblance to any actual persons, living or dead, events, or locales is entirely coincidental.

This book was printed in the United States of America.

To order additional copies of this book, contact:
Xlibris Corporation
1-888-7-XLIBRIS
www.Xlibris.com
Orders@Xlibris.com

4998-MILL

DEDICATED IN LOVING MEMORY

TO MY PARENTS

ERVILLE & LILLIAN DALBEC

AND TO MY CHILDREN

ROBERT, MICHELLE, JENNIFER,

AND BEAU JAMES,

TO REMIND THEM, THAT

DREAMS DO COME TRUE,

IF ONLY, YOU KEEP YOUR VISION ALIVE,

BELIEVE IN YOURSELF,

AND

ABOVE ALL ELSE, TRUST IN GOD

"REMEMBER TO BE gentle with yourself and others. We are all children of chance, and none can say why some fields will blossom while other's lay brown beneath the August sun. Care for those around you. Look past your differences. Their dreams are no less than yours, their choices in life no more easily made. And give. Give in any way you can, of whatever you possess. To give is to love. To withhold is to wither. Care less for your harvest than for how it is shared, and your life will have meaning and your heart will have peace."

Excerpt from "Letters to My Son"
By Kent Nerburn
Published by New World Libraries
Novato, California

ACKNOWLEDGMENTS

I THANK WHOLEHEARTEDLY, the staff at the Crescent City Library for putting up with my demands in person, as well as on the telephone. Their help was always much appreciated. Also, many, many thanks to Lois, for all her encouragements and prodding to complete the story, Ted, for his expert scientific knowledge, and Gerry and Doris for their expertise in the use of my computer program. And, especially to my husband, Carson, for his support, his patience in listening and for his advice. I don't think I could have completed it without all of you.

CHAPTER 1

LUKE STOOD AGAINST the wall listening to the clatter of dishes and utensils. A male voice in the banquet room ballooned, the strident intensity of his laughter a harsh reality in the narrow hall. The sound, louder than the noisy blend of subdued talking, became muted and then riotously broke out again. Someone coughed, the dry sound hanging in the air abrasive against the clear resonance of Debbie's voice. Enunciating each word distinctly and in a concise manner, her voice rose to emphasize something she was trying to make clear to the club members.

They've tuned her out, Luke thought, listening to the whispering murmur-like clamor that filtered through the door. She must be feeling really bad and just about now her eyes would be snapping blue fire. Debbie had proved to be a worthy opponent in debate this year and what a voice, deep, husky and sexy enough to make any guy break out in wild daydreams about her.

Luke's eyes darkened and, raising his hand, he tapped his lips with his fingers. Brow wrinkling in a reflective scowl, his thoughts wandered to the speech contest. This year the topic for the contest was, "Changing our Constitution" a subject only a handful of Americans was passionate about. Somehow, the American people had to become aware of their government's slow encroachment on their freedoms. Citizens here tended to take complacency to a new level. They had to be convinced of the importance of taking an active role in their government and write their congressmen voicing their opinions and convictions.

Luke clasped his hands together and tried to calm himself. Getting up before an audience and giving a speech wasn't that hard, but no matter how much he tried, he couldn't eat. He hyped himself up into a mess of nerves and his stomach reacted by turning somersaults and gigantic flip-flops. The result of all this turmoil was nausea. Breathing in a deep gulp of air to ease his inner fears, he pressed his shoulder against the wall and tried to attain some degree of self control. He tried to remember the basic rules. Think of something pleasant, don't have negative thoughts.

Think positively!

Don't panic!

Laughing silently at himself, he raised his hand and rubbed his face. Concentrate, he thought, mentally badgering himself. Think about something else.

Closing his eyes, his thoughts drifted to the Devils Punchbowl. Piece by piece in a puzzle pattern, he formed a picture of the lake, until he could see it fully like a photograph. Abruptly, in vivid color, the light at the end of the tunnel appeared on the surface of his mind and, the image made his stomach churn.

Raising his hand, he covered his eyes and concentrated walking the trail by the lake. Deep blue like a sapphire, the water shimmered behind his eyelids. Suddenly, he found himself belly-down with Pepper, Rob and Benny staring at the light. Pushing against each other for better positions, they crowded together, and through the ragged edges of the opening, watched the light.

The tunnel was odd. A mystery. Its walls resembled black-marble and for almost fifty feet it sloped downward at a steep angle. The light from their flashlights, shifting into small swirling circles, moved endlessly in the polished shine of the mirror-like walls. In the tunnel's bottom, through a small opening in a pile of rock and debris, a pencil-sized stream of light pierced the darkness with the intensity of a laser beam. The light was brighter than their flashlights and didn't flicker or move.

Luke had been adamant. He wanted to explore further. Grasping his flashlight, he extended his arms over his head and, pushing with his feet, slid into the tunnel on his belly. It was a tight fit. The tunnel closed around him and then anxiously, feeling claustrophobic, he watched the passing reflection of his flashlight's beam of light in the mirror-like walls. Near the tunnel's end, the pinpoint of light beckoned like a star in a dark night. Grunting and sweating, Luke forced himself over small scattered rocks and working his hand through the small opening made it larger. Rocks and dirt fell outward dropping from his sight into a larger area. The tiny arc of luminance grew as he enlarged the hole.

Unable to curb his excitement, he grabbed the edges of the tunnel and, with both hands, pulled and pushed his head through the opening. Gasping, he sucked in his breath and held it. The cavern was enormous and the light awesome. Brilliant. It seemed to come from the ceiling and was brighter at the north end of the immense cavern. Pulling his body clear from the tunnel, he shoved the larger rocks away from its opening. Kneeling on the ground, he yelled urgently back up through the tunnel.

"C'mon, you have to see this. You won't believe it."

The swinging door from the banquet room swung inward, and a cloud of pungent cigarette smoke, mixed with greasy smells of frying food, garlic and spices drifted into the hallway. Rising in disruptive harmony, the indistinct modulation of voices broke into Luke's meditation and he became aware of his surroundings. Reluctantly, he let the image of the tunnel fade away.

"Next Saturday I'll be there, the Devils Punchbowl, I can hardly wait," he muttered. Lowering his hand from his eyes he covered his mouth and nose.

"Phe . . . ee . . . ew!"

The whispered word exploded from Pepper. "How can they stand it in there?" Disgust flashed across his impressive features.

"Puke! Yuck! That smell will rot your lungs out in thirty minutes."

Shifting in his chair, Pepper turned and looked toward the exit sign at the end of the hall. "I wonder if anyone would mind if we opened that door," he whispered. Pitching his voice low, he gave an exaggerated hoarse cough. Raising his hand, he held up his thumb and index finger with a smidgen of space between them. "Youst a wee bit," he added, clutching his throat.

"Ur . . . hak . . . "

Revolting noises erupted from deep in Pepper's throat. The gargling wet sounds, gagging in their clarity, bubbled through the air.

"I'm dyen here, man. As me wee Irish Granny would say, move quick, else you'll find yourself mired to your gunwales in mud." Rising from his chair, Pepper walked toward a door marked an emergency exit.

Luke pushed himself away from the wall and watched Pepper. "I don't think opening the door is a good idea. You should ask someone first before you open it. It might be one that opens for emergencies only. You know, the kind that sets off a blaring sound like a fire alarm."

Pepper hesitated. He wavered, indecisiveness flashing across his face. Frowning at Luke, he shrugged and sat on a folding chair. Sliding on the seat, he rounded his spine and, laying back, thrust his legs straight out in front of him. Pinching his nose closed with his fingers, his eyes danced and his bright humorous smile flashed in the shadowed hallway.

Luke quietly walked the length of the hall and, sitting in a chair next to Pepper, leaned back with a sigh. He started to laugh, the sound from deep within his chest gurgled in his throat. Covering his mouth with his hand, he muffled the noise as his shoulders started to shake. Bending forward in the chair, he rested his elbows on his knees and covered his face with his hands.

Pepper snorted, the sound wet and rude. Pulling his body upright, his chair protested in a singsong of creaks and sharp cracks. The shrill noises caused another bout of uninhibited shaking, the sounds of muffled laughter erupting through their hands in soft snorts and grunts. Their bodies shook uncontrollably.

Leaning forward over his knees, Pepper pressed his hands over his face. Casting a glance from the corners of their eyes at each other, their mouths opened and closed several times, twisting silently. They struggled for control. Yielding to nervous excitement, they helplessly broke out again in suppressed laughter, their bodies shaking in uncon-

THE DEVILS PUNCHBOWL

trollable jerks like Jell-O. Luke shook his head and quietly cleared his throat. He wiped his eyes with a large knuckled hand and tried to control the wild pendulum swing of his emotions. Stiffening his spine, he rose to his feet and, using a remarkable fortitude of inner strength, walked away.

Pepper watched Luke restlessly pace the length of the hall, assessing him with his artist's eye. He moved gracefully with his head held high, his footsteps a mere whisper against the cracked linoleum floor. His nose, short with a high bridge, was set above a wide mouth and a strong jaw ended in a determined stubborn chin. With high cheek bones broadening the triangular oval of his face, his profile resembled a statue of some ancient mythical God. Large blue eyes prone to laughter were set deeply in his strong-boned face.

"A for-real hombre," Pepper whispered.

Luke could be one stubborn ass, he thought, didn't suffer fools gladly and, was at times sharp in his criticisms. Sometimes his dry witticisms provoked such extreme annoyance in others, they got up and walked away. Pepper snorted again, an ugly sound in the quiet hallway. Rubbing his eyes, he concentrated on bringing Bella's image to the forefront of his mind. Now there was beauty and someday he would paint her, maybe nude. The thought pleased him and he smiled a devilish grin.

Luke covered his mouth and broke out again in convulsive nervous laughter. Shoulders shaking, he gulped the sound and stopped pacing. Sucking in a deep breath, he faced the wall. He hated to lose control and was disgusted that he had. I've got to get back on track, he thought. Fast!

"Okay. This isn't the way to begin," he mumbled.

"Get serious."

He stared at the wall and admonished himself for letting their laughter get out of hand. Glancing at Pepper, he grinned, his teeth, in the dimly lit hall, a flashing brightness for a brief moment.

In a graceful, hurried movement, Debbie pushed through the swinging door. Excitement danced across her face as she mouthed. "Ha, you're on next, Luke."

"Are they receptive or are they still sitting like automated humans staring off into space?" Pepper whispered. "I don't think they listened when I gave my speech." Walking toward her, he swung his arms and hunched his shoulders to relieve his tension.

"Nah.! Same old people," Debbie said, grinning at him. "Some of them didn't even have the grace to look in my direction or stop talking. They didn't really listen to the words I clearly enunciated through this big mouth I've got. I got no respect, because after all I'm just a kid, a girl-kid at that. I don't know nothin from nothin."

Giggling, she glanced at Luke. "And . . . my legs got a lot of attention from the old men. Some of them didn't look at my face at all, just my legs. A few, I could tell had lechery in their adulterous hearts. Poor old things."

Debbie laughed again, a subdued echo of her real laugh, her face glowing with suppressed humor. Deep dimples flashed around her mouth and pinpoints of light sparkled in her blue eyes. Turning toward the door, her hair moved in shimmering dark waves around her body. "SH. . . . HH. Listen! Mr. Stanfield is introducing Luke."

Pepper and Debbie quietly stepped toward the partially open door, and listened, to the cool cadence of Mr. Sanfield's voice. . . . "And . . . now our next contestant, a senior at Del Norte High, a student who has achieved the very best in scouting honors; is an Eagle Scout and has been awarded a Medal of Merit by the Boy Scouts of America National Court of Honor. Folks, please welcome, Luke Webster."

Luke turned and raising his hand in the air, displayed his large thumb. Moving it several times upward toward the ceiling, he grinned at Debbie and Pepper.

"Freaky," he mouthed silently.

"Luck, Luke, break a leg," Debbie whispered. Watching his hand as it disappeared from the edge of the door, she smiled at Pepper and, moving quietly, sat in one of the folding chairs against the wall.

Luke moved through narrow aisles created by club member's chairs and, smiling at Mr. Sanfield, whispered modestly. "Thanks for the praise, it wasn't necessary, but it does give my morale a boast." Mr.

THE DEVILS PUNCHBOWL

Sanfield clapped Luke on the shoulder and, quietly stepped away from the podium.

Glancing at the attending members of the club, Luke observed again how diversified the population of Crescent City seemed to be. A sprinkling of young, middle-aged and elderly men and women filled the banquet room.

Strangling on a barely suppressed bubble of laughter, he fought the urge to break out in a wild fit of giggling. Quietly moving the microphone to a different position, he stared at the top of the scarred podium.

Laying his notes out in chronological order, he concentrated on mastering the up and down seesaw of his emotions. Somewhere inside him there had to be an area of calm. He just had to find it. Focusing his eyes at a man sitting in the very back of the room, he started to speak. "Good evening, ladies and gentlemen. I'm glad to be here tonight and I thank each of you sincerely for giving me this opportunity. I especially want to welcome our two esteemed congressmen that represent our district." Pausing, he studied the expressions on a few of the member's faces and waited patiently for them to stop clapping.

"The topic of the contest tonight is one of great controversy, "Changing our Constitution". I did extensive research on the subject and all of us should be more aware of our government's slow encroachment on the freedoms given us by our constitution."

Luke shuddered, his belly muscles quivered and, a lump that felt like the size of Mt. Shasta, formed inside his stomach. Pressing his palm against the top of the podium, he shuddered again, his thoughts meshing in his brain, as fried circuits did inside a computer. And as if seeking a place to hide, his tongue slapped the top of his mouth, sticking there with spit that had the consistency of super glue. Thinking, he wouldn't be able to dislodge it, his panic returned and he gulped, his tongue swelling into what felt like a whole boiled egg. Swallowing convulsively, the movement of his throat muscles, was so painful it brought tears to his eyes. Glancing at his notes, he picked up the appropriate card and forced his tongue to move.

Flipping his last cheat card over, Luke looked up and stared intently at the men and women sitting quietly at the tables. "In summation, ladies and gentlemen, we as a nation must guard our Constitution and all the liberties it gives us—zealously. We have freedom of speech, press, religion and to bear arms, and we must guard all of them from overzealous Presidents and Congressman. We must guard it against do-gooders and passiveness, and if we allow even one change to our constitution, next year they will take another. They will keep hacking away at our freedoms, until most of them are gone, gobbled up by the wolf-like hunger of the government for absolute power. The constitution guarantees you and I will live with freedom; don't sell it short and don't give it away. The constitution is your safeguard against tyranny. Guard it with your life."

"Thank you . . . "

Luke paused, glancing at the faces watching him. "I'd like to leave you with one thought. Beware and fight against a Machiavellian government at all costs. If we don't already have one, it's making its appearance in every aspect of our government, local, state and federal. Our forefathers, Franklin, Jefferson, Davis, Adams and even Abe Lincoln would have slammed the door on it long ago. If you don't know its definition, look it up in your dictionary. You'll be surprised at what you can learn from one small word. The word is Machiavellian."

Luke stepped back from the podium, raised an eyebrow at Mr. Sanfield, grinned, and nodding his head inched his way across the room. Pushing through the swinging door into the hallway, he shook his head at Debbie and Pepper. "I bet over half of them didn't know what I was talking about," he complained.

"C'mon, lets eat," Debbie said. "I'm starved and it'll take Sanfield an hour to get them to vote. Remember, we get a free meal, whatever the restaurant's special is tonight." She grinned and rolled her eyes. "Hope it's good."

"Yeah, let's eat," Pepper agreed. Angling his wiry six-foot frame forward, he rose and, raising his hands, finger-combed his hair. Impatiently, he pressed the unruly curls on each side of his head until they laid flat.

Luke, stacking his papers and notes, glanced up at Debbie's and Pepper's departing backs. Shoving papers into a file folder, he sighed, his thoughts tumbling over each other. I must be a fool. I bombed! Stumbling in the poorly lit hall, he swung the door open and, blinking rapidly in the sudden bright light, entered the restaurant.

CHAPTER 2

LUKE PUSHED ON the wobbling pile of books in his locker. It's a mess, he thought, examining its cluttered contents. Bella's arm brushed against his and he stepped to his left giving her more space to open her locker. Glancing up as she jerked the door open, he watched as she dug through its bottom for a book. Damn, he thought, her locker's a lot neater than mine. Keeping a firm grip on his books, he shoved again on the teetering mass.

Bella peeped at him through long, mascara colored eyelashes and he smiled at her, a quick flashing grin. Glancing back at the contents of his locker, Luke tried to find his chemistry book. It was a bright blue, so it should be easy to spot between stacked books and crumpled, wrinkled papers. His eyes wondered again to Bella. She is a dumpling, he thought, just like Dad says. He must mean she's well rounded, when he calls her a dumpling.

About five four, her nose was tiny, set between wide-spaced brown eyes and dusted with a generous sprinkle of freckles. Her mouth was wide, the lips perfectly shaped, and she was always smiling. Grinning at Luke, deep dimples flashed in her cheeks. Pulled to one side and clasped with a huge flowing bow, curly platinum blond hair fell past her shoulder to her waist. She was a bright ray of sunshine, wrapped in a feminine package and Pepper liked her with a passion that had no boundary.

"It's a good thing we're nearly finished for the year," Bella said, glancing at the contents in his locker. "Your locker's a mess, it needs cleaning. Wow, does it ever!"

THE DEVILS PUNCHBOWL

"How can you tolerate such a mess? How do you ever find anything? I guess guys are naturally messy. Guys are probably the cause of Mr. Chester finding rats lately. I say, clean up your act!" Pitching her voice low, Bella quipped hoarsely, imitating Mr. Olsen's voice. "Please, clean up your act there's no sense in being slovenly!"

"Really, really good. Huh!"

"Huh!"

She laughed, a tickled deep throaty sound. "I finally learned Mr.Olsen's voice. Sounds just like him, don't you think?" Digging her elbow into Luke's side, Bella stepped back, slammed her locker door closed and walked away. She looked back at him smiling mischievously.

"Clean up your act," she shouted, in a perfect imitation of Mr. Olsen.

Luke laughed and waved at her. Pushing again against the pile of books, he swore under his breath. He tried to make order out of chaos and the pile wobbled again. He scowled impatiently. Slipping a book out of the middle of the stack, he slapped it on the top of the teetering pile.

Someone hit Luke's shoulder and he swung around, losing his grasp on the books. The wobbling pile started to slide, and stepping backward, he watched the spewing contents scatter over the floor. Frowning, he looked down into Debbie's bright blue eyes. Exasperation flashed across his face.

Debbie smiled at him and shrugged her shoulders. "Sorry, did I cause this," she said. Glancing at the scattered books and papers on the floor, she knelt and picked up his math book. Tilting her head, she glanced up at him. "Congratulations again, Luke, on winning the speech contest last night." Laughing, she started to stack books and papers in separate piles.

"I'm going to be late for chemistry," Luke grumbled. Falling to one knee, he picked up a stack of books and, rising to his feet, shoved them back in his locker.

"I don't think it really matters anymore," Debbie said. "Being late I mean. We've only got today, part of tomorrow and then we're gone.

I'm sort of unhappy we're leaving all of this behind." Laughing aloud, she continued to pick up Luke's papers, stacking them in neat piles. Rising to her feet, she handed him a stack of papers. "I can hardly wait," she added humorously.

In undulating waves the three-minute bell blared its warning call through the halls. The loudly expressed noise of jeering insults, laughing voices, slamming of locker doors, and the rush of running feet escalated to a heightened pitch. Emptying, the noise in the halls fell into muted, barely heard reflections of sound.

Sighing, Luke slammed his locker door. "Thanks for helping me," he said. Giving Debbie's shoulder, a quick squeeze, he sprinted along the hall and stopped suddenly. Pivoting, he yelled. "See ya in the parking lot." Grinning, an infectious happy motion of his mouth, he walked backward, and waved at her again before slipping around the corner.

Debbie picked up a piece of paper and crumpled it with her hand. Walking slowly, she headed for the windowed school's office. Last day, she thought. She pushed the door open and went through the swinging gate at the counter. Pitching the wadded paper into the waste basket, she smiled.

"Hi, Mrs. Mitchell, anything special you want me to do today?" she asked.

"No, just put the mail in everyone's box," Mrs. Mitchell said, glancing up from her computer. "I haven't had time to do it. Then you're excused. You've been a great help this year, Debbie." She smiled, her face puckering into a thousand new wrinkles and, blinking rapidly behind the shiny brightness of her glasses, she tried to hide her burgeoning emotions.

Picking up both the box and stack of in-house mail, Debbie started to put the mail in alphabetical order. Stooping, she shoved the last envelopes in Ziedman's box and placing the empty mail bin under the cabinet, picked up her small bag from the floor. Pushing through the swinging gate, she left the office. It was almost time for the school day to end.

Wistfully, she stood at the apex where the long empty hallways met. The halls were silent, and along the southwest wing, light halos

THE DEVILS PUNCHBOWL

hung in golden streams from dingy windows. A synchronized rhythmic murmur of voices hummed along the hall. She stared at the bits of sunlight cast on the floor, trying to imagine how many students had talked, laughed and walked through these halls into distant nebulous futures.

Shivering, she smiled at her imagination, and stopping her melancholy musing, she waved pensively at Mrs. Mitchell through the office windows. Giving one more reflective glance back over her shoulder, she turned and walked toward the west exit. Pushing through the doors, she left the building and walked toward Luke's car.

Leaning against the trunk of the car, Debbie expelled a long moody sigh as she watched the emptying of Del Norte High. The students in drabs and spurts poured through the doors, flooding the lawns and parking lot. Every kind of shape was represented, a decoupage of moving color in a spectacular presentation of tall, thin, short, dumpy, fat and wide human beings. Some of us will achieve a lot, she thought, but most of us will have to leave here, because we all need jobs.

Looking to her left, Debbie spotted Benny and Lily. Holding hands, they talked and laughed as they walked through the parking lot. They had liked each other since the seventh grade and felt they were hooked together by an invisible bond. They really were a beautiful couple.

Lily, tall and thin looked like what her name depicted, a gentle and delicate flower. Graceful, she seemed to float along the blacktop. Long, honey-colored hair pulled back with barrettes swung lightly behind her. Laughing at something Benny was saying, she looked up at him with large green eyes. Benny bent sideways and nuzzled her ear. She ducked and sidestepped, bumping into Joseph, Del Norte High's reigning football hero. She said something to Joseph and, laughing, patted his back.

Watching them continue to sift their way past cars and students, Debbie thought about their singing. Maybe. . . . Just maybe, they would get a lucky break in their music. Music was a passion for Lily and Benny; they could play almost every instrument. Lily even played the harp and both of them could sing like birds. When they harmonized on their guitars, everyone stopped and listened. They were composing a special song for the senior prom, and so far, they had managed to keep it a well-kept secret.

Sighing, Debbie's thoughts wondered again, as she watched the homebound students. Even though she tried not to be, sometimes she was envious of Lily's voice. Laughing at herself, a giggle bubbled in her throat, and spying Luke, she waved as he started to walk across the lawn.

Pepper, in his haste to reach Luke, shoved his way through a crowd of slow-moving students. He sprinted across the lawn. He had to talk to Luke before he reached Debbie.

"Hey. Hey Luke, wait up," Pepper called running toward him. "Is it still on for tonight?"

Luke stopped and waited for Pepper. "Did you ask Bella if she could use her mother's van?" he asked "We can't do it if she can't, because my car's too small. To pull it off we have to be in one car."

"Bella called her mother during lunch break," Pepper explained. "She said she could use the van, as long as she was careful. This is going to be the best joke I've ever pulled on Bella. I bet she pees in her pants."

"Yeah, but remember, if we can't pull it off just right, no one will laugh. The laugh will be on us," Luke said. "It'll have to be after I get off from work and it has to be pitch black before we get to the graveyard. Otherwise, it won't work."

Pepper turned and watched the door for Bella, his eyes flashing a bright blue as he glanced back at Luke. His classical features, tall muscular body and ready humorous wit made him a favorite with teachers and students. Pushing his hand through tousled hair, he smiled nervously, breaking out in a chuckle. Glancing at his feet, he drew an imaginary line with his shoe and with a surfeit of nervous energy turned to face Luke. He shifted slightly and rubbed his fingers over his plush, shiny black mustache.

Luke, watching him intently, realized how much Pepper enjoyed having enough facial hair to grow such a magnificent mustache. It set him apart from the other male students. Most of them didn't have enough of a beard to shave every day.

THE DEVILS PUNCHBOWL

"Sure, I know all that, everything's in place, I think," Pepper said ruefully. "Benny's going with the girls. We're supposed to meet them at the graveyard."

"Who chose Benny to go with the girls?" Luke asked, waving at Joshua and Stevie Carson across the lawn. "I thought he was going to be part of the scaring."

"Bella told Lily she wouldn't go to the graveyard with just girls," Pepper answered. "It was too scary. So Lily volunteered Benny. I asked him if he minded, and he said no. But he was kind of disappointed in being left out of the scaring stuff. The scaring is going to be the best part." He rubbed his hands together, grinning broadly. "The girls were really puzzled about why we had to meet them in the graveyard."

Pepper laughed boisterously aloud, and spotting Bella walking through the school's door, he waved. "I think we can pull it off. I'll pick you up at eight. And don't stop to talk to someone inside the store. It irritates me when you do that. You should wear old pants too, because when I scouted the area where we have to crawl, it looked wet. We sorta picked the wrong night, because the weather forecast said heavy fog, so that means everything will be dripping." Walking toward Bella, he turned and grinning happily, waved.

Luke waved back and then pulled his Bulls ball cap a little lower on his head. Shrugging, he shook his head in resignation. Somehow, after talking to Pepper, his misgivings about tonight were worse. Taking a few steps backward toward the parking lot, he turned and saw Debbie waiting patiently.

Deb was the most beautiful girl in the high school, he thought and one of the smartest. She wasn't tall like Lily, but just right, about five-seven with the longest legs he had ever seen on a girl. Her face was perfect with large blue eyes framed in the darkest eyelashes and, her mouth, curved and soft was made just for kissing.

Walking up to Debbie, Luke slipped his arm around her. "Hi, guys, are you going to Sams, to pick up some Pepsi, or are you out of here, like I am? I have to work from five to eight tonight, so that means getting home early to do my chores. How about it, Deb, are you riding with me?"

"Well, it's Thursday and my Mom works until seven, so I'll have to cook tonight. I guess I should go home. The twins will be there and they need me to play referee."

"I've got to finish packing my gear for my hike into the Punchbowl," Luke said. "Pepper told me earlier he was already packed." Turning to Benny, he asked. "You ready yet?"

Benny shook his head.

"Uh-uh," he replied. Looking at Luke, he grimaced.

Benny was six-foot-three with wiry muscles and a loose skin. They teased him constantly that he would never grow enough to fit his skin. He was hollow-cheeked with a strong chin, his nose straight and sharp. His thin angular face shadowed suddenly and an expression of anxiety crossed it.

"I don't have much packed," he exclaimed. "I've got everything collected in the middle of my room, but I need to organize and weed out. Hell, I'll never make that six-mile climb unless I can eliminate some of it. Tomorrow I've got graduation rehearsal and two classes, so I'll finish my packing then."

Poking him on the arm, Lily pointed her finger at him. "What's the most important thing we have to do tomorrow, Benny?" she asked.

"I can't think of anything happening tomorrow, can you, Luke?" he asked. Luke and Debbie laughed together at the indignant expression on Lily's face.

"Okay, I'm not playing your silly game," Lily said, turning her back on them. "You know we have to practice tomorrow for the senior prom. We have to harmonize our song."

"But, Lily, what's more important, the prom or going to the Devils Punchbowl?" Luke asked. He laughed at the hot, indignant look that Lily threw at him over the top of the car.

"Okay, guys," Debbie said, interrupting their teasing game. "It's our last high school prom. Just think, after tomorrow no more classes, just the prom and then a week from now. . . . Yea, graduation! Okay, Luke, take me home in your trusty rust bucket. It must be true love for me to ride in it."

Luke opened the car door, and glancing up, watched Benny walk away with Lily.

Benny hugged her, said something, and looking back, smiled at Luke. Happiness lit up his face making his hazel eyes dance and he waved his left hand over his head at Luke. "We've decided we'd like a taco, so we'll be at Christina's if you and Deb change your minds," he shouted. "If you hurry, you might have time."

Luke shook his head at him and waved. Settling himself on the car seat, he shut the door and smiled broadly at Debbie. "You have to really watch what you say around Susan B. Anthony," he said in an exaggerated whisper. "Her feelings get hurt really easy."

Debbie laughed, hitting Luke on the shoulder. "You're ridiculous, especially about this old car. You must know, giving a car a name is dumb." She giggled and hit his shoulder again. "You're impossible."

Luke joined her, grinning broadly, humor lighting his face. "Let's go, Susan," he said. Gently turning the key, he started the engine.

Dropping Debbie at her house, Luke glanced at his watch and whistled softly. He didn't have much time to go through his backpack again. Just enough to have a snack and change clothes. Well, maybe a quick once-over, he thought, parking his car behind his mothers.

Walking into his room, Luke hoped his mother wouldn't catch him trying to gulp his sandwich and a huge glass of milk in his bedroom. Mom hated anyone to eat or drink in the bedrooms. Number one rule of the house, eat in the kitchen. Shrugging his shoulders in resigned apprehension, he hoped he wouldn't get caught. But using Murphy's law, he usually was.

Sitting on the edge of his bed, he stared at the camping equipment laid out in the middle of the room. Chewing happily, he picked up his clipboard and glanced at his list. Everything was checked off. All he had to do was stuff all of it in his backpack.

"Wow, there's sure a lot of it," he muttered. Anxiety set in and his stomach took a flip as he surveyed the camping gear. Looking at his watch, he swore and, gulping his milk, set his empty glass on the floor. Stripping off his pants, he quickly changed into his Safeway uniform. Grabbing his keys, he ran through the house, yelling as he slammed the door.

"Bye, Mom, I'm off to work."

CHAPTER 3

LISTENING TO THE words of a favorite rock and roll song on his CD, Pepper waited for Luke in the Safeway parking lot. Humming softly, he glanced at his watch, eight-fifteen, where was he? There he was just inside the door talking to Barry, the most cheerful clerk Safeway had, always had a good joke to tell and didn't seem to mind screaming kids or slow women. Starting the engine, he pulled up to the front of the store and pressing the truck's horn, waited impatiently.

Luke walked through the door, waved at Barry and pulled the door of the truck open. He climbed in and pressed his back against the seat. "You're going to have to stop, so I can change," he said, throwing his gym bag on the floor. "I didn't have time we were really busy tonight."

"Okay, no big deal. I'll drive to Front Street. The library parking lot should be empty this time of night," Pepper said.

Turning on 101 South, Pepper gunned the motor and, accelerating, turned into the right-hand lane. Turning right on Front Street, he slowed to a stop in the parking area near the library and shut the engine off.

Luke opened the truck door and standing in a wedge made by the open door, stripped off his uniform. He pulled on a pair of worn Levis and a red sweat shirt with a faded Del Norte High Speech Team logo on it. "I guess I'll be warm enough, it's the one I got in my sophomore year," he said, grinning at Pepper.

"Looks like its kind of small to me," Pepper quipped. "You're a lot heavier now. Are you sure it's muscle and not fat?" he teased. "A few more pounds and you won't fit through the tunnel at the Punchbowl."

THE DEVILS PUNCHBOWL

"SH . . . HH." Luke answered, looking apprehensively at the dark parking lot. "You never know who's out there listening. I've learned a lot since our camping trip last year. The world has mighty big ears. Remember our vow never to talk about it," he admonished, climbing into the truck. "Like your Granny always says, sometimes whispers are heard around the world. If you listen closely enough you can hear them on the wind."

"You know, I really don't understand some of that Irish stuff she quotes. But after hearing it repeated over and over, what she says kinda makes sense," Pepper said, laughing aloud. "I don't know if that's a good sign, or not."

Shifting into low, Pepper slowed the truck and turning on Highway 101, drove north. Pulling into a left-turn lane, he stopped at the intersection for Cooper Street. Whistling softly, he waited for the light to change.

"I wish the rest of the world had as much sense as your Granny," Luke said, watching the red light. "I'm going to miss Rob not going with us to the Devils Punchbowl this year. Go, the light's green. Are you going to park at Big K Mart?"

"Uh-huh," Pepper answered, turning into the Big K Mart parking lot. "Rob's not getting to go with us to the Bowl is a real pisser. He knows a lot more about tunnels and caves than the rest of us. It sucks that the Army ordered him to camp early." Glancing at Luke, he rubbed his nose thoughtfully. "But you know, we do have one consolation, he'll be there for the last two days." Braking, he pulled into a parking space and set the emergency brake.

Opening the door, he stepped down and picking up a paper bag from the truck's bed, flipped the switch to lock the door. Walking quietly through the parking lot, they turned right on Cooper and plunged into the brush next to the road.

"Benny was supposed to tell Bella to park up close to the old section, where all the beautiful tombstones are," Pepper said. "Have you spotted Bella's van yet?"

"No," Luke said, curtly.

Stark frustration lining his face, his apprehension grew as he stared nervously into the depths of the graveyard. "This doesn't feel good to me, Pepper." Tombstones appeared and disappeared in the murky fog as dead people by the hundreds floated across the surface of his mind. He shivered at the bizarre image. The night was black and heavy vapor in sheer, gauzy wetness clung to their faces and clothes.

Moving cautiously, Luke passed looming objects distorted by heavy fog. Stepping carefully, they walked over bumpy, uneven ground toward the back of the cemetery. "There's Bella's van parked way up near the top," he whispered, pointing toward a hill on the west side of the graveyard. "See it?"

"Yeah, barely," Pepper said, waving to part the fog in front of him. "I hope Benny had her park where I told him to. This is going to be perfect," he chortled gleefully in a soft whisper. "If we go up here and just over a little, we can climb through the next hedge. Her van is parked right next to that one."

Walking around marbled ornate headstones they crossed a paved cemetery road and climbed a small hill. Pushing through a row of shaped bushes, wet with dripping leaves and branches, they emerged into the oldest part of the cemetery. Pepper clutching the paper sack to his chest crouched low next to a hedge.

"We have to stop and put our ghost masks on," he declared abruptly. His voice deepened thoughtfully as his head swung in a circle. "Sure is dark!" Opening the sack, he pulled the masks out, offering them to Luke. "You can have your pick, they both look evil," he stated. Peering upward, he tried to see Luke's expression in the dark. "Well, hurry up and choose one, you know we don't have all night here," he added brusquely.

Luke shifted his feet, staring at their dark surroundings as wisps of claustrophobic vaporous fog drifted through the graveyard. "Yeah right. And since I'm standing in the dark and getting soaked to the skin, just hand me one of the damn things. I don't care. Let's get this over with! I feel like the biggest and most gullible asshole in the world."

Pepper laughed, the sound, muted and low. "Asshole, maybe, but not the biggest. What's a friend for if we don't do each other big favors?" Rising to his feet, he handed one of the masks to Luke.

"This is going to be fun. I can hardly wait to see Bella's face. Besides being scared she'll probably laugh herself sick." Pepper turned toward the street lights on Cooper, and moaning made sucking noises through his mask. "How did that sound? Scary! Can you see me?" he asked, his voice slightly garbled by the tightness of the mask.

"No, I can't, and you sound like a pig. What in hell are you making sucking noises for?" Luke replied, derision making his voice rise.

"I was practicing," Pepper replied. "The first thing I'm going to do is ask Bella for a kiss. I'm going to give her one right through the mask. One she'll never forget. Hey, you know the paint on these masks is supposed to glow in the dark."

"Spooky, huh!"

"Walking behind the hedge, we'll look like floating demons just dug up from the grave. We'll be absolutely grotesque." Pepper chortled, the tightness of the mask changing the sound into a merry grunt.

They crouched low behind the hedge, pulling long pieces of gauze over their arms and, fastened a collar made from an elasticized material around their throats. Closing with Velcro, the collar hid the end of the mask, and the ragged pieces of material attached to it completely covered their upper torsos. In the dark the white strips of sheer nylon floated like smokey vapor around them. Pepper turned and looked at Luke. "This is going to scare them into next week," he said.

"Yeah, you look awful and sound worse," Luke said, pressing the mask to his face. He laughed hoarsely, the sound nervously muted. "Especially the hair, half of it's missing. Maybe, it's supposed to be that way. How are we going to do this, crawl along and pop up every once in a while?"

"Yeah. We don't want them to see us until we get kind of close," Pepper answered. He laughed, the low bass sound distorted with a rippling resonance of apprehension and anticipation.

Crouching low, they walked for a short distance behind the hedge and then, dropping to their knees, started to crawl along the muddy ground. Water dripped steadily, but gently, from every leaf, and drifting fog wrapped them in a soft vaporous blanket. Stopping, they stood and looked over the hedge. "A way to go yet," Luke grumbled.

Starting to crawl again, Pepper stopped abruptly. "Psst, Luke. . . . You hearing, what I'm hearing, or is it my imagination?" he asked. Turning, his head, he peered at him through the narrow slits in the mask.

"All I've heard is a kind of panting," Luke replied. He squinted back at Pepper through the mask's eye slits. "I thought it was you."

"I'm not breathing that heavy," Pepper whispered, indignation lowering his voice in harsh protest. "Do you hear it now?" he asked.

Sitting back on their heels, they listened intently, twisting to look in every direction, and watched for any furtive movement in the dark. The foghorn on the end of the jetty blared its lonely and desolate cry, its bleat muffled by fog trumpeted through the blanket of vaporous dark. The fog in the graveyard thickened, and in the quiet night the constant sound of dripping water, was a continuous pitter-patter of drip . . . drop . . . drip . . . drip . . . drop.

Luke rose to his feet and looked down the hill toward Cooper Street. Car lights on the road formed dim irregular halos through the fog, and vaporous streams of wetness moved in erratic clusters around the beckoning lure of the lights next to the County yard.

"No, I don't hear or see anything," Luke muttered, dropping to his knees.

"Let's go."

"Hahhh, hahhh, hahhh."

The heavy sound was close, and crawling a few feet further, they slowed, placing hands and knees with exaggerated care on the ground. The panting whispered along the hedge, and pausing when they did, the sound wet and labored, became louder.

"Hahhh, hahhh, hahhh."

Rising to their knees, Pepper and Luke stared into the foggy, impenetrable darkness. Nothing! There was nothing, just blackness. Anxiety welled up inside Pepper and his mouth turned dry. Seconds passed as they strained to see.

"You didn't bring a flashlight, did you?" Luke whispered. Fear lodged in his throat, and he coughed softly, trying to clear it. "This is a frigin graveyard, Pepper, and we're not the only things crawling along this

THE DEVILS PUNCHBOWL

hedge. Something is tracking us and it sounds like it's right beside me."

"No, I didn't," Pepper whispered. "I didn't think we'd need one. Listen!"

"Hear anything? I don't," Luke whispered urgently.

Apprehension grew inside them, bursting in a rapid illogical pattern on their minds. Straining to see and hear through the thick veil of heavy fog, Luke tried to crush the nervous tremors that ran through his body.

Fog drifted along the ground and, rising like spectral phantoms, vanished into the hedge. Breaking into fragments it resembled spiritual entities and Pepper's superstitious mind roamed wildly along unchartered paths. Seeing and hearing nothing, his mind quieted and he snorted in disbelief.

"Shit."

"The panting has to have a logical explanation. Maybe it's just our imaginations," he whispered. "Let's go. We're almost in position where we can start scaring the girls." Plowing through wet rotting vegetation, they wrinkled their noses at the rotten smell fouling the area and paused to listen when they heard the panting again.

"Hahhh, Hahhh, Hahhh."

"Hell, Pepper, that must be something huge to pant like that. Maybe it's a ghost of a St. Bernard." Luke's voice rose, a grotesque, grating whispering, barely heard through his mask. "Or maybe it's a shadow demon, you know a dead person that can only make sounds. Maybe it doesn't know how to appear."

Their bodies stiffened. The thought of demons, ran like mad dogs through their minds. Staying on their hands and knees, they silently watched and listened. Luke could hear his heart beating in his ears, its thumping, almost in rhythm with the spattering drops of dripping fog. Breathing quietly through their mouths, the sound grew into a rasping, sucking intake of air.

"Hahhh, Hahhh, Hahhh, Hahhh."

The panting shattered the silence. The foggy darkness embellished the sound, breaking it into hot, heavy syllables that swamped Luke and

Pepper in a deluge of terror.

"Hahhh. Hahhh. Hahhh."

"I'm out of here," Pepper wailed.

Jumping up, they ran toward Bella's van. Running next to the hedge, their shoulders and heads bobbed above its top. The ghoulish white masks shimmered in the dark and long strands of stringy hair floated behind them. Slapping them like wet spaghetti, the long pieces of glowing material danced around their bodies. The sound of their breathing whistled through their masks, harsh, hard and desperate.

"Hahhh, hahhh, hahhh. . . . "

Slipping in slimy vegetation, Luke turned to look over his shoulder. The panting, intensifying in clarity, was loud, deep and distinct, and it came from behind him.

Mentally, he cursed.

It was close enough to bite his ass. Sprinting forward in a burst of speed, his foot slipped sideways in rotting leaves, tangling with Pepper's running feet. Falling heavily on the saturated, muddy ground, they scraped their masked faces for several feet through layers of moldy wet leaves. They grunted curses and, sucking in a huge gulp of air, their breathing escalated in a rasping sound of outrage and desperation.

Luke wiped muddy leaves from around his mask's mouth. Gagging, he tried to spit. "I can't believe it I've got mud in my mouth. Get away from me, Pepper," he yelled, shoving on him.

"Move. You're the one that tripped me," Pepper grunted, pushing on Luke's heavier bulk. He spit and wiped a clod of mud and wet leaves from his mask. He spit again and then wiped his mask's mouth with his sleeve.

"Listen," Luke whispered. Desperately, he strained to hear.

"Hahhh, Hahhh, Hahhh."

"That thing is still close to us," Luke said. "It sounds like its standing right over there." Breathing harshly, he rose to his knees and pulled on the rubber mask. The more he pulled, the tighter the suction formed around his nose and mouth. Raising his arm, he swiped it across the mask's mouth, and vigorously rubbed it several times. Shoving a finger through the slit made for the mask's mouth, he wiped his

THE DEVILS PUNCHBOWL

lips and spit again. Silently, holding his breath, Luke peered through the masks eye slits into the foggy, murky darkness.

"Hahhh. Hahhh."

Jumping wildly to his feet, Luke stumbled and started to run. Leaping up on two bent legs and one arm, Pepper lunged and grabbed the back of Luke's sweatshirt. In a mighty leap forward, he pulled himself up and jerking on the sweatshirt, rushed past him.

Luke swore. "Asshole, Pepper," he panted, through clenched teeth.

"Sorry, but I'm faster than you," Pepper yelled.

"Follow me."

Bella, seeing movement in the rear view mirror, gasped, and gasped again, sucking in a huge gulp of air as she turned around.

"Look? What are they?" she screamed.

Benny looked over his shoulder at the silhouetted forms racing toward the van. Covering his mouth with his hand, he almost laughed aloud as Lily shouted. "Quick, let's go. Start the car, Bella."

"Let's go, Bella. Move . . . hurry . . . hurry, they're getting closer," Debbie yelled. Turning in the seat, she watched the running demonic shapes. They disappeared, vanishing in the misty darkness. Fog drifted, and the running demonic figures appeared again, somehow, they had got through the hedge. Debbie screamed. "They're running toward us, quick lock the doors."

"Hurry up, Bella, they look like dead people," Lily yelled. She screamed, a high, uneven treble that ricocheted bullets of sound inside the van. Benny covered his mouth with a large hand and twisting in his seat looked behind him.

Bella's hands shook as she turned the key in the ignition and pressed the lever for the headlights. Frantically, she glanced in the rear view mirror and screamed in terror as one of the ghoulish things pounded on the back of the van. The engine caught and pressing her trembling foot down hard on the gas pedal, it howled in protest.

One of the creatures fumbled with the door handle, trying to open the door. "Op . . . En the door," it garbled and panted. It screamed, the sound obscene and hoarse. "C'mon. Hey," it sobbed breathlessly. "O. . . pen the . . . dooo o r! Let us in! What are you doing?"

Bella squealed and Lily and Debbie screamed again, their terror forcing them to shrink against the seat. Debbie yelled, her voice warbling to a whimper, as one of the demons pounded on the van's window. She shrank away from the door, pressing herself against the center console between the seats.

The thing left wide, muddy patches across the pane of glass, and mud mixed with water, dripped from the tattered, ripped clothes it wore. Screaming incoherently, its mouth opened wide, showing massive teeth. Sucking lips smeared a pasty white into a deep hole in its head, it garbled a moaning sound and scraped frantically along the van. "Op . . . En the door," it snarled. Running along the van, distorted sounds and deep grunts poured from its mouth.

Noises, desperate in tone, erupted from the throat of the one at the back of the van. Slapping the back window, it frantically ran around the van's side, and pulled repeatedly, on the handle of the locked door.

Bella flung the gear lever into drive. The tires spun on the wet ground and, digging for traction, the van leaped forward . . . then leaped forward again. Accelerating, she turned onto a paved cemetery road. Glancing in the rear view mirror, her knees trembled, knocking together as her foot pressed on the accelerator. Glancing again at the mirror, she screamed. "Look! They're running after us." Hysterically, she watched them vanish in the murky, moving fog.

Forcing her trembling leg and foot to press harder on the gas pedal, the van fishtailed on the wet road and slowing, she turned right on Cooper. Speeding west, over the hill by the County yard and turning left on Butte, she sped toward Pacific Avenue. Turning right, she drove into the Pacific Market parking lot and pressed hard on the brake pedal. The tires squealed in protest, as the van came to a shuddering stop.

Trembling, Bella huddled over the steering wheel. Pressing her face into her shaking hands, she tried to resist the urge to cry. Turning sideways in her seat, she glanced first at Debbie and then quickly, at Lily and Benny in the back seat.

"Are you . . . ?"

THE DEVILS PUNCHBOWL

Bella abruptly stopped speaking. Staring at Benny, her body stiffened at the sight of his shuddering, shaking body. "Benny, are you laughing?" Strained and with lost timbre, her voice became a mere whisper. "What's so funny, our screaming? Or do you think those creatures are funny."

Lily raised her head from between Benny's shoulder and the seat. She frowned. He was silently shaking, convulsing almost, his face hidden between his hands. Bending forward, he rounded his back and pressed his face against his knees.

"Benny, you rat! This was a set up," Lily yelled. "That was Pepper and Luke trying to scare us. Jerks! You stinking, malicious jerk! How could you?" Slapping at him with her hands, her face flushed a bright red. "I was scared. I thought dead people were after us."

Laughter exploded from Benny. He howled, the sound uneven and hoarse erupted from his mouth in noisy surges, as he gasped for breath between shouts of uninhibited laughter.

"Oh, God, I've never seen anything so funny." Wiping his eyes with his hand, he choked the words out. "You have to admit, it's the funniest thing that Pepper has pulled lately. All of you were screaming and them running after us?"

"Wait until I get my hands on Pepper. Graveyards, ghosts, what a lot of crap," Bella said. Her voice husky with exasperation, rose and she squeaked. "How could he scare me like that?" Turning her head, she glared at Benny. "You must have been in on it, or you wouldn't have found it so funny."

Suddenly, Bella started the engine. Slamming the gear shift into drive, she turned left on Butte Street and right on Cooper, passed the County yard and cemetery, to 101 South. Pushing hard on the brake pedal, she stopped next to the curb. Looking through the rear view mirror, she made a face at Benny. "Get out, you can walk home," she said angrily. "Maybe, you can meet those two jerk-offs in the graveyard. They'll probably give you a ride home. I'm not! Get out, Benny. I mean it!"

"Yeah, get out. I'm mad," Lily said, nodding her head vigorously. Sliding the van's door open, she moved a little so Benny could get by.

"I'm too angry to be around you tonight."

"Hey, don't blame me, this is Pepper's joke," Benny protested. "You don't have a sense of humor, if you can't laugh over this. This was the funniest I've ever seen. All of you were scared out of your pants, and Luke and Pepper, acted like the hounds of hell were after them." Convulsing, in brief spurts of laughter, he leaned toward Lily. "Come on, it was just a joke," he pleaded.

"No, get out. You're a bunch of dorks. I might forgive you by tomorrow, but not a minute before. Out!"

Gesturing toward the door, the girls chorused . . . "OUT!"

Benny reluctantly got out. "How do you expect me to get home?" he asked, bending to look in the van.

"We don't care," Debbie yelled at him. "Maybe you should take a hike into the graveyard. I'm sure Luke's still in there. In this fog he'll be lucky to find his way out." She shivered. "Gross, a gross joke is what you guys pulled. I really felt like I was seeing dead people. It wasn't funny."

"Let's go, Bella," Lilly said, slamming the door shut.

Turning on Highway 101 South, they looked back at Benny standing on the corner. Debbie glanced at Lily and started to laugh.

"They looked like apparitions from the pits of hell," Bella said. Turning on the seat, she wrinkled her nose at Debbie. "They looked like they were just dug up from the grave, didn't they? Gross lookin, they actually looked half-rotten." Bella shivered, goose bumps running up her arms.

Benny watched the taillights of Bella's van disappear into the obscurity of drifting fog. When the lights had vanished entirely, he crossed the street and walked despondently toward the cemetery. Passing, Big K Mart, he saw Pepper's truck parked beneath a light in the parking lot. They're still in the cemetery, he thought, and breaking into a run, he saw Pepper and Luke stumble through the brush bordering the road. They were limping.

Pepper walked hunched over holding his stomach, and Luke had more of a limp than Pepper. "I guess I'm the only one who saw humor in this joke," Benny shouted. "What in hell happened to you guys?

You're smeared with mud. It looks like you've been rolling in it. When you ran at the van and pounded to get in, it scared the shit out of the girls. They were terrified. Bella could hardly start the engine."

"Jesus, Benny, why didn't you unlock the door and let us in? Something followed us in the cemetery and we couldn't see what it was in the dark," Pepper said, his voice rising in exasperation. "It panted like some kind of ghoul and it was invisible." His breath caught on the impact of his words and he gasped, a spasm of shock and horror crossing his face. "It even followed us after you left. In fact, we ran to get away from it." He looked apprehensively back at the graveyard.

"We were trying to get away from this thing from hell and when you guys drove away, we cut across the graveyard. We kept falling over headstones," Luke interjected. "Then, Pepper playing the all knowing everything God, that he isn't, got so disoriented, he ran in the wrong direction. We went by the infant's graveyard twice. I kept shouting we were running the wrong way, but he was in such a panic, he kept insisting he was right. I have never seen anyone fall down as much as he did. If it was in our path, he fell over it."

Luke's face wrinkled and, becoming grim, his lips thinned in irritation. "You know how Pepper acts when he gets an idea locked inside his pea brain. Nothing stops him. So, like a fool I followed him, because I didn't want to leave him alone in the graveyard. I lost my best Bulls cap too."

Pepper stood staring back at the graveyard. "Oh, shit, stop complaining. We're lucky to get out of there alive," he said. He shuddered. "C'mon, let's get out of here. I'm ready to go home." He started at a fast trot toward the parking lot and stopping suddenly, turned back. Staring at Benny, his expression became puzzled. "Hey, how come you're here and not with the girls?" he asked.

"They kicked me out of the van. Lily was really upset. She told me she couldn't be around me and Bella wouldn't even give me a ride home," Benny said dismally. He tossed his head back with another shout of laughter. His eyes glittered and raising his hand, he tried to rub away his grin. "I guess I'm the only one that had a good laugh tonight."

"I guess! But only because mine and Luke's part of the joke didn't turn out very funny," Pepper said unhappily. "How were we to know that we would meet some kind of demon from hell in the graveyard?" Dismay and alarm deepened his voice. "You said Bella was really scared for a while though?" he asked, staring at Benny's nodding head. "I bet she was, I wish I could have seen it." Punching, Luke lightly on the shoulder, he danced around him.

"I'm pissed! Maybe tomorrow I'll see humor in all of this," Luke said. "Now, all I can think about is falling over gravestones and being stalked by some unworldly being from hell. Let's go! Drop me off at Safeway, so I can pick up my car." Pulling a mask and its collar from his back pocket, he tossed them into the back of the pickup.

Climbing into Pepper's truck, they looked at each other and burst into laughter. "I told you, Pepper, that this joke would somehow backfire on us, and it did," Luke said sarcastically. "We were scared shitless. Probably a lot more than the girls were."

Squeezed together in the cab, they continued to laugh, their voices rising in boisterous hilarity. Pepper gunned the truck's engine and leaving the parking lot, turned south on Highway 101 toward the shopping center.

CHAPTER 4

PUZZLED, LUKE SWEPT his ball cap from his head and, combing his fingers through his hair, jammed it back on his head pulling the brim down over his eyes. Agitated, he rose to his feet and pivoting in front of his chair tried to find Debbie's dark head among the milling students in the crowded room. Her last name was Cardman and she should be in the C row.

Pepper waved to him from a few rows up and he waved back. Some of these students acted confused. They didn't seem to understand the graduation ceremony. All it required was to find your place in alphabetical order. What was so difficult about that? The majority of them must have a bad case of the stupids. And besides, everyone had a list to go by.

Ms. Sawyer waved her arms over her head and shouted into the mike. "Okay, find your place on the list. This can't be that hard. The way most of you are still milling around, I've come to the conclusion, that you don't know your name, or you're confused by the alphabet." Laughing heartily, she watched the moving students. Standing against the podium, her body language spoke exasperation.

"That's better. I guess by talking softly, everyone will hear me easier, than if I shout. I want everyone to look at their list. Find the two people you're supposed to be next to and stand between them. This is important, otherwise when your name is called during the graduation ceremony, someone else will be standing in your spot." Silence became chaos. The students circled trying to find where they belonged in the rows of chairs.

"Okay," Ms. Sawyer said into the mike. "Let's have total silence, so everyone can hear me. I'm going to read from the same list that was handed to you at the door, starting with the letter A. If you aren't in the right order find your place now. There might be a few vacant spots, because of student absences and, if the person next to you isn't here, leave the chair vacant. Able, Martin," Ms. Sawyer said, starting to read from the list of names.

The whispering murmur escalated, and accompanied by major reshuffling, the students became silent as she continued to call their names. Finishing the list with Yest, Donald, she looked up at the attentive seniors. "Now starting with the back row, alternating by rows, the first to the left and the next row to the right, file out into the hall and please stay in alphabetical order. When the music starts, file back into the gym and take your seat. Remember, leave the chair next to you vacant if that student isn't here."

When the somber notes, of pomp and circumstance echoed through the gym, the class became strangely quiet. Listening to the melancholy sound, Luke stared at the students around him. The shuffling of feet was all he could hear in the hall. No one was talking, maybe because they all realized this was it. Their last day of school! Adulthood waited to embrace them, and the prospect of falling into a seemingly unknown void, filled with years of responsibilities, created a lot of mixed feelings. His thoughts were mostly on the exuberant joy of finishing high school, but also, present was the numbing fear that he might fail to achieve his dreams.

I wonder what will happen to all of us, Luke thought. Where will we be in five years? Stepping almost in time to the music, they followed each other and somberly stood before their seat in the straight lines of folding chairs. The class waited until the last student stood before his chair and then, as a coordinated body, in perfect unison, they sat in their designated seat.

"That wasn't so bad." Ms. Sawyer said into the mike. "Just remember where your place is in line and I'll see all of you next Friday at five-thirty. Don't be late," she admonished. Smiling, she added. "Just think. You won't have to hear my next words ever again . . ."

THE DEVILS PUNCHBOWL

"Class dismissed."

Luke slouched in his chair waiting for the rush to subside before he left the gym. He hadn't talked with Deb yet today and he felt deprived. She usually made a point of meeting him somewhere in the parking lot. Come to think of it, he thought, I haven't seen Bella or Lily either. Sitting up straight in his chair, he looked around at the chattering, laughing students. He saw Benny and waved. Standing, he waved at Pepper and twisted to see over the heads of the departing students. He couldn't see anyone in the crowd that resembled the girls, maybe, they were still mad.

"Hey, you seen the girls?" Pepper called, pushing his way through rows of chairs. "I haven't talked to Bella yet today."

"You're not going to get a chance to either," Benny said. Joining them, his expression changed to exasperation, the feeling clouding his expressive hazel eyes. He plopped down and raising his legs placed them on the seat of an adjacent chair. "They decided they wouldn't have anything to do with us today. They're still pissed about the graveyard." His mouth twisted, and raising his hand, he muffled the sound of a wry, humorous laugh.

"You'll never know how you guys looked. You appeared over the top of the hedge and all we could see were these floating ghastly bodies. The girl's were so scared they couldn't move, and when you started pounding on the van's window, they freaked. It was the funniest thing I've ever seen. And the way they screamed I'll never forget it. Right out of the movies. They really thought you guys were dead people." Benny's laugh burst out again.

Luke's expression soured. Fleeting thoughts darkened his intense blue eyes. A frown formed on his face, expressing his dissatisfaction over his part played out in the graveyard. Wiping his hand over his face, he rubbed his mouth. Humor, suddenly changed his expression, and he laughed aloud, a short dry sound.

"I couldn't get the mask off," he said. "It was skintight and glued to my face with sweat. When I finally managed to peel it off my head, I took most of my skin with it. And I have to admit I was just as scared as Pepper was. Common sense tells me that noise had to be a big dog panting, but we'll never know, because I'm never going back. You'd have to be the world's biggest sucker to go back into the graveyard and try to find out. . . . And I'll never be sucked into another one of Pepper's practical jokes." Throwing his hands in the air, he slapped his legs to emphasize his feelings. "You sucked me into participating for the last time," he added, staring at Pepper.

"Oh, you'll help me out again," Pepper said morosely. "You're my friends. Bella's still mad at me though. I tried talking to her last night after we got home, but she wouldn't come to the phone. Sometimes, I think she doesn't have a sense of humor," he added, rubbing his knees.

Garbling a rude sound, Luke laughed and Benny joined him.

"Humor," they chorused together.

"Girls don't know what it is," Benny said.

"Yeah, I know," Pepper answered grumpily. Turning on his chair he watched the line of departing students. "That air head, Logan Marsh actually called me a nerd." Watching Logan's back through narrowed eyes as he left the gym, Pepper's face twisted and he frowned, his eyebrows meeting over his nose as he wrinkled his forehead. "I was working a geometry problem on the computer and I guess he resented it or something." Waving his hands, he dropped them, dismissing the thought with a wry expression.

"You, guys through packing?" Luke asked suddenly, raising his eyebrows at Pepper and Benny.

"I haven't packed anything, yet," Benny answered, shrugging his shoulders. He stared blankly at them, for several seconds. "Being called a nerd, shouldn't bother you, Pepper. Geeks and nerds usually succeed. Ninety percent of nerds grow up to be in the two-hundred and five-hundred thousand dollar pay brackets." Gesturing, he raised his hands, punctuating his words with short, jerky jabs, and abruptly pulling his legs down, straightened in his chair.

"I think if you insult others with words you're either jealous or sadistic. In fact, I don't mind being called a nerd or a geek, I always take it as a compliment and say thank you," he added, glancing at his watch. "I've got to hurry, because I'm meeting Lily, so we can harmonize our song for tonight. It's the only time we'll be together today. I guess she's still mad." His face lengthened, his expression mirroring his unhappy thoughts. "Then I'll have to rush to pick up her corsage and pack for the Punchbowl."

Rising to his feet, he pushed his chair back and turning toward the doors started to walk away. Stopping abruptly, he looked over his shoulder and pointed at Luke. "The limousine will pick you up at five thirty," he said. Turning to Pepper, he placed his large hand on his shoulder.

"It'll be at your house and mine at quarter-to-six. Then we'll pick up the girls. Dinner reservations at the Grotto, are for six-thirty. We have to be finished with dinner a little after seven-thirty. The limousine will pick us up then and drop us off at the high school by eight. That's the plan! Sound ok?" he asked.

"Sounds good to me," Luke said. "I don't think Deb will forgive me if I screw up her last high school prom. And that means no jokes."

"Shit," exclaimed Pepper. A cross apprehensive look appeared in his eyes. "My life will be hell if anything happens to spoil tonight for Bella. I want to make it the best I can for her, then maybe, she'll forget about the graveyard. Bella doesn't forgive easily. I keep telling her she holds grudges."

Benny laughed at Pepper's expression. "Well, holding grudges doesn't sound too good to me. All I can tell you is, join the crowd when it comes to understanding women. My Dad, always says, it's a woman's world, they just don't realize it yet, and somehow, when I'm with Lily, my day has a shine to it." Laughing again, Benny coughed. Holding his hand to his mouth, his eyes sparkled and danced. Turning away, he left, walking between the rows of chairs.

"See ya," he called.

"C'mon, Pepper, I've got to clean out my locker," Luke said, striding down the aisle.

"I don't think I'll go with you," Pepper answered. "I'm going to pick up Bella's flowers and then head home. I've got to check my backpack again, just to make sure I haven't forgotten something. We won't have much time in the morning if we leave by eight o'clock. I'll call you if I think of anything else." Walking away, Pepper waved dejectedly at Luke, his face reflecting his misery over Bella's anger.

"Okay," Luke called, waving his hand at him. "I'll head for home as soon as I clean out my locker. Give me an hour or two to get there."

Luke tugged at his bow tie again. One side just wouldn't lay flat. The tux didn't look too bad, even though the fit wasn't exactly right. Glancing in the mirror as his mother left the room, Luke's thoughts wondered. He grinned, thinking about Pepper's family. They were different. His Dad was from Mexico and had immigrated here in the sixties. During the Vietnam War, he had met Pepper's Mom in England and had married her in three days. She was a nurse from Ireland.

Pepper's grandmother had moved from Ireland to join his family when he was seven. She was wonderful, a witty, loving grandma, who was sarcastic as hell and bit your head off if she caught you telling a lie. But still, without any discrimination at all, she did a lot of hugging. She didn't seem to care who you were. And when she put her arms around you, it felt as if you were sinking into a super-soft marshmallow. Pepper's family was noisy, unpredictable, boisterous and fun. He loved it over at Pepper's house.

Sighing, he thought of Benny. His folks were different somehow. They were older and very quiet. They surrounded themselves in an atmosphere of quiet at all times. Benjy, is what his parents called him, short for Benjamin. Benny and his sister Ruth had been raised with music. When you entered their house, there was always classical music playing softly in the background. An ambience of quiet always hovered within the walls of Benny's house making it a peaceful, tranquil place. And his folks were the richest, his father didn't work and had never been employed here in Crescent City. Their money came from old Europe. No one ever really talked about it, but it had something to do with Austria and Germany.

Rob was a third generation Serbian-Pole. He was all American. Apple pie, pizza and cheeseburgers. His folks were older too and like Luke, he was an only child.

Luke laughed aloud at his memories. Their first year together had been Kindergarten. Rob had been so big, he towered over all the other

THE DEVILS PUNCHBOWL

kids and Benny had been tall too. He and Pepper, had been small compared to them. That's where it had started, Kindergarten at Joe Hamilton, eight years at St. Joseph's Catholic School and then four years at Del Norte High. The four of them from the very beginning had become friends. Loyalty, devilish humor and honor, mixed with a deep sense of caring bound them together. Steadfast and true, they did have some horrendous fights at times, but they loved each other as brothers. They hung together and knew each others innermost secrets and dreams.

Glancing in the mirror, he gave the bow tie another tug. All of them had been so jealous of his being part Indian. He had touted his being part Cherokee, into being the absolute winner in almost every Cowboy and Indian game they had played. Rob and Pepper, had gotten so mad at times they would yell, they had never seen a blond Indian on TV. Benny was different, he had sat back, waiting for everyone to get over their mad, and then he'd grin and start to play again.

Luke smiled again and patted his mouth in a muted, "Wah. Wah. Wah." Shrugging his shoulders in the tight fitting jacket, he left his room. Entering the living room, he smiled at his Dad and went to the window. Glancing at his watch, he waited anxiously.

"You're not nervous, are you, son?" Mr. Webster asked, glancing up from the book he held in his hand.

"Yeah, kind of," Luke answered. "I hope Deb likes the tux."

"Well, I think she should," Mrs. Webster, answered tersely. "Are you being clingy?" she asked, turning to question him. "I've told you that some young women just don't like a man to be too possessive. No woman wants that."

"Love is like a wild bird," she added thoughtfully. "You have to hold it loosely within your grasp and it has to have freedom to grow. You have to learn to trust each other completely, knowing in your heart, that the love you share is great enough to hold you together. I think you should think of it, as gossamer wings that enfold each of you in the greatest partnership God created for human beings. True love is never jealous or selfish, but also Luke, women want a man. Someone who is gentle, loving and caring, but who is also strong and exudes enough testosterone, so she knows your male. Most of all, a woman wants to be loved. And as you get older, you'll find that the woman you finally pick to share your life with, will turn out to be your best friend."

Rising from her chair, she stood, and looking out the window, she handed him a camera. "I think your limousine just drove up. Make sure you take lots of pictures, especially at the gym. You'll love them thirty years from now." Reaching on tiptoe she kissed his cheek and gave him a quick hug.

"Have a good time, Son," his Dad shouted, as he went out the door.

Luke waved to Pepper's parents and grandmother as they stood together on the porch. The Rodriguez's were all smiles. Pepper was their baby and they watched over him like mother hens with baby chicks. His married sisters mothered him too. Bella was different though. She told him where to go and how to get there by himself. No if's and's or but's. No mothering and no excuses. She didn't cater to him or comply with everything he suggested either. She had a big voice and she used it often in her relationship with him.

Two houses up from Peppers, Benny was already waiting on his porch. Running quickly down the steps, he ran across the lawn toward the limousine and waving over his shoulder glanced back at his parents.

"Benjyeee Steinbeck, what are you doing, you'll fall and ruin your clothes?" his Mother, shouted at him. "Be careful!"

"Na . . . ah! I'll be all right, Mom," he called gently. He smiled and waved again at his parents. "Good night."

Luke slid along the seat making room for Pepper and Benny. Slamming the limousine door, Benny laughed. "Now for the good part, I can hardly wait to see Lily."

Benny helped Lily into the limousine as if she was a priceless jewel. Her gown, trimmed in a sapphire blue along the edges of the ruffled skirt and bodice, was a silvery, misty lace. She wore a corsage of white roses the tips of the petals tinted a dark blue to match the piping on her dress. She smiled at Luke and Pepper and settled herself against the leather seat with a sigh.

THE DEVILS PUNCHBOWL

Luke could feel Pepper's apprehension rise as the limousine stopped at Bella's house. Pepper shoved the limousine's door open and ran up the sidewalk. He knocked and Bella's mom opened the door. She said something to him and he grinned, sidestepping nervously. Bella appeared in the doorway, a vision in pale, moonlight-yellow silk. Strapless, the formal gown was skin tight to the waist and then, belled out in yards of ruffles and lace.

Pepper nervously tried to pin his corsage of yellow roses on her formal. Finally Bella's Mom stepped forward and pinned it to the waist of her dress for him. Grinning at him, because he was flustered, Bella gave him a dig in the ribs with her elbow. Pepper whispered in her ear. "Forgive me for last night?"

"Not yet, you jerk, maybe at some point in the next three months," Bella replied. "Be extremely happy that I'm even talking to you." Rolling her eyes, she stepped from the porch and floated down the sidewalk.

Pepper stepped into the limousine and relaxed with a huge sigh next to Luke. "At least she's talking to me," he grumbled to himself.

My God, they're gorgeous, Luke thought, looking at Lily and Bella sitting across from him in the limousine. They look more like women than high school girls. Holding the door's handle as the limousine slid to a stop in the driveway of Debbie's house, he opened it and walked toward the door.

The door opened and Deb stood there, a dreamy fantasy in bright red. Her strapless gown hugged her body to her hipline, then belling out in cascades of scarlet lace, it danced around her in tiny, shiny sparkles of light. She was beautiful, female incarnate. She was sexy and the most gorgeous woman, he had ever seen. His breath caught when he looked at her, his eyes sparkling with tiny blue flames of light.

"Oh, Deb, you're beautiful," he whispered. Taking a deep breath, Luke found he could breathe again. Taking her hand, he rubbed it across his cheek, closing his eyes.

"I missed you."

Fastening his white orchid corsage, with its throat dyed a brilliant red on her wrist, was agonizing. Glancing at Mrs. Cardman, he was certain from her expression that he had done it right. Holding Debbie's hand, they walked down the steps, and stopping for a second, turned to wave at her grinning brothers.

Relaxing, Luke glanced at the three girls sitting on the opposite seat in the limousine. Deb's hair style was the same as Bella's and Lily's. Gathered on top of their heads and pulled to one side, their hair cascaded to one shoulder in a riot of curls. The only difference was the color. Deb's hair was black as midnight, Lily's the color of creamy-caramel and Bella's, a silvery-blonde. Pepper poked him in the ribs with an elbow. Raising his hand, he covered his mouth and whispered. "You're staring."

"I can't help it," Luke whispered back. "They're gorgeous."

"Well, try getting a grip, you're beginning to slobber and pretty soon you'll be drooling," Pepper whispered. He laughed, a modulated rumbling bass. "And if you don't stop soon, spit will be dribbling off your chin."

Stepping out of the limousine at the high school, they all groaned from overeating. Their dinner had been superb, the conversation hilarious and the women gorgeous to look at. They couldn't keep their eyes off them. Even Lily's shape was pushed into something to see, but Bella's and Deb's rose over the top of their dresses and naturally, a guy couldn't keep his eyes from wandering there.

Luke stood watching the limousine driver help the girls from the car. Pepper's self assurance was overlaid with a supple nervous energy. His cheeks were red and his hair was mussed into a mass of black curls. The only cool one of us guys, is Benny, he thought. He looks like he doesn't have a nervous bone in his body. Wish I was as calm as he is around women. Walking from the parking lot felt good and the night air, cooled his cheeks. Touching his jaw, he moved his mouth, his face felt sore from laughing so much during dinner.

Entering the gym, they found themselves in a magical enchanted garden. The senior class had voted Summer Paradise, as the theme for their prom and the committee had done a tremendous job in decorating. Flowers were everywhere, with small nooks for tables and chairs.

The stage for the band was surrounded by a white picket fence, and both red and white roses were laced through a heart-shaped white trellis. A swinging garden gate in its middle, was slightly open, and small gliding benches sat on each side of it against the picket fence. A rock and roll song blared a rollicking, rolling beat of rhythm through the speakers, and lots of couples, were dancing. Strobe lights in flashes of brilliant light picked up the colors of the girl's formals in flashing, swirling color.

The music changed as Luke took Debbie in his arms. With a sigh she raised her arms putting her hands on his shoulders. Pepper grinned at Luke and squeezed Bella tight. She squealed and hugged him back.

Lily, a vision in white against Benny's shoulder, tucked her head into his neck. Benny closed his eyes, completely enchanted by the girl he held in his arms. Immersing himself into the beat of the music, they moved gracefully onto the crowded dance floor.

Clinging together, Luke and Deb paused by the table they shared with their friends. Pepper and Bella were in the flower enclosed bower sitting this fast number out.

"I hate to interrupt, but do you know when Lily and Benny will sing the song they composed?" Luke asked. "Debbie thinks it's the last number of the evening."

"I think so, too," Bella answered. "Is that what you heard?" she asked, looking questionably at Pepper. Poking him, she waited for his reply.

Pepper glanced at his watch. "Yeah, that's right and it should be in twenty minutes or so," he said. "It's twelve thirty."

Watching Luke and Debbie glide to the edge of the dance floor and start to dance, Pepper turned his head and pressed his lips to Bellas. Lifting his mouth, his eyes roamed over her face. He whispered softly, "my girl."

Benny and Lily climbed to the stage amidst whistles and screams. Their beauty as a couple gave them a radiant glow, and their gentle caring of each other apparent in the way they touched. Turning to face the crowd looking at them, they smiled.

"We dedicate this song to all of you, our classmates and especially to each other," Benny said softly. "We hope you'll like it."

The band started to play a haunting melody, and holding hands, Lily and Benny smiled at each other, their husky voice's blending as they started to sing in perfect harmony.

My love . . . Is
Rainbows and magic things
Ringing bells and silver dreams
Sweet touches . . . that promise
Everything
My Love
I'm giving you . . . My heart
My life, my future . . . My destiny
To hold . . . Gently . . . Within your hands
For forever,
I will be . . . His Woman
I will be . . . Her Man
Together . . . We will persevere
Together . . . We go hand in hand
My love and I . . . Are together
As the sea . . . And tides . . . Are melded
To the sun and stars . . . Above
Separate . . . We are spindrift
Only together are we whole
My love . . . And I
Pledge to God . . . Before you
For always . . . And forever
We will be . . . As one
My love . . . Is
Rainbows and magic things
Ringing bells and silver dreams
Sweet touches that promise

Everything
My love and I

Their spellbound audience was quiet, and they harmonized again the last few lines of their song, letting the happy sweet words drift slowly away into silence. Ending it, Benny kissed Lily gently on the cheek.

The couples roared their approval. Their cheering escalated and they yelled for encores. Singing it again, Benny and Lily bowed when they finished, and stepping forward, stood under the heart-shaped trellis. Touching the garden gate they bowed again and whispered into the mikes. . . . "Good night everyone."

Benny and Pepper said good night to Luke and sat back with happy thoughts, as the limousine driver drove them home. Stepping from the limousine, they stopped on the sidewalk and thanked the driver.

Walking slowly up the sidewalk to his door, Pepper called softly. "As me, Irish Granny would say, tonight was a hoot, and we warmed, the cockles of a few hearts." He laughed softly, but heartily, his teeth flashing in the light from his front porch. "And even better, we pleased our girls." Pepper laughed again. "See ya in the mornin. Remember, up early for our six-mile climb."

"Night," Benny called. Running across the lawn between their houses, he ran up his porch steps, and opening the door, stepped inside, closing it softly behind him.

CHAPTER 5

SITTING ON THE edge of his bed, Luke yawned and pushed on his back pack with the bottom of his boot. Five hours sleep, just wasn't enough, he was still tired. Excitement had begun to burn through him like streaks of fire, and small shivers, he couldn't control, flowed like cold syrup along his spine. This year had been long and the anticipation of waiting for this day, agonizing.

"I can hardly wait," he whispered. "Today's the day. Punchbowl time.

The spelunking equipment they needed was borrowed from Rob, and split up between them, well hidden in the bottom of their packs. Luke picked up his clipboard and flopped back on his bed, he had to check his list one more time. He had plenty of tea, coffee, and powdered milk, ten packages of lemonade and Kool-Aid, eight packages of dehydrated casseroles, and four humongous potatoes. There was a pound of bacon for breakfast, three-dozen cracked eggs in a thermos and he had prepared six individual packages of biscuit mix. There was just enough in each package to make a dozen biscuits or a dozen pancakes and Mom had made a double batch of his favorite jerky. Two boxes of energy bars completed his food list.

Luke's eye skimmed the page, mentally checking off, four pair shorts, T shirts and socks, two pairs of Levis, two shirts and extra batteries for their headlamps and flashlights. He smiled. This was it. He was ready. Tied to the back of his pack was a small folding aluminum oven and Pepper carried a very light folding grill, its top made with holes like Swiss cheese. Pepper had received it as a birthday gift

THE DEVILS PUNCHBOWL

from his folks, and folding together like an accordion, it made a small neat package for carrying. It was an ideal stove top for over an open fire, and the oven fit perfectly, on one side of it. Benny carried the frying pan, a small sauce pan and a baking pan. And I've got the water pot, a larger sauce pan and my fishing pole. Luke laughed to himself. They really camped in the rough, in style.

The doorbell pealed an intrusion to his thoughts and Luke could tell it was Pepper. He was nervous. Rolling to the edge of his bed, Luke sat up. Rising to his feet, he picked up his backpack and a small shotgun. He left his bedroom just in time to hear his Mom, say. . . .

"Hi, Pepper."

"Hi, Mrs. Webster, is Luke ready to go?" Pepper asked. Spying Luke at the end of the hallway, he asked. "How many pounds you carrying? My pack weighs forty-seven pounds."

"I'm carrying fifty-one," Luke answered. Dropping his backpack against the wall, he carefully laid the shotgun beside it. "Dad says a bit much, but we're going to eat well." His blond hair fell over his forehead and, brushing it back with a large hand, he slapped his ball cap over it.

"Bye Mom, see you Wednesday or Thursday evening, and don't worry." Picking up his gear, he balanced it in his hands and went sideways through the door.

"Okay, boys, have a good time," she answered, following them down the sidewalk. "Be careful! Oh Luke, Dad has a Doctor's appointment next Wednesday. If you come home then, we won't be here. We'll be in Medford."

"We'll be careful, Mom, so long," Luke answered, lifting his backpack into the back of Benny's truck. "And don't worry about my being here Wednesday. I think we're staying until Thursday." Sliding the shotgun behind the seat, he waved again over the top of the truck.

"Luke," she called, walking toward the truck. "You haven't had breakfast."

"We're going to eat at the Hiouchi Cafe," Luke replied. "Pepper wants to have the biggest breakfast they have. You know the Diet Special the one Dad really likes." Waving at her as she turned to go back in the house, he climbed in the truck and buckled his seat belt.

Shifting the truck into low gear, Benny eased it into the street. Turning left on Ninth Street, he headed for 101 North. "Do you guys feel anxious?" Benny asked, turning onto the highway. "I kept thinking this day would never, ever get here. I'm really nervous."

"I'm nervous too and I've been carrying a pot full of apprehension all morning," Pepper said anxiously. Rubbing his hands together, his expression changed rapidly into an abstract of wrinkled brow and lines of anxiety.

Accelerating, Benny changed gears and turned east on Highway 199. Giant redwood trees formed a thick canopy overhead, and in some places along the highway, the sun's rays never reached the ground. Driving through semi-sunlit areas into shaded ones, shadows deepened into dark pools along the edge of the road. Crossing the Hiouchi bridge, Benny slowed the truck close to the bridge's rail, and they glanced down, at the beautiful clear water of the Smith River. It was a perfect jade green, the best color in the world for steelhead fishing. Driving past the entrance into Jedediah Smith, State and National Park, Benny slowed, turning into the parking lot at the Hiouchi Cafe.

Entering the restaurant, they headed for a table next to a window, and the waitress, Laura, followed with a coffee pot in her hand. Removing their ball caps, they noisily settled on chairs as she poured coffee and placed a menu for each of them on the table.

Laura took their orders and gave them to the cook. Waiting for their breakfast, they sipped from their cups and thought of the climb they would have to make. Laura returned with their specials, patty sausage, hash-browns, three eggs, biscuits and gravy. The cook really had given them huge portions. There was no stinting on portion size in this café, no one left hungry.

Eating quickly, they enjoyed the quiet hum of background noise created by conversation from other people eating in the restaurant. Luke wiped his plate with a piece of biscuit, swabbing up the last of his milk-gravy. "How much do I owe?" he asked Benny and Pepper.

THE DEVILS PUNCHBOWL

Benny and Pepper calculated how much each of them owed. "You owe five dollars and sixty cents," Pepper said. "And, you owe a dollar for your share of the tip.

Laying the money with the check in the middle of the table, they said goodbye to Laura. Grabbing their ball caps, they left the restaurant and climbing in the truck searched noisily for the end of their seat belts. They buckled up as Benny backed the truck, and accelerating, pulled onto the highway, heading north.

Benny applied the truck's brakes, and slowing down turned onto Little Jones Creek Road. Pepper yawned, mesmerized by the illusion of trees and brush rushing by the truck in a green-brown blur. Opening his mouth in another jawbreaking yawn, his eyelids closed as they drove deeper into the mountains.

Luke stared out through the window, his thoughts obviously far away. The quiet hum of the engine and the silence in the cab of the truck, made him sleepy. Rubbing his hands over his face, he yawned, and staring sleepily through the windshield at the road, his thoughts turned inward, altering his expression.

"Sometimes, guys, when I think about the cavern, I feel like me, wee Irish granny always tells me, don't bite off more than you can chew, because it might be too big for you to swallow. Don't you think we might be in over our heads, youst a wee bit?" Pepper asked. Glancing first at Luke and then at Benny, his eyes flashed, agitated with fear and a web of consternation crossed his face. "Hell, we don't know what's in that cavern. We could be stepping into a really bad nightmare. Maybe we should have told our Dads about the cavern."

"Yeah, I've had similar thoughts," Luke replied. He watched Benny for several seconds as he turned the truck onto the dirt road, toward Bear Basin and Doe Flat. "I've thought often about telling my Dad. Then when that thought passes, I can hardly control my feelings, my stomach cramps and my heart starts to race. Just the thought of the cavern and what we'll find gives me anxiety. I want to be the first one to explore it."

"I would have liked to share it with my Dad, but he would've told my Mom," Luke added. "Then she'd put her unequivocal large-thumb down on everything. My Mom would be appalled, or maybe a better word is devastated, if she knew I had crawled through those fissures and crevices last summer." Sighing, he slumped in his seat and glanced, at Benny and Pepper. Unhappy thoughts, gave him a pensive look, and moody feelings flashed across his face.

Braking, Benny stopped the truck in the parking lot at the trail head and pulled, on the emergency brake. Opening the door, he climbed out and stretched his long lanky body. Watching Pepper and Luke, emerge from the truck, he grinned. Surprise, at his own thoughts lit his face, broadening his smile.

"I have to admit I've been scared too. . . . But if we go into the cave with the idea of just looking, we'll be all right. I wish Rob was here though," he added nervously. "He'd straighten us out in no time. C'mon. Enough of this shit, let's get goin. We have a mountain to climb." Opening the tailgate at the back of the truck, he started to remove their camping equipment.

Luke started down the trail stepping lightly on the path. He carried his shotgun and Pepper carried the camp gun, a 10-22 Ruger semi automatic rifle. They followed a well-trodden trail for about a mile, passing the trailhead into Buck Lake. Shrugging his shoulders several times to shift the weight of his backpack, he awkwardly raised his arms to balance himself. Stepping up onto a huge fir tree to cross Doe Creek, he thought about the trail ahead. If the Forest Service hadn't been out lately to check on their signs, finding the trailhead into the Devils Punchbowl might be tricky.

Luke paused, finding the trailhead well marked and kneeling to rest for a second, he watched the trail to see how far back, Pepper and Benny were. And finding them right on his tail, he climbed to his feet and started to climb again.

Climbing from one steep switchback to another, he stopped to rest on a jutting ridge of granite rock. Wiping the sweat from his face, he glanced at the shadowed range of distant mountains. Clouds moved restlessly around the top of Preston Peak, its seventy-three hundred feet of awesome craggy rock, black and ominous. Bear Peak, to the south, raised its rugged outline high into the sky, and the V notch, of the Devils Punch Bowl, was barely discernable just below its summit.

Hitching his backpack higher on his back, Luke expelled a deep breath and fell to his knees. Sitting awkwardly, because of the weight of his backpack, he straightened his legs stretching his calf muscles. Tipping his canteen against his lips, his dry throat welcomed the gush of cool water. Exhaling a deep felt sigh, he took off his ball cap, and bending, as far as his backpack would allow, poured water over his head. Wiping his face with his hand, he welcomed its coolness, and stared, at the rocky prominence of distant mountain peaks.

Seeing movement at the last switchback, Luke watched Pepper and Benny walk around a twist in the trial. They climbed the steep incline laboriously, their faces red with exertion. Luke grinned and waved.

Pepper groaned and plopped to his knees beside him. "My God, what a climb," he said. "I must be kinda nuts to endure this every year."

"I know, but look at the view," Luke answered. "Not many people in the world get to see a view like this."

"Yeah, but how many people would really want to if they knew what a strenuous climb it was?" Pepper said, casting him, a shrewd glance. "Not many, I bet."

Benny drank from his canteen, then stared at the towering mountains. "Hard to believe we've climbed nearly two thousand feet in two miles," he said. Falling to his knees, he sat on the uneven surface of the white granite rock. "I don't think anywhere else on earth compares to this." Falling silent, they rested, spellbound by the panoramic view of the massive mountain range. Below them heavily forested slopes fell steadily downward, a vista of dark and light green patches. "Sitting here, I can imagine that I'm looking at the ends of the earth," Benny said thoughtfully. Pushing himself up on his knees, he looked at the wide expanse of deep valleys, mountains and canyons. Southward, the V notch of the Devils Punch Bowl beckoned. "It's almost like you can see forever."

Rising reluctantly, they groaned, and following the edge of the mountain, climbed steadily higher over rough trails. From the summit and far below them, pinnacles of rocky crags raised their heads into a balmy sky. Mountain slopes flowed downward, and resting on the minuscule valley floor, a creek appeared only as a silver reflection. Crossing a small stream, they went east along the trail climbing steadily over a high bluff. Resting again, they drank greedily from their canteens.

Benny clipped his canteen onto his belt, and looked at Luke and Pepper. "C'mon, lift your lazy asses we've still got a long way to climb."

Luke paused at the edge of a meadow and spinning in a circle glanced in every direction. "Go slow, fresh bear signs here," he yelled. From a dug out area under a fallen tree, fresh dirt mixed with snow was piled beside the trail. Looking for grubs and roots, a bear had dug up three or four feet of the ground from under the tree.

"That's all we need is to meet a bear. He must be really hungry to be looking for grubs this high," Pepper said. His eyes skimmed the brush along the edges of the meadow for movement. Not wanting to be seen, many animals hid themselves in deep shadows beneath brush and trees. Unless they moved, a hiker would never see them. Kicking the pile of droppings with the toe of his boot, he added. "This pile isn't frozen, so I would say he's been here in the last hour."

"Are you sure that piles from a bear?" Benny asked. "Maybe, its Big Foot shit? They've had all sorts of sightings of Big Foot again in this area. In fact, the Siskiyou Wilderness Area, has gotten famous, so many people have reported they've seen Big Foot. Let's do a little singing as we climb," he suggested. "If we sing and make enough noise, any animals, or even Big Foot if he's in the area, will be warned that we're passing through here."

"How could you question that pile of scat being anything but from a bear?" Pepper asked. He snorted staring at Benny in disbelief. "I've never heard any reports of anyone finding a pile of Big Foot's shit. C'mon, your statement stinks, Benny. You don't really believe in Big Foot, do you? His voice rising in aggravation, his exasperation at Benny's statement showed, as he kicked at the bear scat before walking away.

Benny started to laugh. "I gotcha, Pepper," he chortled. "I gotcha on that one. Admit it. I gotcha on that one. He laughed happily.

THE DEVILS PUNCHBOWL

"Okay you got me on that one," Pepper replied. "You almost had me, but you better watch it, Benny, because I'll get you next and it won't take me a long time either." Disgruntled, he tried to smile. "Let's sing, maybe, it'll loosen me up a little."

Luke exchanged grins with Benny, and starting across the meadow, Pepper and Benny followed him. He yelled every few minutes a gargantuan war cry, the sound resonating through deep canyons echoed, until it was only a faint noise, barely heard. Hearing the sound of Benny's bell-like voice, combined with the rich, deeper tone of Peppers, he stopped his war cry, and listened, to the clarity and feeling of haunting words soaring over vast empty spaces of wilderness. Scrambling over a rocky bluff, they headed for the shore of Lower Lake. Walking clockwise around the head of the lake, they started the last short climb over the slopes. Turning to the left they followed cairns, small pyramids of rocks piled up by hikers over the years, into the Punchbowl.

Entering the canyon, they stopped for a second to watch speckles of sunlight dance on the surface of the water. The lake, a glacial cirque more than ninety feet deep, shimmered with the clarity of perfect crystal. Surrounding it on three sides' rocky perpendicular cliffs', more than a thousand feet high contributed to its gem-like quality. In its bowl-like setting, shadows deepened the water to the color of a dark blue sapphire.

Covering one quarter of the southern cliff, a glacier, hung its shiny eight-foot end over the water, and surrounding the lake, the almost perpendicular cliffs, were covered with boulders and a thin layer of shale. Scrub oak and pine growing sparsely on the eastern cliff clung desperately to their footholds on the rocky slope. Huge granite boulders split the western cliff, protruding like giant white markers over the lake. The shoreline covered in places with shale-like gravel was meagerly covered with scrubby brush and huge granite rocks. A beautiful natural jewel, the lake was set in a very rough, wild setting.

Deep drifts of snow lined the edges of the shore, and the meager light cast by the sun, caused dazzling sunbeams to dance along the sheets of ice that covered the cliffs. "It's going to be damn cold tonight, so let's get our camp set up," Luke said anxiously. "There doesn't seem to be any other campers, so we have our choice of spots."

"Yeah, we have so many to choose from," Pepper said sarcastically. "Let's take the one your Dad always chooses. The one completely hemmed in by three huge boulders. At least we'll have some protection if the wind kicks up." In the enclosed protected space they prepared a place to sleep. They removed everything that looked like it would poke through their pads, and working quietly unrolled their sleeping bags, shaking them to fluff the down.

Building a food locker along the edge of the running creek, they dug deep into its gravel bed. Stacking rocks, they made a place for their perishable food. Watching the icy water pour through small openings in the stacked rocks, they waited a few moments, for mud and small pieces of gravel to settle to the bottom. Placing their watertight plastic containers and bags in the water, they placed a small rock on the top of some of the containers to immerse them completely. Lifting a large flat rock on top of the walls, they looked at each other and smiled. Benny gave the rock on top an extra pat, making a tighter closure with the top of the walls.

"Just as good as a refrigerator," he announced, with a tired grin.

Searching through a brushy area, they stockpiled enough wood for the night. About six feet from the bottom of their sleeping bags, they built a fire ring with large rocks, and lighting a few small logs set Pepper's grill and Luke's oven over it. Emptying their backpacks, they placed their dry food into two mesh sacks and, pulling them high in the branches of a cedar tree, anchored them there with a rope tied to the tree's trunk. Stuffing their backpacks deep into a cleft under one of the granite boulders, they finished the preparation of their sleeping area and, grinning at each other, rested on their sleeping bags.

"Guess what, I think its fishin time," Benny quipped, his angular face breaking out into loud happy laughter.

Picking up their small folding rods, they trotted to the water's edge and rolling rocks over along the shoreline, searched for possible bait. Finding a small batch of assorted bugs and worms, they collected a few in a baggie, baited their hooks and happily threw their lines in the water.

THE DEVILS PUNCHBOWL

"Who wants to bet with me this year?" Pepper asked. "I'll be the first with a fish and I'll hook the biggest." Smiling, he looked at Benny. "Any takers?"

"Maybe Benny will bet, I'm not," Luke replied. "You have phenomenal luck and I always seem to lose."

Benny jerked on his line setting the hook firmly in the mouth of the biting trout. Carefully pulling it toward shore, he chortled. "Look who got the first fish."

Sitting on rocks at the edge of the lake, they became silent and introspective. The slap of water against the shore soothed them in its rhythm. Shadows deepened around the lake and the surface of the water changed into a deep, reflecting navy blue. Evening descended, and the unfolding night scattered the sunset into a blurry haze, obliterating the stark roughness of the overhanging cliffs, until they were dark, shadowy outlines against the sky. The air over the lake was brisk, clean and heavily laden with the scent of snow.

"I've caught seven and I've already cleaned them," Luke said. "How many have you guys got?" he added softly, not wanting to break the awesome spell of isolation and silence.

"I've cleaned mine," Benny said. Slipping forward on one knee, he washed his hands in shallow water along the shore.

"Mine's, cleaned too. We've got plenty, let's go cook these suckers," Pepper said. "My stomach says it's time to eat."

Climbing to their feet, they left the shoreline, their boots making sharp crackling noises in the loose shale. A breezy breath of cold wind rustled through the canyon, stirring the leafless branches of brush and trees into a rattling, vibrating commotion.

Benny cooked the fish and Luke fixed a beef stroganoff casserole for six. Pepper mixed a batch of biscuits, patting them softly into perfectly round shapes. Putting the biscuits into the oven, he did a quick renovation on their eating and relaxing area around the campfire. Digging with the camp shovel, he fixed three places for sitting. Rolling a large rock to the head of each dug out area, he tried one for a back rest. Finally satisfied, he watched Benny turn the fish.

"I should fill the water pot for tea," he said quietly. Picking up the enameled pot, he walked to the creek and filled it. Walking back to camp under a grey colored sky, he placed the pot on the grill and looked in the oven at the biscuits. "The biscuits are done," he volunteered. "Is the rest of the meal, ready?"

"Yup, the stroganoff 's delicious," Luke said, taking a hesitant bite of the hot casserole. "So get your plate, let's serve this feast."

"I didn't realize I was so hungry," Benny said. The boys laid their empty camp plates on the ground beside them, and sighing with contentment, listened to the soothing sound of their fire as it crackled and spit noisily. "I'll throw a tea bag in the water pot and then we should get our mess cleaned up. It'll soon be full dark," he reminded them.

Groaning, they climbed to their feet and gathered up their plates and cooking pots. Trudging over rocky terrain to the edge of the running creek, they rinsed and rubbed their plates and cooking gear with gravel. Rinsing them a final time, they headed back to the welcoming brightness of their campfire. Stacking everything on top of the oven to dry, they poured themselves a cup of tea.

Shrugging into their down jackets, they sat back against the backrests that Pepper had made, and sipping their tea, munched on an energy bar. Relaxing, they lay watching the sky change from dark grey to black. Venus, the evening star brightened above the dark tip of a mountain and other sparkling bits of light appeared gradually, until the sky was covered with stars. In the east a three-quarter moon rose over the outline of a massive ridge coloring the rocky landscape, a milky white. The boys huddled near the fire, replenishing it from time to time with pieces of firewood.

Luke raised his arms over his head stretching his aching muscles. Yawning, he pushed his legs out along the ground. "What are you thinking, Pepper?" .

Pepper's expression was stark. Hugging his knees, he sat hunched over staring into the fire. Bending further, he laid his chin against his knees. The flickering fire moved shadows across his face, casting it with a brooding, somber melancholy. "Nothin, that's worth repeating. As me Granny would say, a mishmash of a wee bit of nothin."

THE DEVILS PUNCHBOWL

Laughing aloud, Luke turned and looked up at the sky, it was so clear up here on the top of the mountain, he felt as if he could reach up and touch the stars. The feeling was intense, and so powerful, he was completely awestruck on nights like this. Here I am, God, he thought, puny man made in your image, and I'm sitting, on top of your world. We are so tiny Father compared to all this.

Studying the sky, Luke searched for the North star. "You guys remember, what my Dad taught us about finding North? Find the Big Dipper and then directly above it find the Little Dipper. The star on the end of the Little Dipper's handle is the North Star." Pointing with his finger, he added. "See, that one there's the North Star. It always points North. Cool, hah."

Benny slipped further down on his rock, inching his way, until he was looking upward at the sky. "I wonder if we ever will have space travel between stars," he mused. "It seems kind of a waste when you look up there and see millions and millions of star systems. A reasonable person, would have to surmise, that life must exist on the planets circling them. And, isn't that a pisser of a thought, because we'll never get to see any of it."

"Hum . . . mpt," Pepper snorted. "It blows your mind to think we might be the only intelligent beings in the universe. Which could be, you know, everybody's just guessing. There's just as much chance that there isn't any life, as to think there might be life out there somewhere. I've heard and read a lot of hype about people meeting aliens, but no one has much documentation to prove any of it. If they do have any proof, they're keeping it, mighty quiet."

"That's kind of conceited thinking," Luke said. He raised his eyebrows, and then lowering them, squinted at Pepper through a puff of smoke cast out by their fire. "We just can't be that unique." Rising to his feet, he picked up a small limb from their stacked pile and threw it on the fire. "I'm going to brush my teeth, take a whizz and then hit my sack, daybreak comes early."

"Me too," Benny said. "I'm tired and my body is really sore from the climb. You coming, Pepper?

CHAPTER 6

THE SCREECH OF a hawk woke Luke from a dead sleep. Rolling over, he rubbed his eyes with his hand and sleepily watched the sky. Wispy clouds, embellished the black tips of mountains still outlined against a grey-black sky, and he expected, to see the hawk floating on wind currents above the thousand foot cliffs. Yawning, he tried again to see the hawk. The hawk called another screeching cry and then he saw him, way up circling on the wind, his wings straight out, just floating. What a beautiful bird and so lucky to be able to fly like that, he thought.

Pulling his arm completely out of his sleeping bag, he stuck it in the air to test the temperature. It was cold. Forcing himself to sit up, he grabbed his pants and boots. Crawling to the end of his bag, he sat for several seconds examining the fire for telltale signs of embers. Nothing discernible, but maybe there were a few live coals under all that ash. Shoving his legs into his Levis, he pushed his bare feet into his boots and shivered. They felt like chunks of ice.

Continuing to shiver, he put his down-jacket on over his undershirt and poked at the fire. Laying small pieces of wood on a few slumbering coals, he blew on them until he had a small blaze going. Feeding it slowly with larger pieces of wood, he finally was satisfied that it would burn. Picking up the water pot, he went to the creek. Filling it, he went back to the fire and placed it on the grill.

Crawling on his sleeping bag, Luke retrieved his kit from his backpack and walked to the creek. Brushing his teeth, he thought of immersing his body in the icy water. It wasn't easy to rinse yourself in

THE DEVILS PUNCHBOWL

water this cold, it took guts. He laughed to himself as he stripped and tightening his stomach muscles took a hesitant step into the water. By the time he was finished scrubbing his body it was red, but he felt better. Alive!

Running back to camp, he hovered over the fire warming himself. Shivering, he dressed quickly and waited impatiently for the water to boil. Placing more wood on the fire, he watched it burn, until it was cracking and spitting hot. Jogging to the creek he took what he wanted out of their food locker, and juggling, the ice-cold packages, raced back to camp.

Placing the frying pan on the grill, he laid nine slices of bacon in it. Sizzling and curling against the bottom of the hot pan, the redolent, enticing aroma of frying bacon spiced the air as he mixed up a package of biscuit mix for pancakes. Watching the last batch of pancakes cook, he turned them over another time to brown. Putting them in the oven to stay warm, he spooned instant coffee into three cups, then yelled, at Pepper and Benny. "Hey guys, up and atem, coffee's made."

Pepper and Benny sat up, their faces sleepy and disgruntled. Luke handed each of them a cup of coffee. They sat shivering in the nippy air sipping the hot beverage.

"Breakfast in five minutes," Luke said, grinning at their cranky faces. "Hurry up."

Luke watched Benny and Pepper rush back along the trail. Their noses were a bright cherry red and, walking quickly, their breath vaporized, condensing in cloudy puffs in the cold air. Blowing on their fingers, they accepted a cup of coffee from Luke and sat warming themselves next to the fire.

Pouring eggs from his thermos into the frying pan, Luke quickly scrambled them. Opening the oven, he loaded a plate with pancakes, three slices of bacon and scrambled eggs for each of them. Their forks scraped and clattered against their metal plates as they ate.

Finishing first, Pepper sat back with a cup of coffee and sighed. "Are we leaving right away for the mountain, or are we going to pack a lunch to take with us?"

"I'm going to fix lemonade for our canteens," Luke answered. "I can pack energy bars and jerky my Mom made."

"I brought dried fruit we can pack," Benny volunteered, "and pepperoni sticks. There's also a few biscuits' left over from dinner last night." Luke and Benny both turned and stared expectantly at Pepper.

"What?" he asked, raising his eyebrows at them. "You're both looking at me, as if I've got rellanos', or something really good stashed away." With a quick smile, he ducked his head into the rolled collar of his down-jacket.

Luke and Benny dived on him. Wrestling, they pinned him down, slapping him with their ball caps.

"Okay, okay, lay off, quit," Pepper choked. "Hey, you spilled my coffee. Okay, I've got peppers stuffed with cheese, beans and spicy, string beef. This year, I even brought flour tortillas to roll them in."

"Asshole, Pepper," Benny cried out, laying back to catch his breath. "From the way you were acting, I was sure your Mom hadn't fixed them this year."

Working quickly they cleaned the camp. Packing their lunch in small haversacks, they banked the fire with rocks and ash and picking up their equipment, headed out into the Punchbowl basin. Leaving the narrow opening to the lake behind they turned east and followed the edge of the mountain that formed part of the thousand foot high cliffs circling the lake.

Alaska cedar, white oak, and mountain fir rimmed the meadows and valleys, and the green-black of forested slopes stood out as a sharp contrast against a pristine white blanket of snow. Huge black granite ridges jutted into the sky, standing out as stark reminders that this was a desolate, very primitive wilderness area.

Turning north, they cautiously walked a well-used animal trail and watched apprehensively for possible slides on the mountain above them. If a slide caught them on this part of the trail there was no place to go, except down a thousand feet or so.

Climbing steadily upward, they gratefully left the perilous path, hiking into a brushy canyon. Pushing through low-growing thickets of blueberries and stunted Alaska cedar, they stumbled and twisted through

THE DEVILS PUNCHBOWL

prickly brush for several miles, before the canyon broadened, opening into a flat meadow.

"There's that big fir I carved a mark in last year. You guys see it?" Luke called out. Running ahead of Benny and Pepper, he stopped under the fir tree. Turning to face north, he pointed a straight line at the mountain. "Ummm," Luke muttered, as Benny and Pepper jogged up to him. "See that darker green bush that should be about where we covered up the opening. I hope it's there and not covered up by a landslide."

Pepper tried to find a landmark to aim for. "Okay, wait here and I'll line myself up with you," he said brusquely. "Maybe, I'll find it immediately and we won't have to remove half the stuff growing on the mountain," he whispered to himself. Walking further to the east to a rocky area, he parted a few low-growing bushes and searched along the ground.

"Hey Pepper, look for some odd rocks. Remember, we put them on last, we marked it like a cairn," Benny yelled. His eyes never leaving Pepper, he started walking, pushing branches away from him.

"I think this mountain spews out rocks like it's giving birth to litters of young," Pepper yelled in exasperation. "I thought I made an arrow sign, too," he muttered impatiently.

Yelling, "here's something, c'mon, I think I've found it," he turned and waved his hand at Luke.

Racing toward Pepper, Luke burst through a thicket of huckleberries, and found him on his knees, throwing dirt and rocks. Pulling rocks and dry, dead brush away from the fissure, he enlarged it to the one they all remembered. The year before it had been a tight fit for all of them, but Rob had the hardest time getting through it. His shoulders were massive and he had laughed over their comments. He had told them, all it took was persistence, as he wiggled and squeezed his body into the crevice.

Luke flashing a triumphant grin at Benny and Pepper, pulled his hard hat from his head and flipped the switch to turn on its light. Kneeling, he slid to his belly and squirmed through the narrow irregular-shaped opening. Puffing, he held his breath at times, pushing and pulling to negotiate around an especially sharp bend. This part was tough, because the fissure narrowed, until there was barely enough space to force his body through its walls. Pushing his haversack ahead of him, his back scraped the top of the fissure and sharp edges of rocks gouged his belly and chest.

The small fissure was cold and the frigid iciness of the rock leeching through his clothes, cooled the sweat next to his body. He shivered, even though he felt hot, and wrinkled his face in revulsion when his hands slid over small patches of slime.

Grunting, Luke tried to see around his sack. If I remember right, this crack in the mountain is about thirty feet long, he thought, and as he paused, nervous sweat trickling from beneath his hard hat, blazed a spidery trail on his neck. Being in this small cramped space made him slightly claustrophobic and his mind, no matter how much he rationalized, couldn't accept the thought of tons of mountainous rock above him. He kept pushing the thought back, frantically burying it somewhere in the deeper reaches of his brain, where he hoped it would stay, but it always surfaced again.

Pepper's sack hit his feet and, taking a deep breath, Luke surged ahead, the top of the fissure scraping his back painfully. His sack fell to the floor where the fissure opened up into a wider area, and holding his breath, he released it as his hands encountered the floor of the small space. Sighing in relief, he pulled himself free of the crevice.

"Wow EE . . . EE." Pepper yelled, as his head cleared the opening in the narrow cleft of rock. His voice swelling in exuberance, he tried to choke off the rising tide of panic that threatened to engulf him. "First hurdle over. I had to keep saying my prayers to stick myself into so many small spaces. I could never do it if it was longer." Propping himself against the rock wall, he nervously ran his hand around the back of his neck. "I felt the whole friggin mountain was gonna collapse on top of me. Tons of rock just waitin to squish me flat."

Benny's sack landed with a plop and then his arms and head popped through the opening. "I'm relieved to be out of there," he gurgled happily. My mind kept telling me the fissure was getting smaller and somehow, the mountain was trying to squeeze me in there. Scary shit."

THE DEVILS PUNCHBOWL

"We have about sixty feet to go before we hit the small cave," Luke said hopefully. "I think that's about right don't you?" His look was questioning, the beam of light from his hard hat touching, Pepper's and then Benny's face.

"Yeah, at least some of the other fissures aren't as small as this first one. Remember, the last one is the crevice that turns to the right, and it goes almost straight up, then down into the small cave. Let's go," Benny replied enthusiastically. "I can't wait until we get there. The thought of what we saw last summer makes me jumpy. Shit," he added, sucking in his breath! "Makes my heart race!"

They left the fissure, twisting through narrow passages and ancient underground water ways. Moving at a fast pace, they crawled through silky satin-smooth crevices, and then slowed, pulling themselves through small fissures as rough as sand paper.

Luke held his breath, and with a sigh of relief, fell to the floor of the small cave. The hiss escaping from his lips, audible, as his lungs expelled their last remnant of air. Resting for a few minutes, he waited for Benny and Pepper to emerge from the last crevice. Benny's head appeared and then his body, followed quickly by Pepper's grinning head. They both sighed, expelling a gush of pent up air.

Luke groaned and climbing to his feet, began to clear the debris from the tunnel's entrance. "We really hid the opening last summer," he stated. "I think we did a major overkill." Grunting, he rolled a large rock toward the back of the cave. "I hope the light's still there. It'll be really bitchin if it's not." A flash of apprehension rolled through him, turning his guts into knots.

Digging with their hands they pushed dirt and small rocks away from the tunnel's entrance. Glimpsing a small gleam of light, Pepper's face lit up in a broad grin. Pushing himself from his stomach to his knees, he lifted his hands in a benediction. "Thanks Father."

"Holy shit, guys," Luke whispered. "The light seems brighter than last summer."

Slipping to their stomachs they lay flat, bunching together. The moving beams of light from their hard hats formed a vortex in the tunnel walls, reflecting incandescently an omniscient aurora. Moving in an endless reflection, the light spinning in smaller and smaller circles within the marbleized wall, traveled into infinitesimal infinity through its mirrored surface.

Sliding forward, Luke pushed his sack into the tunnel and watched it slide downward. Raising his arms above his head, he slipped into the opening after it, and using his feet as a brake, pressed his boots against the walls, sliding swiftly toward the bright light at its end. Pulling himself free from the tunnel, he lay for a second on his stomach, and rising to his knees, stared at the immense cavern. Nothing had changed or seemed to be different, the cavern was exactly as they had left it last summer. Cautiously, he pressed himself against the wall and stood waiting for Pepper and Benny to emerge from the tunnel.

Pepper's small sack landed with a plop next to Luke. His arms appeared next followed by his grinning face. Instead of on his belly, he had come through the tunnel on his back. Climbing quickly to his feet, he crouched and pulled Benny's sack from the opening.

Benny's arms and head appeared, and grasping the edge of the tunnel, he pulled himself free. Kneeling on the ground, he looked apprehensively at the huge cavern. Warily, he climbed to his feet.

Clutching their haversacks against their chests, they stood against the wall and listened for any sounds of alarm that their presence might have caused. Pivoting, they stared in every direction, watching carefully for movement, their attention completely focused on watching and listening. There wasn't a sound, just the exaggerated noise of their own breathing. Sweat, beaded their faces, and standing perfectly still, their expressions rapidly changed into patterns of awe, mixed with unknown and imagined fears.

"Okay, we're here," Benny said quietly, loudly ejecting a lung full of air.

"Yeah, we're here," Luke answered. "The most important thing we have to remember is, we stick together. No exploring by yourself and no wondering off alone! Where do you think we should start?"

"Let's do it systematically," Pepper answered. "We'll try to look at everything that's here first. After that we'll pick something that really interests us to examine."

THE DEVILS PUNCHBOWL

"Let's start with the tablet cave," Luke volunteered, pointing toward his right.

They hesitated and moving stiffly, their eyes wondered again over the huge mysterious cavern. Deep shadows clung to the walls and roof, and the strange lighting, didn't penetrate or disburse them.

Shuffling along the edge of the circular wall, they moved toward the entrance of the tablet cave. Luke kept his back to the cavern's wall and his head never stopped moving. His eyes flashed, the pupils enlarged with nervous apprehension examined everything, but never lingered on anything very long.

Crowding together, they stopped at the entrance and looked back at the cavern they were leaving. It seemed endless. The vastness of it covered with dark foreboding shadows, stretched a long way into distant areas, where even the mysterious light didn't penetrate. Reluctantly turning their backs they shuffled forward entering a short hall.

The chamber was minuscule. Row upon row of tablets filled a space about the size of a small tennis court. There were hundreds of them neatly stacked together. Some sections, had just three tablets in a stack, others had a hundred or so. Near the back of the cave, tablets lay in disorderly discarded piles on the floor. Benny picked up one of the filed tablets, and leaning into each other, they examined the odd writing chiseled in its face.

Benny running his hands over the surface of the tablet seemed lost in some private thought, his face blank of expression. He grunted and cleared his throat. "I don't recognize the writing. I think these are old, even older than we can ever imagine," he said absently.

Shaking his head slightly, he glanced across the tablet at Luke. "I can't imagine what purpose they had, but let's leave them as we found them." Apprehensively, he shrugged his shoulders. "They're been left here for a specific reason. Look at the walls, can you tell where the light source is coming from?"

Examining the small cave, their eyes wondered over the smooth, black marble walls and ceiling. Glistening, it mirrored their presence in dark shadowy outlines.

"I think the light comes from within the walls and ceiling, because I can't see anything that even resembles a light fixture. Even the floor is that same mirror-like substance," Luke said. Kneeling abruptly, he placed his palm flat against the floor. "The floor doesn't feel hot or cold, just comfortable. Beats the hell out of me!" He shrugged his shoulders, his face expressing his skepticism.

"There has to be a heat source, because it's not really cold in here. Remember, the big cavern has ice in places and that shiny metal thing we saw last year was frozen from the waist down in a large chunk of ice," Pepper said. Looking back at the entrance to the stone tablet cave, he added. "The doorway into this cave is formed in an oval shape and the hall is about three feet long. It probably has an invisible barrier that keeps the heat in here. And maybe, the tablets need to be protected against the cold. I bet that's what it is."

"Yeah, I bet you're right," Benny said absently, still clutching the stone tablet. It has to have some kind of barrier so the heat won't leak out into the big cavern. I felt something when we passed through the doorway, like a tingle. I think it has a barrier, an invisible curtain of some kind, maybe charged electrons."

Laying the tablet back in its cradle, he turned in a circle. "Even the method of filing is unique," he said. "Each tablet is resting in its own rocky cradle, so it doesn't touch the next one. Awesome, this is awesome! There isn't a sound." Beautiful in its expressive clarity, and as if from a wondrous benediction, the inflection in his voice changed. "Listen to the silence." They fell silent contemplating the marbled wall chamber and the importance of its contents.

Luke cleared his throat. "You know, when Pepper's Granny says, quiet, if you're quiet enough, you'll hear the voice of God, I never really knew what she meant before. Now I do," he said reverently, his eyes softening reflectively at his statement.

"Jesus? I don't know if we'll find him in here," Pepper said brusquely. "I don't think me Irish Granny would think so, maybe just the opposite. This looks like aliens to me. I've never heard, read or seen anything like this in all my life." Glancing toward the door, he added humorously. "C'mon, let's look at something else! And please, say a silent prayer, that we don't meet the devil."

Laughing suddenly, Pepper turned toward Luke and Benny. Backing toward the entrance, he yelled. "Let's go exploring!" Clapping his hands together, he laughed again. "C'mon, lighten up. Make some noise! I can't stand all this quiet! It's spooky!"

Pausing in the entrance, they stood quietly, trying to analyze the prickly sensation they felt when passing through the opening. "Hey, are we gonna stick close to the walls and follow the curve of the cavern, or should we go straight across and look at that shiny thing, Pepper found last year?" Luke asked.

Undecided, they tried to see across the immense cavern. "Let's go straight across and, we'll look at that silvery thing. I think it's a robot," Pepper called out eagerly. "Maybe if we examine him, we'll figure out who they are and what they're doing inside this mountain."

"How in hell do you know if the robot's masculine?" Luke asked. "It might be female," he added. His smile became a wicked grin.

"Oh, that's where you're wrong," Pepper chortled loudly. "Everyone with any common sense, knows that a robot or android type being has to be male. Never a female. God forbid a female robot. What will you think of next, Luke? Benny, have you noticed, ever since last year, when Luke finally got to date Debbie, he's had nothing but the female shape on his mind. . . . ?"

"And I don't mean all of the female shape either, just parts of their anatomy." Laughter bubbling from his throat, Pepper danced ahead of Luke and Benny. Laughing hilariously, he roared and spun around. "Have you ever seen a robot with breasts?" he asked, throwing his arms in the air.

"No, I haven't, but I've never seen one with any other kind of appendage either. Especially, an appendage that would show the robot was male," Luke answered. "You're funny Pepper. I know you're always thinking about Bella and the way she's put together, especially her top half. You can't shit me that your thoughts are all that pure."

Benny glanced from Luke to Pepper, and raising his hat from his head, brushed his fingers through his hair. "I never have thoughts like that about Lily," he said. "My thoughts about her are pure, as Pepper's, Irish Granny, would say."

Yelling in exasperation, Pepper and Luke jumped on Benny, pummeling him. "Let off, quit," he yelled. "I give up." Gasping, he yelled again, gurgling the words. "I give up. . . . Give up."

"Admit it then and we won't hit you again," Pepper said, holding Benny down.

"Okay, okay, I admit it," Benny yelled, laughing hysterically. "I have lewd thoughts about Lily. I can't help it. She's beautiful."

Laughing, they lay on the cave's floor and looked at the ceiling. "We needed to laugh. I'm so tense my nerves have been crawling on top of my skin," Benny said.

"I can't believe a normal guy by the time he's eighteen, hasn't had at least a thousand lewd thoughts, I think I've had a million," Pepper said.

Luke turned over onto his stomach. Getting up on his knees, he swatted Pepper with his hand and, looking at Benny, he laughed. "Get off your asses, let's cross this huge space, as Murphy's law says, times awastin."

Reluctantly, they rose to their feet and stared upward at the ceiling of the great cavern. Benny bent and swiping his helmet from the ground, jammed it on his head. "I really don't feel good about going all the way across this cavern," he said pessimistically. "You could put ten five-story buildings in here with room to spare. Let's move, we'll go look at Pepper's silver robot man."

Carefully trudging over the cavern's uneven floor, they walked up a short incline, and passing a cluster of giant quartz crystals, Luke skipped his hand over the surface of one. Jerking his hand back, he glanced at Benny, shaking his head in disbelief. The crystals, some round as giant beach balls, some as square as perfect dice, were spewed out along the floor of the cavern as if they were toys, thrown there, by a giant in a fit of anger.

"They're radiating an energy," Luke said in disbelief. "And what do you think formed them into such uniform shapes? Odd, I think," he added, stopping to glance again at the rock formations surrounding them, "but then almost everything in nature is kind of odd. Hard to believe some of the things she's produced."

Pepper tentatively pressed a finger tip against the side of an immense crystal. "Feels almost like the hum you hear, sometimes, when you put your ear against a telephone pole. They have to be charged somehow."

"Just think, how dark it would be in here without this light," Benny said. He shivered and pressed his hand against the crystal. "I don't know if I could explore this cavern if all we had for a light was the one on our helmets."

Watching warily, they tramped noisily around ancient stalagmite columns and over huge rock piles. "I think the biggest bend in the cavern is to the north. It gets colder up in that direction, too," Luke volunteered absently. "This place must be ancient." Shrugging tense shoulders, he waved his arms in frustration.

"I don't think there's a logical answer for this place," Pepper said. "Part of me wants to explore everything that's here and then roaring through the other part, it says . . . get out of here." Glancing at the ceiling a puzzled expression crossed his face, and staying there, it changed to one of apprehension mixed with a tension that pulled his lips down in a grim contortion of his mouth. "Where in hell is the light coming from?"

Climbing a short rise, they paused to examine a sixty-foot stalactite, its bottom almost touching the floor. Mineral deposits had colored it in irregular patterns of dark hues and it hung from the ceiling, with nothing else around it like a multicolored icicle. Luke touched it as he stepped carefully around it, and even though, dripping water had made it over thousands of years, it was solid, like rock.

Approaching a brightly lit doorway, they stopped, and cautiously stepping close to the entrance, looked through a small hall into a cave with shiny black walls and ceiling. The robot standing at the entrance seemed to be on guard. A sentinel placed there to protect . . .

What? The cave was empty. They stood in its entrance listening, their heads slanted to one side, straining to hear the slightest noise.

There wasn't any, it was a tomb, the silence echoing its stillness, until it seemed to be a palatable thing, they could feel and almost taste.

Pepper ran his hand over the chest area of the robot. "Look at the ice, there isn't a drop of it melted," he whispered. "It's the same as last summer, nothing's changed. The metal's cold, but kind of warm at the same time."

Luke and Benny stepped forward, tentatively touching the robot with large hands. What Pepper thought was warmth, Luke felt as a prickling sensation running up his arm. Benny and Luke exchanged glances their eyes steady and staring. A trace of anxiety darkened Benny's eyes and a slight flush spread over his face. Luke glanced away, his eyes following his hand as he rubbed it over the robot's shoulder.

"I don't think that's warmth, it's more like he's emitting some kind of energy," Benny said. "You see where the ice ends, where I imagine his waist would be, there's no melting. So it can't be a heat source, because it would melt the ice."

They clustered together, each of them examining the robot. He reminded Luke of a spider, his torso being the biggest thing about him. Resembling a gigantic loaf of French bread, his shape was thicker at the top, sloping slightly to form his shoulders. What served for a head was about the size of a football and it was connected to a neck made of circular pleats that looked like it should bend.

The robot's eyes were huge, half closed and wide apart. Placed on the front of the elongated ball and with a split similar to lips, they were the only openings on its head, the rest was smooth metal. His shoulders were tubular, his arm's made from the same material, and one arm was bent slightly, so it had some kind of elbow, Luke thought, but it wasn't discernable. The hands, blurred dark shadows were frozen deep inside the ice and what he had for legs and feet couldn't be seen. Opaque and thickest next to the floor the ice covered his bottom half.

Pepper slipped to his knees and cupping his eyes with his hands, placed them against the ice. "I can't see a damn thing," he muttered crossly.

Luke and Benny knelt beside Pepper. They circled the robot on their knees trying to see through the ice. Rising to his feet, Luke grunted

THE DEVILS PUNCHBOWL

in frustration. "C'mon, let's eat I'm starved." Gesturing with his hand, he pointed at the doorway. "Do you want to eat in there or out here where we can see the robot?"

"Uh-huh," Benny said absently, circling to look at the robot's back. "Let's eat where we can look at him."

"Yeah, let's eat," Pepper echoed. "I'm starved, too." Settling next to the robot, they opened their sacks and divided the food they had brought.

"The rellanos are delicious, Pepper. How many did you bring, enough for tomorrow too, I hope?" Benny said enthusiastically. Stuffing the rest of his stuffed pepper wrapped in a flour tortilla in his mouth, he tried to smile around it.

"Umm . . . mm," Pepper replied. Grinning, he tried to keep his lips closed over the mouthful he was chewing. "Enough for tomorrow and the next day, if we eat just three each."

Luke lay back on his side and propped his head up with his hand. Chewing noisily on a piece of jerky, he tried to bite off another chewable size piece. Staring intently at the ice-encased robot, he leaned forward. "You know, this robot looks to me like he's holding something." Leaning closer yet, he studied the robot's hand through the ice.

"I'm too full right now to move, let's rest a few minutes," Benny said. Yawning, he laid back and moaned, his body sliding down over the hard surface of the rock.

"Yeah, me too," Pepper agreed, laying back on the rocky floor with a sigh. "Look at the stalactites on the ceiling. Some of them are as big as a small house. That rim of flowstone reminds me of the ocean after a storm, it's rippled and foamy like the surf. The foam is even dirty lookin like the surf is after a bad storm." Falling silent, he murmured. "Where in hell is the light coming from?" Sighing, he clasped his hands under the back of his head and through slitted eyes studied the ceiling of the immense cavern.

CHAPTER 7

SOMEHOW JUST LOOKING at the robot made Luke anxious, and the thought, he seems unawares, but is he, crossed his mind. And even though he doesn't move, maybe, he can see us. He rubbed the bridge of his nose and studied the robot intently. His anxiety heightened, peaking to new levels, and it surprised him, because he felt he had everything under control. "C'mon, let's go. This robot's weird. He's almost all arms and legs and his body isn't very big either, he's sort of a cross between a spider and that cartoon, Robot Man, on TV. He resembles a spider more, but he doesn't have enough legs." Laughing, he jumped to his feet and bowed. Touching the robot on the shoulder, he said in a high falsetto voice. "I dub thee Knight Spidery, a knave of this underground kingdom."

Benny glanced at his watch. "It's one o'clock already," he said, interrupting their laughter. "What should we do next? We have about two hours left and then we're out of here."

"Yeah," Luke said. "We want to get back to camp early enough to fish. I hope it's like last night with no one else around. It makes it easier to talk and we don't have to hide what we're doing."

"Remember, where the trail climbs and makes a big bend in the north end of the cavern?" Pepper asked. "Last year we didn't explore up there and if I remember right the light was really bright. Let's go in that direction."

Following the eastern wall of the cavern they climbed a path carved in the natural curve in the cliff's face. Stepping carefully, along a massive ice sheet that disappeared into a deep chasm, the trail narrowed,

THE DEVILS PUNCHBOWL

until it was barely a foot-wide. Moving their feet cautiously, they held their breath, and passing the frozen water, watched its surface reflect the light from their head lamps.

"Have you noticed how much rougher it is up here?" Luke said thoughtfully. "And darker too." He stared down at the rocky trail, and pausing, turned and looked back the way they had come. Filling the end of the cavern, huge stalactites and stalagmites grew from the floor and ceiling of the cavern. "We're a lot higher here than on the open flatter area where the frozen robot is," he added absently. Amazed, at what he was seeing, his eyes followed the beautiful geometric curve of flowstone along the trail. Sprouting from it, enormous chunks of black and white granite bulged from the cliffs' rocky face, its pattern a stark contrast against the creamy color of the flowstone.

Turning at the top of a slight rise, Benny hesitated, looking back along the trail. "My God, look, how beautiful," he exclaimed. The cavern with its artificial light had a bright, surreal, moon-glow and, looking down through the immense emptiness of it, past the waterfall and its icy blue color, an eerie aureole hovered near the ceiling. Stalactites floated like giant icicles through a nebulous pink glow, their anchoring roots hidden by the cloudy, misty light.

Pepper trembled wrapping his arms around his body.

Luke sank back against the cliff, his mind overwhelmed by sensations of alarm. The panoramic view emanated such a strange aura that his mind faltered and became blank. He couldn't believe what he was seeing.

"C'mon, let's go," Benny said. He turned right, following a sharp bend in the trail, and trudging up a steep incline approached the first lighted opening.

Pepper trotting around the bend, shoved on Benny trying to see around him. "C'mon, move your ass, let's go. We'll, look at what's in there, and then, go topside. I'm ready to leave."

"Okay, quit shoving," Benny said crossly. He stepped back against the cliff's face and gestured for Pepper to pass him. "What the hell, go ahead if you want to go faster. Help yourself, go first, I don't care."

"I think it's time for us to leave if you guys are getting irritable," Luke said. "Remember, that's one of the things Rob said to watch for. We've probably been in here too long for our first day. We'll take a quick look and then go topside." Stepping around Pepper and Benny, he silently approached the first lighted opening. Striding forward, he turned into the doorway and recoiled several steps.

"Holy shit," he gasped.

"What is it?" Benny said.

Turning into the lighted entrance, they stared, their eyes darkening with apprehension and, huddling together, they froze, their mouths gaping open. Two robots, stood a short distance from the entrance, their arms raised away from their bodies. One of them, very erect, stared straight ahead into the room, and the other, had his head bent at an awkward angle toward the floor. Neither one moved. The robots, about four-feet tall, had exaggerated long legs and arms. They looked exactly like the one Luke had dubbed, Knight Spidery.

Sucking in a deep breath, Luke slowed his breathing, his chest expanding until it couldn't hold any more air. He exhaled slowly and followed by Pepper and Benny stepped into the cave. Hugging the wall, they circled away from the robots, and stopping, watched for movement.

Approximately, twenty by fifty feet long, the cave was covered in a white, mirror-like, smooth marbly substance. It had three entrances, one on the north end, one on the south, and the one they had just entered. Both the north and south openings glistened with reflected light. The light in the north wall glowed brilliantly, in comparison, to the light in the opening on the opposite end of the room.

Moving soundlessly, they crept forward, stopping next to a pile of four smooth round objects. Stepping around them, they moved toward the entrance in the south wall. They hesitated at the opening and looked back. The robots still stood motionless, their spider-like metal bodies, reflecting an aureole glow. Their feet, small appendages with joints at the ankle and knee didn't look strong enough to support them.

"I wonder how they move," Luke said, waving at the robots with his hand. "They have four fingers and an appendage like a thumb and,

THE DEVILS PUNCHBOWL

their feet have toes. Do you think they communicate with each other? They aren't moving, but, maybe, they can pass messages to a central computer somewhere. Hope not, because the thought scares me. I don't like the idea of being watched."

"I really don't care," Pepper answered tersely, his voice deepening. "As long as they don't move while we're in here."

Cautiously, they passed through a short hall, entering an immense cavern that sloped sharply downward into darkness. Only partially lighted, the cavern was huge, with deep black shadows lining its walls. On the west wall, a robot sat at the controls of a machine that resembled a small riding lawn mower. Almost half of the floor and ceiling had been smoothed out into a continuous slick surface. The vast space on the east side, had no stalagmites or stalactites, just uneven rocky levels of a vast cavern. It had the appearance of having been cleaned recently.

Luke, using the sleeve of his jacket wiped the sweat from his face. "They must be cleaning this cavern so they can convert it into one coated with that peculiar marble stuff," he said. "The more we explore, the more puzzled, I get. Why did they cover so many caves with this marbly stuff?"

"C'mon," Pepper said. "Let's look in the cave on the north end and then head out. I've had enough for one day. My thoughts aren't too good right now."

Fighting feelings of panic, they rushed across the white marbleized cave toward the brilliantly lit opening in the north wall. Their reflections flattening into distorted silhouettes followed them, moving grotesquely in the mirror-like marbled wall.

Benny arrived at the entrance first and placed his hand against the edge of the opening. Hesitating, their breathing escalating to short gasps, they watched the corridor. Longer than the other hallways they had seen, it curved in the middle, and the radiant light, reflecting from the ceiling, walls and floor shimmered in dazzling brightness.

Pressing their backs against the wall, they moved quietly, climbing to where the corridor took a sharp turn. Stopping, they listened apprehensively, staring at the bend for several seconds. Luke shrugged and slowly hooked his head around the corner. The hallway, a perfectly smooth hollow-tube, continued upward in a steep incline.

"Hey, this isn't a short hall to a cave like the rest we've seen. It's a tunnel similar to the one where we entered the great cavern from the small cave," Luke whispered. Pressed against the wall, they peered around the curve, their hearts hammering inside their chests.

They started again, their movements' jerky and indecisive. Their down jackets slid like satin over the smooth surface of the marbleized wall, and their booted feet scraping the floor echoed, the sound magnified by the narrow, hollow emptiness of the tunnel. They stopped near the oval opening at its end.

"What is it?" Benny whispered, clutching Luke's arm in a fierce grip.

Luke yelped softly, pulling his arm away.

Apprehension crossed Benny's face drawing his mouth down in a grim line. "This is out of this world, nobody on earth made this," he whispered raggedly. Shuddering, he crossed his arms, hugging his body.

Luke took two steps further and crouching near the edge of the opening, glanced to his left and then to his right. Tapering inward, the room was round on two sides, and its middle, its deepest depth, sixty feet long. The ceiling was conical, its center the highest area and starting on the left side of the room, a curved convex material covered the wall. The continuous sheet filled more than three-fourths of the room's wall space. It resembles a frosted window, Luke thought, but it doesn't reflect like an ordinary windowpane. Dark, milky streaks colored an irregular pattern across its surface, making parts of it darker than others. Beneath it, a padded console built against the walls, ended on the right side of the room, forming a table in the shape of a teardrop. The table jutted into the room about six-feet along the wall.

"What do you think, should we go any further?" Luke asked, his voice dropping to a whisper. "Maybe it's not safe."

"Yeah! But let's go anyway," Benny answered, grabbing Luke's arm. "What the hell, we're here." He grinned suddenly. "If we don't, we'll be sorry later and accuse ourselves of being a bunch of wimps."

THE DEVILS PUNCHBOWL

Pepper slipped to his knees in the middle of the entrance. Watching warily for movement, he whispered. "I'm staying here, be careful, guys."

Like rats through a maze, a hundred anxieties scoured Luke's mind, leaving in its wake, goose bumps along his spine and, an uneasy dread. Crossing the sixty feet of pie-shaped room, he turned and rested his hand against the console. Sucking in his breath, he jumped as part of it moved, and pushing against Benny, they yelled simultaneously, as a portion of the console opened silently. A small padded stool with a round back swung outward, and a monitor, with a screen much larger than on a computer appeared above it.

Pepper rose to his feet, the nerves along his skin crawled and he broke out in a cold sweat. Rushing across the room, he pushed between Luke and Benny, and looking down, studied the maze of swirling colors in the slanted screen. "What in hell happened?" he said anxiously.

"Luke did it. He pressed on something," Benny said tersely. "What'd you do?" he asked, shoving Luke forward. Press it again and get rid of it."

Luke pressed the rounded edge of the console. They watched fascinated as the monitor with its keyboard slid downward, and the stool, once again became part of the console. Agitated, they nervously examined the room. Their breathing and the nervous shuffling of their feet against the floor, became exaggerated, the sound made audible by the complete and profound stillness of the room. The silence became intense, and Luke thought, he could hear his eyelids blink as he warily watched and listened.

"What an ingenious mind made this," Pepper whispered, his voice a barely discernible murmur. He hovered over the console studying its rounded edge. "You can't even see the line where it opens and closes. Look how the stool becomes part of the curve in the padding. Neat! Sweet and neat! Weird though! I'm telling you, guys, this is weird."

Luke moved to his left where the console ended against a wall and pressed on its curved side. A monitor rose and a stool moved outward. A keyboard dropped into a slot and a voice from the screen, gurgled softly. Startled, terror swamped him in a sickening rush, and stumbling backward, he pushed on Benny and Pepper. Pivoting, they ran for the entrance and stopping in the doorway, looked back.

"Asshole, Luke, you'd better go turn it off," Pepper stuttered. He swallowed convulsively, his lips twisting in a tremble he tried to control.

The screen brightened into a hazy image and spat out another series of low verbal symbols. Receiving no reply, the image waited and in a few seconds, spit his message out into the room again, a staccato harangue of verbal grunts. Receiving no reply to its call, the voice faded into silence and the screen went blank. Different variations of the color blue appeared on the screen, splitting it into a whirling disc.

Luke gulped and almost running, moved swiftly across the room. Pressing a shaking hand on the curved edge of the console, he watched the room for any type of aggressive movement. The small stool slid back into its slot, and the monitor, with its whirling disc and attached keyboard, disappeared back into the console.

"This is the most phenomenal thing I've ever experienced," he called out, his voice rising to a high nervous warble. "I almost can't believe it! Did that image look human to you?"

Laughing softly, in a sharp tone that was more an agitated muffled bark, Pepper stepped away from Benny. His lips moved in a harsh whisper. "No, he was different. He kinda looked human, but he was different."

Benny laughed uneasily. "This is way beyond any technology I've read about," he said. His eyes skipped warily along the long length of the console. "Maybe, this is a secret place of our government. I can hardly believe what I'm seeing. Unbelievable! And, just think, maybe it's something from outer space. What are they doing here? You know . . . here. I mean a place like the Devils Punchbowl. It isn't where I would expect to find something like this. It's too remote."

"Yeah, but I think that's exactly why they're here," Luke answered. He crossed the room, glancing warily at the console. Nervously, pinching his lips together with his fingers, he blinked rapidly, his expression

THE DEVILS PUNCHBOWL

confused. "It's a remote wilderness area and they're well hidden here. They wouldn't expect anyone to find them buried in a mountain. And where are they? There isn't anything alive in here." Swinging around, anxiety washed his face of color and his eyes darkened, the pupils enlarging as fear raced a rampant path through his guts.

"I think you guys are wrong," Pepper said, excitement making his voice rise to a squeaky high pitch. "This place is old."

"Ancient!"

"It's been here a long time, years and years," he added reflectively. "The robots for some reason got stuck here and they've kept it going . . . kinda . . . but they ran out of a reason to go on. Maybe it's like E.T., they're lost and can't find their way home." He laughed at his own words, the sound changing into a high treble-giggle.

"C'mon, let's go," Luke said uneasily. Turning toward the door, he pushed Benny and Pepper ahead of him. Emerging from the tunnel, they crossed the large white-marbled cave. Passing the guarding robots, Luke stopped and picked up a T-shaped object from the floor where it lay close to one of the robots. "Hey," he said to Benny's back. "This wasn't on the floor when we came in here." He waved the object in the air. "I wonder why the robot dropped it."

Examining the tool, Luke couldn't see how the thing worked, but it had to have some function or the robots wouldn't have it connected to their arms. "Should I take it?" he asked.

Benny and Pepper stood in the doorway. Indecisively, they stared at Luke. Raising his eyebrows, he waited for them to answer. "Maybe I should leave it here where he dropped it," he added uncertainly.

Pepper watched Benny's face. Seeing his indecision, he volunteered. "Oh shit. Yeah, take it with you. Examining it will keep me from thinking about Bella. I miss her," he murmured wistfully.

"Yeah," Benny said, his expression changing to a thoughtful scowl. Uncertain, he clasped his hands together. "Maybe we can figure out how it works." He walked through the short entrance hall and started down the narrow path toward the great cavern.

Luke shoved the tool into his pocket, and hesitating, cast one last look at the robots. Following Benny and Pepper, he stepped out on the trail, and stopping next to the ice sheet's edge tried to see its bottom. The blue-white ice flow glistened in the strange light emanating from the ceiling.

"I'm really glad we're going topside," Benny said unexpectedly. He jogged faster along the path looking over his shoulder at Pepper and Luke. "C'mon. I'm out of here. I've had enough for today."

Pepper slipped by Benny and went down the steep incline at a fast pace. Passing the robot encased in ice, he stopped, gave it a pat and then hurried along the trail toward the exit tunnel. He tossed his haversack into its opening and crept in after it, his long legs disappearing from view. Following him, Benny eased in after him, shouting. . . .

"Hurry your ass, Pepper, I'm right behind you."

Luke paused, and lifting his head gazed back into the depths of the vast cavern. The eerie feelings, he'd been having all day, intensified. The hair rose on his scalp and neck, tightening his features into a stark mask and goose bumps danced up his arms. Falling to his knees, he took one more quick look back. Shuddering with the thought, I feel like I'm being watched, he thrust himself upward into the tunnel. Pushing rapidly with his knees and feet, he popped into the small cave just in time to see Benny's feet disappear into a narrow opening.

Running across the small cave, he worked his body into the crevice. Grunting and squeezing himself through small openings that led into long fissures and tunnels, he saw a bit of daylight at a bend in the last one. Breathing rapidly in relief, he sucked in his breath and forced his body around the curve. Crawling over the rough edges of the narrow crack in the mountain, he pushed with his feet and pulled himself through the last few feet of the fissure. He tumbled through the opening and popped into sunshine.

Blinking against the glare, he grinned at Pepper and Benny. Pushing his hard hat to the back of his head, Luke's eyes sparkled like blue gems and he laughed, a boisterous, relieved sound. The curve of his lips and the tense muscles of his face relaxed as he said.

"We made it. Hallelujah!"

"Praise the Lord," Benny and Pepper, yelled.

"Amen, amen," Luke answered them. "C'mon, let's get back to camp." Throwing up his arms, he turned, his face up to the sun. "Feel that sun," he shouted.

"Yeah, feels really good, and what's more surprising, we didn't meet anything today that attacked us," Benny said, his words softly spoken from between tight lips.

"Yeah, I kept feeling that something was going to spring out at us from some secret place we weren't aware of," Pepper muttered.

"I feel like I'm continually being watched," Luke whispered. "Spooky feeling, I hate it." Trudging wearily along the last steep mountain path, they turned into the Punchbowl.

"If you guys will fish tonight, I'll start the fire and put a pot of water to boil," Benny offered. "What kind of casserole should I fix?"

"Let's have macaroni and cheese. It really sounds good to me," Luke answered, looking at Pepper. Nodding his head in agreement, Pepper bent to pick up his pole and left the camp. Luke grabbed his and Benny's pole and quickly followed him. Approaching the lake, they searched for worms and bugs.

Lifting a rock, Luke grabbed a handful of crawling insects from under it and shoved them into his plastic bag. "C'mon, Pep, I've got enough for both of us," he said, turning toward the lake. Baiting both his and Benny's rods he flipped the lines out over the water. A purple haze shadowed the lake, the forerunner of approaching darkness. To the west, a splash of brilliant light shimmered across the sky, and the mountains, becoming dark ominous outlines, turned black. Pulling in one fish after the other, they soon had twenty pan-size fish laying on the bank. Gutting them, they tossed the offal into the lake, and trout rushing toward the free meal, churned the water's surface into a frenzied white froth.

Luke laughed, a hearty bass-sound that rebounded against the thousand-foot high cliffs surrounding the lake. "They must be related to sharks," he said, continuing to laugh at the ruthless action of the trout. Climbing to his feet, his eyes wondered over the perpendicular cliffs, settling on the bulky outline of the iceberg hanging over the darkening water. Holding his arms out, he shook his hands and wiping them impatiently on his Levis, watched smoke from their campfire disperse itself amongst the skeleton-like branches of brush along the shore. Moving languidly skyward in small wisps and puffs, it disappeared into the grey blanket of coming night.

Climbing the short bank, Luke and Pepper walked quietly toward their camp. Drifting through the air the savory aroma of melting cheese teased and tantalized, pulling them like a lodestone to the warmth of the fire. Sniffing enthusiastically, Luke rubbed his belly. "Ambrosia, huh! I'm ready for a cup of something hot."

"Are you guys ready, everything's done?" Benny asked, carefully turning the last fish over in the hot grease. "I'm starving. The fish really smell delicious." Throwing two tea bags in the hot water pot, he turned and picked up their tin plates.

Luke and Pepper hurried to the fire. Benny handed them each a plate and they fell silent eating with gusto. Benny poured them each a cup of tea, placing the steaming cup next to them on the ground. Sitting back, they sighed in relief, their bellies were full.

They rested until the mountains were the color of black ink and deep shadows invaded the camp. Levering himself up from his prone position, Pepper groaned, and piling the plates and utensils they had used into the big frying pan, headed for the creek. "Stay put, Benny, "he said. "You cooked, so we'll clean up tonight."

Luke walked back into camp and piled the plates on top of the oven to dry. "I'm going to clean up and then sit next to the fire for a while," he volunteered picking up his kit. "If I sit now, I'll never get up again. I need a good wash. I stink. Are you guys coming?" Shouting, they laughed as they ran to the creek. Throwing off their clothes they immersed themselves in the icy water and scrubbed their bodies clean. Drying themselves, they pushed their damp feet into their boots and raced, buck-naked along the trail toward the camp.

Wrapping his soiled underclothes together, Luke remembered the robot's tool and pulled it from his jacket pocket. Tossing it to Pepper, he climbed over his bedroll and shoved his rolled underclothes next to

THE DEVILS PUNCHBOWL

his back pack. Returning to the fire, he poured tea for everyone and sat next to Benny.

Pepper studied the tool, turning it over in his hand. "There isn't much to this, it's shaped like a capital letter T and has six small indentations on the arm." His mouth broke out in a huge smile and glancing up his eyes danced with reflections from the fire. "Do you think we should press the buttons?"

"I don't see why you couldn't. The robots don't move, so my guess is, it won't work." Benny answered. He huddled deeper into his jacket, bringing his feet closer to the fire.

"Toss it here, Pepper. I don't think we should start pressing buttons," Luke said anxiously. "We have no idea what would happen if we did." Sitting close to the fire, he examined the tool. Laying it on a flat rock near him, he lay back and watched as flames danced erratically amongst the burning logs. The wood crackled and popped and a fitful breeze sent an erratic swirl of drifting, pungent smoke, through their camp.

Benny yawned turning the sound into a loud groan. "I'm going to bed," he abruptly announced. "I'm never going to get warm this way." Rising, he walked to their stockpile of wood and picking up two large logs brought them back to the fire. Throwing them on top of the burning logs, he stood watching small pieces of burning ash float skyward.

Pulling off their clothes, they crawled into their bedrolls, and yawning occasionally, stretched, settling into the warmth of their sleeping bags.

Luke whispered, "Gi . . . night you two."

"Night, gi . . . night," was whispered softly in response.

Snuggling deeper, they relaxed and watched the sky turn into a soothing enveloping black blanket. The firelight dimmed as the wood burned and a log fell with a sharp crack into the waiting bed of red-hot coals. The spit and hiss of burning logs settling further into the welcoming heat of their own devastation, disturbed no one, Puffs of smoke, curling and spinning lazily, spiraled upward, until drifting over a wider area, they vanished completely in the murky black of the night sky.

CHAPTER 8

PEPPER ROSE FROM his bedroll and stood near its bottom. Chilling rapidly in the cold air, he threw on his jacket and slapping his ball cap on his head, pulled on a pair of faded Levis. Slipping his bare feet into his boots, he sighed, expelling a cloud of vaporous air. Gathering a few small pieces of wood, he knelt and, removing the top layer of ash, piled them loosely on a few hot looking coals. Blowing gently, he watched the first tendrils of fire lick hungrily at his pile of small sticks. Laying larger pieces of wood in alternate rows over the meager flames, he waited for it to get hot. Rubbing his face with his hands, he removed his ball cap and combed his fingers through his hair. Yawning, he raised his arms over his head, and stretching upward, relieved the cramping ache of sore muscles.

Tilting his face, he stared, at the mountainous peaks outlined against the sky. Yawning again, he groaned, his mouth stretching as wide as it would open. Rising, he picked his kit up from the end of his sleeping bag, and walking to the fire, grabbed the water pot from the grill. Another cold morning, he thought as he started toward the creek.

Stopping abruptly, Pepper suspiciously watched the deep encroaching shadows surrounding the camp. His nerves leaped along his skin and he strained to hear. There wasn't a sound, just an occasional sharp cracking noise from the fire and the lap of water on the shore of the lake. Pausing, he listened intently for any quiet, sneaky noises, and then, started to walk again.

Slipping his soap back in his kit, he sat back on his heels and stared at his surroundings. The water gurgled over the rocky bottom of

THE DEVILS PUNCHBOWL

the creek, and for several seconds, he absorbed the tranquil melody of singing water. Climbing to his feet, he tried capturing the sound inside his mind, and moving quietly along the edge of the creek, filled the water pot from a font of cascading water.

Walking pensively back to camp, loaded with breakfast things from the cold box, Pepper slid the water pot on the grill. And sitting on a rock, he watched the fading night break into day. The sun broke the black outline of the mountains, lighting their tops in a rim of fire. Morning sun, with its warming light came late to the Devils Punchbowl and the cold icy night came early. Throwing two tea bags in the pot, he placed it on the side of the grill, and opening a can of chili set it on the grill to heat. Scrambling eggs in the frying pan, he dumped the can of chili on top and mixed them gently with a spoon.

Unwrapping a package of tortillas, he filled a tortilla with a layer of eggs and chili, a small layer of salsa, and topped it off with a sprinkle of cheese. Tightly rolling each tortilla, he laid them in rows in a biscuit pan and placed the pan on top of the oven to stay warm. Pouring hot tea for everyone, he poked Benny and then, Luke on the foot, yelling, "rise and shine you two, times a wastin. C'mon, up already, here's your tea." Watching them sit up in their sleeping bags, he handed them each a cup.

Squatting next to the fire, Pepper noisily sipped from his cup. Laughing abruptly, his intense blue eyes danced, and he gave Luke and Benny a darting glance. Setting his cup on the ground, he picked up the robot's tool from the rock where Luke had placed it the night before, and aiming at a small log, pressed the button on the left side of the T.

"Bang," he shouted.

The log rolled along the ground, and Pepper's eyes rounded, the pupils enlarging to stark black holes. His face blanched a sickly-white, and stumbling, he lurched to his feet, spilling his cup of tea. Stumbling again, he fell to his knees, dropping the tool.

"Holy shit, did you see that?" he wheezed. Opening his mouth he closed it. His lips trembled and his mouth, opening and closing several times, gapped open. He gasped for air. Taking a deep breath, he scrabbled along the ground and pulling himself up on a rock, sat, hunched over his knees. Rounding his shoulders, he rubbed his palms against his legs, and tried to control his excitement. Closing his mouth he opened it again sucking in a huge gulp of air.

"Shit, oh shit," he muttered.

"I didn't see anything, Pepper," Luke said, his eyebrows lifting in skepticism. Exasperated, he climbed to his feet, and stood, on his sleeping bag. Shivering, he picked up his clothes and balancing his cup of tea, walked toward the fire.

"What'd you do, Pep?" Benny chortled, following Luke. "Is this a joke to get us out of the sack?"

Pepper spread his hands and raising his arms moved them wildly through the air.

"No, No," he yelled.

"Watch!"

Jumping to his feet, Pepper picked up the tool. Aiming it at the log, he pressed the button and the log rolled several feet.

Luke dropped his clothes and setting his cup on a flat rock, ran toward Pepper. Benny followed. They watched intently, as Pepper maneuvered the log over the contours of the ground. A few seconds passed and glancing at each other they reacted, all speaking at once, trying to be heard.

"Hey," Benny yelled. "How's it doing that?"

"Weird! Damn, ow . . . ww," Luke shouted. Stepping carefully, he raised one foot and held it. "I just stepped on something sharp." Balancing himself, he tried to examine his foot. Shivering, he turned, and followed Benny to their sleeping bags. Throwing their clothes on, they stamped stocking feet into their boots and with flapping laces ran across the camp.

Pepper sat overwhelmed. Grabbing his hat from his head, he pushed his hand repeatedly through his hair, until it stood up in wild spikes around his head. Luke and Benny stood next to him looking at the tool where he had laid it on his knee.

"Which button did you push?" Luke asked, as he and Benny hunched over him.

THE DEVILS PUNCHBOWL

"Ph . . . ee . . . ew," Pepper roared, rearing backward. "Get away from me. Your breath stinks. You smell like rotten fish."

"Phew!"

"Yuk!"

"Go, clean up. Besides, breakfast is ready and it'll be ruined if we don't eat soon."

Luke and Benny scrambled for their kits, their somber expressions overlaid with uncontrollable excitement. Dashing toward the creek, they glanced back at Pepper, and grinning suddenly at each other, ran faster.

Pepper picked up the tool and thoughtfully, returned to the campfire. Sliding the pan of rolled tortillas into the oven, he poured himself another cup of tea. Laying the tool on the top of a flat rock, he examined it with a discerning eye.

Opening the oven, he pulled out the pan of rolled tortillas and grabbing, three camp plates, filled them. Granny called this dish his speciality, because she said it was the only reason he had hair on his chest. The salsa was hot, but combined with chili beans, eggs and cheese it was delicious. It was just the right thing to eat on a cold morning, because the salsa raised your body heat several degrees. No one shivered after they ate it.

Luke dashed back toward the fire shaking water from his blond hair.

"Hey, don't look so worried," Pepper said, handing Luke his plate and, a cup of tea. "It's scary, but even last summer we knew that the cavern was way out. Way beyond us anyway, and now, I think, way beyond anyone living on planet earth." Sighing impatiently, he grimaced and then grinned. . . . "I've been thinking."

"Hey Benny," Luke called. "Pepper's actually been thinking." Swinging around, he glanced up at Benny, and laughed. Impatiently, he waved his hand through a cloud of smoke spiraling around him, his eyes watering from its biting sharpness. "Isn't that a switch? He usually acts and then thinks. Sorry Pep, but you're the butt this morning." Taking a sip of his tea, he grinned at him.

"No shitin," Pepper interrupted. "We've got to experiment." Leaning over the hot grill, he handed Benny his plate and cup of tea. Sloshing the hot liquid over the cup's rim, it ran over his fingers unto the grill, the sizzling drops dancing and popping across its hot surface.

"Ow, ooh, ow," Pepper yelled, slipping his fingers into his mouth. "That hurts."

Sitting close to the fire, they ate quickly huddling over their plates. Luke, between bites of his tortillas kept glancing at the tool. "Pepper, what you said about experimenting sounds good," he said. "But, if something happens that's way out weird, how would we control it? If we don't really know how something works, or better yet what it does, we can't indiscriminately push buttons. We could get into a lot of trouble that way."

"I'm not saying we should act like fools and just start pressing buttons," Pepper argued. "I'm saying, we should investigate a little bit of what we find here." He moved his hands in frustration. Raising his eyebrows, he looked over at Benny. "Don't you agree?" he added plaintively. "I know Rob would agree with me if he was here."

"Yeah, kind of, Pepper," Benny answered. Pushing his hand through his sandy brown hair, his eyes brightened in thought. Agitated, he ran his fingers through his hair again, pushing the strands into wild tangles that haloed his head.

Benny hesitated not satisfied with his answer. "I think we should do a little investigating, but like Luke says, we have to be careful too. I think we've stumbled unto aliens." His voice low and muted, he stared thoughtfully into the fire. "Maybe they're just robots, but they're still alien." He raised his eyes and stared at Pepper. "I don't think this place was built by humans. I'm still scared of touching something, we don't know anything about. What if we pressed a button and those robots started to move? What in hell would we do then?"

"Okay, I agree," Pepper said, talking through a mouthful of tortilla. "If something weird happened, I'd be the first one out of there. He laughed, his expression a mixture of contrition and pleased knowledge. "But still, I think we've got to try to gain some knowledge from all this. What made the robots stop here? Why are they buried here in a remote

THE DEVILS PUNCHBOWL

area in northern California? We haven't found out anything yet and if we don't experiment with some of the stuff, we'll never know."

Taking a sip of his tea, Luke grunted and swallowed hastily. It was cold. "I agree, kinda. Remember, we said we'd try to look at everything first. How about the next level through the opening in the ceiling, in what I'll call the main room? Maybe we should call it the bridge. I want to go through that hole and look around. . . . And, what about that big cavern, they're cleaning it up for some reason, I think we should explore it?"

Luke rose to his feet, and piling their plates in the frying pan, started toward the creek. "I'll clean up, you guys pack us a lunch. My canteen is over there with the climbing gear. Fix fruit punch Kool-Aid for today, and make sure, you fix each of us a rellano wrapped in a tortilla. They're delicious."

Pepper and Benny hurried to pack their lunch. Benny tied the strings tight, and looking up, watched Luke return to the campsite juggling utensils.

Picking up the tool from the rock, Luke aimed it at his haversack and pressed the left button. The sack moved and raising his arm it rose hovering in the air. Moving his arm toward his body, he flinched as it rushed toward him. Lowering his hand, he released the button and the bag fell gently to the ground. Laughing nervously, he glanced at Benny and Pepper. He pressed the button again and they watched in awed silence as the bag moved, hovering several feet above the ground.

"I wonder how it's doing that?" Benny whispered, scrubbing his hands over his face and through his hair. "I don't see how something so small could have that kind of power. There isn't a beam of light or anything else that I can see for an energy source. A brooding expression flashed across his face. His eyes focused and still, stared intently at the bag.

"Hey," Pepper interrupted, his voice rising. "Benny, your hair belongs in some weirdo camp. It's sticking up in every direction. It makes you look nuts." Casting his eyes around the camp, he rolled them upward toward the sky, showing his disgust. "Let's go. It takes almost two hours to get into the cavern. We're wastin time."

Packing up their gear, Luke picked up a length of rope with an attached three-sided hook and coiled it several times around his shoulders. They hurried away from their camp trudging under a gray sky, brightened occasionally by weak sunrays penetrating the cloud layer, and shivering, hugged their down jackets against their chests.

Crawling through the crevices and tunnels seemed to get easier and faster each time they did it, Luke thought, but he doubted that the way into the cavern was any less difficult. The reason it seemed easier was, they knew instinctively at what turn and narrow area to push, pull, or wiggle their way through.

Pulling himself free from the end of the tunnel, he rose to his feet, and wondered away from the entrance, to wait for Pepper and Benny. Massaging the back of his neck, he tried to rub away the apprehension he was feeling. The sensation persisted, raising the hair on his neck and arms. His agitation grew and stepping back against the cavern's wall he glanced in all directions. Lifting his hard hat, he combed his fingers through his hair, and jerked his hand away as it crackled and snapped. Lowering his arm, he watched tiny, blue flames appear and disappear between his moving fingers.

Luke shook his head, confusion clouding his perception of what he was feeling. He walked toward Pepper standing at the tunnel's entrance, his senses and thoughts, stymied by something he didn't understand. Benny plopped onto the floor like a dead salmon, and grinning like a Cheshire cat, pulled himself to his knees.

"Hey, let me show you something that's freaky, weird," Luke called. Lifting his hard hat, he combed his fingers rapidly through his hair again. Tiny lancets of blue flame arced between his fingers and the sound of snapping and popping circled his head. Laughing nervously, he stared at Pepper and Benny.

"My God, what is this place," Benny whispered. His features grew taut, stiffening into a mask, and pulling himself to his feet, he backed toward the cavern's wall, pressing himself against it.

Pepper whipped his hard hat off and pushed his fingers through his hair. Nothing happened! Throwing his arms in the air, he looked at

THE DEVILS PUNCHBOWL

Luke in disappointment. "Somethin's happinin to you, what's doing that?" he asked.

"I don't know," Luke answered, his eyes darkening to a perplexed shiny blue. His face shadowed as he glanced apprehensively at the huge cavern. Running his fingers through his hair again, Benny and Pepper, watched arcing blue lights dance around his head.

"There has to be a reason that it's happening to you and not to Pepper," Benny said. Fleeting thoughts flashed incoherent wonder across the planes of his face and his baffled expression suddenly changed. "I bet it's the tool!" He nodded, as if agreeing with himself.

Luke sank to one knee and laid the robot's tool on the ground. They stared at it. "It must be the tool," he thoughtfully surmised. Handing the tool to Pepper, Luke rose to his feet and watched as he put the tool in his pocket.

Pepper removed his hard hat, and placing it gently on the ground, vigorously rubbed his unruly curls with both hands, until a blue haze of winking, arcing lights haloed his head.

Luke and Benny's mouths dropped open. They watched silently as blue flames arced, and danced, over Pepper's hands. Meeting Benny's eyes, Luke shook his head. "I don't understand why it's suddenly doing this. It didn't do anything like this at camp this morning. Give it back, Pepper." He held the tool in the palm of his hand and they stared at it. It was a perfectly formed capital T with six slightly indented areas on one side of the crossbar. He shrugged, the gesture dismissive.

Shrugging his shoulders again, Luke for several seconds stared at Pepper and Benny. Perplexed, he raised his hands. "Let's go," he said, shoving the tool into his pocket. "We've got a lot to explore. We'll experiment with this later."

Passing through the immense cavern, they quickly climbed the narrow trail, passing the ice sheet. Pepper turned around and walking backward for several feet, faced Luke and Benny. His expression usually a blend of humor and happiness was solemn. Dimples flashed as his mouth opened and closed several times. Rolling his eyes, he turned around and continued walking along the path.

"What's wrong, Pep?" Luke asked. "You look like you're thinking dire thoughts."

"No. Not dire, just heavy and confused," Pepper answered. Turning again on the rocky path, he faced Luke and Benny, his eyes skipping past them, watched the vast cavern over their shoulders. "Have, either of you experienced the feeling of how insignificant we are? When I'm in here, this place makes me feel like I'm smaller than an ant. The feeling is so intense at times, I feel like I'm being crushed by it."

"Yeah, I've had the feeling," Benny answered, sweeping by Pepper into the lighted doorway. He turned back to look at him. "It's like a pressure, and sometimes it gets so bad, I can hardly tolerate it. In fact I've had the most jumbled, mixed up feelings ever since we found this place last summer. In the past year, every time I thought of this cavern, it was like I went off somewhere else. Sorta spacey." His eyebrows met between his eyes and his features twisted, wrinkling into a terrible grimace. "It's almost like this cavern isn't part of this world, like it's kind of lost in time. Oh hell, listen to me!"

"I feel diminished by it," Luke said. This place, or maybe, I should say whatever created it is way beyond us in technology. I think we've stumbled unto something from back in time, or maybe this is something from another dimension. I keep thinking all sorts of bizarre things, and I know, some of them are so far fetched they can't be true. Sometimes, I feel like I'm dreamin."

"Yeah, I've felt that way too. I think this place is really old," Pepper answered. He paused and a blank expression crossed his face. "I'll tell you . . . if you won't laugh," he added, staring fiercely at Luke and Benny.

Pausing again, Pepper's words tumbled out in a torrent, tumbling over each other. "I've thought often that we might have stumbled into something from the future. Maybe, these robots are from the future and for some reason they got stuck here."

"I'm having the same kind of thoughts," Luke said. "They just keep rolling over and over through my head, and sometimes, it gets so bad I can't shut them off." Tension deepened his voice, and nervously biting his lips, he frowned, shrugged, and pushed ahead, passing the two robots. Pausing, he looked back at Benny and Pepper. "Let's start in the bridge," he suggested. Climbing steadily upward through the intensely lit tunnel, they stepped through the oval opening. Everything, looked the same. The indirect lighting from under circular panels in the ceiling was still bright and the continuous covering above the padded console circled the room. On the left side near the wall, the opening in the ceiling yawned like a black hole, and quietly pacing across the large room, Luke stretched, trying to see where it went. The lighting on the next level was less intense, and looking upward, he thought, it's very subdued. The opening wasn't large perhaps a yard across the middle. Rubbing his mouth thoughtfully, he stepped away and joined Pepper and Benny at the padded console.

"What do you think of this idea?" Benny asked, as Luke joined them. We're going to open every one of these panels where there's a chair. We didn't seem to get into trouble yesterday when we opened a couple. Maybe we'll find something that will help us figure out how this thing works."

"I think it's okay," Luke answered. "But let's be really cautious and stay together. That way if something weird happens we can run like hell."

"I suggest we start at one end, "Benny said. Leading the way, he walked to the opposite side of the bridge where the console formed an extension that jutted out into the room.

"I think this is a door," Luke said, walking between the wall and the teardrop-shaped extension to the console. Examining the room carefully, he pivoted turning in a circle.

Pepper and Benny shouted and rushing around the edge of the table, they pushed by Luke. Benny ran his hand along the wall searching for any indentations that would open it. The door's surface was cool, satin smooth to the touch and like the console it felt padded.

"Forget it," Luke said, pressing on the rounded padded area on the table. They stood silent, watching a padded stool move outward, and then, a keyboard attached to a monitor, emerged from inside the console. The screen about five-feet across remained blank and the cabinet door next to Luke, silently slid open revealing shelves spaced about every twelve inches. Inside, three to a shelf, were odd shaped objects made in an elongated circle. Formed continuously with no break, an oval disc, with a silver segmented wire attached to its center was fastened to a two-inch metal band.

Luke picked up one, and holding it in his hands, he glanced at Pepper and Benny. Handing Pepper the one he held, he picked up two more, giving one of them to Benny. "What do you think?" he asked. "Looks like headgear, to me."

"Me too," Benny answered, placing the circle of metal on his head. It wasn't a perfect fit. Squeezing it together, he pressed it to both sides of his head. The shiny oval with its attached wire was centered in the middle of his forehead.

"Hey Bro," Pepper chortled, trying to fit the band of metal to his head. "You look like a doctor who's about to look into one of mankind's many orifices. Hey, put the thing with the wire sticking out at the back of your head and sort of slant it. Slip it down on your forehead. It's similar to a hat and the metal disc fits flat against the base of your skull. See." He laughed, waving his hands. "Fits better, but I don't know what to do with the wire, it must be six-foot long." Examining the end of the segmented wire hanging over his shoulder, he added. "Looks to me like the end of this wire must plug into something."

The plug was square and split into three round prongs. Each round prong was split into six segments and each segment was a different size. "Different kind of a plug," Luke murmured. "I've never seen one made like this." Looking up, his face brightened as he looked at Benny. "Look at the keyboard, maybe, this plugs into it."

Benny slipped forward on the stool and bent over the keyboard. Luke and Pepper hovered over his shoulders. Pepper moved to the left side of Benny's stool and examined the end of the segmented wire carefully. Propping his butt against the padded console, he felt movement, and jumping away several feet, he yelled. "Shit." Turning quickly, he watched a stool silently move outward from its position in the console.

Pepper laughed, a short hacking sound and striding around the small teardrop-shaped table, pressed the curved padded section every

THE DEVILS PUNCHBOWL

few feet. When he reached the table's end, nine stools faced the screen. Solemnly, the boys stared at the stools. Silent, their eyes skipped past the large screen, traveling over the long length of the console circling the room.

Plopping on the nearest stool, Pepper slumped forward over the console's edge, and folding his arms on the padded surface, rubbed his face on his sleeve. Resting his chin on his left arm, he blinked several times. "I don't see anything that looks like a receptacle this might plug into," he said, waving the end of the wire in a circle through the air. Dropping it, his right arm scraped the table's padded top as he waved his hand at the stools and screen. "And all the stools face the screen, so I'm going to guess that this screen has to be a communication device. It's probably used to gain information or maybe to send.

"Hell," Luke laughed. "I know what it is. Whatever these beings are, they sat around here and watched porno movies. They're just like us, horny as hell and love all that touchin and movin in rhythm."

They howled, a veritable deluge that filled the room with a cycle of bass and deep bass sounds. Rising to a high treble of nervous giggling, it continued until it bordered on the edges of hysteria.

"Shut up, I can't stand anymore," Benny exclaimed in desperation. Breaking out in hiccups, he held his breath, attempting to stop his hiccuping. "This has to plug into something," he yelled. Sheepishly, he grinned and tilting his head stared at Luke. "How many of these are in the cabinet?"

Luke stepped to the cabinet and counted quickly, "there's nine," he answered. His face brightened suddenly. "Hey, that makes an instrument for every stool around the table. Pepper, look for a receptacle at each position."

Benny grabbed the edge of the console, and moving his legs, turned sideways on the stool. Twisting his body, he watched his fingers move along the fold in the console's padding.

"Ah . . . hic . . . hic . . . Uh," he said between hiccups.

Bending further, he twisted his head and looked at a small receptacle built into the wall under the rolled edge of the console. Running his fingers along its edge, he straightened on the stool and looked across the width of the table at Pepper. "Feel just along the edge of the padding there should be a jack for every seating area. There's one here."

Pepper rose and placing his hand on the rolled edge moved around the oval shaped table. "There's a jack at every stool, eight of them, nine counting yours." Dragging the end of the cable from his shoulder, he sat in the stool next to Benny, and twisting sideways, slid the plug into the small receptacle.

Benny hovered over the keyboard, leaning toward the screen. His legs were too long for the height of the stool and his knees rubbed the wall under the console. Turning his thumbs up, in an A-ok gesture, he broke out in a huge triumphant grin. They watched the screen expectantly.

Nothing happened.

It remained blank.

Luke looked at the screen in disappointment. Glancing at Benny's and Pepper's faces, he couldn't tell what they were thinking, but they were looking at him as if he had an answer. "Don't look at me," he said. "I don't have a clue what we should do next, but I guess to make it work, you'd have to press a few keys on the keyboard. Do you think we should take a chance and press keys?"

Benny and Pepper stared up at Luke. Indecision ran rampant over their faces and question marks gleamed in their eyes. They looked like they were searching for an answer, but were coming up with negatives. Benny, dropping his head forward studied the odd symbols. Minus marks, a circle, some short, fat and longer marks that looked like elongated capital S's were on the buttons. They weren't anything like the keys on his computer keyboard. These keys were small indentations in the material that the keyboard panel was made from. The symbols, raised slightly, on the top of each indentation were odd in their simplicity. He shook his head and looked up at Luke.

"Let's not press any keys," he suggested. "We'll look at everything that's built into the console, first. Then after we look up there," he said, swinging his hand toward the ceiling, "we'll come back to this screen."

THE DEVILS PUNCHBOWL

Laying his hands on the top of the console, Benny rose, unfolding his long body awkwardly from the stool. "I'm certain that this console, or whatever you want to call it, wasn't made for six-footers like us. It definitely was made for smaller beings. So, I think this ship was manned by aliens a lot smaller then us. And, I don't think it was manned by the robots." Removing the circle of metal from his head, he dropped it gently next to the screen.

Trailing behind Luke, Benny punched Pepper lightly on the shoulder. "I think this place was built for a bunch of little people. The kind your wee, Irish Granny is always spoutin about." He laughed at Pepper's expression. "You know, the kind of little people that are wizened and wear only the color green." Raising his arms, he held his hands on each side of his head and wiggled his fingers. "You know the kind that wear those little pointy hats." An expression of trepidation crossed his long face and he frowned. "Where's your sense of humor, Pep? You must have lost it."

"Hey," Pepper yelled. Holding up his hands, he gestured toward the console. "Wait, a second, I have an idea."

"What?" Luke asked apprehensively.

"I think we need to escalate our exploring, so we can see a lot of what's here today," Pepper said. "Let's open every panel in the console without stopping to investigate how it works. We could spend all day in here looking at all this stuff. I'd like to go through that hole up there," he added, swinging his arm toward the ceiling.

"Okay," Benny said. "Where should we start?"

A perplexed expression on his face, Pepper studied the console. "I'll start over here on this end," he said, walking toward the opposite side of the room. "We've opened two on that end. Benny, you sort of stand in the center as a guard, in case we get in trouble. And Luke, and I will keep pressing, and opening these panels, until we meet in the middle. There's a lot to open, must be sixty or seventy feet of console in here."

Luke pressed on the next place where he thought another screen would be, and without pausing to watch what appeared at each place, they each opened seven areas around the curve of the console. Pressing on a section where nothing happened, he turned to watch Pepper press repeatedly on the padded console.

Pepper had opened the monitor they had seen the night before and it garbled and grunted its message, spitting it out into the room. They met near Benny in the center of the room and stared apprehensively at the stools waiting for occupancy by something or someone.

Benny stared at Pepper and Luke. "Look at the space between these stools, it's almost exactly in the middle of the console," he said reflectively. Throwing out his arm he waved his hand. "There has to be something just about here and I think I should open this one?" Striding forward, he pressed on the padded area. Nothing happened. His eyes flickered, gauging the distance between stools, and moving to his left, he pressed a section of the rolled edge with both hands.

A screen nine feet in length and four feet wide moved silently upward, and settling at a forty-five-degree angle, a large keyboard slid into a slot above the stool. Behind the covering above the console, starting on the left side of the bridge, a dark shadow started to move. The boys stepped warily backward, and shuffling awkwardly, huddled together.

Anxiety grew inside Luke, a wild thing that wanted to engulf him. He grabbed at Pepper and Benny's elbows, and clutching them in a tight grip, apprehensively watched the dark shadow follow the curved expanse, until it disappeared. Without a sound the movement stopped and sucking in a tight breath, they gasped. Stepping swiftly, but silently backward, they hesitated in the entrance and got ready to run.

Something inside the covering started to flow, and softening, it dissolved, melting rapidly like hot wax into its frame. Brightening, it cleared, revealing a vast panorama of mountains and valleys. Stark, rocky ridges became dark forested slopes that flowed downward, forming deep gorges and valleys surrounded by nearly perpendicular cliffs. The vista seemed to go on forever until at some point in the far distance it met the sky where it had no perceivable end.

Dark masses of ominous clouds circled Preston Peak. Lightning forked in the moving clusters, its constant battering action lighting their billowing shapes in brilliant reds and pinks. Circling the rocky

THE DEVILS PUNCHBOWL

peak the wind and lightning whipped and twisted the cumulominbus clouds into grotesque shapes. Pushing against each other, they moved in exaggerated, helpless puffs around the mountain's top. The boy's shuttered at the flagrant display.

Luke, whispered as if to himself. "I can't believe it." He stared at the mountains. Puzzled, his expression changed to one of abstraction, his thoughts and feelings clearly exposed on his expressive face. Reluctantly, he moved his eyes from the awesome view beyond the bridge and stared at Benny and Pepper. "Hey, notice we're not hearing any thunder in here. This place must be soundproof. And notice too," he added moving forward into the room. "It looks from here like this place is sitting on the edge of a precipice. How can that be?" Cautiously, he stepped again, his face expressing his inner turmoil until he was against the console. Bending over its top, he looked at the drop outside the massive window.

"Yeah," Pepper whispered, barely moving his lips. The muscles of his face, stiffened, fear shadowing the mirrored wetness of his eyes. "I thought we were deep inside the mountain."

Benny's face went blank. He withdrew into himself his eyes strangely empty. He nodded several times and seemed on the verge of saying something, but only gulped, the muscles in his throat moving in a spasm of awkward, anxious movements. "This is a spaceship," he yelled. "There's no doubt in my mind; this is a spaceship. This covering that we can see through, looks like glass, but I bet it isn't. It has to be a special kind of windshield." Glancing out through the window at Preston Peak, wild emotion welled up in his eyes. "Hey," he said, his voice sinking to a barely heard murmur. "I think we found a spaceship."

Luke and Pepper stood silent, startled into a new awareness by his words. The screen at the end of the console erupted again with its message. The sound in its verbal continuity was so alien they stood immobilized, mesmerized by the sound.

"Well, as me Irish Granny would say, this time we really fell through the hole in the outhouse and we're up to our behinds in the dark stuff," Pepper said quietly. Overwhelmed, his voice thin and reedy, he walked forward and plopped heavily on one of the stools. Pressing his body against the console, he propped his head up with his hand, never taking his eyes from Preston Peak. "Let's eat. All of this gives me a sickenin feelin in my stomach."

"Okay Pepper," Luke agreed, sighing heavily. "Since you're closer, turn that screen off, so we don't have to listen to that gibberish and, like my Dad says, we'll sit and assuage our empty guts. Sighing again, he plopped onto a stool, and leaning forward, rested on his elbows. He shuddered, staring at the limitless space that dropped in an awesome panoramic view of the wilderness area surrounding the Devils Punchbowl.

CHAPTER 9

"I DIDN'T KNOW lightning was so red," Benny said, pointing at Preston Peak. "You can see streaks of it in those clouds. Sorta reminds, me of the northern lights. I wonder if it strikes the ground on the peak. Spooky watching it." He bit down on his biscuit and chewing vigorously, his eyes narrowed at the spectacular view.

For a few seconds, Luke squinted through the window at Preston Peak. Leaning back in the stool, he clapped his hands and laughed, a laugh brusque and elated, filled with a mixture of derision and alarm. "I can't believe I'm sitting here in a spaceship, and I'm watching a display, of the most awesome fireworks on earth."

"C'mon, let's go through that hole in the ceiling and see what's up there," he said. "What would you like to do? I feel . . . I don't know how I feel, I'm mixed up and Pepper looks as if he's had enough experimenting for one day. I'm stunned. This," he waved at the view beyond the expanse of window . . . "blows my mind! Why would aliens build and then abandon all this? And where are they? All these thoughts run like mad dogs through my head. I can't stop thinking them. How about you, Pepper, you ready to go?" he asked.

Pepper lay stretched flat against the floor with his head cradled in his arms. His eyes were closed. Groaning, he opened them and lifting his arms over his head stretched along the floor. Rubbing his face on his outstretched arms, he groaned again.

"I don't know. Let's go through the hole in the ceiling first and then we'll explore that room where the robot is riding the machine." Sitting up, he clasped his knees against his chest, and the expression in his eyes turned dark and moody. "As sure as I have an Irish Granny, this is a spaceship," he said, placing his hand flat on the floor. And when I think about it my brain becomes confused, because I don't know what we're going to do with all this." Agitation chased by a rush of frustration crossed his face. "Sometimes I feel tormented by my own thoughts."

Luke wiggled on his seat, trying to fit himself more comfortably into the small space between the stool and the console. The silence on the bridge was overwhelming as he meditated on what Pepper had said. This was an alien world in here, different from anything that they had ever experienced, and he was keyed up with it. It was a continual brushing of something along his nerves that he couldn't put a name to. Searching inside his head for a word that fit, what did come to mind?

Alien! Luke's hair rose on his head, the full implication of the word settling like a black cloud on the surface of his mind.

"Talk about heavy," Pepper exclaimed! C'mon, let's get physical. We'll climb through the hole in the ceiling and stay just long enough to see what's there. Then, we'll explore that cavern where the robot on the machine is. Maybe a little exercise will help my stress, erase all my doubts and clear up all my ambiguous thoughts."

Pepper smiled, his demeanor changing into one of expectation was enhanced by a hearty, humorous grin. "How's that for an embellished statement? If I start talkin like that all the time, I'll sound just like Luke. Sweet, huh!" He laughed and rolling sideways, jumped to his feet stamping them noisily against the floor. "C'mon, make some noise all this quiet gets on my nerves."

"Hey, shouldn't we shut down this windshield?" Benny called to Luke's departing back.

"Yeah," Luke answered. Stopping abruptly, he watched Benny press the rounded padding on the console. The large screen slid downward and from the frame surrounding the long expanse of pane-like material a thick liquid started to flow. Changing to a milky opalescence, the congealing liquid rapidly altered the clarity of the windshield. The cover starting at the right side of the bridge rushed by, changing the windshield's color once again, to a frosted, darker, creamy-streaked hue.

THE DEVILS PUNCHBOWL

"Awesome. Awesome," Benny whispered. "That must be some kind of metal shield that covers the windshield when they're in deep space." Grabbing up his gear, he flung one more glance over his shoulder at the console. Crossing the room, he stood next to Pepper and watched Luke tie knots several feet apart on a rope.

Luke threw the rope with its pronged three-sided hook up through the opening. Pulling on the rope in short sharp jerks, he tried to force the prongs into the edge of the floor around the hole. The hook and rope slithered downward, and jumping backward to get out of its way, it thumped its way past them, rolling several feet, before it came to rest against the wall. Watching the hook they turned to see each others reaction and burst into laughter.

Luke stepped to the wall and picked up the hook. "The floor's smooth as glass, these prongs will never penetrate it. They'll have to be hooked around something before we can climb the rope."

"Well, looks to me like one of you will have to stand on my shoulders," Benny volunteered. "I'm the tallest."

"Yeah," Luke answered. "I'm heavier than you, so I guess Pepper will have to be the guinea pig."

Benny positioned himself under the opening, and crouching slightly pressed his hands on his knees to help support his rounded back. Pepper grabbed Luke's hand and kneeling on Benny's back rose unsteadily to his feet.

"This is harder than you guys think," Pepper said, waving his arm to balance himself. Benny straightened his back slowly and Pepper stepped to his shoulders, lifting himself upward toward the hole.

"Yeah, it doesn't feel to good to me, either" Benny yelled. "You're hurting me, don't dig your heels into my shoulders."

"Sorry," Pepper gasped. Clutching Luke's raised hand and waving the other for balance, he grabbed the edge of the opening and in one fluid motion caught it. Swinging one foot, he hung suspended for a second. Luke grabbed his swinging foot and pushed him upward. Yelling, Pepper pulled himself through the opening and laying flat on his stomach, looked around.

"What's up there?" Luke shouted.

"Wait a minute," Pepper said. Quietly, he sat up and looked down through the opening. "The room's small and it's round. I think it's a hallway. Looks like some storage cabinets and some doors. The doors are recessed in the walls and one of the cabinets is slightly open. I can see shelves. There's absolutely nothing up here where I could anchor the hook."

"Do you think you could brace yourself against the edge of the opening, so one of us can climb the rope? Maybe wrap the hook around your body and I'll use the rope to steady myself," Benny said. An anxious expression crossed his face and he laughed nervously. "That is if I can get up on Luke's shoulders."

Luke threw the hook up through the opening and Pepper caught it in one hand. Bending forward, he put his hands on his knees and Benny held the rope between his hands.

"Ready, Pepper?" he called.

"Yeah, no," Pepper yelled, "wait a minute, wait a minute, don't jerk on the rope." Wrapping it around his body, he slipped two of the hooks on his belt. He braced himself with his legs on each side of the hole and twisting the rope around his hand once, watched Benny.

Benny stepped up onto Luke's back, and slowly straightened, until he was almost upright. Grabbing for the next knot in the rope, he labored to climb the rope.

"Don't you dare fall on me?" Luke yelled.

Benny laughed. "For Christ's sake Luke, shut up," he mumbled. Another spasm of laughter overtook him. Seizing the edge of the opening, Benny let go of the rope. Swinging free, he grunted, laboring to pull his body up through the hole. Pepper grabbed Benny's arms and pulled, helping him until they lay sprawled on the floor.

"Okay, my turn," Luke called. "Just make sure you've got your feet set solid, so I don't haul Pepper through the hole. I don't think he'll break his neck by falling through it, but he might break mine if he falls on me. Yell, when you're ready."

Pepper sat with his legs spread, his feet propped against the edges of the opening. Bracing himself, he felt Benny pulling back on the hook. "Okay," he yelled.

THE DEVILS PUNCHBOWL

Luke grasped the rope and straining to lift himself, twisted his legs around it for leverage and climbed. Pulling himself up between Pepper's legs, he grabbed the edge of the opening and plopped onto the floor. Rolling to his side, he examined the perfectly round place.

"Hey, a thought just came to me, that's real disturbing," Pepper said, looking down through the opening. "How do you think those robots get up here? I'm sure they don't carry around a ladder or a rope." Turning over on his back, he pointed at the opening in the ceiling. "They'd have to use some kind of tool."

"Remember, if we're going to explore the cavern with the robot on the machine, we don't have much time to look around up here." Pushing himself up, Luke stood and walked to the door that was partially open. He ran his hands over its surface, and reminding himself that everything in this place was different, he sighed heavily and pressed against the partially opened panel.

The cabinet opened, revealing shelves from floor to ceiling. The familiar robot's tool, each one in its own small nesting area, filled four of them. Larger tools filled the lower two shelves and glancing, at the instruments, Luke couldn't imagine what they could be used for. The shelves, a radiant material, gleamed, their edges a darker hue of misty light.

Pepper, stretching to reach past Luke, gently picked up one of the T-shaped tools. "Since, there's so many I'm taking one and I think Benny should have one too," he said. "Tonight in camp we'll do a little experimenting and I think it'll be more fun if we each have one."

Benny picked up one of the tools. Putting it in his pocket, his eyes flickered nervously and he backed away from them. "You should put the one the robot had back on the shelf, Luke, and take another one," he advised. "Those shelves are probably some kind of system to recharge the tools and, the one you have is probably run down. No telling what the life of the tool is, but it might be similar to a battery."

Luke slipped the tool out of his pocket and examined it. He flashed a grin at Benny and carefully laid the tool in the cabinet. The glowing edge of the shelf began a pulsing rhythmic movement. Picking up two tools from different shelves, he slipped them into his jacket pocket. "Why'd you take two?" Pepper asked.

"You remember that article I showed you on antigravity," Luke answered thoughtfully. "The experiment they did actually picked up steel bearings and made them spin in a circle. I think these tools interfere with the polarity in the gravity field. I can't figure out any other way that it would pick up my backpack this morning. It has to form a field of power around the object you're aiming at and become part of it. Who knows? But I think whatever's happening, it somehow, shuts off the pull of the earth's gravity. The result then, enables the tool to lift and move the object."

"Tonight we'll experiment and I think each of us should have two of them. Maybe, it will give us additional power," he added ruefully, grinning at Pepper. Picking up two more, he handed Benny and Pepper another tool, and stepping away studied the small area. The place, like Pepper had said was perfectly round, its walls covered in a silvery-gray, metallic material that reflected dully in the recessed light from the ceiling. Dark bands, one about two-feet from the ceiling and another about four-feet from the floor circled the room.

"Hey guys," Benny said. "Have you noticed there isn't a sound? Not even a whisper. Everything here is quiet. My ears hurt from so much silence. This ship must have a power source that doesn't make any noise when it runs. Let's get these doors open." Crossing the small hall, he stood before one of the closed panels. The panels were thirty-inches wide and recessed several inches into the wall.

Luke paused and watched as Benny searched for a way to open the door. Turning in a circle, he counted five of them plus the opening in the ceiling that went to another level. Glancing at Benny, he surmised by the movement of his fingers, he hadn't found anything yet. Standing back several feet, he studied the recessed area. Now if I was one of those four-foot robots, where would I put a pressure button to open the door, he thought. Striding forward, he crouched and laying his palm against the dark band, pressed inward and the door slid upward.

"Hey, press on the dark band," he called.

THE DEVILS PUNCHBOWL

Pressing on the colored bands, they moved into the middle of the round hall, and watched for movement in the open doorways. The room they were facing was dark, the light from the hall didn't penetrate or soften its total blackness.

Circling to their left they shuffled forward several feet and stood in the entrance to a well-lit, pie-shaped room. There were no windows and, its smallest end was the doorway where they stood. Cabinets lined the walls and an island of white counter top marched down its center. It looked similar to a lab with various instruments placed along the flat surface of the counter. Long ganglion tubes protruded from the walls at the back of the cabinets, and they lay, like coiled snakes along its pristine whiteness. It looked very sterile.

Huddling together, they awkwardly stepped sideways, and pushing against each other, looked into the third doorway. The corridor was short and narrow, its right wall covered with four, evenly separated floor-to-ceiling patterns. They reminded Luke of hieroglyphics. The passage was empty. There wasn't a window, or door visible. Brightly lit, it contained nothing, but the strange symbols on the wall. It was a corridor that went nowhere.

Stepping past the entrance, Luke felt a pulsing rhythm-like vibration run through his body. "Hold it," he yelled at Benny and Pepper as they started to follow him. "Something's happinin here." He stepped again and the oscillation increased. He could feel it through his boots, crackling along his skin, raising the hair on his legs. The feeling grew and he felt it saturate his bones. Stumbling backward, he stepped back into the hall and stood by Benny.

"Whoa, try that, guys. See what you think."

Benny stepped first and Pepper followed him into the oddly marked corridor that had no doors. Stepping again, they stopped and gaped at Luke over their shoulders. Standing for a moment, their expressions changed. Mystified and apprehensive, Benny turned and pushed on Pepper, backing him toward Luke in the hall.

"Weird," he whispered. "I'm not going back in there."

"Me neither," Pepper said. "I didn't like the feeling."

Clustered together, they stared into the small passage, their fascination of its bizarre strangeness captivating. "Let's go," Luke whispered. Stepping softly, they moved sideways, until they were standing at the fourth opening. From the doorway, past a short hall, a dimly lit area broadened into one that they couldn't fully see. A faint glow reflecting upward toward the ceiling illuminated the far end of the room.

Must be a window, Luke thought? Hesitating, they clutched each other's elbows and stepped reluctantly to the edge of the threshold. "Should we enter?" Luke whispered. "After experiencing that last one, I don't know if we should."

"I'll stay here," volunteered Pepper. "How would we open the door if all of us stepped inside and it closed automatically? One of us has to stay here to make sure we could get back."

"Good thinking," Benny said, absently patting Pepper on the back. "Luke can be the guinea pig. He laughed, a few barks of jittery sound and waving his hands, gestured wildly. "I have to admit this place makes me kinda a scardy ass."

"Scares you," Pepper scoffed! "As me wee, Irish Granny would say, it isn't anything like being scared, that I am, but, me arse is feeling, the misgivings of me stomach, so I feel we should quit this place already." Clasping his fingers over Benny's shoulder, he squeezed it in a tight grip and they both turned to look at Luke. Pepper laughed. "You can call me wimpy, I feel about as brave as a bowl-full of wet noodles."

"Don't look at me, as if I'm the big decision maker here; I'm not," Luke said. Stepping toward the doorway, he threw his hands in the air and turning around faced them. "If the door closes behind me, I don't want to be alone in there either and, I don't think that makes me a wuss, or a wimp. I think we should be cautious, in case we meet something alive in here. If one of you will stay here, I'll go see what's down this hallway." Stepping over the threshold Luke pressed himself against the wall. Waiting for some weird thing to occur, he stood there and silently watched where it ended.

Nothing happened.

Glancing up, he turned and grinned at Pepper and Benny. "I guess I'm kind of a chicken," he whispered. He shrugged and laughed softly.

"Maybe even a wuss." Carefully, he inched his way along the narrow hall. What looked like an empty room ahead was filled with shadows and dead quiet. The soles of his boots scraped against the floor, and occasionally, the rubbing action emitted a squeaking sound. Lifting his feet higher, he glanced back at Benny and Pepper hovering in the doorway. Nervously, he waved, his eyes flickering an odd, electric blue. The muscles in his face tightened, his face lengthening as his breath escaped through his mouth. Rubbing the palms of his hands on his pants, he went down on one knee and peered around the corner of the passage.

The hall widened expanding into a huge room. Three large machines and some smaller ones were parked along its walls. Rising to his feet, Luke slipped silently around the corner, and listening with each cautious step, he turned his head often, watching for any movement in the hovering shadows, that might reveal a hidden alien.

A slight tremor skipped along the surface of his skin. Alarmed by his feelings an overwhelming strange sensation swept over him, and creeping through his mind, was the wild thought, he was exploring something that he shouldn't have seen. He knew with a deep feeling of foreboding that somehow this was a mistake. They shouldn't have discovered the cavern and all its secrets. Fear raced through him biting into his raw nerves with jolts of adrenaline. His muscles tightened, bunching under his clothes as sweat peppered his skin, and taking a deep breath, he exhaled slowly, trying to purge his body of built-up stress. Advancing further, he circled to his left, until he was standing over an enclosed space, where the floor dropped to a small platform that circled a machine.

Huge grappling hooks locked the machine in a space especially created for it. What he had thought was a window was a raised area in its middle and it covered most of the machine's top, almost like a bubble. He couldn't see anything of its interior as the raised bubble-like area was colored a soft blue, a perfect color if you wanted to camouflage it, he thought. Not very large, perhaps twenty feet across and as round as a silver dollar, the machine, lit from within radiated a fluorescent glow. " Looks like a flying saucer," he whispered.

Something brushed his elbow and he screamed compulsively, emitting a short, breathless expulsion of his breath. Jumping down four feet to the platform surrounding the machine, he recklessly climbed the side of the strange vehicle, his feet scrambling for leverage on its smooth surface. Frantic wild streaks of desperation ran through him, and pressing himself against the bubble-like canopy, he reached for handholds that weren't there. Hearing an explosion of breath and laughter, his face turned red. Propping his elbow on the canopy, he turned his head and looked up at Benny.

"Sorry, Luke, I didn't mean to scare the shit out of you. I thought you heard me coming," Benny said. Again, laughter exploded from his mouth in sudden bursts of sound. Bending, he crouched to the same level as Luke. He gestured backward, throwing his hand up to Pepper, and yelled. "It's all right. I just scared the devil out of Luke. He's now so pure, he's going to be canonized for sainthood."

Bending forward, he clutched his stomach, and howled, his voice rising and falling. "Fun . . . ny! You leapt right out into space, Luke, I'd say about ten feet." Knuckling his eyes with large, bony hands, he wiped away tears with his palms. "God, I needed to laugh. What a tension reliever. I've been so nervous my body feels sore. I can't remember ever being this tense. Nothing compares to this, not even the first time I sang publicly. Just a minute, Pep," he yelled. "I'll just take a quick look." He wiped his face again, grinning at Luke, his eyes brilliant and shiny with tears.

Glancing around at the room, Benny shrugged his shoulders in resignation. "I haven't a clue, have you?" he asked. Turning again to face the machine, he looked at Luke, his voice deepening with suppressed emotion. "Have you thought of why we haven't met some type of being in here? This is a huge ship, something had to fly it here."

Luke, shielding his eyes with his hands, pressed them against the glass-like bubble. He strained to see through the blue canopy. "Yeah, I've thought of all that. It's like the place has been abandoned. And I've also thought of this. Why? And no, I don't have a clue. We've found something awesome here. Not of this world. Something like the Roswell incident, but we know for sure this one's true. I'm glad we found it,

THE DEVILS PUNCHBOWL

even though I have moments when I can hardly control my fears. And Benny, the thought of aliens never leaves my conscious mind. When we're exploring, I expect to meet some awful apparition around the next corner with six arms and legs. The feeling's so strong it overwhelms me. At times, I'm swamped with the feeling. I guess it's terror."

Luke's voice dropped to a whisper, a whimsical note adding implication to his words. "I think this is a flying saucer and I'd like to fly it." He patted the canopy lowering his head to watch the action of his hand. "Just think what Rob's missing! We're the first here. Odd, we haven't found anything that looks like a place for garbage or a toilet. Maybe this ship is manned by robots. That's not too far fetched you know."

"Okay, Pepper," he yelled, in response to Pepper's frantic waving. "Just a minute." Stepping away from the canopy, he walked the width of the ship's flat surface. Stepping onto the platform that circled the machine, he turned again to stare at it, and shaking his head, forced himself to turn away.

Benny held out his hand, and Luke grabbed it, jumping the four-foot drop. Clapping Benny on the back, he walked away. "You stay, I'll go relieve Pepper from guard duty."

"What's over there?" Pepper called, giving Luke a questioning look, as he walked toward him. Luke pressed his back against the wall and sliding downward, he plopped, pushing his legs straight out in front of him.

"It's some kind of machine," Luke answered hesitantly. He shrugged. "I think it's a flying saucer. Get over there and look at it. Benny's waiting. And hurry, I've got to take a whizz."

"Me too," Pepper called, waving his hand back at Luke. His long, Levi clad legs jogged along the passageway, his boots scraping the floor noisily.

Luke watched Pepper and Benny. When they talk, they use their hands a lot to express themselves, he thought. Pepper, in one of his argumentive moods, held his hand out, palm first.

"Hold it a minute," he yelled.

"You hold it a minute. I'm right," Benny hollered back.

"Hey, c'mon," Luke called. "I've got to take a whizz and we want to look into each of these rooms before we leave." Rising to his feet, he walked to the threshold of the fifth door. This room wasn't lit. He paused in the doorway and took off his hard hat. Holding it at arms length, he flipped the hat's light switch to on. The circular beam of light pushed feebly against the wall of darkness, and casting its beam around the walls, he couldn't see much of anything, just vague outlines.

Pepper and Benny rushed through the door, from what Luke had named the docking room at a run, almost sliding into him in their rush. Glancing at them, he raised his eyebrows and gave them a questioning look.

"Something after you guys, or what?" he asked.

"We didn't see you in the doorway, so we thought you had left us," Pepper answered anxiously. "Remember our pact, we never leave each other. Stick together like glue, Rob told us. Three's always better than one in a sticky situation."

"Well, I don't think you need to worry about me leaving you," Luke answered with a snorting chuckle. "I'm not going anywhere without you guys. Turn your lamps on, let's look at this room. It's the only one without any light and it's sure black in there."

Removing their hard hats, Pepper and Benny pressed the switch to turn on their lamps. Luke advanced into the room crossing the threshold. The room widened about four feet from the door, spreading out in the familiar pie shape and their lights didn't do much to lighten the gloom. Pressing himself against the wall, Luke moved warily, stopping against a small padded structure with a raised lid. Shining his light into it, he stepped back and quickly flipped the light's beam around the room.

Pepper and Benny shuffled forward holding their hard hats high above their heads. The light from their lamps cast a peculiar greenness to their faces and bathed their bodies in an incandescent glow in the darkened room. Nine structures lined the walls, their lids in an upright position. "I'm going back to the door, you guys examine the room," Pepper whispered. "I'll be the lookout and watch our backs." Backing

THE DEVILS PUNCHBOWL

slowly through the short hall, he stopped in the threshold and casting a quick look behind him, pressed himself against the wall. Watching Luke's and Benny's light beams dance the length of the dark room, a peculiar thought came to him, strengthening as it became full blown in his mind.

"Psst."

"Hey."

"Psst. The way they're padded they look like coffins to me," he said softly. Their muscles tensed and breathing shallowly, a surge of fear raced through their bodies. Stepping back toward Pepper in the doorway, Luke swung his arm, skipping the light beam from his lamp over the room. It didn't illuminate much and caused more shadows to form within the dark room. "Stay here," he muttered. Walking swiftly, and staying near the line of coffin-like structures, he examined each one.

Benny and Pepper watched Luke, his light a moving beacon in the dark, his body a bulky shadow against the backdrop of coffin-like structures. Reaching the room's end, the weak output of his lamp outlined his body, and in the dense blackness, he looked like a gigantic shadow-being cut out of cardboard. The light beam swung erratically in giant gyrations against the walls as he moved his hat in a wide arc.

The end of the room widened considerably, but contained nothing but the strange padded structures. Luke walked back along its right side and joining Benny and Pepper, he said. "I think this is a room for the robots to ride in. The coffins are small about five-feet long and narrow." Stepping forward he aimed his light on a lid. "Notice how the inner part of the lid is padded too. I imagine when it's closed against the bottom it conforms to their bodies like a cocoon. Look at this! There's even a latch to secure it on the inside."

"So," Benny interrupted, his voice a barely heard murmur. "I guess we can surmise that they traveled here from a great distance. A place so far away that even their robot bodies had to be protected during the journey!"

"Yeah. Like through what scientists are calling a worm hole. They really don't understand worm holes yet, but I've read they kinda cheat time and space. Like using a short cut through an alley. I'd bet my life that these beings came through a time warp, and they had to use more than the speed of light, plus an added boost from a worm hole," Pepper said. "I've read that speed actually can bend space and time. God, I wish we knew how it all worked."

"Let's go," Luke demanded suddenly.

Leaving the dark room, they paused to look into each of the rooms. As they left each lighted doorway, Benny said dreamily, "the dark room, the lab, the aircraft room, a room filled with cabinets and a passage that goes nowhere and does weird things to you." Pausing by the opening in the floor, he pointed to the corresponding one in the ceiling. "We still have at least one more level to explore; or maybe more," he added, straining to see through the opening.

"I'm going to swing from my hands and drop to the floor," Luke said abruptly. "I hope I don't break an ankle doing it." Picking up their rope, he dropped to his knees and tossed it sideways through the opening. It struck the wall below with a solid whack and fell to the floor. Sitting on the edge of the opening, he launched himself through the hole in one swift movement. Hanging momentarily by his hands, he released his hold and landing on his feet, rolled. "It's easy," he shouted upward, at Benny's and Pepper's watching faces.

Benny lowered himself slowly through the opening. He grimaced and screwed his face into a scowl. He hated the thought of dropping to the floor.

"C'mon, Benny, let go, you're only about six-feet from the floor," Luke called.

Benny dropped suddenly and with his knee's bent slightly for balance, he stood as gracefully as an Olympic gymnast. Smiling broadly at his success, he moved from beneath the opening.

Pepper hanging by his hands for a second, swung his legs and dropped, tumbling several times. He slammed against the wall and lay there, grinning at Luke and Benny. "I've never claimed to be the most graceful one of us, have I?" he quipped, before climbing to his feet.

CHAPTER 10

LUKE STOPPED IN the middle of the bridge and stared at the console. Backing a slow step at a time toward the ship's entrance, his gaze tracked the console's length. Except for the screen that garbled out a message, every one of the screens was turned on, their respective stools waiting for someone or something to sit in them. "Hey, wait a minute," he called. "Let's close this down for the night," he suggested, waving his hand at the screens.

"Yeah," Pepper said. "Let's make a habit of leaving everything like we found it." Pressing on the padded edge in front of each chair, they watched the screens move smoothly and silently into the console. They took one more lingering look at the bridge of the spaceship and stepped awkwardly backward in slow, sliding steps to the spaceship's entrance.

"Awesome, way out weird, but awesome and feel the silence. It's beyond oppressive it's so quiet in here," Benny said softly, pausing in the doorway. "When you consider everything we've found in here, my mind tells me so much silence is way beyond normal. Notice," he added, skipping his fingers along the entrance to the ship, "the wall to the spaceship is about twelve inches thick and I don't think this door closes like the inner doors from top to the bottom. It must close like a pocket door."

"Yeah," Luke said, examining the oval opening. "There's a definite separation between where the tunnel begins and where the spaceship ends."

Walking quietly, they backed away from the entrance sliding along the glassy marbled walls of the tunnel. Benny slowed and patted the wall. He stared back at the oval opening. "I wonder why they covered so many of the caves and tunnels with this marbly stuff? Doesn't make sense does it?"

"None of this makes sense. I'd like to know why we haven't found anything alive in here?" Luke said quietly. "Or even dead. Something happened here, because we haven't found anything but the robots."

Pepper reacted. His eyes widened, the pupils enlarging and his mouth opened and shut several times. His hands moved wildly expressing his anxiety. "Shit. Don't mention findin aliens alive in here. Maybe they'd attack us, have you thought of that?"

"Yeah," both Benny and Luke answered.

"Lots," Luke said quietly. "Every time I turn a corner or we discover another cave." Following the gentle curve of the tunnel, their demeanor changed with the heavy burden of their burgeoning thoughts. Serious and somber, they trudged steadily downward, until they could no longer see the entrance into the spaceship.

Entering the large empty room, Luke followed Benny and Pepper as they crossed it, his eyes wondering over the smooth glassy surface of the white-marbled walls. Pausing, as they passed the two robots standing in the entrance, they stopped. "I still don't understand why they aren't working," Luke said "And though," he continued thoughtfully, "they appear to be turned off, maybe they're just in a waiting mode." Smiling, he twisted his head raising blond eyebrows in high peaks on his forehead . . . "Scary shit, huh."

Pepper placed his hands on one of the robot's shoulders. Crouching on one knee, he stared at its face. Whatever gave them movement, or cybernetic animated life was gone. Their eyes were empty, like they had been shut off, maybe they were shut down at a master switch somewhere. He shivered. Voicing his thought, he asked loudly. "Do you really think they're turned off?"

Benny looked at the robots. "What do you mean turned off?"

Pepper shrugged. "Like, maybe something in the ship turned a switch and cut their power source. You know, like we do an electric light."

THE DEVILS PUNCHBOWL

"C'mon," Luke said abruptly. "I'm got to take a whizz," he added, walking through the short hallway into the cavern.

"Hey, wait up," Pepper called, hurrying after Luke.

Benny crouched, and falling to one knee continued to stare at the robots. Examining the appendage like jointed fingers on the robot's hand and its longer thumb stuck on one side of its palm, he tried bending them, but they wouldn't budge. Inserting his finger inside its mouth, he moved it in the cavity, feeling for a tongue. Pressing harder, he suddenly grimaced and pulled his finger free. "Yuk," he whispered.

"Hey," Benny said as Luke, walked toward him through the hallway. "They seem to be jointed and must have a full range of motion just like us."

Luke watched Benny try to lift one of its legs, but it didn't move. "Let's go," he said, spying Pepper entering the cave. It's almost three o'clock and we're getting short on time."

"C'mon," Luke repeated, glancing over his shoulder at Pepper and Benny.

"Hey, wait up, I'll only be a second," Benny called. Dashing for the entrance, he jogged through the hallway disappearing into the cavern. Beginning to whistle, the notes trembling with emotion filtered softly through the hall into the cave.

Following the curve of the wall, Luke paused over the pile of balls studying them. Squatting on one knee, he lifted one, balancing it in his hand. It was a heavy substance and was pressed into a sphere the size of a baseball. Laying it gently back on the pile, he stood and walked toward the south end of the room. Approaching the entrance, he stepped just inside the opening. The dim lighting in the immense cavern, strengthened the hovering shadows lining the walls, and its southern wall steeped in darkness had no end.

Nothing had moved, he thought, the machine and its robot rider still sat where they had found it. The gigantic size of the cavern was awe inspiring, and his mind had a hard time registering and cataloging, what he was seeing. It was like his brain couldn't accept the picture his eye was imprinting on it. No noises broke the silence. I bet if you dropped a pin in here it would sound like a bomb, Luke thought. He wanted to shout to break the tomblike stillness. Even their whispering voices and the subdued sound of their movements was swallowed up by so much empty space. A faint cold breeze moved through the door, brushing his face, and he sniffed, there wasn't even a hint of an odor.

Sighing, he stepped back to the entrance, looking for Pepper. He was standing in front of the robots, making grotesque faces at them. Benny walking back through the entrance exploded, his expression changing to a medley of bright, sunny emotions. He laughed boisterously, pounding Pepper's back and with a loud whoop they started to stamp their feet. Patting their open mouths, they whooped. . . .

"Wah . . . ah, wah . . . ah, wah . . . ah."

Bending back and forth from the waist, they whooped and, abruptly, standing straight and tall, made their feet go in a frenzy of movement. Circling the robots several times, Benny danced away from them, leading Pepper as they patted their mouths around the curve of the wall toward Luke. He grinned at them as they approached. "What's the name of that kind of dance, wild Mexican, wild Irish or wild German Jew?"

"Nah. None of those," Pepper answered between whoops and yells. "This is genuine, one of a kind, plain, good old American Indian." Finishing breathlessly on a last whoop, they laughed exuberantly.

Grouped together in the short hallway, they flipped the switch to light their lamps, and entering the cavern walked past the robot on the machine. Following the natural curve of the cavern's wall the trail became smooth slick rock. Faltering in spots, they stepped carefully, gripping the rocky cliff-face for balance. Descending into darkness, the incline steepened, plunging ever downward on a narrowing path. Their lights moved feebly against the cliff's face and shadows jumped, hovering in dark patches ahead of them.

Benny slipped on a section of slippery rock and, cursed a steady stream under his breath. Pressing his body against the wall, his hands and fingernails scraped the cliff's rocky face, as his feet sought traction on the trail.

"Hey, slow down," Pepper shouted, watching him.

THE DEVILS PUNCHBOWL

Gripping sharp edges and small crevices, they shuffled downward. The trail leveling slightly, became a less hazardous downward plunge, and their breath accelerated by anxiety, slowed. Luke braced himself against the curved wall, and forced himself to go at a slower pace. Stopping, he glanced back at Benny and Pepper. Benny tried to grin, his mouth splitting in a grimace that showed his anxiety.

Luke paused and anchoring his feet poked his head around a sharp right-angled corner. Narrowing, the huge cavern ended in a fissure barely five-feet in width, and he could see in the distance, a faint illuminance that pierced the total black of the darkness.

"C'mon," he whispered.

Passing the sharp angle in the cliff's face, Benny and Pepper followed him into the tunnel-like opening. The trail ended in a junction, with another branch to the fissure they had just descended. Y-shaped, it angled off in a northerly direction, its opening masked in complete and total darkness. The long leg of the Y-shaped fissure, went upward at a steep incline for approximately fifty-feet, and, narrowed again at its end in a three-foot wedge of light. Reflecting off the white granite ceiling and walls, the light shimmered in the narrow passage. They paused and stood quietly watching, fighting an oppression they couldn't define. Their long descent in total darkness and the heavy weight of absolute stillness pressed against them.

Falling to their knees, they crawled upward through two-inches of snow-white sand, and flopping on their bellies, cautiously stuck their heads through the narrow opening. Starting with a small trickle, water had tumbled and rolled through the Y-shaped fissure, and over eons of time, had formed a torrential cataract of water. Falling over the edge of a thirty-foot precipice, it had gouged out of solid rock an underground grotto. Dry now, without a sparkle of water anywhere, a robot, very alone and small, stood next to a machine on a dry bed of sand.

Benny plucked at Luke's sleeve, drawing his attention away from the robot on the dry riverbed. "They have to be mining for something," he whispered. "Otherwise, none of this makes sense. Why are they digging in an ancient riverbed, inside a mountain?"

"I agree," Pepper muttered. "They're mining for something. But what?" Leaning forward over the edge of the precipice, he compulsively put the knuckle of his index finger into his mouth and, chewing on it, watched the scene below for movement. There was none.

"Everything about this place makes me uneasy," Luke said. "When I try rationally, to put together all that we've found here, my mind labors, like the neurons in my brain have stuck together. I've got a feeling in my gut that these robots are waiting for something to happen. They're waiting! And somehow they've shut themselves off, maybe to conserve energy." He shrugged in frustration, his shoulders rising stiffly to his ears.

"Shit, c'mon," he exclaimed, uncoiling the rope from his shoulder. Removing his hard hat, he flipped the light button to off. "Turn your lights off. Let's take a look down there and then we'll get out of here." Slipping the hook around a rock, he circled it once with the rope pressing the prongs into the dirt behind it. Pushing the hooks in deep to secure them, he duck-walked close to the opening and, threw the end of the rope over the lip of the cliff. Giving it several hard tugs, he crawled to the edge of the precipice.

Luke disappeared over the edge and Pepper frowned watching him. Taking a handful of rope in both hands, he pushed himself backward through the three-foot opening and over the rim. Hand over hand, he followed Luke, and Benny after nervously watching them, laboriously lowered himself, his feet noisily scraping the cliff's face until they touched the sandy bed.

They stood listening, watching for movement in the small grotto. Stepping away from the base of the granite cliff, they approached the robot. Glancing toward their left, Luke pointed at an opening about thirty feet away. It was to the right of the jutting face of the white granite cliff they had just descended and was brightly lit.

Clearing his throat several times, Luke rubbed his face with his hands. He tried to put the pattern of his thinking into some kind of cohesive thought, looking for a different perspective on what they had found. "You know, I feel like my mind has blown a fuse. Like I said, maybe these robots are in a waiting pattern. But then, if they turned

THE DEVILS PUNCHBOWL

themselves off to conserve energy, why leave the lights on. See what I mean . . . if we think they've stopped to conserve energy, then on another train of thought they're wasting it by leaving the lights on." He shrugged, his face wrinkling in frustration as he stared at Benny. "What'd you find?" he asked, striding forward. Dropping to his knees, he knelt beside him.

"This looks like gold to me," Benny answered, picking up another gold-colored object buried in the sand behind the machine. "In fact, I know it's gold. They must be doing something with gold. But it doesn't look like they're keeping it. It's buried in the sand! It's scattered all over here."

Luke scooped up huge handfuls of sand uncovering round topped pieces of gold. They were all uniform in length, about four inches, and looked, like small versions of gold ingots. Staring at the gold, he rose and walked to his left to examine the machine.

Kneeling, he lowered himself to his stomach and looked under the machine. From an opening in its belly he glimpsed a dull shine of gold. Rising, he examined the small box connected to its side. Feeling with his fingers, he felt what he thought was a hinge, so there had to be a way to open it.

He eyed the machine with growing irritation and turning his head looked for Pepper and Benny. The sand swirled as they moved and scooped, the shine of the gold bars they had uncovered in loosely piled stacks.

"Hey, stop! Hey!"

Benny and Pepper looked at Luke, surprise and incomprehension flashing across their faces as they become aware of what they were doing. They stared at the piled gold and rising to their feet, stumbled through the deep sand.

"Remember, we don't have much time to explore," Luke exclaimed. "C'mon, let's see if we can open this box. Look at this," he added, pointing with one of his fingers. "I think these chunks of gold are made inside this machine." Dropping to their knees they examined the box. A large flange connected to a tube with a flat bottom and rounded top, was fastened to the underside of the box. It lay directly over a flat shiny surface.

"I think you're right, I see some gold in the tube's opening," Benny said, laying flat against the sand. "Just think a machine that produces gold," he muttered. Pressing along the edge of the flange with his fingers, he laughed, a soft, choked sound and rose to his knees. "Just like the goose that laid the golden eggs."

Rising to his feet, Pepper walked around to the front of the machine. Looking for a control panel, he hovered over Luke's head. Finding several buttons on the machine's left side, he pressed the smallest one. The box popped open. Luke and Benny lunged backwards, surprise lighting up their faces.

"What happened, it opened?" Benny asked Luke. "Did you find something to press?"

"I did." Pepper answered, waving his hand at the control panel. Bending forward, he looked in the box over Luke's shoulder, it contained small chunks of a white silvery metal.

"What do you think it is, Luke, you're better at identifying metal then I am?" Benny asked.

Luke sorted through the pieces in the bottom of the box, picking up a few of the larger ones. "It's really heavy," he answered absently, moving them around in his hand. Looking thoughtful, he glanced at Benny. "Here," he said, dropping a few pieces of white metal in his hand. "I think it's platinum. I think these robots, are extracting platinum from the gold."

"We learned in a geology class," Luke said, glancing up at Pepper, "that platinum is really scarce and not found in many places. But sometimes if you find a lot of gold, you'll always find some platinum."

"Don't you guys think it's odd that they discarded the gold?" Pepper said, his expression changing to one of puzzlement. "Why would they want platinum over the gold?"

Luke picked up another handful of metal from the bottom of the box, and sifting it through his fingers, shrugged. "I don't have a clue, but I'd guess, it's because platinum is used in electrical instruments and it's also used as a catalyst. The robots must need it for their instru-

THE DEVILS PUNCHBOWL

ments and maybe, even to run their spaceship. Maybe they combine it with other metals, like uranium. They have to use some kind of fissionable material and no tellin, if the spaceship is a time machine, it must need a lot of power." His voice trailed into silence and, meditating, his mind sorted through what he had just said.

Benny moved the pieces of white metal in his hand. Suddenly rising to his feet, he dropped them back into their box and gestured toward the brightly lit cave. "Let's look in there and then get out of here. I'm tired."

Trudging laboriously through deep sand, Pepper felt weird. Everything seemed to be a little bit unreal. Even the dry riverbed was slightly out of focus, sort of surreal. His breathing quickened and he blinked several times to clear his vision.

"Hey guys, are you feeling kind of bitchin, or is it just me?"

"Me too," Benny answered. "It's like I'm on the edge of a cliff and about to fall off and I can't save myself. How about you, Luke are you feeling anything weird?"

"I've felt that way for a couple of hours," Luke answered, stepping into the cave. "I think we've been in here too long."

Long and narrow, the cave reminded Luke of a fantasy story. A fairy tale. About thirty-feet wide and one hundred feet in length, its ceiling soared above their heads, and in every shape imaginable, stalactites hung like giant icicles. In disorderly bunches, satin-smooth white-quartz rocks, resembling giant eggs, lay tossed on the rocky floor. An opening on the opposite wall and directly in front of them, was black, no light penetrated its darkness. Another opening on the furthest wall to the east, was brightly lit.

"Let's look in there," Benny said gesturing toward the dark entrance. "It's the closest. We'll take a quick look and then let's leave. We'll investigate this cave some more tomorrow."

Walking toward the dark entrance, they removed their hard hats, and turned on their lamps. Bunched together in the doorway, they clutched each other's elbow and slowly edged their way into the cave. The beams of light cast by their lamps, pushed feebly against a dark so black, they stopped.

Shuffling forward, Luke removed his helmet and cast the beam of light from his hard hat on the ceiling and walls. Swinging it toward the northwestern wall, a shiny surface leaped out at them. "Hey Benny, aim your light on the ground where we're stepping," Luke suggested. "We don't want to step off into a crevasse."

Pepper laughed nervously at Luke's words and tried to imagine how big the cave was. "Let's go toward that shine, Luke," he said. "We'll go over there and then get the hell out of here. I don't like the dark."

"Neither do I, Pep, neither do I," Luke whispered. Shuffling their feet on the rocky floor, they advanced toward the shiny surface and like a sponge, the dark absorbed the golden, circular beams of light from their hard hats.

"I think it's a frozen waterfall," Luke said cautiously. Bending awkwardly from the waist, he peered at the shiny surface. "Yeah, that's what it is. We must be directly underneath that one up in the big cavern. Hey! Wait! The ground slopes a lot here. Be careful."

Dropping to their knees, they crawled to the edge of a large fissure, and falling to their belly's, aimed their lamps downward. The frozen water fell endlessly, their lights appearing as grotesque shadows and shapes on its mirrored shiny surface. There was no relief to the blackness in the deep chasm and Luke imagined it dropping for miles.

Benny swung his arm in a wide arc along the rim of the crevasse. Abruptly, he stiffened and pressing his hard hat against the ground, focused its light on something he saw to his left and just below them. Holding the hat perfectly still, he found it again, and grabbing Luke's sleeve shook his arm.

"Look where I'm aiming my light," he whispered. "See that dark shadow when I pass it over the waterfall? What is it?"

"I don't know," Luke said. Squinting, he could barely see a dark shape in the ice. "Pepper, aim your lamp where Benny and I have ours focused."

Pepper moved his lamp until its light beam joined Luke's and Benny's. Stiffening against the ground, they recoiled, backing crablike, until they were several feet from the edge of the crevasse.

THE DEVILS PUNCHBOWL

"Did you see that? Did you see that?" Pepper whispered. "It's some kind of great beast! Let's look at it again." Crawling awkwardly, they fell on their bellies and focused their lights at what they had seen.

A huge animal lay captured in the ice flow, the black outline of its body warped by the opaqueness of its tomb. His head pillowed on its front legs was massive, his tail crookedly bent almost at a right angle.

"It's a cat. That's the biggest cat I've ever seen," Benny said, his voice gently rising. "See where the chasm makes a curve, let's go around it, it might be a little clearer over there."

Crawling along the edge of the chasm, Pepper led the way, until he was against a white granite rock. Aiming the beam of their lamps downward, they stared at the huge cat laying on the ledge, his body pushed against the rocky face of the cliff.

Pepper spying another opening behind the frozen ice sheet, pushed himself up on his knees. Staring at it for a second, he stood and casting the light from his hard hat on the ground, watched where he stepped. "Hey," he called, standing in the mouth of the opening. "Here's another cave."

Stepping forward several feet, the beam of light from his lamp flashed across the waterfall's glassy-crystal surface. Resembling waves on an incoming tide, the water frozen in ripple-like ridges, wasn't thick and had a translucency resembling waves on a seashore. "Beautiful," he whispered, swinging the lamp's beam of light over the waterfall's surface.

Luke and Benny watched Pepper's light flow magically through the frozen water, a shadowed star of moving brilliance in its dark mass. "Hey, Pep, move your light over the waterfall again?" Benny called out.

Pepper flicked his light over the water again and catching a glimpse of something in his peripheral vision, focused his light on it. Steadying the beam, he moved it over the object. "Jesus, Mary, Joseph," he yelled. Aiming his light at the ice sheet, he stumbled backward, until he had passed the small cave's entrance and backing over a rock, fell to his knees.

"Hey, I'm outa here."

"I said I'm leaving," he yelled. Frantically, scrambling to his feet, he looked fearfully over his shoulder at the mouth to the small cave.

"C'mon, I'm leavin."

Luke and Benny jumping to their feet ran toward him, their lamps flinging jerky, gyrating yellow spots over the dark ceiling and walls. "What is it?" Luke yelled. Grabbing Pepper's arm, he stopped him from running past him. "What's wrong? Is something in there?"

Pepper tried to speak, his mouth moved, but no words came out. Closing his lips tight against his teeth, he squeezed his eyes shut, and moaned from deep within his chest, a deep distressful sound. "Look in the cave, it's our worst nightmare come true. I don't think it's human or a robot." Pepper's voice rose, the pitch reedy and weak. From deep in his chest he yelled. . . . "I think it's an alien."

"I found a frig . . . in alien!"

"Are you sure?" Luke asked, casting a frightened look at the dark opening. Hesitating, he stopped and stared at Pepper. "Was it moving?"

"No! Not moving," Pepper whispered through set teeth. Vigorously, he shook his head back and forth, to emphasize the no, he had uttered.

"Okay, we'll have to go see what it is," Luke said reluctantly. Focusing the beam of light from his lamp toward the cave's mouth, he tried to penetrate the darkness behind the waterfall. His reluctance apparent in every step, he shuffled forward, forcing his feet to move where his brain commanded them to go. Benny clutched his arm on his left side and Pepper gripped the back of his jacket. Hesitant, they approached the mouth of the cave, riffles of fear scouring their skin. Stopping at the entrance, Pepper released his grip on Luke's jacket.

The cave wasn't large and, with small heavy steps noisily scraping the rocky floor, they entered the dark as midnight opening. Luke pressed his shoulder against the rocky wall and held his breath until he was forced to breathe again. Sucking in air, it whistled and hissed through his teeth, and his chest heaved as a lightheaded feeling, passed over him. "Where Pepper?" Luke asked, forcing the words through tight lips.

THE DEVILS PUNCHBOWL

"Clear back against the wall, to the right, almost against the waterfall. It's laid out on a block of ice," Pepper whispered. "You can't miss it."

Focusing their lamp beams on the waterfall, Luke felt Benny's trepidation build as his movements became stiff, calculated and slow. He was moving in typical Benny style. Experiencing a sudden burst of panic, he hesitated. Their beams of light chasing each other across the water, gave the frozen ridges a riffling illusionary illuminance, as if they were wet and flowing. They tread softly, their attention focused on the back of the cave and on what lay centered in the small yellow circle of their light beams. Warily they approached it.

Luke's shoulders sagged and his breathing escalated. Gripping Benny's arm, he stopped and, swamped in a rising tide of apprehension, stared at the alien. He was dressed in a shiny suit, similar to the metal the robots were made of, but it looked soft, almost like supple leather. A hinged visor in the helmet lay toward the top of his head. The only exposed part of its body was the face and it looked familiar, its features human. Parted over small even teeth, the lips, curved and full, were set below a crooked nose. Large, partially open eyes dominated its facial structure, the eyelids with a pronounced epicanthic fold covered dark irises.

"I've never seen eyes like this on any animal on earth," he whispered. Sparse, graying, brown wisps of hair lay on the alien's forehead. His skin, pale and porcelain white, had a luminous texture, like he hadn't been out in the sun much.

Luke thought, he's in some kind of deep sleep, or very dead, and he voted mentally for very dead, because he looked to be very frozen. "Hey," he whispered, turning to look at Benny. "Do you think we should touch him? He looks dead."

"Uh-uh," Benny replied emphatically, shaking his head from side to side. "You know, how some cultures carry on about their dead. It might be taboo or something if we did. Then we'd have caused an intergalactic war just because we touched him. Our whole world might perish because we examined him." Starting to laugh, Benny covered his mouth with his hand and, choking, swallowed the sound.

Luke joined him, their bodies shaking. Clutching each other, their voices rose to a howl, a high-pitched mixture of terror and excitement.

"What in hell, are you laughing at," Pepper demanded. His voice rose to an intense nervous whisper. "Here we are buried in this mountain and we've found the most God-awful creature imaginable and you're laughing."

"Shut up!"

His voice rose again, belligerent and anxious, desperation deepening it to a harsh loud whisper. "Hey, I said, shut up." Flushing a bright angry red, he watched Luke and Benny's silhouetted bodies in the dim light cast by their hard hats. "Your acting nuts. C'mon, let's get out of here. I've had it! This is way too much for me. I want to see a little bit of the sun before it sets."

Luke and Benny threw one more fearful glance at the frozen creature, and then, walked away, their bodies convulsing. Benny aimed the beam from his lamp on Pepper hovering in the doorway.

"Okay, Pep, we're coming," he choked out between gusts of laughter. "You don't know what Luke and I just did in there. We almost started an intergalactic war."

Luke and Benny broke out in another bout of high-pitched giggling. Standing in the mouth of the cave, Benny started to hiccup and they grinned at each other. Leaning against the wall, Luke slapped Benny on the back several times. Aiming their lights on Pepper, they grinned broadly at his discomfiture.

"Okay, okay, let's go," Luke said.

Shoulders hunching with suppressed emotion, their bodies shook in uncontrollable jerks, and following the curve of the wall, they passed the frozen waterfall heading toward the lighted entrance. Thankfully entering the brightly-lit cave, they walked across it, and stepped, into the deep sand of the riverbed. Stopping near the robot, Luke picked up a bar of gold and shoved it in his pocket.

Watching him, Benny and Pepper did the same. Benny squeezed the gold for several seconds in his large hand, and then, put it in his jacket pocket. Their eyes skimmed the dry riverbed, their awareness of their surroundings rising to a feverish pitch. Turning around, they

THE DEVILS PUNCHBOWL

stared warily back at the opening, and dragging their feet, plodded like old men to the face of the white granite cliff.

Grasping the rope, Pepper swiftly scaled the face of the cliff. Reaching the top, he watched Benny laboriously climb the rope, and thought, of what his Mom had told him about Benny. She had said, his growth pattern was different, so he hadn't yet grown in width to fit his length, but once he filled out, he was going to be a huge man. A musical genius, and softly spoken, he was generous to a fault, and he possessed a worldly wisdom way beyond his years, caused by the influence of old world parents and grandparents. "Benny sees the world through gentle eyes, but he's also a lot more suspicious of people than Luke and me," Pepper whispered to himself. "He places no trust at all in the goodness of human nature, and always says, most people have very little of it. He was always saying, you better watch it, they'll kill you for a nickel."

Pepper grinned at Benny and rising to his knees, offered his hand to help him over the edge. Benny sighed with relief, grabbed Pepper's hand and raising one knee to the rocky edge, pulled himself over the rim. Crawling several feet, he sat on the ground, releasing a huge expulsion of air.

Luke's head appeared above the edge of the drop, and throwing one hand upward, grasped Pepper's hand in a tight grip. Pulling hard, his feet noisily scraped the rock straining to find toeholds, and scrambling over the rim, he lay on his stomach next to him. Pushing himself to his knees, he grunted.

"C'mon," he said, coiling the rope over his shoulder. "Let's go and we won't stop to look at things. I'm bushed and I need a little bit of sunshine to make my day end on a happy note." Sucking in a deep breath, he crawled until he could stand, and rising, to his feet waited for Benny and Pepper.

Walking rapidly they climbed the trail steadily and silently. Passing the robot on the machine, they walked into the brightly lit marbleized cave. Rushing by the two guarding robots to the cave's entrance, they moved swiftly by the massive ice sheet, and followed the trail downward into the great cavern. Pepper patted Sir Spidery, the half-frozen robot on the way by, and jogging ahead, disappeared into the narrow entrance tunnel.

Benny, forced his mind into a blank state of emptiness, and moving swiftly through narrow fissures, pulled himself around corkscrew curves and deep crevices through the mountain.

Luke followed them and eventually emerging from the last fissure, he sighed deeply, glad to be free from the bulky presence of massive rocky ceilings and walls. Piling brush and rocks over the fissure, they hid its entrance and walked away.

"It's a gray day. We might have guessed everything would be overcast," Pepper said. "There isn't even a glimmer of sunlight." His voice turned grumpy, low and harsh with disappointment. "Let's go! What a day," he added, sighing heavily.

They walked, hugging the face of the mountain and carefully watched where they put their feet along the narrow path. Mesmerized by the view over the edge of the trail, it drew their eyes downward to harsh ridges and valleys. Clouds drifted a thousand feet below them and in thick scattered bunches of soft billowing heaps, they covered the slopes and valleys in a moving mosaic of shadows as far as they could see. Hiking over a granite ridge, they entered the opening into the Devils Punchbowl, and sighing in nervous exhaustion, found sanctuary in their camp.

CHAPTER 11

BENNY LAY BACK against his rocky backrest and patted his stomach in gratification. It was full. Pepper had fried the fish extra crispy tonight and they had been delicious. He was giving the frying pan a good scrubbing at the creek, and Luke, had left to have what he called, a sluicing of the daily grime and stress sweat from his body.

He laughed softly to himself. Luke at times came up with the most graphic descriptions, describing everything he saw in lewd detail. He saw humor in everything, even in a person's bodily functions. Tilting his head back against the padded collar of his jacket, he watched the sky. The camp was clean, and the dishes and utensils washed. There wasn't anything else he had to do, except move his lazy ass enough, to walk to the creek and bathe. Sighing at the irritable thought that he had to move, he scrunched lower into his jacket's collar and curving his spine against the hard ground closed his eyes.

The low-drone of Luke's and Pepper's voices got louder. Luke yelled and Pepper laughed. Luke must not have liked the ice cold water, Benny thought. Opening one eye, he lifted his head and watched them as they hurried along the trail.

"I still don't see why we can't press buttons on the tool," Pepper argued, dropping the frying pan on the grill. "We'll never learn what the tool does unless we do. Benny, how about you?" he added, nudging him with his foot. "Are you in favor of experimenting with the tool . . . ? Or what?"

Luke stood next to the fire, throwing his clothes on. Pushing muscular arms into the sleeves of his shirt, he raised them and pulled it over his head. He gave Benny a questioning glance and pulling his towel free stepped into his shorts. Pulling on a clean pair of Levis, he wrestled with the buttons trying to get them to work through the buttonholes. Everything was stiff when it was cold, nothing worked right, he thought. Taking a deep breath, he exhaled slowly, trying to relax.

Benny lay lazily contemplating, Pepper's question. Sitting up, he hesitated and then grinned. "I don't see why not," he answered, looking up at Pepper. His face brightened with enthusiasm. "I'd like to experiment too, it's the only way we'll learn what their functions are." Glancing at Luke pulling his boots on near the fire, he frowned, and then, pulled the two tools out of his pocket. "As long as we're careful, I don't see how pressing the buttons can hurt us in any way. How about it Luke, before I dunk my ass in cold water tonight, we'll have a little fun?"

"Okay," Luke said reluctantly. "Let's do a few things with the button we pressed first, that one we know moves things." Slinging his jacket on, he picked up his wallet, knife and camping paraphernalia and shoved all of it into his Levi pockets. He tugged his ball cap out of his jacket pocket and pulled it over his damp hair. Discarding some trash into the fire, he sat on a nearby rock and watched Pepper.

"Hey, press gently and the rock barely moves," Pepper said, glancing at Luke and Benny. "If you press down hard and hold it, it moves a lot faster. Move your arm up and down and it lifts the rock or lowers it."

"I'd say a lot faster," Benny chortled, experimenting with his tool. Lifting his arm, he aimed the tool at a rock until it hovered in the air. Holding, a steadily increasing pressure on the button, he moved the rock out over the lake, and dropped it with a large splash into the water.

Luke held the tool in the palm of his hand. Pressing the button on the left side, he aimed it at a rock near the water. Nothing happened. Holding it close, he examined it and frowned. This tool had four buttons on the crossbar and two indentations on the leg of the T. One was

THE DEVILS PUNCHBOWL

marked with a circle, with a dot in the middle, and the other was marked with a star.

"Hey, this one's different, look at your tools," he shouted. Rising to his feet, he examined the tool again. Walking around a large rock, he squatted, and balancing on his heels next to Pepper and Benny, showed them the indentations marked by the circle and star signs. Pulling the other tool out of his pocket, he examined it. It was different, it had six buttons on the cross bar and the leg of the T was plain.

"This tool is different," Benny surmised, bending his head to examine the instrument. "It must have another purpose."

"Yeah." Pepper agreed.

"I tried pressing the left button like we did on the other tool and nothing happened," Luke explained. He rose and walking several feet stood next to the fire. "Okay, watch this. This tool must be similar to the other one. I'm going to try something different. I'm gonna press two of these buttons simultaneously, and aim the tool at the log laying next to the big rock."

Blinking several times, he took a deep breath and pressed the left button at the same time, as the button with the dot in the middle of a circle. The log vanished and then reappeared, landing with a crash next to the fire.

Yelling, Benny and Pepper jumped to their feet and ran toward Luke. Luke's mouth fell open and sitting abruptly, he licked dry lips, confusion racing rapidly across his face.

Pepper grabbed his arm and held on. "How'd, you do that?"

Luke studied the tool in his hand. "I don't know. Just about the time I pressed the buttons, I thought it would be a good log for the fire tonight. And". . . sucking in a deep gulp of air, he let it out with an explosive whoosh. "Then, it appeared next to the fire." Laying the tool on a rock next to him, he pushed his hands through his hair. "I can't believe it."

"I want to try it," Pepper said, his excitement barely contained. "What buttons did you push?"

"I pressed the left one on the bar and the circle with a dot on the leg." Luke answered.

"Be careful, Pep," Benny cautioned. He sank to a rock, his body stiff with tension.

Pepper looked around the camp. Lifting the tool, he aimed it at a small tree branch and hesitated. "What did you do again Luke?" he asked quizzically, looking at him. "You pointed the tool, pressed buttons and thought the log would make a good one for the fire tonight. And then, it vanished, reappearing next to the fire."

Luke nodded.

Pepper aimed, pressed the buttons and thought the branch would look good on his sleeping bag. The branch vanished and reappeared, landing with a soft thud on his bed-roll. Running to his bedroll, he picked it up and held it in his arms. Walking to the fire, he knelt next to Luke and Benny, cradling it in his arms.

"Did you guys see sort of a flash of light around the branch?" Luke asked. Rubbing his mouth, he sighed, frustration dulling his eyes. "I thought I did."

"Uh-uh, I didn't see anything," Pepper answered. Glancing at Benny, he shrugged and Benny raising his eyebrows, shrugged too.

Reaching for his ball cap, Luke picked it up and shaking the dirt from it, placed it on his head. Wearing perplexed expressions, their minds explored what they had discovered.

Benny, sitting beside Luke showed the most apprehension. He cleared his throat several times, bewilderment etching his face. "Just think," he stated, staring intently at Luke and then at Pepper. Clearing his throat again, he started to speak and stopped. Shrugging several times, he looked at his hands clasped on his knees. "Just think, what the public would do if they ever found out about this. We would be mobbed. Even our government would probably kill us for this kind of knowledge. The more we find in the cavern, the more afraid I am."

Glancing at Luke again, Benny's eyes opened wide, the pupils dilating to the edge of the iris. "It could be worse for us than it was for the Jews in Germany. We'd be hunted and persecuted, just like my grandparents were. What we've found here is big, way beyond us. We've got to be careful, because we could be hunted by our own government, and by foreign ones too." Shivering, he hugged his body. "Sometime,

THE DEVILS PUNCHBOWL

if you guys are interested, I'll tell you what happened to my grandparents. I'll tell it like they did, in graphic detail just what the Nazis did, so you'll never forget it."

Pepper stood and threw the branch on the fire. Sitting abruptly, he stared at the billowing cloud of smoke it created, and hugging one of his legs tight against his chest, he rested his head on his upraised knee. Absently, his expression blank and stark, he picked up Luke's tool and handed it to him.

They became silent, thinking about Benny's words. Words spoken in such simplicity and without innuendo, made their innermost fears surface to ripple along already frayed nerves. None of them could imagine a government that would kill them. Not here in America.

The wood burned, snapped and popped. The flames danced a macabre movement along the branch's length and devouring it, turned the bark to a white ash. They became preoccupied with their thoughts, watching in lethargic fascination the mesmerizing, flickering movement of the flames.

Deep in introspection, Luke tried to correlate his thinking and at first didn't believe what he was seeing. Wiping his eyes, he closed them and dragging his hand over his face, shook his head. Opening his eyes, he watched a black bear move quietly along the shore of the lake. His steps were silent and he made no noise. Startled, Luke jumped, and grabbing Pepper and Benny by the shoulder, shook them.

"Run, there's a bear," he yelled.

The bear frightened by Luke's voice turned and ran back toward the lake. Suddenly, he spun in a circle, causing a torrent of shifting, moving shale, and ran in a hopping stiff-legged motion toward the campsite, challenging them. Stopping abruptly, he watched them climb the boulder, and realizing they were no threat, he ambled closer. He wheezed as he walked, his breath forming puffs of cloudy vaporous mist in front of his snout. Slowly, but warily, he entered their camp. Raising his head, he sniffed again in their direction, eyeing them with flat dark eyes.

Luke scrambled up the side of the largest boulder that made up part of the enclosure for their beds. His hands and feet scraped its surface to find minute cracks for leverage, and experiencing a sense of euphoria, he propelled himself straight up the face of the boulder. Pepper and Benny followed him, casting backward glances at the huge bear.

Black as ebony and colored a reddish-brown on his neck and legs, the bear stood suddenly, his fur rippling over his body in shiny waves. He sniffed the air. Standing upright, he watched the boys intently, as they frantically climbed the almost perpendicular side of the boulder. Grunting soft noises, he lowered himself to stand on four legs, and lifting his head, sniffed again.

The boys stood on the rounded top of the boulder trying to stay upright. Clinging to each other's jackets for balance, their boots slipped and slid on its smooth surface. "Now what in hell are we going to do? I forgot to grab our guns," Luke said. Exasperation drove his voice higher. "I should kick my own ass for this one!"

"What'll we do if he charges, this boulder isn't that high?" Benny asked. "He doesn't seem to be afraid of us or the fire. Their camp oven banged as it fell over and he cringed at the noise. "We've got to do something, he's going to wreak our camp."

"Yeah, but what?" Pepper asked. "The fire didn't stop him and I'm not going to challenge him. Are you? I think he would win in a wrestling match. Maybe we should yell at him though, it might frighten him away."

"I don't think so," Luke whispered. "We could yell until we were blue, but I don't think it would faze him. He's not afraid of us, I can tell by the way he's acting. We've got to frighten him enough, so he won't come back. I don't want him hanging around when we're asleep." They became silent as they watched the bear eat their leftovers from dinner.

"Listen, I have an idea," Luke said. "The only thing is I don't know if it'll work. Let's try to send him somewhere else with these tools. I know," he added with a broad grin, "let's send him to Sacramento. The perfect spot is the El Dorado Hotel. Remember, we stayed there during our eighth grade graduation trip to Cal Expo. It'll be the best joke ever. No one will ever know how the bear got there." Precari-

THE DEVILS PUNCHBOWL

ously balanced, they laughed, and grinning at each other, swayed like tall trees.

"Remember the garden with the beautiful fountains. I mean, the Spanish one with different levels of patios and terraces. Okay, have you both got that picture in your mind. Remember it's the biggest fountain. There's three of them and it's the one in the middle of the biggest terrace."

"Got it?"

"This is impossible, Luke," Benny whispered. "You don't know if it'll work. There's a big difference in moving a small log and moving a five-hundred-pound bear." Benny's voice rose, strung out and taut with tension. "We'll probably make him mad and then he'll attack us. "And . . . shit . . . ," he wailed. "This is going to be really hard, we need to use one hand just to stay balanced on this rock."

"Oh shit. It might not work and if it doesn't, we'll do something else. I'll go down and get our guns, maybe, he'll run if I shoot near him. Let's try the tool first," Luke said, looking down at the bear. "He doesn't look like he's ready to leave any time soon, and I'm already tired of being perched up here with you guys on this rock. You both stink. And Benny, think of the alternatives. He could suddenly get it into his pea brain to attack. No tellin, what a bear will do."

"Okay, now on the count of three, press the left button on the arm and the button with the circle and dot in it. Make sure you press the right ones," Luke cautioned. "One . . . make sure you're picturing the fountain . . . two, three."

Pressing on the correct buttons, Pepper's hands trembled and his eyes never left the bear. Swaying awkwardly, his feet slipped and he fell to one knee on the smooth surface of the boulder. The air around the bear flickered. He vanished.

And Luke vanished with him.

Pepper's hands scraped frantically over the rocky surface, his fingernails digging into small crevasses and cracks, to slow his downward plunge. He slid faster, his feet searching for toeholds, and rocketing over the edge, he landed on his feet, driving his leg bones with a teeth-jarring jolt into his hip sockets. Tumbling backward, he fell on his rear and with a small whoosh flopped on his back, his breath exploding from his chest. His thoughts scrambled, and a descending dark veil hovered, ballooning inside his head. The swelling cloud swept him up in a wave of circling darkness and, he heard Benny screaming from far away. Something about Luke.

Benny yelled, a deep croaking sound of fear and horror, the anguished undulating pattern of his cry echoing over the lake. Rebounding off the sheltering cliffs, it split into fragments and faded in a soft echo against the mountains.

Eerily, everything stilled and a soft blanket of silence covered the camp. A deep twilight silence that sometimes is heard in the wilderness, where everything stills and time seems to become frozen. Nothing moves! A silence so profound that it crushes your senses, so you feel that you are alone, perhaps the last person on earth. And if you strain hard enough you'll swear you can feel and hear the earth move.

He stood frozen, his boots riveted to the top of the boulder. The echo of dead silence burst inside his brain, paralyzing him. The sound of water slopping against the lake shore faded, and sucking in his breath, he held it. His muscles didn't respond to the message his brain was sending, and he stood stiff, useless and blank for several seconds.

Everything righted gently, the cloudy edges along the perimeters of what he could see in the distance bubbled, and sharpening into a knifelike focus, lost their fuzziness. The noises around the camp, at first a soft distant murmur, increased in volume and the sound of a tree limb snapping made him jump and he yelled. Kneeling, he scrabbled for holds on the rock. Shivering violently against its rough surface, he searched for places to put his shaking feet, and slid downward, digging his fingernails into crevices to stop himself from falling too rapidly. Instantly running when his feet touched the ground, he ran to Pepper and shook him. Pepper's head rolled against the ground.

Benny ran to the camp fire and grabbing the water pot sprinted for the creek. Slipping, he fell to his knees, dropping the pot. It rolled, its tumbling action a clattering noise over his harsh breathing, and stopped its rolling action, against a large rock. He eyed it as if it was an enemy.

THE DEVILS PUNCHBOWL

Panic in huge dark patches blossomed in his mind, and spreading rapidly, caused the muscles of his body to cramp and shake. He panted and starting to hyperventilate, broke out in a cold sweat.

Climbing to his feet, he ran after the water pot and grabbing it in a tight grip, jogged to the creek. Plunging the pot in the frothy water, he pivoted and one foot slipped between two wet rocks. He fell, dropping the pot, and, it emptied, floating for a second before the current swept it away from him. It came to rest in a small eddy near the shore.

He cursed and jumping to his feet, ran, slipping and sliding over mossy rocks on the creek's bottom. Grabbing the pot, he filled it to its brim and scrambled ashore. Instantly running, water sloshed over the rim, wetting his front and he stumbled awkwardly, his breathing erratic and labored. Sucking in a deep gulp of air, he exhaled, his breath evaporating in a cloudy vapor near his face. Hesitating for a second, he hovered over Pepper's prone body, and not realizing that he was conscious, jerked the bottom of the pot upward, pouring ice cold water in a drenching deluge over his head and face.

Pepper sat up with a deafening bellow.

"What in hell," he roared.

Pepper swiped at the water running over his face. "What in hell did you do that for?" he roared in frustration.

"I'm sorry!"

"Sorry. . . . "

Benny dropped the water pot. "You don't understand," he gasped, dropping to his knees. Wringing his hands, his expression mirrored his desperation. "Luke disappeared. He vanished with the bear." Benny blinked rapidly his eyes filling with tears.

Pepper stared at Benny.

"He couldn't have," he sputtered. "You're pulling a joke! You're, shitten me!"

Jumping to his feet, Pepper ran through the camp. Scraping the mass of wet hair from around his face, he stared wildly at Benny.

"What in hell happened?" he yelled.

"I think when you slipped on the rock, you brought your tool forward just enough to hit Luke," Benny stuttered. Rising to his feet, he stumbled after Pepper, following in his wake as he rushed again in a circle around the camp. "He's gone! He disappeared with the bear."

"Jesus, Mary, Joseph, what have I done?" Pepper said, sinking to a rock next to the campfire. Staring fixedly at the flames, his eyes filled with tears. Agitation worked the muscles of his face. "Jesus, Benny, what did I do?" he repeated.

"Well, nothing," Benny answered. His voice, deepening with suppressed emotion, trembled, and his eyes filled with tears. "You fell off the rock. Whatever happened to Luke is just as much our fault. You can't blame yourself. We should have done something else to scare the bear away. It was a mistake to use the tool." Swiping his jacketed arm across his eyes, his throat muscles tightened causing a painful spasm and he gulped noisily. "A big mistake!"

Benny shook and clasping his hands together, tried to suppress the movement. "We don't know enough about the tools and how they work. After all they belong to aliens." He shivered uncontrollably, and tried to enunciate his words through trembling lips. "As far as we know, Luke could be on another planet. No tellin where he went."

Staring at the campfire, they both trembled. Benny fell to his knees by Pepper. "Knowing Luke like I do, he'll be back," he said. His voice roughened, emptying of emotion. Gulping air, he gripped Pepper's shoulder, and shook it slightly, trying to offer something that would console him. "I'm sure he'll be back." Rising to his feet, he picked up a log and threw it on the fire.

"Were you watchin when he disappeared?" Pepper asked. He stared at Benny, misery twisting the muscles in his face. Grief, darkened his eyes to the color of a purple anemone, and burying his face in his hands, he hunched over his knees resting his elbows on them.

"Yeah, I was watching, because I was standing a little behind him. The bear vanished and then Luke. One minute he was here and the next he was gone. He just seemed to . . . "

"Wink out!"

CHAPTER 12

SOMETHING SQUEEZED LUKE, compressing him into a cocoon that felt and clung like plastic wrap. He couldn't move. A pulsing vibration of heat rippled over him causing his body to dip and sway as if he was riding a wave on his wind-board. Dropping into a trough with a sickening lurch, he rode a crest to a new peak. He dropped again, this time it felt like a mile before he evened out just riding a wave. A pressure formed within his inner ear, increasing, until he thought his eardrums would burst. The muscles of his body rebelled, bunching under his clothes and his dinner surged upward into his throat.

I can't vomit, he thought.

Don't vomit!

The pressure in his ears became an agony. He tried focusing his eyes, but he couldn't get his eyelids to work, they felt as if they were glued shut. His feet hit something solid and he sat with a jawbreaking jolt on a narrow ledge, biting his lip and part of his tongue. The pain in his mouth became so intense, his eyes watered and his head started to ache. Swinging his arms around an object he sensed was in front of him, he grasped it in a death grip. A fine spray of water misted his face and opening his eyes he closed them again, scrunching his face into a wrinkled mask. Everything was grey, filled with murk.

Water misted his face again and turning his head, he opened his eyes into slits. Surrounding him, an obscure grey wall pressed against an out of focus, blurred misty sky. He could see his left foot immersed several inches in water and just above his head, on the very top of the ornamental pillar he was hugging, a small cherub angel poured water from an urn into a pool. Several feet past his foot the clarity of the water became a flat color, coalescing with the air around it. Beyond that there was nothing, just moving, obscure shadows, and where the sky should have been a gray veil of darkness hovered.

The veil pulsed, and in dark surf-like waves, split, and Luke, looking up, could see a night sky shimmering with a sparkle of stars. His surroundings brightened, the clarity of each object standing out in outlined relief. He swung his head straining to hear the musical melody of falling water in the fountain. The silence was complete, profound, covering him in a thick blanket of isolation. He was inside a bubble, a hollow empty space, where even sound didn't penetrate.

Dropping his arms, he straightened suddenly against the cherub-topped pillar. The murk surrounding him shifted, and across the pool, three men dressed in formal-wear stood staring intently at him. Apprehension grew inside his brain and a numbing paralysis crept over his body freezing his muscles.

Everything stopped.

Something primitive and elemental burrowed its way into his brain. Fragmenting into something he didn't understand, his senses and thoughts changed as he watched the fleeting expressions on the men's faces. He froze stunned by the clarity of his thinking.

Danger!

Defensively, as the concept swept over him physically and mentally, he switched his mind away from the absurd thought. Something he had never felt before flared into existence and he tried to grasp the elusive sense. A vague exhilaration invaded his body changing everything that was familiar. Analyzing the sensation as it prickled his skin, the feeling became acute and so intense, his mind went blank.

He blinked!

Fear and horror mixed with confusion made the men hesitate. The suppressed terror they were feeling was clearly reflected in the mirrored glassiness of their eyes. They continued to stare at him, until suddenly the terror faded and something else surfaced in their glassy-enlarged pupils. Something primal, dark and disturbed.

THE DEVILS PUNCHBOWL

Luke read it in their eyes the minute their brains kicked in, with the thought . . .

GET HIM!

It was all there for Luke to perceive with a comprehension he didn't understand. Their purpose was a malevolent spark he could feel. He was the prey and barely suppressed, a dark baleful invidious gleam appeared in the dilated pupils of the men's eyes. A spasm of hesitation crossed their faces and, they watched him with a cold and ominous stare. Two couples from an adjacent garden area, also wearing evening dresses and tux, ran toward the watching men.

Luke, fascinated by movement with no sound, watched intently. It was like he was somewhere else looking through a window into another place. Somehow disconnected, but he knew the men could see him. Their expressions told him that.

Time slowed creeping by in immeasurable seconds. He swallowed, his tongue moving convulsively within his mouth. Touching his bitten lip with his tongue, he tried soothing the sore spot.

Crazily, everything surrounding him moved. Tilting, his immediate environment wobbled and shiny illusionary cracks appeared in the air. A brighter light within the cracks shimmered and peeling like an orange, the layers pulsed, almost as if they were alive.

Focusing again on the men watching him, he became aware of the women's heels clicking a steady clacking beat of sound against the cement sidewalk. The fountain gushed and water in a million drops of pattering, fell back into the pool. Blending with the noisy sounds of city traffic, it became a deluge of noise, deafening, the moment suspended as the torrential din poured over him.

The center of the fountain burst into another pattern of sparkling water, as a strident bellow of a frightened animal erupted. Whipping through the air in waves of urgency, the cry drowned out the gentle whispering ripple of cascading water. Becoming a roar, the cries rose, undulating in awesome ferocity. A rising chorus of screaming voices mingled with the roaring of the animal.

Stopping, the approaching couples changed direction and running like deer they climbed a gradual terraced incline. The women with their evening gowns clutched up around their knees, stumbled, their heels on their shoes sinking into the lawn. One fell to her knees and scrambling to her feet, she left a bright red shoe embedded in the grass.

Luke stood as the men turned to look toward the sound. Panic marked the horrified expressions on their faces. One of them pointed and yelled . . .

"Governor."

He started to run and stopping abruptly, looked over his shoulder at Luke. Indecision appeared in his eyes and then a medley of emotions played across his face. White lines appeared around his mouth as he fought his indecision. Confusion was followed by a scowl, and then a dark, blank expression flashed across his face. The blank look stayed as his face emptied, becoming void of feeling and expression.

Spinning in a circle, the bear stopped his loping run and ran in the opposite direction. Pandemonium broke in a tidal wave of screaming voices as the crowd became aware of the wild animal. They ran, in a frenzied stampede of frightened people, pushing and kicking, to get away.

Roaring a balling-plaintiff cry, the bear smacked a small cherub angel perched on the low wall of a small fountain. Falling from the edge of the decorated cement, the angel split into fragments, and its head rolling along the sidewalk, stopped with a distinct wobble at the edge of the lawn.

The horrendous, shrieking grew in volume, men and women's voices blending in a blanc mange tremor of terror. Luke trembled at the extreme pitch of uninhibited screaming, the noise breaking around him in waves he could feel. He ducked and pulled his ball cap a little tighter on his head, his down-jacketed, Levi-clad body conspicuous and, out-of-place, amongst the formal-clad crowd of men and women. Scampering, he hunched low and skipping to the right of the fountain ran up a small grassy incline. Hiding behind a massive oak tree, he watched a mass of people running toward him and listened intently for the bear. If I can get close enough, I'll have to send him back, he thought. What a huge mistake this was.

THE DEVILS PUNCHBOWL

No joke!

He grimaced, his eye's dark and grim. Closing them for a second, he pushed the thought away and erasing it from his mind, his resolve deepened, he didn't have time for negative thoughts. Fighting down an instinctive reaction to run with the crowd, Luke tried to subdue his desperate feelings of flight. An overwhelming surge of panic, swept through his body, and he glanced wildly at the hysterical people running past him. Something cool raced through his brain. He became calm.

The same three men in tuxes moved slowly through the running crowd. They watched Luke, their eyes tracking him with a malignant focused stare.

Dodging a zigzag pattern around hysterical people running away from the bear, Luke's legs propelled him forward in a desperate mad dash. His mind became fixed on the intensity of emotion radiating from the people closest to him, and a feeling, of wanting to react to it clawed its way through his guts.

A large woman propelled herself forward and in a sudden burst of speed joined a group of desperately running people along a bricked garden path. The gown she wore, a gray-sequined, sophisticated mist of tissue lace, was ripped at her waist, and hanging in shreds, it flapped and billowed behind her. Gray satin slippers hugged her feet and pale gray nylon stockings had been scraped from both her knees and blood ran twisting, erratic patterns of red down her legs, puddling in dark stains on her shoes. Her feet slapped the sidewalk in perfect precision and naked fear ran a gauntlet of emotion across her face. She ran frantically, her eyes opened wide and with each labored breath, she sucked her lips inward tightening the muscles of her face. Between breaths her mouth hung open and her double chins and jowls bounced and danced to the rhythm of her gait.

Watching her, the bizarre picture of a guppy crossed Luke's mind. Shaking his head to rid himself of the grotesque thought, he pulled his eyes away and focused his thoughts on the bear. Waiting for a break in the running mass of people, he glanced for a millisecond over their moving heads trying to keep the bear in sight.

The large woman glancing over her shoulder at the charging bear, squealed, a high-pitched guttural sound. She swerved drunkenly and, suddenly raising one arm, shoved on the back of the man next to her. He tumbled, falling heavily to his knees. The woman grunted, and finding a small opening in the crowd, turned in a tight right angle, plowing straight into Luke. Knocking him over backward, she fell on him in an expulsion of fishy breath, her sweat peppering his face in a sprinkle of small drops. People fell around them like dried leaves in a strong wind and piled in groups of three or four, they lay gasping to breathe, their air choked off by a deluge of overwhelming panic.

The woman grabbed at Luke. She clutched him and at the same time she used her knees, legs and feet to push him away. Luke glimpsed terror in the woman's eyes, a dilated hollow blankness. He moaned and raising his hands pushed her until she lay on her side next to him. Turning on his stomach, he dragged himself forward several feet along the paved walk, until he felt it might be possible to rise to his hands and knees. "My God, all I can see is legs and feet," he whispered frantically from his prone position. He rolled, trying to protect himself from being stepped on, and pulling himself to his knees, tried to rise.

A man appeared beside Luke, and raising his arm, his eyes expectantly skimmed the crowd, searching for someone. His mouth opened to yell, just as a hand in the middle of his back, shoved him violently forward, and his yell, prematurely stopped in an expulsion of breath, came out as a bleat. He fell over Luke and cursed. The screaming rose a decibel higher, as people continued to push on individuals around them. They crawled in their haste to rise and finding an open spot hysterically climbed to their feet. They continued to run and it didn't seem to matter in what direction they ran, just to keep moving was enough.

The woman in the torn gray-sequined dress was on her hands and knees crying for help. Glancing at her, Luke leaped to his feet. Touching her shoulder, he whispered, "sorry, so sorry," and starting to move, pushed himself through the crowd.

Standing in the middle of the second pool, the bear watched the stream of running people. Swinging his head in a wide arc as they appeared in his peripheral vision, he ran forward several times, chal-

THE DEVILS PUNCHBOWL

lenging them if they got too close. The white froth of flowing water cascaded over him, wetting his fur. His breath whistled through his nose and low menacing growls emanated from deep in his throat. He moved in a circle churning the water looking for an escape route. He acted confused. Agitated. Abruptly, rearing up on his back legs, he raised his head, and sniffing the air, the confused expression in his eyes changed to a wild rapacious gleam.

Think of somewhere, Luke thought desperately. You don't have much time and he looks like he just smelled food. I got it. I'll send him back to the trailhead that goes to Buck Lake.

"I hope this works," he whispered anxiously. His mind churned, ideas flashing like neon bulbs inside his head. Has to work, he thought, there's no alternative.

Picturing the sign lettered Buck Lake in his mind, Luke dodged running people and ran straight at the bear. Jumping over the decorated, carved wall of the fountain, his booted feet slipped over the pool's bottom as a geyser of white water, in millions of sun-drenched rainbows, danced over his head. Moving warily, Luke's eyes became fixed, his mind intent and focused. He stopped about five-feet from the bear, aimed the tool and pressed buttons.

The bear vanished.

Sucking in a deep breath of relief, Luke turned his head and met the eyes of one of the men wearing a tux. A spasm of fear ran the length of his body. What he saw reflected in the man's eyes wasn't good. Leaping forward, he ran to the opposite side of the pool, and jumping over its edge, crossed the sidewalk, entering an immense formal garden.

Don't look back, don't look back, he kept telling himself. Waste's time, remember what Dad says, waste's time.

He looked back.

Women sat where they had fallen, their escorts on their knees trying to comfort them. They whimpered, their face's white, strained and terrified. A fat man supported by his elbows on the step above him, sat with his back against the bricked steps to a terrace, and cursing intermittently, he watched the scattering crowds of running people.

Luke raced upward through the hotel's ascending terraces and gardens. Jumping three steps, he ran swiftly over a bricked split level terrace, his booted feet slipping in the residue left by people as they dropped small plates of hors d'oeuvre and drink glasses. He pushed and shoved his way through the tumbled snarl of chairs and tables, their striped umbrellas a tangled ricochet of blurred color in his vision.

A bartender behind a portable bar stood with a glass in his hand, frozen in place. His mouth hung open, his face expressing shock at what he was observing. Two very huge men stood on the bar's top watching the crowd. Huge containers of wild orchids circled the lanai-shaped bar and terrace, their musky scent hung heavy and sweet in the warm air. The absurd thought, they have an odor, so they're probably imported from Hawaii, went wildly through Luke's mind.

He surged ahead, breathless, running in the opposite direction then the screaming mass of people. The slap of footsteps and the sound of labored breathing was close behind him. Someone shouted . . . "There he is."

Dodging between trees, Luke glanced back at his pursuers. They stood out in the dusky twilight, their dress shirts appearing as streaks of pale-white movement between ornamental bushes and trees. They pursued him with a vengeance calling out their positions to each other. The two women hampered by the crowd, ran toward him, their evening gowns a bright smear in his vision. They were fast, probably runners, he thought. A bullet, with a solid chuck, immersed itself into a massive oak tree next to him. A woman and man shouted together.

"Stop!"

My God, they're shooting at me, raced through Luke's mind. An electrical current of fear and adrenaline surged through his body. His breathing accelerated into a desperate sucking infusion of air and panic pulled his legs forward in a burst of speed. Chest laboring, as he tried to breathe, he pulled himself through a quarter-acre of rose gardens. He swore as thorns tugged and tore at his clothes. Leaping over a bush, he thrust himself into a hedge and forcing a way through its clinging branches, stumbled out on a sidewalk next to a wide boulevard.

THE DEVILS PUNCHBOWL

Traffic was heavy and, the headlights on the bumper to bumper cars, glowed dully in the twilight. Glancing again toward the hotel grounds and his pursuers, indecision caused him to hesitate. Someone shouted . . .

"He's in the street."

An adrenaline rush raced through him again, a powder keg of power and fear, making his muscles bunch as spasms rolled in painful cramps through his back and legs. His heart pounded wildly in his chest and sucking in great gulps of air, he looked back at the pursuing men and women. Forcing his muscles to work, indecision left as he leaped out onto the highway. Dodging between vehicles, the people driving them blew their horns shrilly and long at his moving silhouette. It was a horrendous avalanche of honking and blaring horns coming at him from every direction. He glanced frantically behind him toward the hotel, and making it to the center divider, between the east and west running boulevards, he jumped to its top. Balancing on its narrow rim, he paused.

Gasping, he labored to breathe through his open mouth, his chest expanding painfully. A salty sweat, dripping from beneath his ball cap burnt his eyes and, he blinked rapidly to clear his vision. Sweat soaked his shirt beneath his down-jacket and he opened it a little wider, fanning his face with one of its edges. He became aware of the tool biting into his hand, and shoving it into his jacket pocket, zipped it closed. Senses raised to a fever pitch, and with new cognizance, he watched everything around him, recognizing inherently what was a danger to him. His subconscious and conscious mind sifted through the panic of his incoherent thoughts, logically processed what he could use to his advantage and dumped the rest. Picking up every nuance of his physical body, his brain registered each pain and shut down his nerve endings in that area to help him in his flight for survival.

A pickup, with two men in its cab slowed; they turned toward him, their faces masked in shadows. His pursuers shouted.

"He's on the boulevard."

Traffic slowed again and taking advantage of it, he leaped out onto the highway. Dodging by the trunks of slow-moving vehicles, he made it to the other side. Racing for the corner, he ran around it, leaving the cursing and horn blowing behind him. He ran for three blocks, passing blurred faces of people watching him as he raced by.

Turning a corner into a busier street, he came face to face with a cop car pulling up at the curb. Pivoting, he raced back around the corner as one of the cops opened the door on the moving vehicle.

"Hey, stop," the cop yelled at him.

"Stop, or I'll shoot!"

Screw it, Luke thought, panic spreading a gut-wrenching rampage through his mind. Power raced through him, obliterating everything, but the fixed intent of getting away.

He ran.

The cop pursued him.

His long legs propelled him through the streets of Sacramento, until he could run no longer, Luke slowed to a hip jarring jog. Sucking in huge gulps of air through his open mouth, his chest painfully heaved as he gasped, struggling to breathe. The muscles of his legs started to tremble and he felt sick almost to the point of vomiting.

Slowing to a fast walk, Luke eyed the people he passed with apprehension. He expected at any moment for someone to point an accusatory finger at him. Approaching an alley splitting a block in two, he paused for a second and turning into it hugged the building. The alley actually had a stop light, and directly in front of him on the opposite wall, a huge sign read, One Way Traffic Only, No Pedestrians Allowed. He ignored it and sprinted toward the light on the opposite end. He prayed as he ran that at this time of day there would be no traffic.

Emerging from the alley, he went to his left and leaning against the building tried to slow his heartbeat. This street wasn't so heavily traveled by vehicles, it showed by its open markets that it was used mostly by local people who probably lived in the area. Casually, pressing his back against the cool brick building, he lifted his foot up behind him and leaned heavily on it. He needed the rest. Watching everything around him, he eyed the intersections for cops. His breathing slowed and sucking in a deep shuddering breath, he wiped his forehead with his sleeve. His heart wouldn't stop pounding, it still beat wildly like a jack hammer in his chest.

THE DEVILS PUNCHBOWL

A storm of shouting voices suddenly burst from within the alley and he gasped, sucking in another deep breath. No luck, he thought wildly, the pursuit of him wasn't over. Trying to look casual, when his brain was on fire with the word run, he walked quietly, but stiffly away from the alley. Passing a health food store, he noticed a small space between it and the adjacent building. A sign placed high on the building's wall flashed on and off in bright red letters, Best Dry-cleaners.

Raising his arms over his head, he slipped sideways into the space between the buildings. It was a tight fit. His jacket scraped the rough brick and his Levi clad ass, rubbed the stuccoed side of the health food store. Plowing through papers a foot deep, he soon had scraped together an accumulation of debris more than two-feet deep on his left side. Twisting his neck, he looked down at the pile.

Glancing at the distance between him and, the opening at the end of the buildings, he did a quick calculation in his head. The pile on his left side would be taller than he was by the time he got to its end. Lifting his feet one at a time, he tried scraping some of it to his right side. He labored in the close narrow space trying to move the debris. Stopping, he twisted awkwardly to look at his feet. There isn't much room to maneuver, he thought, and his feet were almost as long as the space between the buildings. Working diligently in the close airless space, he scraped minute pieces of the foul stuff beyond him. Sweat, soaked his shirt and he labored to breathe. Sucking in a breath through his mouth, he gagged and leaned wearily against the warm brick.

The air trapped between the buildings smelled bad, like old pee and city slums. It's been trapped in here for years, Luke thought, gagging again at the pungent odor. No cool, freshening breezes found their way between the buildings to clean and blow away the rotten smell of human habitation and its accompanying decay.

Trembling, an all encompassing fear swamped his mind and a cloud of panic took over, swelling into a tangible mass. He moved his feet in a faster slide through the debris, accumulating another large pile of papers, and with a claustrophobic desperation in his movements, he pushed his way through it. Starting to shiver uncontrollably, he broke out in a cold sweat, and bracing himself against the building, allowed himself a moment of respite, wiping his wet face against his jacketed raised arm. Glancing up, at the narrow aperture at the back of the buildings, the gleam of light, beckoned. His vision blurred and he blinked rapidly to clear it.

"Jesus, I don't want to be caught in here," he whispered. Praying silently, he quickened his steps as full, pitch-black night descended, giving an intense gloomy atmosphere to the narrow space.

His clothing scraping against the buildings, rubbed a sandpaper grind along his nerves, and he tried sucking in his gut to make himself smaller, so he could move faster. But it didn't work, the buildings still pressed against him like tight bands.

Approaching the opening at the back of the buildings, a cascade of relief flooded through him, and he blew through his mouth an explosive expulsion of pent up air. Tucking his head down, he inched it out just enough to see a six-foot hedge separating the health food store from the dry cleaners. The area on the left, belonging to the health food store had a patch of grass and sheds lining its boundary. The dry-cleaning side was blacktopped. Trucks lined its area, their signs proclaiming them to be the best dry cleaning establishment around.

Emerging from the narrow opening inch by slow inch, he walked quickly hiding in shadows, until he found a small cutout area in the hedge. He wedged himself into it and trying to move silently worked his way deeper into its center. The snapping of breaking branches seemed loud to him and he stopped to peer out through his leafy hideaway. Watching and listening, he quietly continued to bend branches, until he had made, up away from the ground, a simulation of a small seat for himself.

Forcing himself into the tight area, he sat carefully on the hedges resilient branches. Sighing heavily, he inhaled a huge breath, and blew it out, slowly. Thank God, this hedge has no thorns, he thought. Zipping up his jacket, he settled further into the shrub, forcing the branches down. Moving some of them, he laced them together until he had made a small platform, and resting his arm on it, pressed his sweaty face into the crook of his elbow. He tried to relax. The down of his jacket sleeve felt good, but it wasn't a pillow.

THE DEVILS PUNCHBOWL

Resting, his body shuddered, and his leg muscles cramping painfully, tightened into knots the size of golf balls. The sound of his erratically beating heart in his ears eventually drowned out the noisy banging of the cleaning plant.

He slept.

City noises woke him often and he shivered because he was cold. Thank God for Gore-Tex, my boots kept my feet dry, he thought. He found himself listening carefully for any sign of alarm in the noises made by the sleeping city. The night was dark and seemed, endless. Ends of twigs and branches poked him constantly and he restlessly broke off the more painful ones. Moving his body around on his uncomfortable seat, he stretched, trying to work the kinks out of his aching muscles and dozed again.

Luke woke, startled by a burring sound somewhere near him. An engine sputtered, coughed then died into silence. Three different sirens wailed; their sounds muted by distance, were lonely and plaintive cries. For a moment he didn't remember where he was, until everything that had happened to him intruded on his consciousness. A miserable reverie, he thought, and lifting his hand wiped away the drooling saliva from his cheek. So miserable, I wish I could blot it out.

Grimacing in disgust, he wiped his hand on his pants and listened as someone tried again to start one of the dry-cleaning trucks. The starter didn't have a chance. The guy was ruining it. He didn't let up, just kept pumping the gas pedal and grinding away. Resisting the temptation to walk over and help him, he sat quietly in his leafy bower, watching and listening.

With a wrenching squawk, the truck door opened and then slammed shut. The crackle of steps on the blacktop told Luke the guy was leaving. Finally. The backdoor to the dry-cleaning plant opened with a squeal, and closed with a bang, the abrasive sound echoing, along the quiet street.

Bent awkwardly, Luke tried to stand in the small hollowed out space. Sharp ends of branches stabbed him painfully, and resembling a crippled old man, he moved, pulling himself from his cramped position in the hedge. Stretching his body, he muffled a groan as a new set of aches settled in his muscles. Walking in deep shadows created by the line of parked vehicles, he removed his cap and used it to brush himself off. Slapping his cap one last time against his legs, he gave up, realizing it wasn't helping. The dirt and grime seemed to be stuck permanently to his Levis and jacket. Glancing up and down the dark street, he started to walk and, almost jogging, left the area.

CHAPTER 13

AIMLESSLY, SEEKING THE deepest shadows, Luke wandered wraithlike through the empty streets of Sacramento. His stomach grumbled and glancing at his watch, he whispered, four o'clock."

Pausing in the mouth of an alley, he watched for movement in its cluttered darkness. Seeing none, he ventured into its dark depths, his eyes searching the shadows. Shuffling his feet, he stepped quietly through inky blackness, and twice, stumbled over something he couldn't see. Kicking an empty can, it rattled and clattered, rolling over the pavement. The noise made his heart stop and he flinched, shrinking against the backside of a Dumpster. Blending into its shadow, he glanced back at the wedge of light that was the alley's entrance. Cautiously, raising his hands he fumbled blindly, stepping between garbage cans and Dumpsters, until he stood against the wall of a building.

Listening to the hiss and clatter of his pee hitting the wall, Luke aimed its stream in another direction. The sound intensified, a hollow drumbeat of moving liquid as it hit the side of a garbage can. He started to laugh and before the sound could emerge from his mouth, he choked it off in the back of his throat.

Something goosed him in the ass, and stumbling forward two steps, he hit the side of a Dumpster. Emitting a startled gasp, he jumped and continued to move until his back was pressed against the building. His heart beating an erratic clamor within his chest, he started to tremble as fear rising in a gushing tumult, swamped his senses. Peering into the dark space in front of him, he tried to see what had pushed him.

A dark shape moved in the narrow space, materializing as a darker shadow. It snuffled where he had peed and banged against the Dumpster. Luke backed away from the wall and moving swiftly, but carefully around the garbage cans, looked back into the gloomy shadow at the shape. It wiggled and jerked in a squirming contortion of movement. Raising its head, it snuffled again, a soft pleading noise.

It's a damn dog, Luke thought, staring at the shape.

A dog.

The dog ran forward and sat next to Luke. Snuffling softly in its throat, it raised its head and looked up at him. Except for its eyes that glowed a shiny reflective red in the light from the street, the dog wasn't visible in the pitch-black gloom in the alley.

Hearing the engine of an approaching truck, Luke stiffened and, holding his breath buttoned his Levis. The sound of the truck escalated into a pattern of sharp complaints as the driver downshifted. Standing perfectly still, he listened intently as vague street noises filtered into the narrow space between the two buildings.

Approaching the alley's end and its wedge of pale light, he pressed himself against the side of the building becoming part of its deepest shadow. Poking his head around its corner, he watched a driver stack crates on the sidewalk across the street. Stacking them neatly, near a green double door, set into an alcove in the front of the building, the driver cursed in a low monotone. He cursed his words in a ritual, the liturgy of sound in perfect harmony with the rhythm he used in stacking the crates. He never stopped. The sign above his head in bright red and blue letters read, Porkeys, The Best Place to Pig Out.

The driver finished and the motor of the tailgate whined in protest as it closed. Swinging the door of the truck open, he glanced warily at the empty street and swiftly climbed in. The engine of the truck wailed as the driver accelerated, leaving behind a puff of air that smelled of gasoline.

Luke watched the street, the rising sun coloring the building tops in a blush of red gold. The dog sitting as close to him as possible poked its nose on his leg. "Go away, Dog, you can't follow me. Go away. . . . "

THE DEVILS PUNCHBOWL

"Go away," Luke whispered again, flapping his arms. Leaving the alley, he crossed the street the dog tagging his heels. Stopping near the stacked crates, he whispered again. "Go home, Dog." Seeing movement near a building in the next block, he watched a man approach the lighted intersection.

Pivoting on the sidewalk, the man pressed his hand to his face. Luke could barely make out his facial features, but he could see he was smiling to himself as he stood on the corner. Abruptly, throwing his arms up and away from his body, he started to sing. The words of the song, poignant in their meaning about a life sorely lived, rushed along the street.

Luke moved quickly into deep shadows next to the restaurant, and the dog followed. Sitting close, her head touched his leg, her haunches and backbone standing out in bony relief.

The man finished his song, his voice tapering off, until it was a faint murmur. He bowed to the opposite three corners of the intersection, and suddenly jumping off the curb, he started to dance, his feet a white blur of movement in a bright, new looking, pair of tenny shoes. Kicking and twirling, to an imaginary tune, he moved diagonally across the street, his body motions, graceful and yet clumsy. Leaping, he crossed the curb with a flourish and bowed again to the three opposite corners. Laughing aloud, he clapped his hands in obvious delight and walked toward Luke. Watching his hand slide over the worn bricks of the building, he hummed and sang softly, completely engrossed in himself and the words of his song.

He was small, a very thin white man. One side of his threadbare Levi jacket, hung halfway down his left arm, the collar hugging his elbow. Like attachments on a puppet, his wrists and hands protruded from too short sleeves, and hanging loosely, appeared as appendages strung together with string. A thick rope was tied around his waist, the ends swinging a wild pendulum arc around his knees as he walked. The legs on his black baggy pants were too short, ending well above his ankles and, black socks sagged in bunched circles over the tops of his white tenny shoes. Spying Luke, the man hesitated and stopped. His voice became a whisper of sound, barely heard.

Warily, the man watched Luke.

Luke glanced at him from the corner of his eye, apprehension growing in his empty belly. The man suddenly broke out in a huge grin. Wrinkles worked into his face showed in defined relief the pathos and direction his life had taken. An inch-wide livid scar, following a deep crevice along his jaw, pulled one corner of his mouth downward.

Watching him, Luke stepped away from the building, stopping near the stacked crates. They contained vegetables and fruits, the tomato's red and juicy looking, glistened in the early morning light. Stomach rumbling at the thought of food, his eyes ran over fresh cabbage, broccoli, carrots and bananas.

"Man, I's can see's what you're been thinkin," the man said, in a soft singsong manner, deeply punctuated by a southern patois. Laughing, a deep humorous sound, he slapped his thigh. "If we's only had an icebox, we sures could eat real good. He laughed again, the sound ringing out happy and full-toned along the empty street. His voice, deep and lyrical, surprised Luke, coming from such a small man.

Luke laughed. "Yeah, I guess a guy could, if we only had a place to keep it."

"Fine dog you got there, a female, huh," the man said. He held his hand out, his palm up to the dog. The dog backed away from his hand, hiding behind Luke. A slow whine erupted from her throat.

"She's not mine," Luke said. "I don't know who she belongs to. Just a stray, I guess."

"Awful thin," the man answered. "Like me, needs a home, but she's free and that's the best part, no worries, cept of course where to eat and with a spread like this, I sures do eat good." Slapping his thigh again, he laughed, a boisterous, bawdy sound.

"So long," Luke said. Stepping around him, he continued down the street, the dog at his heels. Glancing over his shoulder, Luke watched him hover over the crates of vegetables and fruit.

"Oh what the hell," he whispered, "they won't miss a few and he looks like he needs something good to eat. And so do I," he added, glancing at his watch. "It's almost five o'clock. I've got to find a restaurant that's open. I'm starving. How about you Dog, are you hungry?"

THE DEVILS PUNCHBOWL

Laughter bubbled in his throat and he stopped walking abruptly. Guiltily, he cast furtive looks along the shadowed street. I can't believe I actually asked a dog if she was hungry, he thought.

Watching for any sign of law enforcement, he walked continually until he felt, he had covered miles of pavement. Trotting diligently beside him, the dog never deviated, her nose stayed as close as possible to the proximity of Luke's left leg. He was two blocks away from the Capitol building before he found a restaurant that was open. The sidewalk along the building was wet and it glistened with a dewy freshness in the early morning light. Potted flowers of a bright red hue, gave the place a happy look, giving it character and presence. Postage size, it wasn't very large and had just opened for the day.

The open doorway, about ten-feet wide seemed to welcome the passerby. Lining the high ceiling, heavy oak beams every four-feet, added to the room's spacious feeling, and deeply carved wainscoting, stood out in marked relief along oak-covered walls. Round tables circled with oak stools marched in perfect order down the center of the room.

A miniature oak counter was built along the wall, with oak stools lined up before it in a soldierly manner. It was a place where you could sit or stand to eat and drink. The floor, laid in a cris-crossed pattern of wide oak planks was oiled to a bright-sheen and meticulously clean. The rich aroma of fresh coffee spiced the air and a huge sign stated gourmet coffee in every blend possible, even one that said plain.

In what Luke thought must be the kitchen, two men, stood behind a glass enclosure laughing heartily. They glanced up as he walked through the door, their smiling faces a mirror of happy humor and when he paused to tell the dog to sit in the doorway they watched him.

The men, one white and one black laughed again, their faces expressing merry animation. The glass diminished the sound and the resonance of their voices was just a mellow echo in the room.

Luke stepped to the counter and studied the menu printed on the wall above shelves that contained a large collection of coffee beans. The gallon jars of beans labeled in bright red letters were displayed to catch the eye. And they did, he thought, because they caught his and he wasn't much interested in coffee beans.

Glancing at Luke who had moved to stand at the register, the black man raised his hands and shouted. . . .

"I can't believe it!"

Leaving the kitchen through a swinging door, he kept laughing. "Can I help you?" he asked through his laughter. His voice, deep and melodious resonated from deep within his chest.

Luke smiled and placed his order; four croissants with jack cheese, eggs and ham, a carton of milk and a large coffee, to go. Luke gave the man a twenty-dollar bill and he counted out his change. He then spoke into a small mike at the register, ordering Luke's choices for breakfast.

Luke stepped back and nervously sat on the edge of a stool. Pulling the brim of his ball cap lower on his face, and bending forward, he placed his hands over his knees. Staring at his left wrist, he watched the second hand of his watch. Glancing up twice he checked on the dog. She didn't move much, her eyes darting from Luke to the man behind the counter were apprehensive and she watched Luke with wistful eyes, her ears raised to expectant points on her head.

The black man walked to a window and put his order into a bag that was labeled, Capitol Grounds, We Grind Only the Best Coffee for Gourmands. Glancing into the bag, he went to the swinging door and pushing it open slightly, spoke softly. Shrugging, he shook his head. He shrugged again and walked away. Picking up the bag, he smiled and moved to the register area. Luke rose and met him at the counter. He handed him the paper bag. The white man busy with something behind the glass enclosure raised his head and stared at Luke.

Hunching his shoulders, Luke pulled his head down into the rolled collar of his jacket. Turning sideways, so he didn't face the men directly, he mumbled, "please may I have a cup of water for my dog? You can charge me for it if you like."

The man glanced in surprise at Dog and then complied with Luke's request. He filled a large cup with water and quietly placed a lid on its top. Snapping it down snugly, he returned to the counter and handed it to him.

"Thanks," Luke said. Tugging his hat further down on his forehead, he turned and walked away.

THE DEVILS PUNCHBOWL

The white man stepped to the swinging door and pushed it open slightly. "Nah., couldn't be," the black man said, as Luke followed the line of tables down the middle of the room. "Hundreds of kids walk the streets, some are homeless and, they all resemble, seen one and you've seenem all, because they all dress alike. Stinking, dirty and unbathed." He laughed heartily, the sound following Luke as he stepped over the threshold into the street.

Luke jogged, hugging the stuccoed walls of sky-high buildings. With Dog running beside him, he turned the corner at a intersection and ran. Holding the bag containing his breakfast and, the cup of water tight against his chest, he set a steady pace toward the southeast, away from the business complex and government buildings.

Approaching, what he hoped was more of a housing and apartment area, Luke found on the corner of the intersection, a glass enclosed bus stop. With the dog sitting between his legs, he sat on the bench against one end of the enclosure and opened the bag. Opening the boxes, he unwrapped two of the croissants and tearing them apart, placed them on a wrapping paper on the ground. Pouring water into one of the croissant boxes, he set it down next to the paper. The dog sniffed the croissants and then the water. Lifting her head, she stared at Luke.

"Go ahead, girl, eat. They're yours," Luke said. Bending, he patted the paper. "Eat. Drink." The dog eyed the sandwiches. She lowered her head and, trembling, delicately mouthed a piece of croissant and ham. Smiling, Luke opened his own, wolfing down his two croissants with his milk. Rising, he stood for a second watching the street. Stepping over the dog, he strolled to an overflowing trash container and, threw the bag and milk carton on top.

Inhaling a deep soothing breath, he opened the tab on the cover of his coffee and drank thirstily. It wasn't very hot anymore, but he hoped it would revive him. Sitting again on the bench, he watched the intersections, patting Dog's head every few seconds.

There weren't many people on the street, only a few night stragglers despondently dragging their feet and, ho-humming their way along the sidewalk. They looked in every garbage container they passed, digging through it as if they expected to find a lost treasure

Across the street, a black man and woman exited an apartment building, and for a few seconds, they stood talking near the entrance. The man wore a three-piece suit and the woman in a dark dress with a huge white collar looked neat. Kissing her goodby, he walked west to the corner where he turned around, and smiling broadly, raised his arm. Gesturing in a grand manner, he kissed his palm and blew on it.

The woman waved and pressing her fingers to her mouth blew on them. Smiling, she watched him, waiting until he disappeared around the corner. Crossing the street, she entered the bus stop and sat on the end of the bench. She ignored Luke and the dog.

Luke kept glancing at her and Dog downright stared. He hoped she wasn't afraid of staring dogs, because Dog's stare wasn't friendly.

The woman acted like they were invisible. She held a rolled newspaper and, snapping the elastic band, dropped it on the sidewalk. Reading the headlines, she opened the paper to another page and read silently most of the time. Occasionally, she whispered the words, as if she couldn't quite believe what she was reading.

The woman laughed suddenly, the sound ironic, flowered into hearty mirth. Pressing her hand gently against her mouth, she glanced at her watch. Folding the paper twice she laid it on the bench. "What will they think of next?" she muttered to herself. "Give me a break!"

A bus approached the intersection, its brakes squealing as the driver braked to stop. Rising, the woman picked up her paper and stepping to the heaped, garbage-filled container threw it on top. Strolling to the edge of the curb, she impatiently tapped a very high-heeled shoe against the sidewalk. The door opened with a whooshing explosion of air and the woman stepped up into the bus.

Luke watched the bus accelerate, leaving behind in its wake a nauseous, reeking cloud of diesel fuel. Pushing himself up from the bench, he walked to the garbage container and picked up the lady's discarded newspaper. Holding it against his chest, he turned and watched the street. Nobody seemed to be interested in him and what he was doing. Settling himself inside the glass enclosure, he smiled as Dog laid

THE DEVILS PUNCHBOWL

down. Laying her head gently on his boot, she eyed him from the corner of her eye as if to say is this all right. Sighing, he turned the pages of the newspaper back to the front page. Huge letters leaped out at him.

GOVERNOR'S $1,000. A PLATE FUND RAISER, INTERRUPTED BY APPEARING AND THEN DISAPPEARING BEAR AND MAN. Last night, at approximately seven o'clock, a massive bear, suddenly appeared fifty feet from where the Governor and First Lady stood in the midst of a crowd of two thousand or more.

Quoted by some as mono size, and weighing nearly one thousand pounds, the bear roared a challenge to the people attending the black tie affair, charging some. He ended his mad dash to get away by throwing himself into a fountain. A few of the participating patrons of the Governor's fund raiser, said:

"The bear was standing upright in the center of one of the fountains, when a young man wearing a ball cap, charged straight at him through the water. He aimed what looked like a cross at the bear, and the bear magically vanished. The young man kept on running."

He was pursued by the Governor's bodyguards, but disappeared into the night after he crossed Sutter Boulevard. The Governor's edict of no news coverage and cameras at the affair acted against the authorities, because no pictures were taken. Witnesses, describing the young man varied:

He was or wasn't wearing a ball cap, pulled over light or dark hair, fair featured, bearded, very dirty looking, wearing tennis shoes or boots, Levis and everyone thought, a dark jacket. Anyone seeing a similar dressed individual, should notify their nearest police station. The city and state police would like to question him, as to what he had to do with the appearance of and disappearance of the bear. Do not try to apprehend him, as he might be a dangerous individual.

Furtively, Luke glanced up and down the street. Folding the paper, he shoved it to the inside of his jacket and without looking worked the zipper closed. Pushing himself up from the bench, he stood for a second and forcing himself to feel a moment of calmness, quietly walked away. Dog stayed close, trotting next to his left leg, her nose nearly touching it.

Somehow, Luke thought, I've got to get back to camp without being apprehended. Strolling as much as possible in dark shadowed areas, he followed tree-lined streets for many blocks.

Entering a small child's neighborhood park, he twisted through and around the playground equipment. Spotting a circular slide, he climbed its enclosed steps with Dog at his heels, and laughed, at her ability to climb the ladder. She did it awkwardly and didn't let Luke get very far ahead of her. Worming his large body into the small enclosed area at its top, he patted the dog's head and made room for her. He relaxed. Surely no one, would notice him up here, he thought and it would give him a little time to think.

Closing his eyes, he thought of Benny and Pepper. They would be frantic by now. This was Tuesday morning and, glancing at his watch, nearly six o'clock. Rob was supposed to be home. Thinking of him, Luke grabbed at the idea that snapped and ran unchecked inside his mind. He would appear, or he thought, almost laughing aloud . . . teleport into Rob's bedroom. To keep from laughing, he pressed his hand against his mouth, and tilting his head, looked through the plexiglass enclosure at the small park. If Rob was home, it would be the surprise of his lifetime. He silently laughed again.

A Sacramento City police car crept by the play area, its engine barely heard. A red door, on a large Victorian home opposite the park, opened suddenly, and a small oriental woman wearing a bright blue apron, ran lightly down a long set of stairs. Stopping at the curb, she gestured at the policemen.

Luke watched the police car as he thought of Rob. He should be home and just about ready to leave for his two-days at the Devils Punchbowl. The thought, something's wrong, broke like a hot streak across his mind. I've got to get the hell out of here.

The police pulled to the curb and backing up a short distance, they talked through the window with the woman. She gestured toward the playground.

THE DEVILS PUNCHBOWL

Digging the tool out of his pocket Luke's fingers shook as he held it. It's going to take all the guts I've got to point this thing at myself, and press the buttons, he thought. Wow, I wish I had the wisdom Dad has right now. I wonder if he would say. . . .

Go for it.

Fire away.

"Well, what should I do with you, Dog. I hate to leave you here," Luke whispered. Frowning, he moved his hand gently over the dog's head. "I guess I'll take you with me. Where I'm going, you'll have a better life than here. I know my Mom will love you a lot. Here go my conjuring skills again."

Putting his arms around the dog, he pressed her to his chest and pictured Rob's bedroom in his mind. I hope his Mom hasn't moved the furniture around since the last time I was there. Holding the tool against his jacket, he put his fingers on the correct buttons and closed his eyes. Concentrating, he thought of the rug beside Rob's bed and picturing it like a camera within his mind, pressed buttons. . . .

He winked out!

This time the transition was faster and the vicelike, continuous compression of his body more evenly distributed. His perception of falling was swift, and for several seconds, he couldn't breathe. He rode a huge wave and then dropped like a stone into a trough. The urge to open his eyes was intense, and he tried lifting his eyelids, but they wouldn't move. They lay like immovable pieces of lead against his face, and his inner ear swelled, until he was sure it was going to pop through his nose.

Whop! Luke hit the floor beside Rob's bed. He landed on the rag rug, curled in a fetal ball with the dog clutched to his chest.

Rob yelled a guttural grunt from deep inside his throat. He jumped on Luke, one of his powerful hands squeezed his neck and the other pounded him several times on the body. Luke tried to shout, the sound garbled, and he gagged, his voice and breath choked off by Rob's hand. Shoving Dog to the floor, he desperately pulled on Rob's fingers. Dog laying next to him growled weakly, pushing her nose against Luke.

Rob's recognition of him came late and driven by reflex and desperation his fist connected with his chest, several more times. Releasing his throat, Rob's facial muscles worked into a grotesque mask and a sick pallor gradually whitened his face. He stared at him. With his knee pressed in his stomach, Rob patted Luke's cheek with a shaking hand. "God, I'm sorry," he said, the deep bass of his voice hoarse with emotion.

"Rob, are you all right?" Mrs. Polasky called, from the living room. "What was that noise? It sounded like something crashed against the house."

Luke gagged again sucking in a huge gulp of air. Hastily, he put his finger to his lips to silence Rob. Pushing him away, he scrambled to his knees and picking up the dog, painfully walked several feet on them into the open closet.

"Just a minute Mom, I haven't got my pants on," Rob called. Undoing his belt, he walked to the door, and opening it, watched Luke, with his finger to his lips shake his head at him. "I didn't hear anything, Mom," he yelled down the length of the hall. "My backpack fell off the bed, maybe that's what you heard." Lifting it from the floor, he laughed. "I don't know if I'll be able to walk up the switchbacks with this much weight. Those frozen steaks you gave me, must weigh two pounds each."

"I know, but the boys will really enjoy them," Mrs. Polasky said, stepping to the threshold to the living room. "You did tell me they were probably tired of fish by now. The steaks are frozen and I doubled the Ziploc bags, so if they start to defrost they won't leak inside your backpack. You're a little white son, are you sure you're up to hiking that six-mile climb into the Punchbowl?" Sniffing slightly, she smiled at Rob and turned away.

"I'll make it fine, Mom, and I'm sure the guys will love the steaks," Rob called to her retreating back. "I'll just repack this. There has to be a way I can balance the load, so it'll be easier to carry." Closing his bedroom door, he walked over to his bed and sat heavily, the mattress sinking several inches, protested with a loud snapping noise.

"What in hell is going on, Luke?" he demanded, his voice pitched low and strained in its harshness. "You just appeared out of the air in my bedroom, almost like in a magic show! If I hadn't seen you do it and hit you in a few places, kinda hard I admit, but you startled me. . . . Which I already said I was sorry for. This sounds like I'm going nuts, or maybe this is a nightmare," he whispered, staring hard at Luke. "I must be bonkers and I'm hallucinating."

He curved his body over his knees and closing his eyes tight, worked his massive hands over his face and head. Opening his eyes into mere slits, he watched Luke through the split fingers of one hand.

"Nope, you're still there," he whispered.

Luke climbed to his feet inside the closet. Holding his ribs, he groaned. Sucking in his breath, he tried breathing gently. It still hurt. "Hell Rob, you hurt me," he complained, pressing his hands against his sides.

Rob snorted. The sound sharp and loud in the room.

The dog whined an answer.

"I could have killed you. Think about that!" His golden, brown eyes rounded again at the thought, darkening with suppressed fear.

"Yeah," Luke answered. "I'm sorry, I choose to teleport into your bedroom. I should have waited for you at the trail head to Buck Lake. But, you were the closest answer to a problem I was having in Sacramento and I couldn't think of what else to do. So, without thinking it through enough, I acted, instead of thinking. . . . "

"I guess," he added thoughtfully, "that's something I've been doing a lot of lately." Blinking rapidly, he stared at Rob and lifting his cap pushed his hand through his hair.

Rob's face lengthened in disbelief, and twisting his mouth into a crooked hard line, his chin dropped in skepticism. "Teleport, what in hell are you talking about and what in hell were you doing in Sacramento? I thought you guys were at the Punchbowl? I was just shoving my stuff into my backpack to head-up there."

Hearing, Mrs. Polasky's footsteps in the hall, Luke pressed himself further into the closet. Rob stood, smoothing out the blankets and quilt on his bed. His Mother knocked softly. "Baby, it's almost seven," she said. "If you want to have time with your friends, you better get going."

"Okay Mom," Rob answered, through the door. Silent, they listened intently to the soft swish of her slippers sliding over the carpet as she left.

"Listen," Luke whispered. "I've got a problem with the dog. I couldn't leave her in Sacramento. She's starving to death. Do me a favor and drop her at Dr. Petes. Tell him to give her the necessary shots, feed her well and I'll pick her up on Thursday evening."

He pushed the door of the closet open a little wider and stepped into the room. "I'll meet you at the trailhead to Buck Lake and I'll explain everything then. Just wait for me there. Don't leave the sign area."

Luke chuckled. "Undoubtedly Pepper and Benny think I'm dead or that I've been transported onto some God-awful alien planet. They're probably in a dead panic, by now." Pulling the tool out of his pocket, he smiled jubilantly.

"You won't believe what we found in the cavern," he said. "And you won't need to climb the switchbacks, so bring along more of that steak your Mom was talking about. All we've had is fish and casseroles lately." Patting the dog's head, he picked her up and placed her in Rob's arms. "And be extra careful around the sign to Buck Lake, there might be a starving bear hanging around there." Grinning, Luke thought of his bedroll between the huge granite boulders and pressed buttons. . . .

He winked out.

Rob his arms filled with Dog stood with his feet riveted to the floor staring at the space where Luke had been. He shook his head to break the intense mesmerized feeling. Forcing himself to walk across the room, he waved a large hand through the air where he had been standing. Sinking to one knee, he laid the dog down and moved his hand over the carpet. Luke had vanished.

Rising to his feet, his eyes darkened, stark and blank. Opening the window, he picked up Dog and stepping over the sill ran to his truck. Opening the truck's door, he laid her gently on the seat, and running back to the house, climbed silently over the sill. Grabbing his gear by

THE DEVILS PUNCHBOWL

the strap, he raised it to his shoulder and with an anxious, hasty look around his room, threw the bedroom door open. "Bye, Mom," he yelled, rushing from his room. "See you Thursday evening."

Closing the front door with a bang, he ran for his truck.

CHAPTER 14

LUKE APPEARED IN the middle of his sleeping bag. Sprawling flat on his stomach, he turned over to look for Pepper and Benny.

They were in their sleeping bags and Pepper's eyes were open. He stared sleepily at Luke, watching him for a second, and grabbing the edge of his sleeping bag, pushed it away from his face. Sitting up he started to yell, and hesitating with his mouth hanging open, stared bleakly at him. Twisting his body, he flung himself forward, grabbed a handful of his jacket and raising his fist, punched him on the shoulder. Wiggling, his legs hampered by his sleeping bag, Pepper wrestled him over on Benny.

Luke yelled . . .

"Stop!"

He pushed on Pepper and blocking his blows with his arms and legs, he yelled again as Pepper swung at him.

"Hey, stop!"

"Stop!"

"Hey, quit," Benny yelled. "Quit, I don't want to get up yet," he muttered. Turning over, he pulled on his sleeping bag and met the bulky weight of Luke's body. Shoving on him, he pushed him away and sat up with a sharp curse. "Luke, my God, Luke," he yelled. Emerging from his sleeping bag in a wild tangle of arms and legs, he enthusiastically whooped, pounding his back.

"Hey, quit guys," Luke shouted. Twisting his arms over his head, he tried to protect it from their fierce slaps. "I know you're glad to see

THE DEVILS PUNCHBOWL

me, quit," he repeated. Laughing suddenly, he crawled away from Pepper and Benny. "I've been punched enough today and besides, you stink. Do you ever?"

"PH . . . EW. What a stink, I can tell by your smell you didn't wash last night."

"Where in hell have you been, Pepper and I nearly went nuts here? We thought we'd have to tell your folks you disappeared," Benny said. His voice trailing into silence, he stared at Luke, and laughing abruptly, flopped backward on his sleeping bag.

"You're full of shit, Luke," Pepper yelled. Jumping to his feet, he kicked at the restraining folds of his sleeping bag. Kicking it into a ball, he raised his foot and gave it a heave over on Benny.

Benny jumped to his feet and angrily kicked Pepper's sleeping bag. Raising it with his foot, he kicked it over onto Luke's bag. Shouting a few choice curses, their voices rose. Relief mixed with happiness warred with tension and distress made their eyes bleak. The turmoil of what they were feeling flowered into extreme aggravation, and stepping to the edge of their bags, their stance showed their annoyance and displeasure. Shivering in the cold air, they stood in their underclothes and stared in self-righteous indignation at Luke.

"What you did is inexcusable," Pepper said. Angrily, he hugged himself as goose bumps broke out on his legs and arms. "Right now, I'd like to beat the shit out of you and kick your ass up between your shoulder blades. You know what you're always telling me about using my brain. Well I don't think you used yours. What happened to you and where in hell, did you go? And why didn't you come right back?" He sputtered, his voice breaking up. "You came back now, so you could have a lot earlier than this. Damn, my grief was so great, I was about to jump off the nearest cliff. I thought, I'd killed you," His voice broke. "I didn't know how I was gonna face your folks."

"Okay. Okay, I'm sorry. I admit I should have tried to come back earlier. I had a feeling you'd be worried and in a panic. But I was in trouble too," Luke explained. "A lot of trouble!"

Squatting, Luke piled logs on the fire and gazed thoughtfully for a moment at the flames. Rising, he smiled. "Now, here's what I propose.

Let's go wash. I have an urge to sluice my body off in ice cold running water. I stink! Then let's fix something to eat, really quick. I had something earlier, but I'm empty now. I have to meet Rob down by the trailhead that goes into Buck Lake." Glancing at his watch, he grimaced. "C'mon, we'll have to be fast. I'll tell you what happened to me while we fix breakfast and eat."

"How in hell can you meet Rob at the trailhead?" Pepper asked belligerently. He stiffened, his voice rising again showed his anger and his eyes snapped blue fire at Luke.

"I'm going to use this," Luke answered, pulling the alien's tool out of his pocket. He smiled and glanced down at the tool. "This is the most magical instrument you could ever imagine." Looking up at them, his eyes glazed over with his thoughts. "C'mon, let's get with it, we don't have much time."

Tearing into their backpacks for clean clothes, they laid them on their sleeping bags and, ran for the creek. Scrubbing their bodies clean in the icy water, they ran for the shore, shivering in the cold air. Racing back to the fire, their wet muscular bodies gleamed in the morning light. Shouting and teasing each other in an excess of young male exuberance, they quickly dressed.

Pepper dashed to the lake with his fishing pole and came back in ten minutes with six dressed trout. Making an envelope out of foil, he placed the fish, a tablespoon of oil, one of water, a sprinkling of salt and pepper and sealed the edges tight. Carefully sliding things around on the grill, he set the package of fish over red-hot coals.

Dicing three potatoes in a frying pan, Benny placed it on the grill. Waiting for breakfast to cook, he sat wearily next to Pepper with his back against a rock and tried to rest. They listened avidly to Luke's words, their eyes tracking him as he made biscuits and shoved the pan in the oven. He poured them each a cup of tea and their mouths dropped open when he said he'd been shot at.

"You're, shittin us. You're kidding!" Benny yelled, sitting straight up.

Luke continued to talk, his hands busy checking their meal, telling them what happened to the bear and the frightening experience of being chased by cops. Benny and Pepper were skeptical, until he showed them the newspaper he had thrown on his sleeping bag.

"Believe me, they shot at me," Luke said in affirmation. "I was scared, but I think they were more scared of me. They saw me appear and were so frightened by it, they didn't want to get near me. They watched me though." He shivered. "They watched me like wild predators do their prey." He stared for a second into the fire, remembering. "You know it was uncanny what I was feeling, but I knew what they intended before they did it. It wasn't so much that I could read their minds, but, I subconsciously knew what they intended. It bothers me that I kinda knew what they were going to do, it was like all my senses were working at maximum peak. I felt charged with something I've never felt before." Dishing up their food, Luke handed them each a plateful, and they sat silent, too busy chewing to talk, completely engrossed with their meal.

Mentally and physically exhausted, Luke sighed, and glancing at Pepper's and Benny's, tired faces, knew they were too. It showed. A wave of fatigue swept over him at the thought of having to explain it all again to Rob. Glancing at his watch, he popped the last piece of his biscuit into his mouth. "I've got to go," he muttered, between his mouth's chewing action. Licking the grease from his fingers, he grinned, and patted his jacket pockets. "I've got to have one of your tools for Rob to use."

"You're not going without me," Pepper stated forcefully. "No way!"

"I'd like to go to," Benny stated emphatically, staring at Luke.

"Okay, I'll stay here. I'm tired of talking anyway, here's the tool," Luke said, handing it to Pepper.

"What's it like?" Benny asked. "Do you go through some kind of black void or maybe a tunnel? Or do you remember?"

"When you first press the buttons, its sorta like your body is compressed inside a bubble or vacuum. It's almost a pressure you can't stand, but it's also kinda instant, so you're not feeling that way for a long length of time. A different kind of pressure builds inside my head and it affects my ears. Feels like my ear drums are going to burst, but then, you land and, as you appear the feeling goes away."

"Okay," Luke added enthusiastically. "Which one of you will go first. Make up your minds, because Rob's waiting. Probably impatiently." Silently, he watched their faces and laughing abruptly at their expressions, walked to the fire. Picking up the tea pot, he poured himself another cup.

"It's easy, guys."

Pepper and Benny stared at their tools. Indecision marked their faces and they sat with their mouths open. Pepper lifted his head as Luke moved toward them, studying him intently as he lowered himself to the ground.

Luke sat with an expulsion of breath and leaning forward placed his cup of tea on a flat rock. Crossing his legs, he glanced over at the lake. Peaceful here, he thought.

Laying a tool on Luke's knee, Pepper picked up his own and placed it next to it. "You go. We'll wait here, but you have to promise not to stay too long."

"Sure," Luke answered. "As soon as I show Rob how to use the tool, I'll be back." Picking up his cup, he sipped the hot beverage. "Too hot," he muttered, setting the cup back on the rock. "This is a fabulous way to travel. Beats walkin." Pressing buttons on the tool, he laughed a nervous high treble and, thought of the flat surface next to the Buck Lake trail sign. An airy whisper of sound, echoing faintly, lingered where he had been sitting.

Benny gasped, the emotions he was trying to control passing in quick succession across his face. Horror predominated, but one of incredulous wonder was the last one that appeared, and it stayed, working the muscles of his face. He cleared his throat. "This is the weirdest, Pepper," he said. His eyes skimmed the area around their camp, and his voice softened, his expression turning thoughtfully inward. "I hate to sound like some kind of wimpy wuss, but I'm glad I didn't go. It looks so far out, I can't really believe it. This is weird."

"You know, Benny, anything Luke can do, we certainly can," Pepper said. "You know how he always puts on this superior, arrogant attitude. Remember, when we were little, he could talk us into most

THE DEVILS PUNCHBOWL

anything he wanted. He's a talking fool, but he's not getting away with this one."

"What do you mean?" Benny asked. Moving slightly, he twisted his head and, stared at Pepper. "He gave us a choice, we could have gone. I don't think he really wanted to go."

"Yeah, but I think he really did. He gave us the impression that it was kinda frightening, so we'd automatically choose not to go."

Benny sat staring at his empty cup in his lap and for a second, he thought of what Pepper had said about Luke and his arrogance. He was arrogant, but Pepper was too, in fact all of them were about the same in that department. They excelled, so consequently, he always felt a certain amount of arrogance came with the territory. As long as you didn't get to feeling you were the very absolute best, a certain amount of arrogance was good. It certainly made him feel good. Smiling, he raised his head and looked at Pepper. "I agree, we can do anything Luke can, that's a given," he said. "But I think we're just as arrogant as he is, he just shows it more. You go first. I'll wait until you get back."

"Okay," Pepper said, readily agreeing. "I'll come right back so you can try it. I think the flattest area around there is in the middle of the trail. There's a lot of brush and trees next to it, so I'll think about the trail. I'll picture that and on the count of three, I'll press the buttons. I feel like a wuss. What if . . . I appear in some foreign place, maybe even another world?"

Vacillating, Benny and Pepper watched each other. They laughed, the sound low, gravelly and sporadic with nervous tension. Pepper's hands moved, his agitation showing as he clenched his fists. Picking up the tool, he pressed it against his chest and counting together . . . "One, two, three." They giggled.

Pepper winked out!

A nervous wail trailing his disappearance, diminished softly in the space he had occupied. Benny stared at the spot mesmerized by the sound.

Landing in the path directly in front of the sign to Buck Lake, dust and dirt erupted around Pepper, covering him in a coat of fine dust. Fright had changed the color of his complexion to a sickly-white, and muffling a deep groan, he curled into a ball on the ground. Pushing his legs straight, he stared in empty-eyed confusion at Rob and sitting up, looked around for Luke.

Luke grinned at him. "Not too bad," he said. "How'd you like the sensation of moving through a void? At first I feel a flash, like heat is traveling over my body and then it wraps me tight. It's the wildest ride I've ever had."

Pepper leaped to his feet his eyes expressing a wild haunted look. Shivering, he shook himself. "It's awesome, there's no words to describe it," he whispered, more to himself then to Rob and Luke. With shaking hands, he brushed the clinging leaves and dirt from his pants, and launching himself at Rob, slapped him heavily on his back. "It's a good thing you're here, you won't believe what we found in the cave," he said in a rush. He knelt next to him, his voice a harsh whisper and arching forward pressed his hands against his knees. "Most of it is unbelievable. I even found a frigin alien! Sometimes, I think I'm having a nightmare it's so bad."

Pepper twisted his body to look down the trail. Anxiously, he looked at Luke. "I've got to go right back. I promised Benny. I'll see you guys up top. Don't be long. God, I'm glad you're here, Rob," he repeated, patting him again on the back. Pressing on buttons, he grinned roguishly.

"I agree," Luke replied, handing Rob a tool. "I'm glad you're here too." Stepping forward to the main trail that led back to the parking area, he stood listening intently. "We've got to get out of here, we're really taking a chance that someone will see us." Anxiously, he glanced sideways from the corner of his eye at Rob. "The tool's simple to use."

"Yeah," Rob said. He thought for a moment and then looked down at the tool. "I'm cool. Makes me nervous though."

Benny landed hard not far from Rob on the side of the trail. He lay for a second, grinning squeamishly at Rob. Sucking in a deep breath, he gasped, and climbing to his feet, brushed dead leaves from his clothes. Dragging in another deep shuddering gulp of air, he stated. "It's been freaky here without you."

THE DEVILS PUNCHBOWL

"If you get to feelin sorta like a wuss, don't feel bad," Benny said hastily. "The rest of us feel that way most of the time. Believe me your inner anxiety will get worse when you see what's inside the caves. Sometimes your nerves will crawl like your being stuck with hot needles." He laughed, a dry sound with no humor. "C'mon, let's go back to camp."

"Yeah, let's go," Luke interrupted. "Just remember to picture where you're going to land. Try to picture it like a camera even to some small details. You shouldn't have any trouble. The only problem is you haven't been up to the Bowl yet. Remember where those campers tried to bury their garbage last year, well, that area is still the same, it's nice and flat with no big rocks."

Benny fell to his knees by the tree. "If I can do it, you can Rob. There's nothing to it. "It took all the guts I've got to use this tool. "I'll stay here and we'll press these buttons together."

"I'm out of here," Luke said, lowering himself to the ground. "This kind of travel could get to be a habit, especially to the Devils Punchbowl. It eliminates all the work. I'll take your backpack with me," he added, and picking it up by its strap lifted it to his shoulder. "Wait until you try the tool, I think you'll like it. Gives me a rush." Raising his eyebrows several times, he laughed. "Beats feet anytime." Resting his arms on his knees, he raised his eyebrows again and laughed boisterously.

Benny and Rob stared at the spot where Luke had been sitting. His laughter trailed him, streaking into silence, and where he had been sitting, crushed grass, blade by blade curled back into an upright position.

"It's really easy, Rob," Benny said, without much conviction. "And I imagine it'll get easier as we learn to use these tools. I think they must do a lot of what we'll consider miracle type things. C'mon, put your fingers here and here. See, it's the left button on the arm of the T and the other one is on the bar. It's the one with a circle and a dot. On the count of three, we'll press the buttons together. Make sure you're thinking of that flat area up at the Punchbowl," he cautioned.

"One, two, three," Rob said, his lips moving silently.

Benny waited a second, and then pressed buttons. Appearing on his sleeping bag, he laughed exuberantly and jumping up, walked to the fire. "I can't believe I did that," he exclaimed, waving the tool in the air. "When I first pressed on these buttons, my guts twisted into knots and I expected to land on some foreign soil facing an alien or something from another planet. It sends me sorta into a spin. I actually feel lightheaded." Laughing again, he turned to look for Rob. "Where's Rob?" he asked.

"He didn't appear," Pepper answered. Scanning the camp, he raised his head and looked at Benny with a worried, questioning stare.

"I watched him use the tool, he disappeared," Benny said. Anxiety tightened his mouth into a straight line. "He must have landed around here somewhere."

"Let's give him a few minutes," Luke said.

Rob landed in a heap beside his bed, the thump causing a vibrating rumble to echo in his room. His Mom's vacuum continued for several seconds and then went silent. The house settled into a blanket of quiet stillness, and he imagined her standing, with her fingers pressed against her mouth. Her head would be cocked to one side, and she would be listening intently for any unusual noises.

Rob slid, pulling himself under the bed, and holding his breath, hoped it wasn't moving. The overhang of his quilt swayed next to his face, and he watched it for a second, before grabbing the edge of it.

Mrs. Polasky's feet in her bedroom slippers, whispered over the carpet. She walked the length of the hall and cautiously turning the doorknob, pushed on the bedroom door. Her head appeared in the opening and then her body. She examined Rob's room. Walking to the open window, she looked through it at the carport. Closing it slowly, she locked it with a faint, scraping click. Pivoting on her heels, she stared with quick darting glances into each corner, and opening the closet door, moved the clothes along the bar.

"I don't know what's happening here, but I don't like it," she whispered. "Loud banging and thumping. . . . "

"Humph. . . . "

THE DEVILS PUNCHBOWL

Rob, from his hiding place under the bed, watched his Mother's feet and part of her legs walk to the door. She turned and examined the room again. Slowly, closing it, her eyes surveyed the room, watching it keenly for any sign of movement. Snapping it closed, she waited a second and then snapped it open again.

"Humph . . . !"

"No explaining it, must be outside," she said, closing the door a tedious slow inch by slow inch. Leaving it slightly open, she suspiciously watched the room through the crack. Glancing nervously into the shadowed open doors of adjacent bedrooms, she turned and walked away.

Rob waited, and holding his breath, slid cautiously and silently from under his bed. Listening acutely, to the humming sound of his mother's vacuum cleaner, he sat on the floor, and pictured the flat area at the Punch Bowl, but the lake kept interfering. Sighing in frustration and disgust at himself, he pressed firmly on the buttons.

Landing on his butt, he fell backward with a huge splash in the lake. Bellowing like an angry bull, he pulled himself to shore, and leaping to his feet, sprayed a cascade of water drops around him. Water ran over the rugged planes of his face, past his neck and in dark spreading stains soaked his shirt. Anger colored his skin, changing it to a bright red hue.

Luke, Pepper and Benny laughed. Continuing to laugh, they watched as he jerked his clothes off.

"Shut up," he yelled, his anger forcing it to a hoarse low bass. His eyes, thickly lashed and widely set below a broad intelligent brow, flashed a golden brown fire.

They teased Rob often, calling him, No Neck, because he was massive, the muscles in his neck corded and so pronounced they seemed to be part of his shoulders. He easily flares into anger Luke thought, watching him, and when he's mad, he portrays it with a passion. Oozing male magnetism and charm, his charisma was devastating, and his smile so captivating, girls at school simply fell over themselves to be near him. He suppressed a smile, thinking of the envy that he and Pepper tried to hide, over how many girls were attracted to Rob. Benny had always had Lily, so he wasn't envious at all.

Jerking a dry shirt from his backpack, Rob's shoulders started to shake. Glancing at them for an instance, his eyes danced with suppressed humor and he grinned. "I kept thinking of that area over there," Rob said, flinging his arm out and pointing at the flat area near a huge cedar tree, "but the damn lake kept interfering. I tried picturing the area under the tree and then, the blue of the lake would creep in. So, at the last minute, a flash of my bedroom went through my mind. That's where I went. I landed on the floor in my room and my Mom came running to investigate. I hid under the bed and I barely fit," he added ruefully.

They laughed.

Pepper snorting every once in a while, lay back against the side of a huge white rock, and rubbing his face wearily, wiped away all trace of his laughter. "Okay guys," he said looking at his watch. "It's nine-fifty and we have only about two days left to explore. There's a lot for Rob to catch up on. How are we going to do it?"

"I think we'll save time if we use the tools to transport ourselves," Luke suggested. "It takes us two hours from here to go along the cliffs and climb through the fissures into the big cavern. If you and Benny transport first, then one of you can come back with a tool so Rob can use it.

"Benny nodded his head in agreement. "Rob, do you think you can picture the big cavern enough to teleport yourself into it?" he asked.

"Yeah, I think so. I should, because for the last nine months, that's all I've thought about. At times I thought I'd go nuts thinking about the tunnel and cavern," Rob said absently, pulling dry socks on his feet. Opening a side pocket in his backpack, he removed his boots, and pulled them on, lacing them tightly to his feet.

"How was the dog when you left her, Rob?" Luke asked.

"She was all right. She shook a lot though and Dr. Pete was concerned, because she was so thin." Rob glanced at Luke. "He said with a good diet and, a lot of care, she should be a healthy animal in no time at all."

Pepper looked up. "What dog?"

"I forgot to tell you. When I was in Sacramento, I found this dog, actually I should say she found me. She was hungry and dying of thirst,

THE DEVILS PUNCHBOWL

so I brought her home with me. I'm glad Dr. Pete thinks she has a good chance to live a healthy life. Let's get going," Luke suggested abruptly changing the subject. Climbing to his feet, he looked at the pile of dirty dishes. "Let's finish fast, so we can get to the cavern."

Luke headed for the creek to wash dishes, and Benny and Pepper packed lunches. Rob rummaged through his backpack, taking out items to put in their food storage bags.

"Rob, did you bring something we could put in our lunches?" Benny asked.

"I brought a package of cheddar cheese, salami and a box of Ritz crackers," Rob said. He held each item up for them to look at.

"Yum, the salami and crackers will taste good," Pepper said, leaping forward to take the packages from him. "What else is in there?" he asked, bending over Rob's shoulder to look into his backpack. "Do I smell chocolate?"

"No peaking," Rob said. Grabbing his backpack he held it close to his body. "I brought some surprises. Here's each of us an apple and orange."

Pepper stepped away, laughing. "I hope the surprises are really good ones, like, maybe some of your Mom's chocolate cake. I'm starved for something really good to eat."

"Come on Pep, let's get these sacks packed. Luke's finished with the dishes," Benny called. Wrapping cheese wedges in with slices of salami they put an apple and orange into each haversack, and closing the tops handed one to Luke. Picking theirs up, they stood by the fire and waited for Rob.

"What kind of juice did you put in our canteens?" Luke asked.

"Strawberry Kool-Aid and it really smelled good," Pepper said, watching Rob tie the anchoring rope for their food sacks to the tree. "How are we going to do this? Who's going to be first to go into the mountain?"

Luke stood near the fire with his haversack over his shoulder. "Why don't you go first, Pepper?" he suggested. "Then Benny. I'll stay here with Rob and come in last. Remember, one of you has to come back with a tool for Rob."

Pepper looked skeptical. "Are we going to meet where the tunnel opens into the big cavern?"

"Yeah, it's the only place that Rob's familiar with. Make sure you wait for us there," Luke answered.

Rob watched Benny and Pepper, his eyes focused and intent. He raised his hand and gripping his chin, a solemn expression settled in his eyes. Pepper and Benny dropped to their knees. Sitting on the ground facing each other, they grinned and pressed buttons.

"I can't accept this, Luke," Rob said "My rational mind keeps telling me it isn't possible, even though I've pressed these buttons and actually was transported somewhere twice by a small tool. Teleportation! Unbelievable! And it's instantaneous. One second you're here and the next you're gone. I can't believe it." .

Luke, with his legs drawn up to his chest, sat waiting for Benny or Pepper to reappear. Leaning forward, he propped his arms on his knees and smiled. "It's not so bad for me now and it gets easier every time I do it. You should have seen my hand shake when I pressed the buttons to teleport myself into your bedroom."

Benny appeared on his sleeping bag, and for a second, he was an illusionary shadow. A standing, indistinctive shape, and he crumbled in a heap on the bag, as if boneless. "Has to be an easier way?" he mumbled. Handing Pepper's tool to Rob, Benny eyed his somber expression, and hugging his knees, took his alien's tool out of his pocket. "You've already done it twice, Rob, it's fantastic." Grinning broadly, his expression turned triumphant, and pressing buttons, he vanished.

"C'mon, Rob," Luke said. "Let's go."

Rob tried to fix a picture of the immense cavern and the tunnel where they had slid down into it inside his mind. Holding the tool in his hand, he raised his eyes and looked at Luke. "Okay," he said. Watching where he placed his fingers on the tool, he glanced up at Luke again. Whatever he was thinking, in myriad variations flashed over his face and, each thought, changed his expression. He frowned, grinned suddenly, pressed buttons and . . .

Winked out!

CHAPTER 15

ROB APPEARED AGAIN almost instantly beside Luke. "What in hell happened?" he asked. "It didn't work."

Luke frowned. "What were you thinking? You had to be thinking about something else." He rubbed his face with both hands and shook his head. "Try again, but tell me first what image you pictured in your mind."

Rob sat thinking thoughtfully, his brow wrinkling. "I was picturing the tunnel and the cavern in my mind. I had a clear picture of them."

Luke glanced at Rob, studying him. Holding up one hand, palm out, he waved it several times. "Wait! Wait a minute, let me think on this." Picking up the tool, he sat staring at it, contemplating what had happened. Frowning slightly, he glanced again at Rob. "It has to be that your primary image was the tunnel. It couldn't move you there, because it might have harmed you. Sitting as you are now, you wouldn't fit. That has to be it," he added triumphantly. "The tool will only transport you where you can't be harmed. It has built in safeguards. It won't put you somewhere that could be dangerous to your life or squash you into a smaller space." Fleeting thoughts raced through his mind. Studying the tool his face sobered, and listening to an inner voice, he thought of what he had said. He lost his frown and grinned broadly at Rob.

"Try again! This time, think only about the cavern and picture yourself standing against the wall, near the tunnel's entrance, but don't picture the tunnel."

"Okay, let's go."

Luke appeared in the cavern a few moments later than Rob. Grunting as he landed, he involuntarily pushed his legs straight out, striking Rob with his booted feet behind the knees. Hitting the ground on all fours, Rob slid several feet, his joints locked in awkward positions. He groaned, the sound, a low grumble erupted from deep in his chest, and pushing himself up to a sitting position, he turned and glared at Luke.

Watching Luke and Rob, Benny and Pepper laughed, the sound choked and muted. Turning their backs, they walked away their bodies shaking.

Staring hard at Pepper and Benny, Luke's chin jutted forward and a gleam of anger leaped into his eyes. "Right now, assholes, your humor isn't appreciated," he shouted. "You're acting like a couple of jerks." He rose to his feet and held his hand out to Rob. Helping him to stand, he walked away and brushed himself off.

"Your lights on, Luke," Benny pointed out, laughter bubbling out between words. Wiping his eyes with a large bony hand, he hiccupped and started to laugh again.

"I know it's on," Luke said, glaring at him. "I turned it on deliberately. I thought I'd try to see as I was being pulled through space. But no go," he added, releasing a deep pent-up breath. "It squeezed me tight and my eyes closed, so the light didn't help me at all." Exasperation changed the expression on his face, and frustrated, he turned to Rob. "How do you want to do this?" he asked. "All of us go with you while you explore, or just one of us?"

"I think I should be the one to show Rob everything that's on the lower levels," Pepper said, interrupting Luke. "You and Benny, can do a little experimenting in the spaceship. If there's just two of us, it shouldn't take too long, maybe, two hours. The most interesting parts to look at, is the body of the alien and the gold. The tablet room isn't much of an interest, since we can't read the language. We'll just take a quick look in there. Are you guys going to use the tool, or walk up the trail past the frozen waterfall? Rob's going to have to walk, until he gets familiar with the different caves."

"I think I'll use the tool," Benny answered, glancing at Luke with a questioning look. "I'm going directly to the spaceship. Maybe, I can make one of those machines do something I can understand. What about it Luke, walk or teleportation?"

Luke nodded. "I'm going to use the tool," he answered. He grinned, listening to Pepper's voice instructing Rob to take off his hard hat and rub his hands through his hair.

"What the hell for?" Rob asked. "Are you blind, I don't have any hair, I'm bald?"

"Let's go," Benny suggested. Grinning at each other, they sat and listening to Pepper's determined, argumentive voice, pressed buttons.

Luke landed a little easier. He tried relaxing his muscles and didn't resist the pulling squeezing force that pressed against his body. Benny hit the floor hard, toppling like a pin in a bowling alley.

"Hey, Ben," Luke said. "I think the secret of these landings is not to resist the pull of the tool when you're being transported. Make your body sort of boneless. I just tried it and my landing was a lot easier. Lifting himself to his feet, he walked toward Benny. "I think if we learn to relax, and with a little more practice, our landings won't be such bone-crushers."

"Maybe," Benny answered. Rising to his feet, his hazel eyes held doubt mixed with humor. "I've been so apprehensive about landing that automatically I cringe and tighten all up when I press the buttons. With a thoughtful nod, he acknowledged this and he laughed, his expression lightening. "I've been so tense ever since we started to explore the cavern, it amazes me that I even function."

Luke swung around, apprehensively eyeing everything on the bridge. "Let's open this up and see what the weathers like on Preston Peak, and then, let's experiment with the machine on the end, the one with the head gear. It must do something, because it has head gear."

Breaking out in laughter at his statement, he stopped and waited for Benny. Together they approached the console. "Just think Ben, maybe we'll discover a new kind of music, so alien and out of this world, it will revolutionize the music field. Maybe even the way we listen to it. Something like that virtual reality thing they've got going right now."

"Wouldn't it be something if it even became part of you?" Benny said. Dreamily, he pressed the curve on the console. "I mean, somehow inside of you where you would be hearing it, not with just your ears, but feeling it within each cell. You'd be entirely immersed in the sound using your whole body."

They watched the huge screen emerge and the dark sliding cover beyond the windshield rushed by, disappearing into the wall of the ship. The substance within the windshield melted like hot wax, disappearing into the frame and, the sixty-foot windshield cleared. Glancing at each other, Benny and Luke grinned, awe mirrored in their eyes.

Clouds tossed about by villainous wind currents covered the sky toward Preston Peak. Their billowing vaporous bodies moving rapidly beneath a mountainous cumulus layer formed ominous, vaporous dark streaks that fell toward the peak. Luke imagined the downpour as they emptied their watery contents on the mountain.

Nervously wetting his lips he looked over the console's flat top at the abyss. "Damn, this ship is perched right on the edge of the mountain, and when I look down, I have the feeling that most of it is sitting over empty space."

"Yeah, and look at the overhang, its jutting over what I imagine is the edge of the spaceship," Benny said. "I wonder if there's trees growing on the mountain above us?" His voice trailed away to a soft whisper. "Sometimes I just can't believe I'm here, seeing all this."

Shuddering, Luke forced himself to look away from the awesome spectacle and, with Benny following him, he walked the length of the console. Pressing the curved edge, he watched the screen rise into view. Opening the door to the storage area, he picked up two of the headgear and placing one on his head, handed the other one to Benny. Sitting on the stool, he pushed his booted feet under it and leaned back to study the keyboard.

Benny pressed on the curved padding next to Luke and watched a stool emerge from the console. Dropping heavily unto the seat, he gently placed the silver band over his forehead and, bending, plugged the end of the cord into its receptacle.

"You know Ben, I don't see how we're going to do this, we don't know the keys and what their function is. I hate to press buttons when

THE DEVILS PUNCHBOWL

we don't know what they do. We'll probably get into a lot of trouble that way."

Luke raising his hand scrubbed it over his face. Yawning, he rubbed his whiskers and then his mouth, pinching his lips together. Examining the keyboard, he turned the stool slightly and stared at Benny. "Let's assume that a minus means a minus and what looks like a zero is a zero," he said and then grinned. "Hell, they could really mean the opposite. What do you think?"

"Let's press two keys simultaneously and see what happens," Benny answered. Last time nothing happened when we plugged into it. So to make the thing work we've got to press keys. Screw it, let's just press a couple of keys and find out." Tapping his teeth several times with a long finger, he twisted his head and glanced at Luke, his expression pensive and thoughtful. "But. And that's a big but, one of us can't be plugged in. One of us has to be here watching, sorta on guard, in case there's trouble and we have to pull the plug. You want to be the guinea pig or maybe I should. You got to be the pig with the tool, so I think I should go first on this one."

Luke pulled the end of his cord out of the receptacle. "You go ahead. In this case I'll be the monitor." His brow wrinkled in thought. "Just remember, if it turns weird, try to give me a signal. I'll give you three minutes. That should be enough time for you to experience whatever the machine does. Then I'll pull the plug. And I think we should write down what keys we press." He looked out of the corner of his eye at Benny. "We'll never remember what keys we've tried, or if it works or doesn't." Pulling a small crumbled notepad from his jacket pocket, he asked. "What should we press first?"

Benny glanced at the keyboard. "Let's try the minus and the swizzle or S," he said. A short, explosive giggle escaped him and he sobered suddenly. Watching Luke, he took a deep breath and blinking his eyes rapidly in nervous expectation, wiggled, pressing his body against the stool's back.

Pressing gently on the keys, Luke stared intently at the monitor. Lighting up, black and green lines flashed across the screen and, horizontally and vertically, four stars formed. Circling each other as if attracted by a magnetic polarity, they danced a peculiar, individual, whirling rotation, producing a prism. Retreating, they started to spin, and melding became a whirling disc that filled the screen. Intensely lit, it spun until it was the size of a small coin and rapidly expanding, the circle filled the screen. Pulsating in a charged, rhythmical motion, it brightened again, and the image of a pyramid appeared on the edge of a vast lush plain.

People strolled along a path, laughing and talking, but Luke couldn't hear any sound. Hell, not being plugged into the machine was a disadvantage, he thought. You can't tell what's going on. Recognizing Benny on the screen, his body grew rigid with tension.

Benny walked on a wide smooth surface, merging with a group of men that were all dressed alike in a long robe of rough weaved cloth. Even their haircuts were similar. They seemed to be having a good time. All except Benny. Wild eyed, he looked scared, and he stuck out like a sore thumb in his jacket and Levis. A man brushed by him, touching his shoulder, but he didn't seem to be aware that he had actually came in contact with him. He must be invisible to them, Luke thought, glancing at his watch. Two minutes to go.

Benny separated himself from the crowd, and following a path to his left, walked toward the pyramid. His head turned often, his eyes darting in different directions, and suddenly looking back over his shoulder, he threw up his hands. A breeze ruffled his hair and he laughed. Luke could tell it was one of triumphant exultation.

The Benny in the flesh, sitting next to him with a weird contraption on his head, was poker faced, almost as if he was asleep, or in a catatonic state with his eyes open. Luke tried to analyze what he was feeling. His face, flushed a bright crimson red, was blank, and his lips hung slack, his mouth wide open. Perspiration trickled from beneath the silver metal band on his head. He didn't seem to be in trouble.

Glancing at his watch again, Luke thought, thirty seconds, and raising his head, watched Benny on the screen stroll down a path. Suddenly, directly over the pyramid, a dark object appeared in the sky. Hovering, it sent beams of light down into the stone. The crowd of

THE DEVILS PUNCHBOWL

men ignored it, but Benny, with one of his hands raised to shade his eyes, watched intently.

An immediate, uneasiness engulfed Luke. Rising several inches on the stool, he leaned toward his left and pulled the plug to Benny's headset from its receptacle. Raising his head, he watched the screen. It went blank.

Benny's long, lanky body sagged on the stool and pulling the headgear from his head, he laid over the edge of the console. "That was mind-blowing. The noise from the crowd of men awful and what weird clothes. I want to go back. I want to find out where I was. It wasn't a place I recognize."

Nervously clearing his throat, Benny sat straight on his stool and eyed the screen. "It was wonderful. I walked this path with a crowd of men. I think it has to be the past, during the time when they built the pyramids. Probably Egypt, since that's where most of the pyramids are. The air was hot and humid and the smells were awesome. Musky with a breeze filled with odors. Spicy, I've never smelled a place like that before." Sighing, he smiled again, tentative at first, it changed into a full face-splitting grin. "They spoke, I could hear them, but it wasn't a language I recognized." Delighted, he laughed aloud. "I can't believe it."

"Okay," Luke said tentatively. "There must be thousands of possible choices. We used a minus and the swizzle. Let me try the zero and the symbol with a dash and period above it." Writing the symbols in his notebook, he laid his stub of a pencil down and plugged the end of his cord into its receptacle.

Leaning forward on his elbows, Benny watched Luke settle himself comfortably. "Now you have three minutes and if it looks like you're in trouble I'll pull the plug," he said

Turning to face the keyboard, Luke pressed the keys. Vertical and horizonal slashes of light formed a whirlpooling disc across the screen and brightening suddenly expanded into a picture of no-color. Stark, dismal and black, huge mountainous cliffs rose sharply against a desolate skyline.

Benny watched the screen. Luke appeared in its center, his arms wrapped around his torso. He looks cold, Benny thought, his clothes were puffed out around his body, as if he was stuffed with feathers. Dust devils swirled around him, obscuring everything, sometimes even him. Walking so he faced into the wind, he raised his arm, and tilting his head forward, shielded his face from flying debris. Cupping his jawline with his hand, he stared at the barren landscape from under his sheltering arm.

Benny glanced at Luke. He had begun to shiver and his teeth were chattering. Reaching across the padded area between the stools, he touched his hands. They were ice cold.

Luke walked to the rim of a cliff and cautiously stepped to its edge. Perpendicular, it was part of a larger mountain chain that circled a crater so huge, its dimensions were undeterminable. The basin, as far as he could see was littered with pitted and scarred mountain-size holes.

A large lighted object appeared near the edge of the skyline, its tail leaving in its wake a mile-long-trail of fire. Falling to the bottom of the crater, it exploded in a flash of brilliant light, and upon impact, its accompanying shock wave tumbled Luke backward, head over heals. Rolling along the ground, in a hurricane mass of flying rocks and debris, his body became obscure, until he was completely hidden in a cloud of dust.

Benny jumped up and darting around the back of Luke's stool pulled the plug from its receptacle.

Luke huddled in his seat. His body shook, his skin colored an ugly shade of milky-blue. "My God," he shuddered. "It was cold, Benny. Colder than any place, I've ever been." His teeth chattered against his lips and he closed them in a tight, thin line to control them.

"Where in hell do you think you were, Luke? You must have been on another planet. I can't imagine anyplace on earth, being that stark. On the screen it was like I imagine our world was millions of years ago."

"I even thought my eyeballs were going to freeze," Luke muttered. "My guts were so cold, if I'd stayed much longer I would have had

THE DEVILS PUNCHBOWL

hyperthermia. I never want to go back to that place. Get this Benny, our bodies are actually feeling what's happening on the screen. My ears are ringing from that explosion. You said it was hot and your face here was flushed. I could see you were sweating." Turning on the stool, he faced Benny. "If I'd spent another few minutes there, I think I would have frozen solid."

"Yeah, your teeth were chattering, so I knew you must be really cold," Benny said. "Do you feel sore, you took quite a tumble?"

"Yeah, a little," Luke replied, moving his arms and shrugging his shoulders. "I feel like I've been really tense, my muscles are stiff. Nothing serious, though. I wish we knew how this works. Then we could choose where we go, instead of doing it randomly. You notice how the monitor goes blank when we pull the plugs. Swiveling on the stool, he stared quizzically at the keyboard.

Hearing a noise, their heads swiveled apprehensively toward the sound. Jerking the headgear from their heads, they leaped to their feet as Pepper, crumbled jelly-like to the floor.

"What's wrong?" Luke yelled.

"C'mon!" Pepper yelled breathlessly, barely managing to enunciate the word. "We found another opening in the ice wall behind the alien, and, when Rob stepped close to examine it, he slipped, went down on his ass and slid through an ice tunnel."

"Is he hurt?" Benny asked.

"No! No! He says he's all right," Pepper shouted, sucking in a deep breath. "And that's not all . . . he's down there with four aliens and they're laid out like it's a mortuary.'

"C'mon!" Pepper yelled again. "Rob, thought, you guys should see the aliens. C'mon, c'mon, Rob's all alone, let's go."

Pulling the alien's tool from his pocket, Luke rushed to the opening in the ceiling, Benny and Pepper at his heels. "First, I'm going to get a set of these tools for Rob," he said. "You'd think this tool would somehow elevate you through these openings."

Benny and Pepper stood below the round opening, listening intently for the sound of Luke's landing. The sound vibrated through the hole and, grinning at each other, their hands slapped together in a high five.

Luke chose two of the tools from the cabinet, and putting them in his pocket, walked to the opening in the floor. He looked down at Benny and Pepper grinning up at him. "I'll meet you by the gold machine," he said. He glanced at the T-shaped tool in his hand and pressed buttons.

Pepper and Benny moved, putting a small space between them and using the alien's tools, followed Luke.

Shaking sand from his clothes, Luke watched Pepper and Benny's bodies appear in a millisecond of dark fusion beside the gold machine. Our landings are still too hard, he thought, there has to be an easier way. Shoving the tool in his pocket, he turned and followed Pepper.

Entering the dark cave, Benny and Luke turned on their hard hat lights, and stopping for a second, waited for their eyes to adjust to the lesser light. Carefully crossing the rough terrain near the frozen waterfall, they suddenly heard Rob's voice. His words in a rhythmic cadence, soared upward into the cave. The words of the ribald army song resounded, deep and mellow through the fissure.

"I have a girl that lives in town, she doesn't love me, cause I let her down . . . sound off . . . one . . . two . . . three. . . . FOUR! I got a girl her name is Sue. . . . "

Entering the cave behind the frozen waterfall, they could still hear the distant cadence of his words. The narrowness of the tunnel had changed the timbre of his voice and, as if disembodied it floated eerily up through the ice tunnel.

"Hey," down there," Benny yelled, interrupting him. "Ready or not here I come." Rob's song stopped, his voice suddenly chopped off. "Come on down," he sang through the tunnel. "It's only me and the scary boogers down here and we're having a hella good time."

Squatting next to the black opening, Luke propped his hand against its edge. "Is the tunnel very long?" he yelled.

"Kind of," Rob shouted, his voice a low rumbling resonance through the tunnel. "I nearly lost it during the descent. I mean, I panicked so badly I thought I'd pass out . . . so I don't really know how long it is. It curves toward the bottom though that I do remember. I was so thankful when I landed on something solid that even the dark didn't bother

THE DEVILS PUNCHBOWL

me too much." He laughed skeptically. "That is, until Pepper sent down his hard hat and I saw what I had for company."

"Watch it, Rob, I'm a comin," Benny shouted. Sitting on the edge of the narrow opening, he lay on his back and disappeared into the yawning dark depths of the ice tunnel.

Luke glanced at Pepper. "You next?" he asked. His blue eyes danced in the dim, reflected shine cast by the light on his hard hat.

Pepper hesitated.

"You should go next Pepper, or you're going to be left up here in the dark. Remember you have no hard hat."

Pepper twitched, his body trembling in a slight shiver. "Thanks for remembering, Luke." Grinning, he slid into the tunnel.

Giving Pepper time to clear the exit below, Luke carrying a bucket full of trepidation, pushed himself through the narrow opening a few seconds later. Plummeting downward through a circle of opaque ice, the light from his hard hat cast a pattern of flashing brilliance on its polished sides. Landing on his feet, he hesitated and made a quick survey of the cave. It was small, maybe forty by sixty feet and the floor, ceiling and walls were covered with a thick layer of ice. The ice was smooth and shiny as if something had carved and then polished it into a glossy, smooth surface. Along two walls, aliens lay on ice platforms carved to fit the shape of their spacesuits. The shields on their helmets were raised, their positions identical to the alien in the small cave behind the waterfall. Luke crossed the space carefully, his boots slipping on the ice floor. He stooped and ducking around Rob, focused the light from his hard hat on the alien.

"I think she must be pregnant," Rob said in a hushed tone. She's the only one with this huge mound for a belly."

The alien's face was smaller than the others, more feminine. Gently curved, her lips were full and soft looking, and like the alien in the room above, her eye sockets were out of proportion to her facial features. Eyelids lined with straight black eyelashes were closed tight against slightly rounded cheeks. The helmet covered most of her hair, but what was showing was a shiny jet black. Rob gently laid his hand on the mound that was her belly. He looked at Luke.

4998-MILL

"Sad, huh," he said.

"Yeah," Luke whispered. "Are any more of them female?"

"I can't really tell on the rest of them, they all seem to resemble each other. I only guessed on this one, because I think she's pregnant," Rob answered.

Luke stepped along the ice biers, moving his hard hat's beam of light over each individual alien. They did look similar. You couldn't tell from their features whether they were male or female.

"Hey," Luke said, joining Pepper for a closer look at an alien. "Have you noticed how different these aliens are from the one up behind the waterfall? These have a lot more hair and their eyes are different, they're still as big, but they don't have that marked epicanthic fold. They look younger too, I'd say a lot younger," he added. Moving his light over the alien's face, he bent forward and hovering over the ice bier examined him. "Maybe, we should undress one and examine it. Then we'd know how they're made physically. Can't tell much when they're completely covered with these space suits?"

Pepper jumped four times, his legs a scissoring blur as he slipped and slid across the length of the cave. Pressing his back against the wall of ice, his arms swung wildly. The muscles covering the planes and angles of his face twisted, and then pulled tight, outlining them in bold relief. His expelled breath, in agitated gasps, vaporized in cloudy puffs in front of his face. He looked like a pagan and his features mirrored his shock and horror.

"You can't do that," he shrieked. His wide, sensuous mouth fell open, forming a perfect circle. "It would be a sacrilege. You would have to be a ghoul! You're not doing that while I'm here. You wouldn't?" he demanded of Luke. "Besides they might still be alive. We don't have any proof that they're dead. They might be in some type of suspended animation for all we know and the suit protects them."

"I'll be damned. I didn't say I was going to do an autopsy. I thought we would open one of their space suits a little, just to see how they're formed. What's wrong with that?" Luke demanded. Staring at Pepper, his eyes darkened and his face turned grim with disappointment. "Ghoul," he scoffed. His expression changed to a scowl, showing his

THE DEVILS PUNCHBOWL

irritation. "Damn, how could you ever say I was ghoulish. You're the one that wants to study forensic medicine. If you thought unhooking their spacesuits and looking at their bodies a sacrilege, what will you do when you have to dissect a corpse. Jesus, Pepper you make me mad sometimes."

"What about it?" Luke asked, turning to Benny and Rob. "Should we look at one, or leave them as we found them?"

"Nah. I vote to leavum," Benny said, looking green in the phosphorus like-glow from his lamp. "I couldn't undress them. I say like Pepper, too ghoulish."

Luke's expression changed to grim frustration.

Rob looked indecisive. Picking up Pepper's hard hat, he stepped forward and handed it to him. "I fixed mine, Pep, you should put this on," he said. Gloomily, he turned and stared at the aliens. "I don't see how we could hurt them by taking a helmet off and look at their head. But let's not disturb the one that looks pregnant. Let's leave her like we found her. Has that got an okay from you guys?" he asked, turning to face Pepper and Benny.

Pepper and Benny eyed each other. Pepper finally shrugged his shoulders. "It's all right with me, I'll look, but I'm not touching it."

Benny nodded, his hazel eyes perplexed and huge in his angular face. He gulped. . . . "Me neither!"

Rob and Luke carefully searched for fasteners on the alien's helmet. "I can't find any on this side, I guess, we'll have to turn him over," Rob suggested. "Maybe the hinges are attached on the back of his space suit."

Pepper trembled, his face a mask of alarm.

Benny stepped along the wall, until he had a clear view of the alien. Glancing at Pepper, he made a face showing his apprehension, and rolling his shoulders several times, tried to relieve his tension.

Luke and Rob carefully turned the alien over on its side. Lifting it, they pushed, until they had the body resting on a rounded two-inch wide ledge behind the ice bier. The body slipped on the ledge's rounded edge and fell back into its carved resting space. "Let's tip it toward us," Rob suggested. "And then, unto its belly, that way we'll use our bodies to support it. Damn hard to move something that's stiff as a board. On the count of three raise your end."

Muscles straining to hold on to the space suit, they raised the alien, turning him onto his side. Forcing the body toward them, they rolled him to his belly and rolling him again raised the body onto the edge of the bier. He slid away, and grabbing for holds, they hugged the stiff, space suited form, struggling to keep it balanced on the narrow edge of ice.

"Roll him, just a little toward us, so the back of the helmet is facing me," Rob said tugging on the alien. "I think I can examine the back of the helmet if you've got a good hold on him. Do you think you can hold him on the edge?" he asked. Anxiety tightened his voice and he grinned to overcome it. "He's awkward to handle, being stiff, and the suit must weigh a lot, feels like he weighs a ton when I try to lift him." Grimacing, he flicked a quick glance at Luke and rolling his head to the side, wiped his face on the shoulder of his jacket. "I'll count to three and then let go. One, two, three. You got him?"

Luke nodded.

Releasing his grip on the alien, Rob bent and then folding his knees knelt on the ice floor. Examining the back of the suit, he pulled on the helmet and the body slid. Luke lunged for a tighter grip and losing his hold shoved the alien back toward his carved out space. Frantically, he pushed on the awkward body. His feet slipped on the ice floor and he grabbed for the edge of the bier to keep himself from falling. The top of the alien's body swung outward, teetering over the icy ledge.

Rob raised his arms and held the alien on the bier. Twisting his head around his upraised arm, he stared wild-eyed at Luke, whose feet were slipping on the ice in a frenzied, scissoring dance. "C'mon, grab hold," he yelled.

Luke's breathing accelerated to small sucking gasps of air, and grasping the space-suited body, held it tight. Moving it several inches, the alien slipped again, and for three-seconds, he lay suspended over the edge of the bier, and then, plummeting, toppled on Rob and Luke. Falling in a twisting mass of swinging arms, legs and bodies, Luke slid,

THE DEVILS PUNCHBOWL

and striking Rob, propelled him with the alien laying on his chest, across the ice toward the center of the room.

Rob shoved, and pushed on the alien, the heels of his boots digging deep scaring marks, on the smooth, frozen surface of the floor. The more violent his movements, the faster he slid in rapidly expanding circles.

"C'mon, get it off me," Rob yelled, kicking furiously. "C'mon, he's heavy," and kicking again propelled himself over the ice in a wide circle toward Luke.

"I'm trying," Luke said, through gritted teeth, and crawling several feet, pulled himself up. Standing unsteadily over Rob, he wobbled, and bending cautiously from the waist, tugged on the alien's legs. Gasping, Rob kicked again, striking Luke's legs, and knocking him flat, they both slid in opposite directions across the floor.

Benny and Pepper slapped each other's back, and howling like banshees, collapsed jelly-like to the floor in an explosive surge of released tension. Laughing in spurts and starts they wiped tears from their eyes.

"Watch it, Rob, its got you," Pepper yelled. "It'll probably bite." He howled again, wiping the palm of his hands over his cheeks.

"Get it off me," Rob roared. "It weighs a ton."

Luke crawled toward Rob and carefully climbing to his feet grabbed the alien's foot. "Rob," he yelled anxiously. "Shove on it as I pull." Pulling on the space-suited alien, Luke moved Rob in a six-foot circle. The harder he pulled the faster they moved over the ice. Giving an extra hard yank on the alien's leg, his feet slipped and he fell hard, shoving Rob and the alien in a tight spinning circle across the ice.

"S' not working," he yelled plaintively, shaking his fist. Sitting up, he wiped his forehead and glanced at the collapsed Benny and Pepper holding their stomachs. "Come help me, instead of sitting over there laughing your heads off. This isn't funny, assholes."

"It is from our perspective," Benny yelled back. "You guys are funnier than anything I've seen lately. Hilarious in fact." Covering his mouth, he laughed again his mouth splitting wide in a loud howl. Wiping his face, he turned to Pepper. "Let's helpem, if we don't we'll never get out of here. This has been a regular Laurel and Hardy cartoon. Better maybe."

"Okay, but I'm only touching its bottom half, the feet," Pepper said, laughter bubbling through his words.

Rising to their feet, they carefully stepped across the room, and standing above Rob, dropped to their knees. "I wish I had a camera, this is one for the books," Benny chortled. "You guys will never live this down. I'll remember it always."

"And I'll keep reminding you, in case you have a tendency to forget it," Pepper said. He laughed again and sliding next to Luke, asked. "How should we do this?"

"I think Benny and I can pick up the head part if you'll pick up his feet," Luke answered. Once we get him off of Rob, we can push him over the ice. Lift when I yell, heave."

"Heave," Luke yelled, and lifting the frozen alien, they moved the body, sliding him with undue haste to the ice floor. Pepper releasing his grip on the feet, gave the space-suited alien an extra push toward his ice bier. Sliding rapidly away from them, he started to spin, his weighted top giving him a lopsided wobble like a child's top, when its lost its momentum.

"My God," Benny said, his breath condensing in a puff of vaporous air. "You weren't kiddin when you said he weighed a ton. I thought you were kiddin, Rob. Are you hurt?"

"No! Just my feelins," Rob said. "And maybe a little bit of my dignity. I think it's his body and what they've done to it that makes it so heavy." He grinned and then laughed aloud. "We're going to need a crane to put him back up on his bier." Climbing to his feet, he grumbled. "Let's give it a try. Most of the weight is in the top part of his suit. Luke will take his head, and I'll stand here at his chest, with Benny next to me near his hips. Pepper can lift his feet."

"Remember you're standing on ice, so this isn't going to be easy," Luke offered with a grimace. Bracing themselves with their knee's bent, they placed their hands under the alien. "Heave," he yelled, and each of them, sucking in a deep-seated grunting breath, expelled it in a

THE DEVILS PUNCHBOWL

gargantuan yell. Lifting the alien they threw him into his ice formed coffin.

Gasping, his breath breaking into short bursts of sound, Pepper laughed raggedly. "You still want to examine him, Luke?"

"No, maybe next time. I'm had enough fun for today," Luke answered. He puffed, his breath condensing in a vaporous white cloud in front of him. "I guess I'm the butt today." Pressing the alien gently back into the curve of his ice coffin, he shook his head. "Ghoul I might be, but maybe someday, I'll get to do some tissue tests on them. Someday, maybe," he sardonically added, flicking a disgruntled glance at Pepper.

Unzipping his pocket, Luke removed two tools and handed them to Rob. "This one is like the tool you used to move from the trailhead at Buck Lake. This one move's objects. Since you haven't been to the spaceship, I suggest you appear at the entrance where the two robots are standing. Remember, that huge lighted cave covered with shiny, white marbly stuff. From there, you took the south entrance that leads down here. On the north side of that cave is the tunnel that leads straight into the space ship. If we appear there, we'll walk you through the tunnel to the ship."

"Then I hope we can eat! All of this shit has eaten a hole in my guts and it gives me a feeling of starvation. I can't believe how hungry I get in here. Okay, let's go!"

Luke paused, watching Rob press the correct buttons on the tool. Grinning, at the sound of his yell when the tool began to pull on him, Luke pressed his own.

CHAPTER 16

ROB FOLLOWED BENNY into the tunnel leading to the spaceship, and with Luke close on their heels, they listened to Pepper argue for his viewpoint about the aliens.

"Even though they're frozen solid, I don't believe they're dead," Pepper said. "They're in some kind of suspended state until they're rescued by their own people. "It's logical that if a world or another time lost contact with a spaceship this size, they would bust their asses looking for it," he added.

"If that was true, Pep," Benny said, "then your theory about the spaceship coming through time can't be true. All they would have to do, is input the same sequence of numbers, or coordinates that they used to get here and they'd be here. Your theory sounds good, but it just can't be that easy."

"Yes, it could," Pepper argued. "Maybe it's just a fluke they landed here."

"All of that's good theory," Luke said. "But wait until you use the machine with the headgear. Benny went to the time of the pyramids, and when I tried it, I went to a world that was primal. It was stark with huge craters and bitter cold. A meteor landed not very far from me and the shock wave rolled me over the ground. I almost froze to death before Benny disconnected me from the machine."

"Another thing," Luke added, glancing at Rob and Pepper. "Sitting in the stool on the bridge, your body is reacting physically to stuff that is happenin to you inside the machine. "So, let's say, you find yourself in some bitchin situation, and you were killed, would you feel

THE DEVILS PUNCHBOWL

it sitting in your stool. You'd be dead in the machine, but would you die here on the bridge."

Benny held his arms away from his body and showing his agitation, flapped them. "Now that scares the shit out of me."

Stepping into the spaceship, Rob stood spellbound. "I don't believe it," he whispered. Tentatively, his eyes swept across the wide expanse of continuous windshield. Walking the width of the bridge, he looked at the abyss below the ship and hurriedly stepped back. "You said it closed, show me how."

Benny pressed on the rolled padding, and the six-foot monitor, dropping silently with the keyboard disappeared inside its cabinet. The jelly-like liquid starting to flow, changed the pane to a frosted, milky-white, streaking it in places to a darker creamy color.

"This monitor is the only one that controls the sliding cover," Luke said. "We think it's some kind of metal shield that protects the windshield when its in deep space and maybe a time warp. The rest of the monitors fit into the padded console the same way this one does. To open and close them you just press on the curved side of the console." Gesturing, his eyes glistened reflectively with his thoughts. "I've thought a lot about why the ship's monitors and instrument panels are fitted into the console. It has to be because of the type of travel they use. The ship must come through some heavy stuff, because everything here seems to be protected. All of it sits in some sort of cushioned padding."

Luke pressed the console's curve, and the covering outside the windshield slid by and, the syrupy, milky hued liquid, flowed into its frame. "See how it looks like a clear pane of continuous glass, but I don't think it's glass as we know it. Has to be made of some other material, and I can't imagine what that thick stuff inside the pane is for? But it must be some kind of protection, maybe against radiation when they're in between worlds or dimensions. And maybe this ship was used for time travel. Who knows?"

Rob stood with the fingers of one hand covering his mouth, staring at the wide panorama of mountains and valleys. He was silent, rendered speechless by the view and, the awesome reality of the alien ship. He shook his head back and forth. "Unbelievable," he whispered. "And there isn't anything alive in here. This is awesome, really terrifying. Unbelievable!" Pacing, he circled the length of the bridge, his thoughts skittering in every direction like a vagrant wind. "Unbelievable," he kept repeating.

"Let's eat," Benny demanded, sliding on a stool. "It'll give Rob a chance to look around at the bridge of the ship." Settling himself, he placed his haversack on the floor beside him. Digging through its contents he took out his lunch, unclipped his canteen from his belt and laid them both on the console. Preston Peak caught his eye and he sighed, gray clouds still covered its summit. Bleak looking mountains circled the horizon, most of their tops still heavily laden with snow. Making a sandwich of salami and cheese, he nibbled his way through a half-dozen Ritz crackers.

Luke watched Rob, pace. He stopped about every other turn, and bending, as far he could over the top of the console, looked at the drop below the ship. Every time he did it, he shuttered. Munching on an apple, he stopped next to the teardrop table and dropped heavily on one of the stools. Leaning forward, he rested his body on its rounded edge and picked up one of the headgear dropped there by Luke and Benny. Examining it, he waved it in the air and asked. "Are these the instruments you put on your head?"

"Yeah, they're really flimsy for having so much power," Benny said, turning in his seat to watch him examine the headgear. "I can't imagine how they work."

"I've been sitting here thinking," Pepper said. What are we going to do with all this?" His voice roughening with emotion, he swung his arms out in a depressive gesture, showing his discomfiture. "Are we just going to walk away and leave it, or what?"

Rob glanced up at Luke and then over at Benny. "Pepper's actually been thinking," he mouthed silently. They grinned at each other.

"I saw that, Rob," Pepper said. His expression changed to one of indignation. "You guys are always teasing about my thinking. My thoughts are just as good as any of yours. Between all of us, the only

THE DEVILS PUNCHBOWL

one who can express himself any better is Luke, and I think most of the time, he just uses big words to be asinine."

"We tease because you usually speak before you think Pep," Luke answered. He quietly put the remains of his lunch away, and clearing his throat, glanced up, his eyes skipping over the tight-lipped fleeting expressions on his friend's faces.

Benny's eyes reflected his inner turmoil, and his mouth pulled downward into a grimace when he glanced at Luke. Pulling the angular shape of his chin tight against his throat, he raised his hand, rubbed it across his mouth, and then covering his eyes, leaned forward on his elbow.

Rob sprawled on the teardrop table, his deeply cleft chin and squared jaw propped up with his right hand. The headgear with its silver shine, lay discarded near his elbow. The whiteness of his scalp gleamed in the artificial light. The shadow of his auburn hair lay like a dark mat against his shaven head. The bright yellow blotch of his hard hat lay between his feet, tossed down on the green folds of his haversack.

Rob isn't comfortable, Luke thought, staring at him. Everything around him is minimized by his bulk, and people, most of the time are intimidated by just his size. Which is really a paradox, because he's really very gentle.

Luke took a deep breath, and running his hand impatiently through his hair, shook his head to blow away his wondering thoughts. He glanced at Pepper and recognizing the worry behind Pepper's words, tried to correlate his own into something that made sense. They did have some problems that had to be solved before they left the Devils Punchbowl. His eyes skimmed the bridge, and the word spaceship popped into his mind. It staggered him.

"Okay I agree with, Pepper. We do have some problems to solve and keeping the cavern a secret is the biggest one. But let's do it tonight after supper." Clearing his throat, and for a few seconds, his bright gaze touched each of them. Restlessly, he studied the bridge of the ship until his eyes once again were drawn to the wide expanse of wind-shield. The huge bulk of snow capped mountains, pulled his gaze out-ward to skitter apprehensively over black ridges and deep forested valleys. Reluctantly, he pulled his gaze from the hypnotic view beyond the windshield. "Let's try to go through the opening into what looks like the top level. We'll take a quick look and then, I'd like to experiment with that headgear. Or would you like to try the headgear first?"

Rob raised himself from his slouched position, and touched, the headgear laying beside his elbow. "I'd like to do that. Use the headgear I mean. My mind is sorta buzzed out with all I've seen today."

Gathering around the tear-shaped console, they each picked a stool and choosing headgear placed it on their heads. Luke sat at the keyboard and slipped his notebook from his pocket. "Okay. What keys would you guys like to press? Benny and I pressed the minus with a swizzle and the zero with the dash and period over it."

"Let's try three keys this time," Rob said, looking thoughtful. "What do we have to choose from?" Rising, he walked a few steps and stood behind Luke.

"The keyboard's full of symbols, so the possibilities are probably endless," Luke explained. He laughed suddenly, turning in the stool to look up at Rob. "At least I think so."

"Since you guys tried two keys, I think I'll try three, the minus, that shape that looks like a bird and the parenthesis. Those keys combined, will probably land us up to our asses in snow at the North Pole," Rob said.

"That sounds good, but who's going to stay here and, pull the plugs if we get into trouble?" Benny asked. "One of us has to be the observer."

"I will," Luke answered. "I'll do what we did, you'll have three minutes to look around. Okay! Get plugged in and we'll see where you go, I hope it's better than the one I picked."

Luke watched them insert the end of their cords in its receptacle and settling back on his stool, his features glowed in happy humor. Positioning his fingers over the keys, he simultaneously, but gently keyed them.

The screen lit up flattening into horizontal and vertical lines. Spinning rapidly in a conglomerate melding of colors, they disappeared within a marble-sized whirlpool. Expanding, the scene brightened, flashing a baffling idiom several times, and brightening again, a watery, gray landscape appeared. A forest of sea plants moved sluggishly along one side of the huge screen, and in synchronized movements, a school of fish swam into view. Their bodies, a moving rainbow of color, they darted away, vanishing into shadowed areas along the edge of the screen.

"What in hell, they're under water," Luke muttered.

A long line of large flat stones, some of their edges standing out as black lesions lay along the sandy bottom. They disappeared against a flat grey wall of a distant crumbling city. Surely, that has to be an optical illusion, Luke thought, staring at the odd, distant silhouette of stone shapes blending with murky water.

Pushing himself up a little straighter on the stool, he pressed hard against its back. Rob, Benny and Pepper appeared together on the lower left of the watery scene. Glancing at them, sitting relaxed on their stools, he observed that they didn't have a problem breathing. Being underwater didn't seem to be giving them any trouble.

Luke turned and watched the screen.

The water ebbed, the slow sucking force of its movement, caused their clothes to float and balloon around their bodies. They looked ludicrous, like fat caricatures of their actual selves. A sunken ship lay a short distance away, a jagged hole blown in its side exposed the skeleton of its framework. One-fourth of it was buried under sand and, looking at it through the murky water, Luke surmised its structure was made from wood.

A geyser of air bubbles from behind the ship rose toward the surface. Fish darting into the cloudy air stream, emerged higher in the column of bubbling water, barely moving. Suppressing a laugh, Luke thought, they look lethargic, almost as if they're drunk on some kind of gas. "What in hell could that be," he muttered. Bending toward the screen, he studied the column of air bubbles.

Benny hugged himself and twisting his arms wrapped them around his body. Rob walked toward the ship, the movement of his booted feet churning the water. Dropping his head forward, he watched murky sediment rise in a cloudy mass around his legs. Rubbing his hand along the side of the ship, he walked toward the hole in its side and turning around beckoned to Pepper and Benny. Pepper shook his head and held his hand up. Benny said, an emphatic no. Rob laughed.

Glancing away from the screen, Luke looked at them sitting on their stools. Noticing Benny had begun to shiver, he looked at his watch. "Two minutes, to go," he muttered.

Pepper grinned and stepping closer, stood beside Benny. They watched Rob raise his hand and grasp the edge of the gapping hole in the side of the ship. Benny said something, pointing at the line of stones. Crouching, he knelt and ran his hand over the one he was standing on. Pepper fell to one knee beside him and rubbed his hand over the stone. He shook his head, pointing at the faint illusory buildings.

From the murky depths, a small whale appeared swimming straight at them. Passing directly over their heads they jumped, raising their arms and tried to touch the white skin of its under belly. They laughed, bending like seaweed, as the rippling motion of water around the whale, turned them buoyant, and moving with the current, they bounced like rubber balls along the bottom.

They turned and still laughing, shrugged, staring straight at Luke from inside the screen. Rob stepped up on the huge stone slab, and saying something pointed upward. Pushing with his feet, he launched himself upward off the bottom, and Pepper and Benny joined him, in a frenzy of moving arms and legs.

Glancing at them sitting on their stools, Luke realized that like Benny, Pepper had started to shiver. Twenty seconds to go he thought, keeping tabs on the time. Watching them bend to scrape at something on the slab of stone, he hesitated for a second. Rising to his feet, he rushed around the table pulling plugs from their receptacles.

Rob opened his eyes, they were vacant and introspective, studying something deep within his mind. Removing the headgear from his head, he stared at it.

Pepper and Benny grinned at each other.

"That was awesome," Pepper said. He glowed with enthusiasm, his eyes bright with eagerness. "It was the most incredible experience I've ever had. A frigin, livin fantasy. Let's go back. It was wonderful.

THE DEVILS PUNCHBOWL

We actually were underwater and didn't have to worry about breathing."

"Awesome," Benny answered. He rose and standing next to his stool sucked in huge gulps of air. Stretching his arms out wide, he swung them in circles.

Rob turned in his stool to face Luke. "This is simply more then I can comprehend." A flash of overwhelming surprise settled on his face. "We were underwater. Further underwater, then I've ever been and it actually felt like I was really there," he said. "I felt everything. The siding on the ship, and the displacement of the water as the whale swam by. I actually felt myself sink into the silt on the bottom. Weird, everything about it was way out in the weird category. I thought I saw a hazy spectrum of colors filtering through the water above us, but when I tried to swim to the surface something held me down. It was like I had weights on. I could only get a few feet up, and then, some kind of force would drag me back down, until my feet touched the bottom. I would have liked to break the surface and explore where we were. And I think that was a sunken city we could see in the distance."

Pressing against the back of his stool, Rob turned it to face the screen. "We actually were together. We spoke and I could feel everything, even the water soaking my clothes. This is really weird, way out weird . . . and to top it off, it works by pressing buttons on a keyboard." Clasping his hands, he stared for a second at them as if they were foreign objects, and with a deep sigh, propped his head up with one of them. "You know, I just thought of something. What if it were possible to press a different combination of symbols and we could actually go there and somehow bring back stuff we find?"

They stared at each other and glancing back toward the screen, their minds churned with the things they'd like the complex machine to accomplish.

"Let's go again," Pepper suggested. "This time I get to choose which keys to press. Okay?" he asked, glancing at each of them.

"Sure, okay by me," Rob answered, taking a deep breath. "Who's going to stay here, to man the station?"

"I will," Luke answered. "We could all go, if I could just figure out how to exit this and, bring us back, but until we do, one of us has to stay behind. Rolling his eyes toward the ceiling, he smiled ruefully and shook his head. "If we ever do."

"Get over there, Pepper and pick out some symbols," Rob urged, jerking his chin toward the keyboard. Relaxing on his stool, he picked up the shiny headgear and, placing it on his head, pressed it firmly against his forehead.

"A hell-of-a-lot of combinations to choose from," Pepper murmured, rubbing his mustache. "I'm going to take . . . a plus . . . that odd lightning looking thing . . . and that one there, that funny lookin upside-down F." Laughing, he spun around and retraced his steps. Plopping on his stool, he picked up his headgear and placed it on his head.

"You ready?" Luke asked quietly. Turning to face the screen, he pressed the keys Pepper had chosen. The screen darkened and shifting to a whirling pattern, turned fuzzy, brightening into a lighted area.

A huge place.

Spectators stood leaning against a wrought-iron fence, looking down at a skating rink. Trees' grew in large tubs around the fenced area, their branches reaching skyward toward a glassed-in vault-like dome, made of plain and stained glass panels. The sun shining through the glass panels glowed, bathing the skating rink in radiant color.

"Looks like a mall," Luke muttered, his eyes glued to the screen. "A modern-day mall."

The coalescing huddled figures of Rob, Benny and Pepper, appeared in the center of the rink, their bodies brightening into solid looking images. Fascinated by a girl skater performing a perfect pirouette, Pepper and Benny turned to watch her. Rob stood looking up at the people, looking down at the skaters.

Spectators suddenly pointed downward into the rink their expressions changing into obvious shock. Luke could see when they started to yell. People rose from where they were sitting on benches and ran to stand along the fence. The skaters slowed to stare at the boys, their mouths gapping open in disbelief. Confusion turned to horror, and

THE DEVILS PUNCHBOWL

they ran into each other, falling awkwardly on the ice. Scrambling from their tumbled positions, they continued to watch the center of the rink.

A male skater smashed into Benny, plowing straight through his left side, and his image broke apart, causing indistinct ragged strips of him to float freely in the air. Brightening, his figure glowed incandescently and coalesced again to his shape.

The male skater's legs buckled and he fell to his knees. Continuing to slide over the ice, he twisted his upper body to look back at Benny, a surprised horror stamped on his face. His chin dropped, and the horrified expression stayed as he slid into two children, knocking them flat.

They howled.

Luke gasped, sucking in his breath, mesmerized by what was happening on the screen. He could tell the second the people became silent.

The skaters and spectators gaped at the boys, their expressions a mixture of wonder, fear and terror. Pepper never took his eyes off the skaters, and Benny stood swaying, his arms held slightly away from his body. Rob stared at everyone.

Luke rushed around the table pulling plugs. He glanced at his watch. They had been there exactly twenty seconds. "I hope no one had a camera," he stated into the silence of the room. Waving his hands, he plopped in disgust on his stool and propped his elbows on the console. Overwhelmed by his feelings of frustration, he rubbed his hands over his face, and slipping his fingers through his hair, knocked his hard hat off. It fell with a thump sliding along the floor. Holding his head clenched between his hands, frustration showed in every line of his body. Hunching over the console, he rounded his shoulders and stared at the strange symboled keyboard. Groaning, he sat up straight and stared at Rob sitting across from him. Sliding from his stool, he stood again, his agitation apparent in every step as he walked away. "I think we're in deep trouble," he said, throwing up his hands in a futile despairing motion.

"Why, Luke?" Benny answered. "Are you thinking maybe someone had a camera? Maybe, no one did. And it's logical, to think no one could describe us. We weren't there that long."

"Yeah, don't be so quick to think the worst," Pepper interjected. "How long were we there, it didn't seem that long to me?"

"About twenty seconds is all, but I saw everyone staring at you. I couldn't believe it," Luke said, with a grim twist of his lips. "I knew by the way the people reacted that you weren't invisible like Benny was the first time we used the machine. If we're lucky enough, nobody took your picture, but maybe they'll be able to describe all of you. You know with police composites." Throwing his hands in the air again, he leaned over the console staring down into the void that opened below the ship. His expression a bleak mask, his face wore his feelings like a coat of despair. The drop into the blue-gray vault of the sky went on forever, melting into mottled patches of light and dark green shadows slashed with beckoning strips of sunlight. Between craggy peaks, a pair of vultures or hawks floated effortlessly on vagrant, nebulous currents of air, and they looked like they were playing, really having fun riding the wind.

"Okay, let's not get depressed over something that probably won't happen," Rob said. Emphatic, his voice dropped harshly and he blinked several times. Folding his hands together, he watched his thick fingers form a steeple. "Right now, let's not stew over it. Let's assume that no one got a picture or a good look. The people standing in the spectator section above the rink would be the only ones that could have had a camera."

"Yeah, someone with a camcorder that has a telephoto lens, that can take a picture of a gnat's ass at four hundred yards," Luke said, interrupting him sarcastically. "Who knows, what they'll say or be able to describe. The skater that plowed straight through Benny, shook, he was so frightened. He must have realized that you had no substance that you were just images."

"Well, shut the shit up for a minute, you didn't let me finish," Rob answered flicking Luke, a disgruntled look. He inhaled suddenly, a deep calming breath and then exhaled slowly. He too, wanted to curse.

THE DEVILS PUNCHBOWL

"You've sort of went overboard. For right now we'll assume that everything's all right and nothing can be traced to us. Let's assume that."

Rob paused watching them. "All right? Now there's a couple of levels in this spaceship I'd like to explore." Slapping the padded console in front of him, he rose to his feet. As Pepper's, wee Granny always says, let's have a bit of attitude changin here. No more caterwaulin, or I'll crawl down your throats and gallop your guts out. Now, how do we get me to the next level? I've never been there, so how can I picture it?" Swinging his arm, he pointed upward. "You know, up there."

CHAPTER 17

RELIEF MIXED WITH hope loosened the muscles on Luke's face, the grim expression fading as he stared at Rob. "I thought we'd experiment with this," he said, tossing the robot's tool in the air. "I don't think the robots use the one we've been using for teleportation." Picking up his haversack, he crossed the room, and dropped it on the floor below the opening in the ceiling. Stepping back several feet, he extended his arm and, aiming the tool at the sack, pressed buttons. Raising his arm, the bag jerked upward, rising until it disappeared through the opening. Luke lowered his arm and the sack fell in a twisting erratic spin to the floor.

"That's just like the experiment we did in camp, but we don't know if it will work on humans," Pepper exclaimed doubtfully.

"I think the robots used these tools, for everything," Luke stated. Examining the tool, he blinked several times. "These other buttons must have specific functions, too. Let's try this!"

They crowded together watching Luke's fingers press simultaneously on two of the buttons. Aiming the tool at the haversack, it rose without any hesitation in a steady ascent toward the ceiling. Passing through the opening the sack didn't hover, but continued, disappearing from their view. He released the buttons and they watched the haversack plummet downward, until it plopped on the floor.

"Hey," Benny exclaimed. "It works."

"Just a minute," Luke answered. "Let's try it out here first. Coming down is going to be the tricky part." Pointing the tool at himself, he pressed the buttons and rising several feet, hung there. "This part's

THE DEVILS PUNCHBOWL

okay, but the problem is how do I get down." Releasing the buttons, he fell to the floor.

"Hey, I've got an idea," Rob said, studying the tool. "Try one of the buttons next to it in the middle. It might work." He aimed the alien's tool at himself and rose toward the ceiling. Twisting his fingers, he kept a steady pressure on the indented button and pressing the one next to it, he descended, feather light, until his feet touched the floor.

"Cool," Benny yelled, rushing toward Rob. "You did it."

"Hey, let me try this sucker out," Pepper exclaimed. Pressing two buttons on the tool, his upper torso vanished, and his moving legs, dangled several feet from the floor.

They howled and rushed to stand next to him. Luke put his hand out where Pepper's shoulder should have been. "Pepper, are you all right," he yelled. "Part of you has disappeared all we can see is part of your legs."

"Yeah," Pepper's disembodied voice answered. "I can still see you."

"Press the buttons again," Rob yelled. "You're scaring the shit out of us!"

Pepper's laughter ricocheted into the room and accompanied by shadowed movement, he appeared. "I pressed the wrong buttons. It was worth it, though, your expressions were priceless."

"Explain, Pep, you just scared hell out of us," Benny said. "We're up to our asses in shit, don't joke about this, it's not funny."

Pepper's face flushed. "You're the one that's a pain in the ass. I just explained. I pressed the wrong buttons on the bar. Hell, I didn't do it on purpose."

"Hey, forget it," Rob yelled. Adrenalin in a gushing torrent ran a path of havoc through his body, and an overwhelming urge to run, rushed over him. Clutching the tool, he moved it over the right side of his body. It vanished, as if someone had used an erasure to blot out that part of him. Straddling a threshold into an unknown space, only part of him was visible, the left side. "How can this be, I'm seeing the bridge of the ship with my left eye, but I'm also seeing it with my right? It's sorta shadowed though. This feels odd, its like part of me has stepped through a pocket in the air. I feel wrapped in it." Waving his arm again, his left side disappeared, until the side of his face and his right arm was the only visible part of him. His left eye danced golden lights, and waving the tool over the exposed part of his face, it completely disappeared. And then, slowly, his arm was pulled through a fold in the air. It vanished.

They waited expectantly.

"C'mon Rob, you're giving us anxiety," Luke shouted.

"I'm up here," Rob said, his voice barely audible.

Spinning around they stared at Rob's head. It hung about a foot from the ceiling. Nothing else showed only his head, cut off just below his chin.

"How in hell did you do that? Come down and show us?" Luke demanded.

Rob laughed. His head descended, and for a second, his outlined silhouette appeared as a shadow figure, barely visible.

Benny walked forward and touched his shoulder. "Show us, I can't imagine anything with this kind of power."

"You can move around too," Rob explained. "It's sorta like you're looking through a fuzzy glass wall between you and out here. You see and hear everything, but out here, no one can see you. It's like you've stepped into another space or dimension, but you're still here. And to move you have to use a swimming motion. Can you believe it?" His voice trailed into silence, and perplexed, he stared at Luke, Benny and Pepper. "There must be a way to use this and stay on the floor. And why haven't we met an alien that's alive? I just can't believe they'd leave this place voluntarily." A brooding silence fell amongst them and turning as a group they stared at the bridge of the ship.

"Oh shit, c'mon, let's do something, this silence gets to me. I can feel it pressing like a sheet of lead on the top of my head," Pepper whispered. "C'mon Rob, lighten up and show us how you did that?"

Rob's eyes focused on Pepper. "Okay, you have to press this one, like you did." And concentrating on his fingers, he showed them the proper sequence of pressing buttons to levitate and make parts of their bodies appear and disappear. "This is a hell-of-a-tool."

THE DEVILS PUNCHBOWL

Pressing buttons, their bodies vanished, until only their heads were visible, dangling close to the ceiling. Floating, Pepper turned a slow somersault, and turning a double somersault, Rob snorted, striking his head against the ceiling. Boisterously nervous, they broke into spurts of loud laughter, making faces at each other. Benny's head broke out in hiccups, and Luke's, slowly bobbed its way toward the opening in the ceiling.

"Let's go, we have another level to explore," Luke yelled. They watched his head levitate through the circular opening, and then listening intently, they heard the hollow echo of his laugh.

"C'mon," Benny yelled. Terror swamped him, the feeling so powerful his stomach shook, and trying to control it, he floated to the opening in the ceiling and went through it. Moving into the center of the hall, he waved the tool over his body.

Rob spent a lot of time examining the small, saucer-like ship in its dock. He examined the canopy inch by inch trying to find a way to open it. Finally, giving up, they walked toward the round hall, and Rob trailing behind, cast covetous yearning looks back at the saucer-shaped ship. He was the last one to leave the docking room, and he whispered, in eager, hopeful anticipation. "I'd like to fly it."

Stepping forward they each patted his back in commiseration. "Me too," they whispered. Walking to the entrance to the weird corridor that went nowhere, Rob stepped over the threshold and stood there for a second. Glancing back over his shoulder at his friends hovering in the hall, he put his arms out and touched both walls.

"Weird," he mouthed silently. Twisting his head to look over his shoulder, and standing perfectly still, a pulsing wave of energy, gained momentum in its upward path through the soles of his boots. Sliding his hands along the walls, he stopped for a second, and raising one foot stared at the spot where it had been on the floor. Balancing himself, his hand slid into the center of one of the odd symbols, and bending further to look at his feet, his hand, arm and upper body disappeared through the wall. Jerking himself violently backward, he struck the opposite wall and sliding down its surface flopped on his back. Scrambling to his knees, he crawled to the door and jumped to his feet in the hall's entrance.

Yelling, "c'mon Rob," they grabbed his arms, and turning around ran to the round opening in the floor.

Luke's voice trembled, his incoherent words barely audible. "You all right Rob. What happened? Most of your body went through the wall. It vanished." Crowding together, they stared at Rob.

Rob held up his arm and hand. It hadn't changed, it was still there and seemed all right. Shaking with a fine tremor, he raised his hand, rubbing it over his head and neck. "It doesn't seem to have done any harm," he stated flatly. "I feel the same." He stared blankly, his eyes darting wildly around the hall. He laughed, a short nervous croak. "I just went through a wall! Scary! Holy shit! Where do you think that opening goes? It was dark in there and cold. Bitter cold. Maybe we should experiment and just stick our heads through. I'd like to examine the other side."

"Uh-uh," Pepper whispered. His voice trembling uncontrollably, he tried to form his words, and failing, raised his hand pressing his fingers against his mouth. "We should leave now, I don't think we should go on exploring, this is too much for me. Let's go top side."

"Yeah," Benny said. "We're," he hesitated, his voice faltering. His eyes darted around the hall, skipping over each of them. "We're . . . we're way over our heads, maybe we'll run into something we can't control, what then. . . . " His voice, trailed into an emotional silence, and they stared at each other, their eyes expressing their fears.

"No, we can't leave yet," Rob stated flatly. "Our time's limited and we've only got one more day to explore." Walking swiftly, he crossed the hall and stood near the entrance to the corridor that went nowhere. "We've got to try to look at everything that's here." His expression rapidly changed, its wiggling, moving contortions, expressing horror, excitement, wonder and awe before a blank look of shock settled on his face. Shaking his body like a wet dog, he crossed the circular hallway and slapped Pepper on the back. "It'll be okay, we just won't go in there. That was almost more than I could tolerate." He tried to grin and succeeded only in a weak movement of his lips.

THE DEVILS PUNCHBOWL

Luke studied the dark opening in the ceiling. "Okay, here goes," he said, as he pressed the correct buttons. Jubilant thoughts marching across his face, clashed with ones portraying extreme anxiety. He looked at Benny, Pepper and Rob. Levitating, he twisted his head to the side and looked at Pepper standing below him. "I hope this isn't a mistake," he added, before stepping off into another small hall.

Scanning the area quickly, Luke noticed that the ceiling had no corresponding circular opening to the one in the floor. The hall was round like the one below on the second level, but much smaller. "Hey c'mon," he yelled, watching a starlike object that hovered near the ceiling. Faceted, it glowed, emitting a subdued very faint radiance over the area. Stepping away from the opening in the floor, he waited in the hall's center, staring intently at the shiny object suspended near the ceiling.

The boys drifted noisily through the opening stepping lightly to the floor. Their faces, held a mixture of bravado and apprehension as each of them joined Luke. They stared at the starlike object. "How in hell is it staying up there, I don't see anything attached to it," Rob whispered.

Luke walked around it studying it from all directions. "Beat's me," he said, "think we should examine it?"

"Uh-uh," Benny whispered. "Too weird, leave it alone."

"Okay," Luke said, turning to examine the hall. Placed evenly in the circular walls two small and three larger doors opened off of it. The three large ones were open, their entrances bathed in bleak darkness. The subdued lighting from the hall, scattered an irregular pattern of frosty fluorescence over their thresholds, and shadows lurked where the light didn't touch, adding credence to their fears. They stood quietly, watching.

Stepping forward, they moved quietly, bunching together in the narrow entrance of the room nearest to them. The light from their lamps didn't illuminate much of the soot-black darkness, and new shadows formed, as they held their hard hats high above their heads. Their light beams, small round circles of pale yellow moved over the walls. The room wasn't large, it was narrow near the door and widened again in the familiar pie shape. It was very small compared to the ones on the second level of the spaceship.

"I think I've counted nine of those square shapes," Luke whispered. "And I think they're built into the walls. I see a shine. See it there where I've got my light aimed. Each one of the shapes has a shine. Watch this!"

Luke skipped his light beam over each bulky object, moving it swiftly through the dark depth of the room. A shine appeared momentarily on each one, disappearing when he moved the beam to the next shape. "I think they're similar to the ones made for the robots. They're coffin-like and where the light reflects, it must be some type of lid," he added emphatically.

"Let's go," Rob said impatiently pushing on Luke. "Lead the way, let's examine one of these suckers." Striding past Luke, Rob moved the beam of his light over the lid. The structures were larger than the ones made for the robots, their raised covers a glass-like substance.

Rob, moving the beam of light over the padded interior, caused a surfeit of dark shadows to flicker across his face. "Look at this," he whispered. "There's a tube here that must make a connection with their spacesuits." Cautiously, he lowered the lid, until he was forced to kneel on the floor. "Has to be that," he added? "These guys must need air and protection during their journey. I imagine the window was put in the lid, so a robot could check on them."

Rob laughed softly, the sound a low vibration from deep within his chest. "What, an intelligent observation, that was a statement of pure genius, it should win you an award."

"Hey, Rob," Benny called, throwing his voice upward in a throaty whisper. Standing at the end of the coffin-shaped bed, and bent near the floor, his head wasn't visible, just his body. Appearing as a black smudge at the end of the coffin-like structure, the light from his head lamp gave a sinister bulkiness to his outline. "There's tubing coming out of the wall and it's connected to the lid. They definitely need some kind of air during their journey."

Raising his head, Benny blinked several times in reflective thought, his eyes appearing just over the edge of the coffin-like structure. "So, I think they need air to breathe, and at some point, they must travel through a time warp where they have to be protected. Not only do they need air, but they also need padding as protection, because I think they must travel through some really rough stuff to get here."

"There's nothing in here but these coffin-like beds for the aliens," Luke said, interrupting Benny. "C'mon, let's go."

CHAPTER 18

PEPPER LED THE way back into the round hall and stopping suddenly, pressed the dark band on a small door. "Let's look in here," he suggested.

The door slid sideways, revealing a brilliantly lit passageway that went straight down through the bowels of the ship. Bands of metal that looked like handholds were placed every five feet along the walls of a vertical, cylindrical passage. "Shit. Wow," he shouted. "This must connect to every level. The engine room, guys, finally, I think we found an entrance to the engine room."

Luke stepped to the opening and standing between Rob and Pepper, looked down and then up. The passage going upward didn't go far, and it ended, in a raised banded area that covered a good portion of the bulkhead. Has to be an airlock, he thought?

The reflective passageway spiraled endlessly downward, a brilliant shiny perpendicular tunnel. Luke looked at Rob and they smiled. Their understanding of what they had found, lay in avarice, greedy lust within their eyes. Maybe, Luke thought, they had within their grasp the chance to see the engine room of the spaceship.

Benny pushed between them and Luke stepped back, letting him take his place. Looking down through the gleaming tube, his white-knuckled hand, gripped the edge of the bulkhead, and forming a perfect circle with his mouth, he whistled. The musical notes vibrating along the hollow tube, echoed into its bottom, and then soaring upward, oscillated in perfect pitch along the metal walls. Rob squeezed his shoulder and Benny looked at him.

THE DEVILS PUNCHBOWL

"Do you realize what this means, Rob?" he asked.

Rob nodded.

Luke and Pepper quietly stepped to the next closed door. This one was made from a different material. It wasn't resilient to the touch like the rest of the doors they had opened. Luke placed his palm on the dark band and the heavy door slid sideways. Silently opening on a hidden track, it revealed a storage space filled with crystals, arranged in rows on separate shelves, according to size and color.

From the darkest hues of purple, to the whitest of white, faceted prisms lay next to diamond cut spheres, their surfaces as smooth as satin. Others, shaped stars had sharp extended legs and a few had quills like a porcupine, each spine so finely cut it shook, and as it quivered, it emanated a sparkling jewel-like radiance. Completely covered in fragile spider-web netting, six crystals, the size of basketballs, sat on a middle shelf in deep nests especially made for them. Absorbing, like sponges the beams of light cast by their hard hats, each crystal started to radiate a brilliance that splintered, shooting streams of color in every direction.

Luke closed his eyes against the sudden deluge of flashing, crystallized light, and pushing on Pepper, backed up from the open cabinet door. Turning his head in another direction, he raised his hand and flipped his hard hat light to off. Moving quickly to the cabinet, he picked up a perfectly smooth crystal sphere, the size of a baseball. It warmed in his cupped hands and starting to glow, the walls of the crystal ball vanished, the light radiating from within its circular walls, brilliant, a small sun. "They've trapped some type of energy in these crystals," he said. Beginning to shadow, his body became illusionary, his shape fading along its edges into the air surrounding him.

Pepper poked him. "Put it back, your body is beginning to look funny," he said. "Weird."

Grunting an odd sound from deep within his chest, Luke opened his hands, and dropped the luminous, blazing ball of light, back into its place on the shelf.

Stepping back from the open door, the splintered light beams from the larger crystals flowed through the boy's bodies. Filling them with an incandescent shine, indistinct, faint images of their bones appeared, and emerging from their backs, the light, as fluid as a liquid, pulsed over the inner wall of the ship. Within each cell that formed the wall's structure, the nucleus changed, lighting up with a fiery glow as if it was a star. Icy-cold, it emitted no heat. The wall pulsed, as if each cell had life, and disappeared, in a shimmer of dazzling, dancing light.

"Close the door," Benny whispered, shoving Luke toward it.

Stepping to the wall, he slapped the dark band hard, and the heavy door silently closed, shutting in the splinters of brilliant, shining light from the crystal balls and the flashing rainbow spectrum from the others.

Barely breathing, they silently studied the closed cabinet. Biting his lip, Luke glanced at the wall behind them, it was solid again, and their bodies weren't lit up like light bulbs. "Do you want to take a guess on how they work?" he asked, flicking an anxious frustrated glance at each of them. They slowly shook their heads and no one spoke. Aiming his light at the object floating near the ceiling, he shrugged. "They resemble that thing up there, but it doesn't respond to light like the ones in the cabinet."

Moving heavily, their steps slow and labored, they stepped to the next open door. Stopping in the entrance, the beams of light cast by their headlamps, flickered along a continuous, unbroken silver-covered wall. Stretching endlessly into murky darkness, their lights didn't penetrate the length of the corridor and they couldn't see where it ended. About thirty-feet from the entrance and covered in deep black shadows was a darker black opening.

They wavered in the doorway as Rob's lamp on his hard hat, blazed a path through the darkness, banishing some of the darker shadows. Advancing cautiously, they stepped through the hall's entrance, their lights shooting ahead of them, moving in round yellow circles along the silver-colored wall.

"Psst," Pepper called. "Aim over here. I mean all of you."

Rob removed his hat and raising his arm held it up high. Bunching together, they moved their lights over a dark recessed doorway. Placed just beyond its entrance, a group of nine-contoured chairs' sat in a

THE DEVILS PUNCHBOWL

tight circle in front of it. Grouped slightly apart from each other, each chair was placed, so its occupant would have an unobstructed view of the room. Covered, ceiling, walls and floor with a highly reflective material, the huge, hundred-foot room appeared to be a sitting area.

Their light's reflecting off the shiny material cast brilliant strobe-like streams of light around the room. "Phenomenal," Benny whispered. "The wall's are like mirrors and why so huge. Who would have thought?" His voice trailed off into a murmur, "phenomenal."

Shuffling their feet in nervous anticipation, they moved further into the room and Benny fell loose-limbed and limp on one of the chairs. His feet and legs, from the knee down hung over the bottom edge, and he chuckled, to himself. These too, he thought, were made for a smaller body. Leaning back comfortably, his hand touched a series of buttons along one side of the arm. Thinking that the chair must recline, he pushed the first button and pressed against the chair's back.

Nothing happened.

Benny moved sideways and twisting his neck, looked down at the recessed buttons placed just under the arm of the chair. A radiant glow formed in the hundred-foot room; walls, ceiling and even the floor beneath his chair lit up. Sucking in such a huge gulp of air that it hurt, he sat up straight, gasped, and sliding forward, stood. Grabbing Luke's jacketed elbow, he clutched it.

Everything in the room changed, the ceiling and walls softened, became indistinct, unreal. The ceiling disappeared into an endless blue sky, and where the floor had been, sunlight sparkled over a sea of prairie grass. The grass lay in rows of patterned color, each row a distinct variation of brilliant greens fading into the burnished browns and golds of late summer grasses. A wind, blowing dry and hot across their faces rippled the grass, moving it in the same synchronized motion, of a curling wave on an ocean beach. Small hills circled the horizon and three tiny red moons hovered near their tops.

The wind smelled hot, pungent with dark odors, and the boys stood riveted for several seconds by what they were seeing. Completely disarmed into any vestige of movement, they stood silent, watching two huge animals appear on the horizon. Bellowing, in a roar of deep, guttural challenge, they ran toward each other, their massive hooves tearing out huge chunks of the golden grass. Circling in ever smaller circles, they met, the clash of their horns, an explosion of rubbing drum-like noise. Their snorting bellows filled the room with sound and they reeked with the smell of musk and the visceral lust of wild animals.

Benny's grip on Luke's elbow tightened, and pulling on his sleeve to warn him, he released it, and turning abruptly, he jumped toward the entrance.

They ran.

Stumbling in their rush to move away from the fighting animals, they pushed each other, plunging frantically into the murky corridor. They rushed into the circular hall, anxiety turning their insides to mush, and stopped when they stood above the round opening in the floor.

"What in hell happened?" Rob yelled.

"I have no idea," Luke said. "It just suddenly turned on."

"I think I did it," Benny said quietly.

They turned and stared at him.

Benny's expression was gaunt and haggard eyed in the light cast by his hard hat. He hugged himself, twisting his arms across his stomach, until the seams of his jacket pulled at the shoulders. "I pushed a button on the chair, because I thought it would recline, and shit, was I ever wrong." He laughed, a high pitched nervous sound. "I didn't realize it would turn the damn thing on," he added plaintively.

"It's still going on, so it can't be a threat to us," Luke said. "Before we go any further, let's make a rule. No pushing buttons unless all of us are aware of it." Pausing, he stood silent, trying to calm his senses and thoughts, as nervous fingers of fear, chugged along his body. "I nearly shit my pants. And Benny, I was that close," he added, holding a hand up with a finger and thumb held an inch apart."

"And no touchin. The rule is hands off," Pepper said suddenly. His words punctuated with precision from tight lips were harsh and hollow. "My stomach's still shaking. I want to live through this," he added, glaring at Benny.

THE DEVILS PUNCHBOWL

Benny glared back, his eyes a brilliant green in the shadowed light. "I didn't mean to turn the frigin thing on, Pepper. I thought it was a recliner. What's up your ass? So I made a mistake. No biggie, I'm sure. You're the one that's acting like a jerk."

They retraced their steps, feet shuffling and scraping the floor. Entering the corridor, they hugged the wall and peered around the edge of the door at the room. The shock of what they were watching, staggered them, and reluctantly, anxiety dogging their steps, they moved quietly over the threshold, captivated by the scene. They flinched, at the horrendous, brutal sounds the animal's made hitting each other, and listened, to their labored breathing in their desperate battle for supremacy and survival.

Advancing further into the room, the sounds became louder, punctuated by deep animal groans, until they were experiencing, the harrowing knowledge that they were standing not more than thirty feet from dangerous, wild animals.

Sweat darkened, the animal's hair and thick, clotting blood ran from deep wounds ripped in their sides. The ground trembled from their massive weight, and their sharp hooves tore the soft grasses, mangling it, until open streams of naked dirt marred the uniform rows of golden grass. A vaporous steam rose from the wounded, sweating animals, its odor so real and the smell so thick that it gagged Luke with its veracity.

"Turn it off." Luke said, shaking Benny's shoulder.

"Okay," he answered, his eyes never leaving the animals.

They watched him move cautiously to the chair, and pressing his hand to his mouth, his agitation grew as he crouched on its edge. Bracing himself on one hand, his eyes focused on the fighting animals, he fumbled under the arm for the row of buttons.

"Shit," he whispered. Desperation crossed his face, and forcing his eyes away from the animals, he pulled himself further on the chair. Touching the row of buttons with his hand, he ducked his head for a second and watched his finger press the first one.

The image of the animals dimmed, and their grunting bellows, dribbled away into soft measured sounds. Dwindling gradually into hazy twilight, the sunlight faded, and went out. The room gradually changed, darkening, until it was once again, covered wall, ceiling and floor in a mirror-like substance.

Benny, his chest heaving with the effort, sighed, a heavy expulsion of air. "I'm sorry guys," he said. "I scared the piss out of myself. My heart literally stopped and my knees shook so badly, I didn't think I was going to make it to the hall. God, what, an experience," he added. Laughing nervously, he wiped his face with a trembling hand and raising his other hand clenched them together. "What in hell, makes this work?" Shaking his head in incomprehension, his eyes darkened and became introspective.

Sobering suddenly, his eyes brightened and he pulled himself to the chair's edge. He rubbed his hands together and looked thoughtfully up at them. "Remember, when some show on television, advertised they were going to broadcast some of their shows in Three-D. You know, where you had to have those special glasses. This reminds me of that."

"Yeah, I remember Benny, but here if you noticed, we didn't need any special glasses," Luke said sardonically. "And . . . in that Three-D thing, the actors didn't appear in the middle of your living room. We could actually smell what was happening in this room, the odor from those animals was so putrid, I kept gagging. This was almost too real for me."

"C'mon guys, times a wastin," Pepper interrupted. "No use hashin over old shit, it's four o'clock. Let's explore this area really fast and go topside. I'm hungry, and Rob's Mom sent us some surprises for our dinner. Rubbing his face, he wearily scrubbed his eyes with the palms of his hands. "I don't know if I can stand something else, happinin. This place gives me such stress, I bet I've lost five pounds."

Reluctantly they left the fabulous room, and stopped for a moment to examine each room they passed in the corridor. One had all rounded corners and they thought it could be a kitchen, because it was completely bare of any instruments. Pepper walked in and tried to open what he thought was a cabinet door, but he couldn't make it budge.

THE DEVILS PUNCHBOWL

"Hey. I think we're going in a circle," Benny whispered, looking apprehensively back into the depths of the lengthy black corridor. "There isn't even a glimmer of light in here and, I can't see the entrance anymore. The dark sucks."

Hesitating, Pepper, his humor servicing again, danced forward pressing them back. "I want all of you to take note of this and it's very important. Have any of you seen anything that remotely looks like a shitter? These aliens must do it differently in that department. They have no orifices to do the big job or little job. Consequently, they have no organs for sex. They must reproduce in some weird way."

They laughed. "Now don't you guys feel better," Pepper chortled. "A little dash of humor goes a long way to restoring the good feelings a body should have, so saith me wee, Irish Granny. You know, I could never imagine anything as dark as it is in here. Spooky, makes me have weird feelins."

"I agree with Benny, the walls curve, see how it takes a sharp bend just ahead," Rob said. "And this total darkness gets on my nerves, too. I like to see a little bit of what's ahead of me, so I know where I'm goin." He laughed suddenly, spontaneous, boisterous, rollicking sounds erupting from his open mouth. "At least when it's lighted, it chases away my thoughts about booger's hiding in dark places. What in hell would we do if our lamps went out? Have any of you thought about that?"

Like lighted shadows they crept along the pitch-black corridor, their bodies haloed in the pale light cast by their lamps. Dark shapes sprang to life ahead of them, jumping in weird grotesque movements against the walls and floor.

"The dark's getting to me," Pepper muttered. "I really don't like this much dark. Makes me more nervous. I can actually feel my nerves crawling on my skin. And this isn't really dark this is what I call black. Stark black."

"Yeah," Rob whispered. "This much dark always reminds me that we should be on the lookout for boogers. Why isn't there something alive in here?" His voice, stressed out and nervous climbed several octaves. "All of this adds to the spooky feeling I have and I can't seem to shake it."

Hesitating, they apprehensively approached a curve in the dark hall. Stopping, they ducked their heads and peered around the corner. The hall stretched ahead, its murky darkness intensified by a lighted open doorway near its end. The light pouring through the opening, splashed a beckoning patch against the floor, and it caused a surfeit of deep, hovering shadows, to line the black as night hall.

"Jesus, I'm nervous," Rob whispered. "There isn't a sound in here."

"Spooky," Pepper said.

"Oh shit," Benny laughed, his voice a hoarse uneven bark of sound. "Let's go conquer whatever the hell is in that room and then go topside. I want out of here for today. I've had enough exploring, my nerves are raw."

"Me too," Luke breathed. "This much dark would even scare the Pope."

Stepping into the lighted doorway, they sucked in a collective harsh breath, and in unison, recoiled and ran. Luke stopped when he got to the curve in the corridor, and tried to grab Pepper's arm, as he darted past him. "Don't run," he yelled. "Stop!"

The lights from their hard hats, like golden beacons on a long dark wharf, were strung out in the pitch black of the corridor. The circles of glowing globes were illusionary, and outlined their bodies in pale sur-real light. Rob blew nosily and leaning forward grasped his knees. Benny was the furthest along the corridor and he turned to fully face Luke, his boots a bare whisper against the floor. He swallowed hard, the sound audible in the tomblike silence.

Taking a deep breath, Luke exhaled slowly and started back toward the lighted recess. "This is the same as the rest, the robot isn't doing anything and the alien isn't alive," he said emphatically. "C'mon!"

Reluctantly they followed, and with him, stood staring apprehensively into the lighted room. "Hey, have you guys noticed there aren't any doors in this area, just open rooms," Luke whispered. "So far, everyplace we've been on this ship, the rooms have had a door, but

THE DEVILS PUNCHBOWL

here on this level it's all open." Striding forward, he stood next to the robot.

The alien lay on a padded bench with tubes hooked to his body. He was nude. A cloth similar to a blanket was held in the robot's fingers.

Benny walked tentatively into the room, stopping at the bottom of the bench. "You were wrong Pepper, they definitely have organs and this one, if they're like us, is male," he called out. He grinned suddenly and then laughed aloud. "I'm disappointed though if these creatures are from our future, because their bodies are inferior compared to ours. C'mon, Pepper and study this creature. You're the one that wants to study the human body."

Pepper, the last one to enter the room, stopped about three feet from the bench. "He's definitely male, all right" he said halfheartedly and, stepping further, stood beside Luke.

Rob ran his fingers gently over the alien's forehead. "He's hard just like the ones in the ice cave," he said. "Interesting, because we assumed they were frozen. The robots must use some kind of chemical on them. Maybe to preserve and hold them in suspended animation, until help can arrive from their world. Everything in here must have stopped suddenly, because the robots didn't have time to put him down in the ice cave."

"Notice too, the absence of body hair, but he still has plenty of it on his head," Luke whispered. "And I don't think he has to shave. He does have some muscle delineation, but not like men do in our world."

"What I find most fascinating about them, are their eye sockets," Benny said. Crossing in front of the padded table, he stepped between Rob and Luke to stand next to the alien's head. "They really have huge eyes, twice as big as ours. It makes me think that there wasn't much light on their world, so through evolution they developed differently. I wonder why on some of them, the epicanthic fold is so pronounced and others' don't have it at all. Everything else looks the same as us. He even has nipples and a belly button," he quipped.

A soft voice garbled a sound behind them and they twisted to face the door. Terrified, they jumped, shrinking back against the wall and padded bench. Panic raced through their minds, and bunching together, they stood paralyzed, stiff and immobile. Their eyes didn't waver from the open doorway and, cold chills of alarm ran through their bodies in a gauntlet of rampant waves. They watched.

An alien, a being, a force that they had never imagined they would ever meet, was appearing in the dark corridor. Just beyond the lighted doorway, in deep-set shadows, ectoplasm formed into a smoky wraith-like figure. Knotting together, and then parting, gray mist raveled like string into the black split behind him. The cohesion of fiber and threads that made up the particles of his body moved with a definite purpose within his twisting figure. His arm's moved upward, and a red rimmed white vapor, smeared with dark shadows, followed the motion. It streaked the air around him. And then he spoke. Low and modulated, softly, a bell like resonance as he phrased each word. It was words and sounds that none of them recognized.

Huge bright blue eyes floated in the incandescent vapor. A manifestation of his superior intelligence became evident in the pupils, as gleaming pinpoints of light appeared within their depths, softened, and then, darkened. With an imploring expression, he tried with his facial muscles to convey to them the importance of his message. Pulled back by some unseen force, his gray-white, shoulder-length, curly hair blew wildly around his head. His image wavered, shaking, in its effort to force a cohesive blending of his body parts.

A twisting blotch of vapor, he swayed, his head stretched into an elongated shape, and his eyes in the cloudy substance, became prominent, huge, an intense vivid blue. The hazy mist grew grotesque, and leaning forward, he shimmered with an excess of determination, in his effort to materialize.

Luke trembled and he could feel Pepper shaking beside him. He hesitated for a minute, and then, with grim tenacity, moved his hand, wiping the running sweat from his face. Stiffening his body until every muscle was tight and hard, he glanced quickly at the others. The urge to run was so great that he knew if he relaxed at all, he would start out and never stop.

THE DEVILS PUNCHBOWL

Rob never moved, his face was taut, a profile of a graven mask. Large beads of perspiration appeared on his forehead, and following the rugged planes of his face, ran in drops over his jaw. Puddling in the creases of his neck, they disappeared, leaving wet, dark spots on his collar. His hand squeezed Benny's elbow, as if it was a lifeline.

Benny stood without movement his eyes fixed and staring. One of his hands, clenched into a fist, rested under his chin, the knuckles completely white. His mouth formed a grim line across his face and a muscle jerked rapidly in convulsive movements along his jaw.

Pepper's face had whitened to the color of milky-chalk and the way he was shaking, Luke couldn't imagine how he could stay on his feet. The shakes had him corralled, under a siege he couldn't control. Even his clothes seemed to move of their own volition. He swayed like a tree in a buffeting wind, his feet rooted to the floor.

Luke stiffened, trying to conquer the fingers of panic that were taking over his brain. As he watched the alien, he became mesmerized with his own thoughts, imagining his panic as something he could master. He grabbed for control as if it was a living thing, and holding it tight, shoved the panic down through his throat, until it lay like a red-hot coal in his stomach.

Fading into a misty veil, the alien's features fused again, and from the waist down, he broke apart. The wavering action of his shape pulled on him and lifting his hands again, stringy strands of vapor fell away. He tried to speak, the sound, as if spoken through a hollow tube, from a great distance, became faint. A bizarre whisper.

The vapor faded until a dissipating shadow lingered in the hallway, the molecules of its shape clinging to the air as if it had substance. Scattering into small particles, they pulsed in a slow rocking rhythm, until all that was left, were minute dots of fading light and then, gradually they to disappeared. A soft whistling sound erupted into a screeching howl, and the edges of the split puckered, as if air was being forced out through its narrow opening. Overlapping, it continued to fold itself into an ever smaller piece of darkness, until it was gone.

"Listen, we may have just a few seconds," Luke whispered tersely. "Looks to me like he can't materialize. Let's use the tool and go topside.

I'm going to go to the bridge and close it down. We left that huge windshield open and some of the computer screens on. They've got to be closed down. Any volunteers to go with me?"

"I'll stay," Benny answered. "Rob should go and start dinner, he knows what he brought. All right with you, guys?" he asked tentatively.

"Yeah, okay with me," Pepper answered. "I'm outa here." He blinked rapidly his eyes huge and blank. "Let's go, Rob," he whispered. Staring wild-eyed at the hall, Pepper turned and looked at him.

Rob sighed, glancing at Pepper with dull eyes. "Yeah, let's go. I'll feel more human if I'm out in the open with some sunrays on my head." Fumbling in their pockets for their tools, they looked again toward the dark hall. Trembling, they pressed buttons . . .

CHAPTER 19

WHITTLING ON A small piece of wood, Rob watched his pile of shavings grow. Placing them within the fire ring, he struck a match, and blew gently, until they curled and turned red. Laying several small logs on top, he waited for it to burn down. To successfully bake the potatoes in the ashes, there first, had to be a bed of coals. He slumped forward, propping his elbows on his knees and watched the spiraling smoke.

Glancing at the lake, he shivered, thinking about what he had seen in the spaceship. A trout jumped and wiggling desperately through the air, he watched the sun shine for an instant on its slick-silver body. A shower of rainbow-colored drops flew around him and his tail slapped the surface as he disappeared back into the water. The sound broke the hushed silence of the quiet, wild setting.

Rob groaned and glanced up briefly to skim the cliffs that enclosed the lake. There wasn't much to do for this meal, he thought, his Mom had prepared all of it for them. Steak, potatoes, and even a huge Ziploc bag filled with salad greens and vegetables.

Pepper had already left for the creek to take his bath, and thinking about him, brought an expression of amusement to Rob's face. His mouth broke into a wry smile as he thought about Pepper and his avarice desire for chocolate. His stomach rumbled as he thought of his Mom's chocolate cake with its inch-thick dark-fudge frosting. Pepper would be in a state of bliss when he saw what they had for dessert. Seeing movement in his peripheral vision, Rob turned his head and watched their sleeping area. Benny was appearing on his bag.

Moving quietly, Benny stepped to the fire and held his hands above it. The tightly drawn expression on his face, plus the bleakness of his eyes, showed the consequence of extreme stress. He stood, looking empty and void of feeling.

Luke appeared and fell to his knees on his sleeping bag. A fleeting expression moved over his face, giving voice to the stress that flickered in his eyes. Then it was gone. With an explosion of breath, he plopped forward on his stomach and cradling his head on one arm, stayed there.

Digging beneath the fire with a camp shovel, Rob pushed logs and coals to one side, making a hollow in the hot ashes for the potatoes. He laid them in a row, covering them with another thick layer of ash, hot coals and burning logs. Jumping up, he grabbed his kit and left for the creek.

Benny watched him leave the camp area and decided to go with him. Kneeling on his sleeping bag, he groped in his back pack. Luke still lay face down on his sleeping bag.

"Sorry," Benny mumbled, glancing at Luke.

"What are you guys, doing?" Luke asked. Sitting up, he glanced toward the fire.

"I guess Pepper is already down at the creek washing up and Rob just left," Benny answered quietly. "I just saw Rob bury the potatoes in the ashes and they're really huge, so it'll be at least an hour or so before we can eat. Might as well get cleaned up. Thank God, we don't have to fish tonight," he said ruefully.

Luke watched Benny walk toward the creek, his steps making soft crackling noises. The hoarse shout of Rob's voice greeting Benny echoed in the quiet setting. Broken only by the sizzle and crackle of burning wood, a heavy silence fell over the camp. A log shifted in the fire sending a deluge of sparks and ash into the air and spinning crazily, they drifted aimlessly, turning black. Gases in the smoke sent them spinning higher and starting to spiral they began to float before commencing their gentle, sliding motion back to the ground.

Luke sat, his body stiff with tension, he didn't move and his mind pulled him inward. Eyes, stark and blank lacked any trace of emotion,

THE DEVILS PUNCHBOWL

and he shrugged, hunching his shoulders, trying to dissipate the intense, seething ineptness he felt. But the feeling still rolled through him with the power of a run-away-semi with no brakes. Muscles bunching painfully, he stiffened until his joints ached and feeling the beginning of a tremor he forced himself to move. Idly stroking the sharp ridge of his nose, he groaned and overwhelmed with his dark meditation, smiled grimly.

Rationally thinking about the problems they faced, the dark brooding thoughts faded from his mind and hope beckoned like an elusive light in the distance. His confidence returning, he felt, that together the four of them could conquer this. Their problems weren't insurmountable, even though they were faced with overwhelming odds. Optimism raced a happy path along his nerves, everything, would work out. Digging through his backpack, he found his kit and headed for the creek.

Slowing his stride, he grinned as he passed Pepper and Rob running toward the campfire. They were nude, except for towels wrapped around their waists and boot's pulled over bare feet. Clutching his dirty clothes to his chest, Pepper said through his chattering teeth. "You'll love the water tonight. It's just a mite warmer than an iceberg."

"I'm leaving, Pepper," Rob called. "You can stay and talk, but my ass is frozen and being this cold can't be too good for my gonads." He laughed as he hurried away, the laces of his boots swinging in wild gyrations around his legs.

Shivering violently, Pepper hurried after him, and Luke jogged on toward the creek, passing a blue skinned, red faced, shaking Benny, hurrying back to camp.

Standing in a small ray of meager sunlight, Luke stood in knee-deep water and scrubbed his body. Holding his breath, he sat in the creek and rinsed away the day's sweat. The water was cold enough to stop your heart, he thought, laying backward for a few seconds beneath its icy surface. The pull of the current rinsed his body clean and the rapidly moving water, a roaring symphony in his ears, erased from his mind the day's disappointments.

Springing up, he gasped as cold air hit his wet body. Running clumsily to shore, he stood and rubbed himself dry. Wrapping his towel around his waist, he shoved his feet into his boots, gathered up his dirty clothes and sprinted for camp. Pungent and enticing, the aroma of garlic and frying meat floated in the air, the smell so tantalizing that his nostrils quivered and his mouth watered.

Sitting on the end of his sleeping bag, he pushed his boots from his feet. Grabbing his backpack, he pulled out clean clothes, ramming his arms and legs through underclothes, Levis and sweatshirt. Pulling on his socks and boots he laced them up. Grabbing his jacket, he pushed his arms through the sleeves and accepted with a thankful smile, a cup of tea from Benny.

Curling his cold hands around the warm cup, Luke hunched down close to the fire. Balancing himself on the back of his booted feet, he held the cup with both hands and lifting it to his mouth sipped the hot beverage. "My God, this is ambrosia," he said. "And tonight, we get to eat a meal we didn't have to catch or cook." He laughed. "We're innum tonight."

"Yeah, wait till you taste my steak," Rob said. "It's somethin to die for. We're going to start with salad first, because the steaks are so big, there won't be room on the plates for anything else except our potatoes." Handing them each a camp plate loaded with salad greens, vegetables and a hearty smothering of ranch dressing, they dug in hungrily, scraping their plates clean of every morsel. Rob filled them again with a two-pound New York steak and the baked potato. Opening the doubled foil wrapping on the potato, the heady, tantalizing aroma of thyme and rosemary made their mouths water. Besides a potato quartered and brushed heavily with butter, Rob's mother had put between the slices, thinly cut pieces of carrot, three long green beans and slices of onion. It was truly a meal fit for a king.

Pepper set his plate on the ground and laid back with a groan. "That was the most delicious meal I've ever had," he stated emphatically. Bar none! It even surpassed my wee, Irish Granny's cookin." He laughed joyfully. "You know guys it feels so good to be alive. And Full! And not frightened to death." Abruptly, sitting up he wailed . . . "For a while today, I thought we were gonna die for sure and I wish like hell that alien hadn't appeared. I think his appearance means that some-

THE DEVILS PUNCHBOWL

how, they can communicate with the spaceship. We've got to talk about what happened this afternoon."

"Yeah, we do, but let's wait until after we get our camp cleaned up," Luke retorted. "I suggest, while Rob fixes his bed-roll, we clean up and fill our water pot. Tonight we need coffee, because we have a lot of talking to do and we've got to come up with some answers."

Busily they worked together, doing the chores to police up their camp for the night. Rob pulled their sleeping bags down about a foot and laid his lengthwise at their heads. Walking back to the fire, he looked at the water in the pot, it was steaming, but still not hot enough to make a good cup of instant coffee.

Digging his heels in the gravel Rob squatted next to the fire and thought of their dilemma. He wished he had an answer of how to solve it. The gold laying in its sandy bed passed like a picture through his mind, and a curious, focused idea formed just at the edge of his consciousness. Growing rapidly, the thought spread, giving him a warm pleasant feeling. His eyes remained blank and unseeing, as he watched Pepper lay their utensils on the oven to dry.

Benny spooned instant coffee, measuring it in typical Benny style, into cups from a Ziploc bag. The thought, just how methodical he was ran through Rob's mind. He seemed to do everything in that fashion.

"Must be a learned trait," Rob muttered to himself. Rising, he picked up their cups and handed them one by one to Benny. He filled them with water and, Rob gave a cup to Luke and Pepper with a large piece of chocolate cake. Picking up his coffee and slice of cake, he sat next to the fire. Leaning back on a medium sized rock, he straightened his legs and settled back with a long blow of contentment.

"This is delicious," Pepper exclaimed, closing his eyes after his second bite of cake. "This is stuff to die for! I hope they have chocolate in heaven. I just can't imagine God doing without chocolate."

Luke pulled his legs up to his chest, and balancing his cake on his knees glanced at his friends before taking a bite of his cake. Pepper still looked worried and apprehensive. Benny, stodgily silent, had his usual demeanor of resigned caution. Looking at Rob, he was surprised to find him more relaxed, as if he had come to accept their situation and knew they could somehow surmount it.

"You don't seem to be worried, Rob?" Luke said, giving him a questioning glance.

"I wouldn't say I wasn't worried," Rob replied. "But I've come up with a couple of questions I want to ask all of you. Maybe you won't go along with it, but it certainly would help me. And if you guys vote against it, then I'll go along with that decision."

All of their attention was on Rob, so when Benny spoke quietly, it startled them. "Let's give each of us a chance to speak before we decide the fate of the mountain," he said. "Then let's pick the best ideas out of the pile. We don't want to put us and I do mean us, in any possible danger. I think we've all reached some conclusions and if we combine them, maybe we'll come up with some really good ideas. Since you started Rob, you go first."

Rob cleared his throat and sipped from his cup. He hesitated and then laughed brusquely. "Okay! I want to take enough gold out of the riverbed to pay for my education. My going to Cal Poly Tech is really going to put a financial bind on my folks. The only thing is, I don't know how we could sell the gold without arousing a lot of suspicion about where we got it." Nervously, he cleared his throat again.

"I think it's a good idea," Luke stated. I have a problem with expenses too. The only problem is putting the gold somewhere else. Where could we put it?" He laughed. "We would have to magically find it somewhere else this summer. Somewhere, nowhere near the Punchbowl."

"I don't see a problem with it," Pepper interjected, fumbling for his words. "I'd like to pay for my own education. My folks are taking a second mortgage on their house to pay for mine."

"The only problem with taking the gold is we'll have to go public," Benny said. He frowned, his words dry and emphatically spoken. Twisting his mouth in a caricature of his usual grin, he tried to smile. "I mean, we would have to announce to the world that we had made this fabulous discovery." Thoughtfully, his gaze tracked their faces. "Or maybe . . . we could hide it, so far away from here that no one would

THE DEVILS PUNCHBOWL

suspect that we found it up here at the lake. You know, we can't ever divulge what we've found in the cavern."

A faint red flush swept over his face. Looking down at his folded hands laying in his lap, he raised them in a mute gesture of frustration, and then dropping them, rubbed his palms over his knees. "My biggest concern is the mountain and, protecting everything we've found in the cavern. You guys don't realize what governments do to control people. It's an insidious craving for complete power and control. It's like a disease and some governments will do anything for it. Even kill us. Our only saving grace here in the United States is our constitution, and sometimes, it doesn't even protect citizens from those in control."

"Someday maybe," Benny quietly added, "I'll tell you what the German people condoned and what Hitler did to some of the German people. And most of the population knew what he was doing. He gassed millions, in the name of and for the good of the German people. Look what one man did to Russia. . . . "

"Lenin!" He spit out the name as if it left a bad taste in his mouth. His voice strung out high and thin, he continued speaking. "He had a crazy idea and the people that eventually followed him into power enslaved the Russian people. In a lot of ways that government was worse than Hitler's. Stalin killed way more people than Hitler did."

"I agree with Benny," Luke interjected. "If our government knew about this place, we'd be dead tomorrow. Governments have no remorse about killing you if they feel it's in the best interest of the government. Our history tells us this's true. And if they get caught at it, their excuse is, it was in the best interest of the people. What a crock! They really don't give a rat turd worth of shit about us. That's what my speech was about, saving our constitution. You know, in my research, I came to the conclusion that Benjamin Franklin in his time, had more freedoms than we do. The only dictates he went by were moral ones and they were followed loosely. He believed in one thing most Americans have lost, he firmly believed in the sovereignty of the United States. But . . . he didn't believe in giving the government so much control over its people. Old Benjamin hated taxation. You know he was somewhat of a loose canon. They'd call him a redneck today." He laughed at his comments and they all joined in, their laughter boisterous and happy.

Rising, Luke walked to the fire and setting his cup on a rock poured himself another cup of coffee. "I got off track again. I'd like to be done with this so we could go on to happier things. Like pulling a colossal joke with these tools." He sipped from his cup and quickly swallowed. "Hot," he exclaimed, clapping his hand to his mouth.

"I think we should hide the fissure into the mountain, and the tunnel into the cavern from the small cave. Otherwise, someone else is going to find it like we did. And I don't feel the aliens are a threat to us, but I don't have any factual basis for feeling like that. It's only a feeling I got, when Benny took his little trip with the mind machine. Something else was there and it actually was flying above the pyramids. I think the aliens helped build them for their own use. I really have a gut feeling that some of the pyramids were a kind-of way station, maybe used to boost the power they were using to get here."

"Okay, this is what I've got out of our conversation so far," Pepper quipped. Holding up his hand, he pointed to his first finger. "The aliens aren't a threat to us. Two . . . we don't think taking the gold will cause any problems, as long as we do it in a way that won't jeopardize the cavern. Three . . . we have to swear with our lives that the cavern will remain a secret. Four . . . we've got to cover the opening to the fissure and the entrance to the cave inside the mountain."

"All those ideas sound good, but I can think of a couple more things, that my Irish Granny, would say were worrisome beings." Pepper laughed, the sound ending in a high nervous giggle. "And then, she'd finish with . . . goblins and such that niggle and wiggle like snakes in your mind and leave you no peace. What about us being seen at the skating rink?" he asked. "Maybe, the people will be able to identify us. What then? And . . . what about the tools? Leave them here or . . . ?"

He shrugged, not vocalizing the rest of his words from his last question. Leaving the thought hanging in mid air, he sipped from his cup. Making a face, he swallowed hastily. Rising to his feet, he walked a short distance away and threw the rest of his coffee along the ground. Pouring himself another cup, he stood silently staring at the lake.

THE DEVILS PUNCHBOWL

"All right," Rob said abruptly. "Here's what I think. Early tomorrow morning one of us will use the tool to go into town. The papers from out of town are always at the post office early. Buy one and zip back. Surely, if we made the papers, the story will be in one of the major big ones from the city.

"Wait a minute," Luke said, interrupting Rob with a pleased smile. He glanced at Benny and Pepper. "Remember what my Mom said as we left. My Dad has a doctor's appointment in Medford tomorrow and, they always leave early, so I'll appear in my room. They have a San Francisco paper delivered as well as the Del Norte Triplicate. We should do it that way, it eliminates some of the risk of being seen."

"Okay," Rob said. "Now the problem with tools, I don't have any idea how to solve that one. I'd like to keep them on me though. And I really think we should exchange them before we leave here Thursday. The only problem is, we'll have to hide them."

Pepper dug through his jacket pocket and held the alien's tools in his hand. "Hey, how about this, we can have the old guy at the shoe shop make a leather holder in the shape of a T. We'll havem made with eyes for a shoelace, so we can lace the tools inside. We could even have a secret pocket sewed into our clothes." He laughed suddenly, and lowering his head, studied the tool. "I couldn't have it sewn in my jacket though, because I'm always leaving it behind. I think in my pants would be a better place for me, I've never lost a pair of my pants. One of those ideas should work," Pepper said optimistically. He glanced up his eyes skipping over each of their faces.

"That's a good idea, Pepper," Benny said enthusiastically. "The secret pocket, I think, is a good one."

"I just thought of something else," Luke interjected. "Remember, a couple of years ago when those treasure hunters discovered a shipwreck somewhere off the east coast. I forget the name of the ship, but the government came in and claimed part of it. They claimed it, even though it was lost at sea over two hundred years ago, and is three hundred feet down, sitting on the bottom of the ocean. If that doesn't suck, I don't know what does!"

"Hey guys, I think we're making it harder than it actually is," Rob said. "This really makes it simple. We'll hide the gold in one of our houses. In about a month we'll surprise our girls with sand castles we've made in secret. We'll makem out near Pacific Shores on some property my Dad owns, and we'll makem monstrous size; remember the ones we made for the Fourth of July celebration a few years ago?"

"Remember, Benny, how Lily loved them. And then, when we have the castles just about completed, we'll discover the gold, and present it to our parents. No one needs to know that it actually was never buried. We'll bring a few buckets of sand home from the same area where we've made the sand castles and smear the gold around in it."

"You're a genius, Rob," Pepper yelled, jumping up. I was worried that after we buried it, someone else might find it. It's perfect!" Their mouths splitting in wide, pleased grins, they looked at each other. Happily, they accepted Rob's idea.

"Since Mom and Dad aren't going to be home tomorrow, we'll load up our backpacks and transport the gold to my room," Luke said. "I think of all of us, I have the biggest closet and my Mom never goes into it."

"I think that's okay," Pepper answered. "So far, the only thing I have an objection too, is Rob's suggestion that we wait a whole month before we find the gold. I don't want to do that. The longest I think we should wait is two weeks."

"With that, I'll agree," Benny said, giving Pepper a high five. "When Luke brings back the paper, we can look up gold prices."

"Good idea," Luke said. He yawned and stretching his arms over his head groaned. "My mother has a scale in the kitchen and I'll weigh this." Pulling a gold bar from his pocket, he tossed it in the air, and the small pivoting ingot smacked his palm when he caught it. "I'm going to bed," he said suddenly, climbing to his feet. "I think we've hashed this over enough. As soon as I brush my teeth, I'm getting under some down, it's really cold tonight."

THE DEVILS PUNCHBOWL

Crawling in their sleeping bags they lay back and watched the sky. "What you thinking, Pepper?" Benny asked. "I can hear your brain, grinding its gears way over here." Turning on his side, he raised himself on his elbow and stared at him.

"Nuthin much," Pepper answered sleepily. "I was just wonderin what Bella was doing. She probably really misses me."

Rob snorted. "Yeah like Amy Christine, Mary and Rachael miss me."

"No, they don't miss you, Rob, because you play the field," Pepper said. "You don't settle for just one, you have a half-dozen at a time, after you." He yawned, the noise muffled by his sleeping bag. "Bella really loves me."

Luke and Benny laughed. "I agree, Pep, she must to put up with you," Luke said. "Remember guys, about pulling the most colossal joke in this century. Try to think of somethin, really good like in church. We could maybe dress like angels."

"I'd like to appear up high near the stained glass window behind the altar. It would be an ideal place, you know, on each side of the cross. Be a big joke on Father Paul. The congregation could see us, but he wouldn't. We'd be there for just a second and then vanish," Pepper, sleepily chortled.

"Yeah, but it probably would backfire like most of your jokes do," Benny said, his tone sarcastic. "Tell me, how in hell would we hide Rob's feet? We'll never find an angel outfit to fit us, especially Rob. He'd have more than three-feet of leg and feet sticking out. Picture this. One of the servers could be at the side of the altar when we appear, so he'd be able to see under our robes. And you know, Rob's shorts never fit right, so, his one-eyed willie would be hanging halfway down his leg, just like the ding-a-ling clapper on a bell." He snorted trying not to laugh. "We'd be the first angels ever documented that appeared in jockey shorts." His voice broke, strangling on a shout of uninhibited loud laughter.

They roared!

Their imaginations building hilarious scenarios, they continued to laugh. Benny started to hiccup, and Pepper snorted, causing another burst of laughter.

"Shut up," Benny gasped. "If I keep laughing, I'll have to get up and get a drink of water."

Emitting a soft chuckle every few minutes, Luke relaxed, listening to the soft sound of Benny's hiccups. Pepper's grunting as he turned over and the deep rhythmic exhalation of Rob's breathing was the last conscious thing he heard. He surrendered to his sleepy feelings and drifted with the tranquil sounds of the night.

They slept.

CHAPTER 20

LUKE WOKE AS Benny crawled from his sleeping bag, and opening his eyes, gazed sleepily at his dark surroundings. The sun hadn't appeared yet and the nighttime sky was still a dark gray. It was that in between time, no sun, no moon and no star shine.

Benny sat yawning on the end of his sleeping bag. He pulled on his boots and rose to his feet, his broad-shouldered frame a smudged outline in the darkness. Picking up a stick of wood, he pushed it into the ashes, stirring them until he had a layer of ash-colored coals. He laid several small pieces of wood on top.

"What's happinin, Ben?" Luke whispered, sitting up in his sleeping bag.

"Nothin," Benny answered. "Just had an urgent call to take a whizz and thought I'd start the fire. It's almost five. We've got a lot to accomplish today."

"I wish I could recapture the dream I was having," Luke murmured, scrubbing his face with his hands. "It was all about Debbie and it was a good one and getting better. I miss her." Picking up his backpack, Luke dragged it with him to the bottom of his sleeping bag.

Benny and Luke dressed quietly, emitting soft grunts and wide yawns. Grabbing their kits, they left for the creek.

Rob sat up and rubbed his eyes. Stretching his arms above his head, muscles bulged beneath his undershirt and a repetitious "Ah," was repeated a half-a-dozen times. Unzipping his sleeping bag, he crawled out of it, grabbed his clothes and started to dress.

Pepper moved, just a wiggling lump with nothing showing except the very top of his curly black head. Pulling the edge of the bag down, he exposed his eyes and watched Rob for a second. Eyelids heavy with sleep, he blinked several times and rubbed his drowsy face. Shoving the bag further down, he raised his arms and stretched. Groaning, an aggravated frustrated sound, he sat up. "Is everyone up, already?" he asked, his words sharply punctuated in a grievous tone.

"Yeah, let's get going, Pep, we've got a hell of a lot to accomplish today," Rob said. Shoving his foot into a wool sock, he pulled on his boots and quickly laced them. Pushing himself up, he stomped several times, forcing his feet into more comfortable positions inside them. "C'mon, let's go," he said.

Pepper scrambled, throwing his clothes on over his shivering body.

Rob stepped to the edge of the fire and inspected the water pot. Picking up a few chunks of wood, he shoved them on top of the burning logs, and walking back to his backpack, he grabbed his kit.

Pepper picked up his and they ran for the creek. Joining Benny and Luke, they stood along the shoreline and washed away the sleepiness from their faces. Their tall, muscular bodies bathed in dark shadows, stood out, like paper silhouettes against a backdrop of stark, leafless brush and stunted trees. Except for an occasional yell, as one of them splashed his face, and head with icy water, they were silent. Gathering up his things, Luke left for camp and the rest followed. Standing next to the fire, he stacked their cups and asked. "Any of you have a preference this morning, coffee or tea?"

"I'd like tea," Benny quickly answered. Luke, glancing at Rob and Pepper, raised his eyebrows.

"Tea's fine with me," Pepper and Rob said in unison. Smiling, they gave each other a high and low five. Laughing exuberantly, they went through the ritual and then, accepted a cup of tea from Luke. Sitting close to the fire they sipped the hot beverage and watched the sun paint the sky, in a decoupage of vibrant color.

The lake shadowed between its overhanging cliffs, sloshed a gentle riffling noise against the rocky shore. From far off the strident scolding of Blue Jays was broken by the distant call of a hawk. They grinned hap-

THE DEVILS PUNCHBOWL

pily at each other each time the hawk made its screeching call, and searched the sky, for its circling body. The scent of burning wood hovered in the air, its smoke a pleasant drifting odor, strong and pungent.

Luke tipped his cup draining the last drops of tea from its bottom. "I'm leaving now to get the paper," he said. He laughed aloud, the sound rippling through the camp. "I still can't believe we can teleport ourselves with this small instrument," he added, digging through his pockets for the tool. "Amazing." He laughed again, the sound one of triumph. "If Mom and Dad are still there, I'll have to wait. So don't worry if I don't get back in a flash. Save me some breakfast, I won't be long."

Luke's feet touched the ground beneath a Weeping Willow tree with a soft thud. Surprised at his skill in landing, he grinned happily at his own expertise. The presence of his tree house, a bulky shape loomed over his head, surrounded by leafy branches. He watched his house for a few seconds, and finding the light still on in the kitchen, knew his parents hadn't left yet. He wished they had been gone, it would have made everything so much easier.

Darting from bush to bush along the fence, Luke crept to the back of the house. Pulling the branches of a flowering shrub to one side, he worked himself into a space just below the open kitchen window.

His father burped and his spoon clattered against his bowl. Luke shook his head and grinned. Except for an occasional egg and milk gravy over biscuits, he had the same breakfast every day. It was always oatmeal.

Luke could barely hear the soft rustling sound made by the newspaper. His father suddenly laughed, and slapped the table, the sound sharp and distinct. His chair squealed as he sat back scraping the legs along the floor. All of a sudden he started to sing, his hands slapping the table in perfect rhythm with his words.

> How about those tummy gummers
> Ain't they dummies
> Have . . . n they're fun
> Gummin them tummies
> Gummin them haunches
> Out of their mind

Run around shoutin
It's tummy gummin time
How about them tummy gummers
Lurken in the yard
Waitin for a jelly belly
Gonna catchem off guard

Luke's mothers soft laughter joined with his fathers and the dogs started to bark. "Hush, you'll wake the neighbors," she admonished them, trying to be heard above their barking. "Max, Doodle, hush."

"You're as bad as I am, Lucas, with your tummy gummin song. Sometimes, I get one of those childhood verses we sang to Luke inside my head and I sing it all day long. Just yesterday, I kept thinking, I went to the toilet with my little tin truck, fell down the hole and the pigs ate me up. I just couldn't stop thinking it. Over and over it stuck like a leech inside my mind. I tried everything I could to shake it, even singing a gospel song, but it didn't work, the rhyme was there to stay. It actually became ludicrous after a while."

Silence! Luke peaked over a corner of the sill. Damn! They were kissing and Dad had his hand under his mother's robe. Frowning, he pressed his hand to his mouth and tried not to laugh. Nervous, he slid silently down the wall and sat on the ground. His mother laughed, a pleased sound. What in hell, were they doing!

"You should get dressed," his Dad said. "It's almost six, time to go." His mother's footsteps crossed the kitchen and she laughed softly again. The sound of running water, and then the dishwasher door squealed open and closed. The rustling of paper again and then the window slammed shut. The light in the kitchen went out.

Luke sat pressed against the wall, waiting. A door slammed and his father called. "Here Doodle, here Max." The car engine started and the automatic door opener whined and growled, raising the heavy garage door . . . and whined and growled again, as the door descended. The sound of the car's engine became muffled and gradually faded as they drove away.

THE DEVILS PUNCHBOWL

Luke thought of his room, and pressing the buttons on the tool, appeared instantly on the soft mattress of his bed. He lay back with a grunt, and resting for a second, his eyes skipped over the walls, passing over the sleek black shape of a stealth bomber against a blue-sky background, to the Skyhook prints above his computer. Beautiful prints of an old Army Caribou rescuing somebody. He sighed, his eyes wondering again, until the thought of the guys popped into his mind.

"Shit," he mumbled.

Walking quietly through the house, he found the paper folded on top of the trash container in the kitchen. Picking it up, he glanced at the refrigerator and, opening its door, pawed through its contents. Grabbing a half gallon of milk from its place on the shelf, he set it on the table. Hope Mom doesn't miss it, he thought. Choosing four large bananas from a fruit bowl, he opened the freezer door, picked up a package of frozen sausage, put it in the microwave and pressed the button to defrost.

Opening a cabinet door, he picked up a small kitchen scale and placed it on the counter. Unzipping his pocket, he pulled out the bar of gold and set it on the scale's tray. The arrow on its face bottomed out at the number sixteen. Sliding the gold bar back into his pocket, he opened the cabinet door and put the small scale back on the shelf.

Searching for a plastic grocery bag, he found one and stood tapping his chin waiting for the sausage. The microwave buzzed, and throwing the sausage in the bag with the milk and bananas, he placed the paper on top.

Pressing buttons on the tool, his shadowed image became visible on his sleeping bag and strengthening became solid. Rob sitting on the end of the bag rolled away from him, spilling his tea and jumping to his feet shouted. "Shit, there has to be some way of alerting everyone that you're going to appear. Swinging his hands, he waved them vigorously, shaking off the spilled tea. Wiping them on his pants, he picked up his cup. "Wow," he added with a grin. "My nerves are raw."

Pepper noticed the bag Luke was clutching, and walking around Rob, took it from him. Opening it, he chortled gleefully, throwing the newspaper on Luke's sleeping bag. "Hey everybody, we get a cup of real milk for breakfast. And sausage! And a banana for desert! We're having regular people food," he sang, happily.

Luke picked up the paper from his sleeping bag where Pepper had tossed it and rapidly scanned the front page. There was nothing about the appearance of anybody on it. There it was in large letters on the second page. . . .

Second Time This Week—A Case of Appearing and Disappearing Young Men. In Providence, Colorado, at the Wisdom Valley shopping mall, three young men appeared in the center of the skating rink. They appeared for about fifteen seconds, caused a panic and then vanished. In an interview with an eye witness, a Mr. Glenn Lester of Sunrise Heights, he said.

"I skated right through one of them. It was like they were made of smoke. They weren't real, I swear they were just images."

Most of the skaters and spectators could not give a description of them, accept to say they were young. Many of them thought they were angels visiting the earth. No one had a camera!

A few days ago, a similar incident happened in Sacramento at the El Dorado Hotel. A young man, and a bear, appeared at a fund raising dinner for the governor, caused a lot of havoc amongst the guests and then, the bear vanished.

"It's called unexplainable phenomena," one scientist exclaimed in an interview, "it's similar to raining fish, frogs, crop circles, and flying saucers. Phenomena, have occurred for centuries here on earth, and some of it, quite often, can't be rationally explained."

Tossing the paper to Rob, Luke flung himself on his sleeping bag. Laying back, he laughed heartily. "We beat that one," he yelled. "We beat it against phenomenal odds."

Benny strode from the campfire, and nudging Luke with his foot, handed him a dish filled with his breakfast. "We beat it, Luke. What a deal," he said, handing him a cup of milk. "Our luck held out."

Sitting in a close circle, they ate, enjoying every bite. Luke rose and striding to the fire set his empty plate on a nearby rock. Pouring himself a cup of tea, he grinned, his expression mirroring his happiness. "Anyone else," he asked holding the pot aloft.

THE DEVILS PUNCHBOWL

"Yeah, me," they all chorused.

Pouring for everyone, Luke set the pot back on the grill. Sitting on a small rock, he spread his legs out in front of him and sighed. "Did you make any plans while I was gone?"

"No, we didn't talk much, but the air was smoky with the heavy thinking we were doing," Benny said. He laughed boisterously. "I kept thinking about the mountain and then a picture of Lily would pop in there. Just the thought of her gives me pleasure."

Glancing at each other, Rob, Luke and Pepper laughed. "And how do thoughts of her give you pleasure," they chorused together.

Benny gurgled. "She makes me feel all gooey inside, like a cooked melting marshmallow," he answered. They bounced on him whacking him with their hats, until he yelled . . .

"Okay, okay, stop!"

Walking away, they left Benny in a curled position on his sleeping bag. "Shit," he yelled, raising his head and propping it up with his hand. "I like to laugh, it makes me feel really good."

"Yeah, it does," Rob retorted. "I always thought I had nerves of steel like Superman, but I guess I don't. The cavern has made my nerves raw. At times they feel like they turn into red-hot wires. When we met the alien in the spaceship, I felt absolute terror and I couldn't control it. The feeling got so bad, I almost climbed over you guys to punch his lights out. I'm not kiddin I almost did." He laughed, his face flushing a bright hue. "Rational, huh. Spooky really. I've never experienced feelins like what I had in the spaceship. It was almost as bad as my panic when I went through the ice chute. Talk about terror, you should have felt what I was feelin then. It's not describable!"

"Let's clean up," he said, suddenly. "And transport the gold. That really shouldn't take too, long." Twisting around, he looked over at Luke. "Hey, you forgot to look up the price of gold."

Luke rose and stepping to the sleeping bags picked up the discarded paper. "My mom's scale measures food in ounces and the bar was too heavy for it. When I put it on the platform it made the dial go to the bottom which is sixteen ounces. So, from that I surmised that it was heavier than a pound." Turning the pages, he looked for the selling price of gold on the stock market and looked up suddenly. "Remember, precious metals are weighed in troy weight, but this should give us a rough idea of what they're worth."

"My God," he exclaimed, crumbling the paper down against his waist. "You won't believe it, it's selling for three-hundred ninety two dollars an ounce. That means". . . looking into the distance sky, his lips moved as he calculated the numbers in his head. "Each bar, if it weighs a pound, would be worth more than six thousand dollars."

They roared.

"That can't be, Luke, too good to be true!" Rob exclaimed.

Pepper nodded in agreement and Benny yelled. "Yeah, that can't be true." They stared at him expectantly.

Shrugging, Luke touched his mouth and looking down his lips moved softly as he calculated the numbers. Raising his head, he stared at them. "It's true. Each bar, if it weighs sixteen ounces, will be worth six thousand two hundred seventy two dollars."

Whooping, jumping and stomping they laughed, and slapped each others back. Excitement and elation grew into an exhibition of nervous energy and they howled their pleasure.

"Hey, let's get going, I can hardly wait until we have the gold stored in Luke's closet," Pepper said. "I can't believe it, this is too good to be true, I must be dreamin."

Rob stood and begin gathering up their dishes. "Let's hurry, and we won't pack a lunch, we'll eat here after we move the gold."

Making short work of the camp cleanup, they emptied the contents of their backpacks into their sleeping bags and zipped them closed. Slinging the backpacks over their shoulders, they pressed the buttons on their tools and appeared beside the robot and his machine on the lake bed.

"How many bars do you think our backpacks will hold?" Benny asked.

"Try for thirty, or thirty-five," Luke suggested. "That means two trips for each of us."

Most of the gold bars were easily found, and stacking them in piles of twenty bars each, they grinned happily at each other as they searched.

THE DEVILS PUNCHBOWL

They soon had twelve individual piles stacked unevenly over the bed of the ancient underground river.

"How are we going to do this," Benny asked?

"Picture my room first, and at the bottom of my bed, the red and blue rug," Luke answered. "Land there. My first trip, I'll clear the end of my closet and grab some paper bags from the kitchen." Picking up his backpack by the straps, he placed one of them over his shoulder, and pressed buttons on the tool.

Waiting a few minutes, each of them followed until they were standing in the bedroom. Luke was inside his closet, tossing things out into the room. "I've already got paper bags from the kitchen, empty your backpacks," he called out, sticking his head out around the edge of the door. Backing out, he grabbed his and stacked the gold bars in a paper bag. Lifting it, he placed it against the back wall of his closet.

By the time they had made their second trip, they were grumbling, and watching Rob drop the last gold bar into a paper bag, they gave a collective sigh of relief when he finished.

Luke quickly shoved his things back into the closet, covering the top of the bags with an old jacket to hide them. Stacking his comic book collection on top and old games in front of the paper bags, he wiped the sweat from his face. Closing the closet door, he smiled, and strode to the door. "I've got to get the broom, my Mom will notice this much dirt and sand." Returning with it, he lifted the round rug and shook it. Sweeping the dirt and sand under his bed, he replaced the throw rug on the floor. Grinning, they stood in the door and looked at the room.

"Look the same to you, Luke?" Benny asked.

"Yeah," Luke replied. "I don't see any difference." Entering the room, he pulled his bedspread a little tighter on his bed and rubbing his hand over it, smoothed out the wrinkles. Walking to the doorway, he glanced back at the room. "Looks the same to me, no one will ever know, not even my eagle eyed, mom. We pulled it off so far, let's hope it goes as good in a couple of weeks."

"I'm hungry," Benny stated, wiping his face on the sleeve of his shirt. Grimacing, he laughed, a small shaky sound. Glancing at his watch, he grunted sharply, an amazed expression flashing across his face. "I'm not just hungry, I'm starved, and it's only ten. What about a pizza? Do we dare?"

"Pizza sounds good, but where would you appear," Luke replied. "It's daylight and there's always someone around. I don't think we should risk it. Maybe tonight, one of us could teleport near the Pizza Parlor, but no matter where we appear, there's always a risk we'll be seen."

Standing together in the hall they thought about pizza, until Pepper threw his hands in the air in frustrated exasperation. "Okay, that's out. Luke, let's look in your Mom's freezer, maybe she has something we could eat that won't be missed."

Following Luke, they traipsed through the silent house to the kitchen. He opened the freezer and in resignation shrugged his shoulders. "Nothing," he said. "I'll look in the freezer in the garage." Treading on his heels, they followed him to the garage.

"Uh-huh," Pepper exclaimed. "Neat and sweet, we struck the mother lode." Grabbing four packages of pocket sandwiches filled with beef, cheese and rice, he headed for the kitchen. Putting one in the microwave, he waited.

The microwave buzzed and Pepper handed the first package to Benny. Going through the cooking in record time, they sat at the table gobbling sandwiches and drinking Pepsi's. Gathering papers, napkins and discarded boxes, Pepper shoved them into his backpack. "We can't leave any evidence here," he quipped, sending each of them a humorous look.

Luke carried the cans to the garage, threw them in the recycle-bin and replaced the broom. Stepping back through the garage door into the kitchen, he locked the door. Benny wiped the table and placed the chairs around it.

Glancing around the kitchen, Luke sniffed the air. Everything looks okay, he thought, but there's still a heavy smell of spicy beef and cheese in the air. Crossing the room, he opened the cabinet beneath the sink and picking up a can, liberally sprayed the kitchen with scented-deodorizer. "Let's go," he said, bending to replace the can in the cabinet. He waited, watching as his friends pressed buttons and were teleported. Casting one more glance at the kitchen, he sniffed at the floral scent of

THE DEVILS PUNCHBOWL

deodorizer, and deciding there wasn't a trace of spicy beef odor left in the kitchen, keyed the tool's buttons.

The soft hissing noise of the refrigerator and the clicking sounds made by the clock, as its hands measured their movement around its face were hollow, brittle noises in the quiet, empty room. The misty sweet odor of deodorizer faded rapidly.

CHAPTER 21

A FAINT OUTLINE of Luke appeared against the white boulder and Benny, stuffing his clothes in his backpack, twisted his head toward his image. He grinned, waiting for Luke to materialize.

Rob and Pepper finished with their backpacks and stepping to the fire poured water into cups. Spooning in instant coffee they stirred vigorously, and handed a cup, to Benny and Luke. Luke placed his on the ground and quietly packed his things into his backpack. Blowing a breath out noisily, he picked up his cup and settled near the fire.

Resting quietly they blew on the hot liquid, sipping cautiously. Riffling trees and brush into a frenzied clatter, a cold wind gusted through the bowl-like setting. Smoke from the fire billowed, and the capricious wind, forced it to spiral erratically in different directions through the camp.

Finishing his coffee, Benny lay back on his bed-roll. Sighing, he raised his arms and covered his face with them. "What's next?" he mumbled.

Rob threw the dregs from his cup on the ground, leaving a dark wet streak between his feet. Leaning forward, he propped his elbows on his knees and supporting his head with one hand, he stared at Benny. "We don't have much time, so I suggest we block the tunnels. We should get as much done today as we can. Tomorrow we'll inspect the cavern again and leave. I'd like to leave early tomorrow."

"Me too," Benny said. Sitting up, he laced his fingers together and stretching his arms out, rolled his shoulders forward. "Let's do the tunnel first. It'll be easier than the fissure."

THE DEVILS PUNCHBOWL

Climbing to his feet, Benny nudged Luke with his foot. "C'mon, let's finish this," he added grumpily. "Besides being nervous as hell all the time and frightened almost to the point of dying, now we have to work like dogs to cover the entrances into the cavern."

"Yeah, we know you're one of those lucky farts," Luke said sarcastically. "Privileged! No lawns to mow, no stacking or chopping wood. You and Pepper have never cleaned your rooms. I really feel sorry for you guys." Rising to his feet, Luke stood beside Benny and softly hit him with his cap.

"Let's go," Benny said, digging in his pocket for the alien tool. Walking away from Luke, he turned and stared at him. He started to speak and then turned away, his eyes darkening to a mottled jade green. Turning back, a note of resentment entered his voice, and he spoke in a clear, concise and controlled manner.

"I can't speak for Pepper, Luke, but I've done enough lawn mowing to last me a lifetime. I've mowed more lawns than you have. If you remember right, I did it for years to earn extra money when I wanted something."

"My folks, even though they have a lot, never buy much for Ruth or me. Ruth, baby-sits for her extra money. In lots of material ways, especially in toys, you had a better childhood than I did. Talk about privileged, your parents gave you most of the things you wanted. You're the one that's privileged, asshole. You didn't have to work for anything. You know . . ." Benny stopped speaking, a surprised flush stained his face. "Ah shit," he muttered. "Sometimes you're an asshole, Luke. A big puckery red one. Picture it. I'm leaving. I'll be at the small cave." Picking up two camp shovels, he threw his hard hat on his head.

They stared at the raw emotion expressed on his face. His anger and stiff body language, didn't portray the gentle Benny they all knew. Disturbed, they glanced at each other, and then, back to his disappearing body.

"I don't know why you said that. You must be jealous because I don't have many chores. Remember, I've had five sisters and a granny who do everything in my house. Benny's right though," Pepper said, giving Luke a wry glance. "His folks live frugal lives and other than music lessons, Benny hasn't had many extras. I think you should apologize. What you said was uncalled for and you sounded jealous. Asshole, Luke, or maybe some asshole's wipe. Take your pick." Giving Luke, a disparaging sideways glance from the corner of his eye, he turned and looked at Rob. "I'm leaving," he added shrugging his shoulders. Standing rigidly, his body language one of condemnation, Pepper softly pressed the buttons on the tool.

Rob sighed, and casting Luke a disparaging look, he stared at him. His forehead wrinkling in a scowl, his silence was eloquent in its criticism. "Kiss my rosy red ass, Luke, but what you just said wasn't called for," Rob stated emphatically. "Why would you say something like that? What in hell's wrong? I agree with Pepper, you should apologize."

"I don't know why I said it," Luke said peevishly. "Besides I don't think what I said was that bad. Do you?" His face wrinkled in remorse. "Maybe, it's all that's happened lately, exploring the cavern, my run in Sacramento, being shot at. Some weird things happened to me after Pepper doused me good with the alien's tool. For a while, I was somehow separated from the real world. I even saw cracks in the air. I think, I was in a lost space, sorta in between here and another place. I'd call it another dimension, but I don't really know where I was. I've used the tool many times since and I've never got the same results as then."

He sighed heavily, blowing out a steady stream of air. "I don't know why they took such offense? Maybe it's because our nerves are raw. I have the oddest feeling inside me. Maybe its just exploring the cavern," he repeated. "Haven't you felt it?" He watched Rob, dread mixed with discerning perception lighting up his eyes. "I guess my words came out wrong. I didn't mean anything by them."

Rob sighed again, and frustrated, shook his head. "No, your words weren't that bad. I've said and heard worse from all of you, but for some reason they took offense this time. Maybe it's like you said, has to be the cavern making our nerves raw? Half the time my stress is so bad, I feel like I should take off and run a hundred miles. I get that panicky feeling of fight or flight." He laughed ruefully, irony laced through the sound.

Luke shrugged and, shaking his head in derision, put his hand in his pocket and pulled out the alien's tool. "We better get going," he said, pressing the buttons.

Rising to his feet, Rob picked up two logs. Standing for a second with his head thrown back, his eyes skimmed the closest ridge of mountains. Stepping to the fire, he stirred the coals with the end of a log, causing a cloud of acrid white smoke to billow around him. Pulling the tool from an inside pocket in his jacket, he thought of the small cave and pressed buttons.

Luke felt beads of perspiration form on his forehead. He pushed harder on the large rock, trying to shove it from its rounded indentation in the floor of the cave. It rolled slightly, and he thought, I've almost got it. Shoving on it again, it moved a fraction of an inch toward the entrance to the black marbled-lined tunnel. Benny rushed over to help him and Luke paused. "I'm sorry for saying what I did. Somehow, my words came out wrong, and you guys took offense."

Benny grinned. "Apology accepted, and I apologize, too. Half the time I feel like my nerves are eating through my skin. And I can't tell you why I feel that bad. I knew when you said it, it wasn't anything to get mad about, but I let myself get mad anyway. Shit happens! Let's move some of these damn rocks. His eyes rounded and danced in the lights cast from their hard hats. "After all, with the amount of gold we put in your closet today our wealth is about even. And . . . you know, just because my folks have a lot of money doesn't mean I do."

Grunting and groaning, they wrestled the rock across the cave, until it rested against the pile of debris. Rob fell to his knees to help, and adding his puffing and blowing to theirs, they pushed the large rock until it was on the top of the heap. There it sat like a great king, its smaller subjects, rocks and debris strewn around it in a great pile. Breathing hard, they sucked in each breath, their face's sweaty and red with exertion. Glancing at each other, they laughed exuberantly.

"Hard work, moving rocks," Pepper said. He made a face that narrowed his eyes and pulling his mouth into a circle, blew noisily. "I think we're finished in here," he stated, examining the pile of rocks and dirt. Groaning, he rose to his feet and stepping to his left picked up a shovel.

"Yeah, I think it's enough," Rob exclaimed. "We don't want to cover it so heavily that in an emergency, we couldn't push the small rocks away from the opening to the tunnel. Let's get the fissure into the mountain blocked, so we'll be finished with this heavy shit." Wiping his forehead, he fished in his pocket for the alien's tool, and picking up his jacket, pressed buttons, and left. The others followed.

Luke appeared the furthest from the fissured entrance into the mountain. He landed on a small prickly evergreen, and forcing it against the ground, he tripped on one of the tree's small branches, stumbled and fell. Rolling on the ground his elbow hit a rock, and clutching it with a large hand, he swore under his breath. Sitting up, he swore again, creating a visual picture, in a furious, torrential deluge of descriptive and rude words. Relieved of some of his built up tension, he sat quietly holding his elbow. The boys laughed and turning away tried to hide it.

"We're laughing with you not at you," Benny chirped, staring at Luke's sullen face. "You're not very appealing." His face broke out in another huge grin. "Deb should see the expression on your face right now. Wow, she'd probably run."

Turning his back, Benny slipped his jacket off and picked up his shovel. He started to dig, pitching dirt and small rocks around the fissure with each shovelful.

"Hey guys, I've just thought of something. Why in hell didn't we use the robot's tool to move some of these rocks?" Pepper asked.

Rob groaned. "Why in hell didn't you think of it sooner?" Digging through his pockets, he searched for the alien's tool.

Using the tool to levitate large rocks, they placed them in a loose circle three-feet from the entrance into the mountain. And to give their pile an authenticity of a landslide, they packed a bulky mass of dead brush over the fissure and between the biggest rocks. Standing back, they admired what they had done. The fissure was gone. It resembled just another large pile of rocks and brush that had slid from the top of the mountain.

THE DEVILS PUNCHBOWL

"Move, Pepper, you're in the way," Benny shouted. Watching the huge rock float through the air as if it was a feather, he lowered it on top of the pile. "That's the last one."

Luke sat with his back against a small tree and taking off his hard hat, laid it on the ground. Wiping the sweat from his forehead, he rubbed the wetness off on his Levis and raising his arm mopped his face with his sleeve. "I'm tired. Should we exchange our tools now, or wait until tomorrow?" he asked.

"Uh-huh," Rob grunted. "We should do it now. Our luck's going to run out. I'm surprised we've had the lake to ourselves this long. Let's go. Meet you in the spaceship and don't be long, I don't want to be alone in there. The thought scares me, shitless, what if I met a booger?" Grinning a little lopsidedly, he laughed aloud and pressed buttons.

Pepper and Benny both groaned when they stood. "I'm so sore, I think a lot of hot water and a soak in a bathtub would help my aching body," Pepper said. Laughing together, they pressed buttons, vanishing as they were teleported to the spaceship.

Luke listened to the sounds of the small protected valley. Taking time to rest for a moment, his mind wondered. Broken only by the occasional rustle of dry brush, and the faint, calling treble of some far-off bird, most of it was silent. The Siskiyou Mountain wilderness area was awesome. Sitting quietly, he surveyed his surroundings, relishing the quiet hush of nature at its best, naked and raw. He didn't move, his mind registering each separate noise in the quiet setting.

Examining his apprehension, he tried to analyze his nervous feelings. They had been a constant source of his irritability and, something he couldn't define, was sitting on the edge of his consciousness. And it had been there ever since they had started to explore the cavern. He always had a spooky feeling in his gut that he should look behind him. It never let up. Sometimes the feeling was so formidable, he could feel it growing inside him, a black lump of something he couldn't shake. Even thinking about it, made the hair rise on the back of his neck. Picking up his hard hat from the ground, he grimaced as his nerves puckered his skin, sending small scrapings along his body. Pushing his fingers through his hair, he placed his hard hat on his head, and dragging the tool from his pocket, keyed the buttons on the tool.

Appearing in the round hall, Luke's feet settled quietly against the floor. He smiled, pleased with his landing.

"We've already got our new tools," Pepper said, throwing his hand out to point at the cabinet. "We piled ours until you pick out two new ones. We didn't want you to pick up any of our used ones."

Crouched down on one knee in front of the cabinet, Rob examined the items stored on a bottom shelf. Crossing the hall, Luke stood above him.

"These are really weird," Rob said. Holding up an instrument, he tilted his head and looked up at him. "I can't imagine what they could be used for. Looks like a salad fork with elongated spears on the end. Must be quite a machine?" He grimaced, his frustration showing in his expression, and laid the odd tool carefully back on the shelf. "These are the shelves we took the tools from." Raising his arm, he touched two of them with his fingers several feet above his head.

Laying his tools on the used pile, Luke chose two new ones. Slipping them in his jacket pocket, he zipped it closed. Picking up the tools they had used, he laid each of them in its cradle.

"Are we out of here, or what?" he asked. He grinned to himself, Rob was laying flat on the floor with his head completely inside the bottom shelf, rummaging.

The lights in the small hall dimmed.

And then brightened. Raising their heads, the boys watched the ceiling.

Rob squirmed backward, and jerking his head from inside the cabinet, rapped it hard on the edge of the shelf. He muttered curses under his breath and raising his hand rubbed the back of his head. Pulling himself to his knees, he picked up his hard hat and watched the ceiling. The lights dimmed again. Fluctuating from bright to dim several times, they faded to a faint glow.

And went out.

The boys gasped, the sound blending as each sucked in an audible breath. Hearts starting an erratic thump against their ribs, they held

THE DEVILS PUNCHBOWL

their breath for several seconds, and listening intently, strained to see the door openings in the dark hall. There wasn't a noise, only dead, numbing silence came out of the totally black space that surrounded them. Embellishing the total darkness, it crushed their senses, and involuntarily, they stepped back against the wall. Their breathing quickened to a whistling noisy inhalation and exhalation, and standing perfectly still, they watched the darkness.

Rising to his feet, Rob's boots scraped the floor, his breath, a sucking, noisy rasp, and raising his hand, he pressed the light button on his hard hat. Moving restlessly, they stared at the small round hall.

In the doorway to the weird corridor that went nowhere, subtly moving shadows formed. A darker shadow, almost indistinguishable from ones caused by the gloomy darkness, churned in a shifting pattern of rotating vapor in the open door. Billowing inward, its undefined edges hovered, vague and fuzzy within a darker mass, and meshing, became part of the ship's wall. Deep, within layered stacks of moving clouds an opening formed, a void, a black hole so deep it seemed to have no end.

Luke stared in disbelief. He didn't blink. "Psst, look at that," he whispered. "Look at the door to the weird passage, it's moving."

They stared, straining to see through the moving mist into the weird passage. The door and surrounding wall darkened again, its deceptive twisting edges, indistinct. Illusionary. Murky.

For an instant, a sliver of light flickered along the edges of shifting, moving clouds of darkness and then, it vanished. The boys froze against the cabinet, seduced by a growing fear into watching the moving mass.

"Look at that, the doorway's frigin gone," Rob whispered.

"Vanished," Benny retorted. "It's moving, see it!"

Swirling grey mist choked the opening. Dissolving as quickly as it had formed, the vapor softened, disappearing into the darker reaches of the pitchblack void. Deep and black, a split appeared within the void one big enough they could step into, like Alice did through the looking glass.

Rob's light on his helmet dimmed, and fading into a soft mushroom glow, it brightened and then gradually faded.

It went out.

Breathing in audible bursts, they listened, straining to hear what was happening. There wasn't a spark of light, and bending from their waists, they strained to see. "I'm going to turn my light on," Luke whispered. The resonance of his voice, hollow and empty, hissed through the vacuum-like silence. He reached for his hard hat as Rob grabbed his arm.

"No, don't," Rob said harshly. "I think something sucked all the energy out of mine. Save yours. We might need it later."

They strained again to see into the impenetrable deep black, and shuffling their feet in nervous apprehension, they listened for any distinguishable sound. It was as if they had been swallowed by a bottomless abyss, a hole so deep they were immersed in it. The density of the air in the hall changed, the pressure against their bodies intensifying. Heavy. Oppressing. Pressed back against the cabinet they waited, watching and listening for a whisper of sound or a hint of light. They didn't move.

Wrapped in a claustrophobic blanket of suffocating black, a thickening shroud of paralyzing terror enveloped their minds. They waited, their burgeoning senses, both physically and mentally, acutely aware of every shift in the atmosphere of the hall. Panic seethed through their bodies, scouring their skin with a hundred needle-like pricks as goose bumps rose and danced along it.

A numbing vacuum of silence filled the hall, a quiet, so intense and turbulent, it heightened their anxiety into a palatable sense. Luke could smell their fear, and his thoughts tangled, meshing into a rolling mass of snakelike hysteria. "Somehow, we've got to get out of here," he whispered. Instinct told him to run. "Something's about to happen and it can't be good. I feel it."

Again, they went still, straining to hear and see.

Intensified by the uncanny quiet and impenetrable darkness, the rasp of their breathing, filled the hall. The sound, roaring in their ears, spliced the earsplitting silence into sharp edged pieces, and rang in their heads, like the words from a lead vocalist at a hard rock concert. Tension sharp as knifes, scraped their skin, and fear ran a rampant rampage through their bodies. Immersed in a terror that held them enthralled in a numbing grip, they stirred involuntarily as a cold sweat popped out along their skin.

Pepper grunted a low sound of distress, moving his feet in a nervous skirmish. "I'm leavin," he muttered.

"I wish, but we can't," Luke whispered. "You can't see which buttons to push. What if you pushed the wrong ones? Maybe we could go through the hole in the floor, but it's so dark, I can't even see it. The lights must have gone out everywhere, even in the cavern."

Luke's words hung in the air, tangible and heavy as lead weights, they caused a surge of dread to flow through them, silencing any response to his words. Breathing shallowly, their heads swinging to search every area in the dark hall, they stood stiff and straight as ramrods.

Pepper grunted another low mutter just under his breath, and Benny's breathing, accelerated. He wheezed, his exhalation of air whistling through his mouth.

A rustling, humming noise came from their left and their heads swung toward the weird corridor. A rosy glow of light, pale and indistinct, quivered along the edges of a nebulous rolling mass. It shattered the complete blackness of the dark hall, and the space where the door and wall had been grew, opening into a spinning, circular void that was ink black and empty.

From deep within the hollow sphere small blue-white stars blossomed. Beautiful for an instant against the billowing darkness of the void, they exploded, bursting, into brilliant streaks of arcing light. Gradually, they became layers of flashing brilliance, moving inside an immense, cluster of black clouds. Immediately, another one formed creating a continual design of pale exploding light.

Forming at the very edge of circling darkness, a split appeared. Brilliantly lit, it expanded rapidly, its edges becoming a circle of energized light, and within it wiggling, dark shapes became visible. Solidifying, they became dark, vivid silhouettes. A manifestation of something recognizable. Aliens, four of them stepped from the pulsing light. They glowed in a halo of shimmering brightness, and the radiating circle behind them, darkened along its ragged edges. They were magnificent in every detail, and each of them held a small, perfectly round crystal as bright as a small sun.

The split they had stepped through, moved, and growing larger, it formed within the confines of the darker black void, a lighted, smoky-grey outline. A dry cold penetrated the small hall, a leeching kind of cold, sweeping over everything. Like cold empty space, Luke thought, and trembling, the overwhelming urge to take a whiz was suddenly acute. He gasped, sucking in a gulp of air, so huge, it made him dizzy.

The aliens gestured and, stepping forward, spoke as a unit, their dialect strange and foreign. Each word was carefully enunciated, the syllables measured with exactly the right pitch sounded like a practiced speech. Blank expressions covered their faces and their staring eyes gleamed with fixed intent. They're going to get us, Luke thought, even though they don't seem to be hostile and they clearly want something.

"Perhaps they're feeling exasperation that we found their space-ship, or maybe they're questioning why we're here inside of it," he whispered. To emphasize his words, he squeezed the elbows he was clutching. "Maybe they're just plain mad."

The atmosphere in the hall changed. Air swirled around them and deadening became oppressive and heavy. It pressed against them until they were encased in a pocket of isolation. Luke felt the bubble form. The air stilled, giving rise to a feeling of hollow emptiness, and a thick pressure pressed them back against the wall. Swelling, it grew unbearable until an audible rush of air forced its way through the tiny hall and shattering, popped their ears. Involuntarily, a soft squeal escaped Benny's lips, and raising his hands, he covered his ears, pressing them against the sides of his head.

Abruptly, a raw elemental substance flowed from the void in a deluge of pale waves they could see. They gasped, as small streaks of energized light danced over their clothes and skin, leaving behind minute feelings of being burnt in a hundred places.

Brilliant light immersed in dark billowing shapes, churned within the void, and for an instant, small red slivers of arcing light escaped into the hall. Exploding, they left behind the nauseous odor of ozone.

THE DEVILS PUNCHBOWL

Rustling, as if released by a great pressure, an eerie howling burst through the small space. The split shifted and bending within the confines of the larger void, it spun in a series of multiple contortions, compressing itself into a tighter sphere.

The aliens stood in a straight line, their expression's intent and focused on the boys. A shadow like a wayward thought crossed the first alien's face. He spoke. The other three aliens, leaning forward slightly, so they could see his face, listened avidly to his words for a few seconds, and then, turning their heads, watched the boys.

Rob hunched his shoulders and pulled his neck further into his chest. His hands formed huge fists and the ligaments in his throat stood out like thick ropes. A numbing paralysis took over his body. Releasing his breath, he lowered his shoulders, relieving the pent up panic through his mouth. Sucking in another huge breath of air, he let it go softly past his lips.

The hall became oppressively still. Stirring, the air built into a pressure of rushing, whooshing rattling, as if it was being sucked through a small hole. The sphere spun, forming a dark funnel-shaped tunnel behind the aliens, and at its narrowest end, a spark of light blazed in the distance. Where the aliens stood at the largest end of the funnel, the lighted edges flickered, moving rapidly in a circle. The funnel darkened, the light at its smallest end intensifying. It opened wider and for several seconds, they watched an odd orange-purple light form in the narrow end of the funnel.

Benny digging his fingers into Luke's arm, nodded at the strange light. Brightening, the dark funnel spun clockwise, the whorls of its circling pattern a darker black, as it moved at a dizzying speed within the confines of the void. It reminded Luke of a tornado laid down on its side.

"I think they're images, similar to what we were, when we used that mind machine on the bridge," Rob whispered. "They're like a hologram, a three-dimensional figure right out of some other world or dimension. I have no idea if they can hurt us, so be careful what you're doing." Rob continued to whisper his voice a harsh monologue.

"Hold your hands up. Palms out. Pepper, you've got a death grip on my shoulder, let go, you're hurting me," he said urgently.

Pepper pressed himself against the cabinet. Panic and suppressed fear narrowed the features of his face into a mask. They stood huddled against the tool cabinet and wall, trying to make their bodies smaller and insignificant. Another rush of adrenaline accelerated their breathing and sucking each breath as if it was their last, they reluctantly raised their hands shoulder high.

An ethereal glow emanated from the aliens covering them in a blanket of luminance, a faint glowing light. Their features had a similar and perfect symmetry, as if they had been born from the same linage. They wore shirts and form fitting pants tucked into a sock-like boot. All of their uniform was tinted in soft phosphoresce greens, and except for the size of their eyes, they looked very human.

Their expressive eyes were different.

Calculating.

Commanding.

They mesmerized, and made the alien's faces appear out of sync, giving them an unearthly presence. Well-defined eyebrows arched on broad smooth foreheads and long dark lashes lined their eyelids. The huge, staring eyes revealed an anxious, hollow-emptiness and with dilated shining pupils they expressed a strange apprehensive intelligence.

The first alien in line was blond, his hair cut off just below his ears. He spoke more than the others and seemed to be their leader. The other three aliens, standing slightly behind him had variations of curly, light and dark-brown hair, and it was cut to fit their scalp like a glove.

Gesturing, the aliens looked at each other as if questioning each other's actions. Speaking, they gestured toward the leader, and turning back to stare at the boys, their mouths opened in wide beguiling smiles. Turning slightly, they made a sweeping motion toward the funnel-shaped-tunnel behind them. They waited.

Suddenly the leader spoke again, and copying the boys, they raised one of their arms, holding the hand palm out, toward them. The other hand, held close to their bodies, clutched the sun-like crystal. The size

THE DEVILS PUNCHBOWL

of Rob's hands would have made two of theirs, but they did have four fingers and a thumb, like the one they had examined on the third level of the spaceship.

The aliens and the boys stared at each other with their hands in the air. Silent, they stood perfectly still, warily watching each other.

It was a standoff. An impasse.

No one spoke!

"I'm out of here, I can't take anymore," Pepper whispered through stiff lips. "I can see the buttons now, so I'm warning you get your tool's out . . ."

"I'm leavin. My minds tripping, I'm spaced out bonkers."

Luke, cautiously lowering his hand, unzipped his jacket pocket. The alien's watched Luke's movements, their eyes focused intently on his hands. Pulling the tool from his pocket, he palmed it, and holding it tight against his chest, surreptitiously flicked his eyes at it to be sure it was the right one. Glancing at Rob, Benny and Pepper, he saw, they too, had palmed the tool, and the fingers of their other hand, hovered over it.

The alien's lowered their arm, and palm up, they held out their hand. It was a movement of supplication. Entreaty. They stepped forward and spoke simultaneously. The tone of their voices crackled oddly, their words intense in their ferocity. Air swirled again through the circular hall and a supple pressure pushed them lightly against the wall. The funnel-shaped circle, behind the speaking aliens, dimmed, its lighted edge blending with the darker void.

They sure as hell want something from us, Luke thought. The grating rasp of their voices scraped along his taut nerves, raising the hair on his neck and scalp. He listened, an awareness sweeping over him, something, he couldn't quite grasp. His features tightened and a dark smudge crawled inside his mind. A hot tenacious web of heat followed, and insidiously, with light digs and jolts spread over the surface of his brain.

"They're doing something to my mind," Luke shouted, the intensity of his voice sending a shrieking sound through the hall.

Gesturing apprehensively, their expressions changing to startled surprise, the aliens stepped backward, closer to the black spinning funnel behind them. The alien at the end of the line, suddenly screamed, his foot caught in a cloudy, moving mass of intense darkness. Slipping further, as if he had stepped into a deep hole, the thick, dark mass, flowed over him. Amidst shouts of extreme anguish, his image faded, and he vanished in a flash of shifting, brilliant light.

Stepping backward again, toward the funnel, a spasm of fear flashed across the alien's faces. Wearing an expression of horror, the leader stopped, and speaking harshly, a short and emphatic speech, waved his hand in a chopping gesture. Hesitating, their eyes intent on the boys, they resolutely stepped forward again. Behind them, the circling lighted edge of the funnel, spun, and growing larger, moved closer to the aliens.

The boys, horrified at what they had seen, screamed and stepping further away, huddled against the wall. Blinking several times, Luke stared at the aliens and tried to control the surge of wild panic that tried to engulf him. He trembled unconsciously, horrified at the signals his brain was trying to deliver to the rest of his body.

"I'm leaving, press your buttons."

"C'mon! Let's go."

They winked out.

CHAPTER 22

APPEARING ON THEIR sleeping bags, the boys fell to their knees, sprawling awkwardly on their stomachs. A tidal wave of disbelief went through Luke's mind, and his muscles, felt like they had been glued to his bones. Sitting up, he stared at his surroundings with an unseeing gaze, his ability to analyze, he thought, was impaired. He had absolutely lost his cool somewhere. It was gone. Plopping backward, he covered his face with his arm and sucking in a deep breath blew it out, expelling the air from his lungs. "That alien sounded like he was in agony when he stepped into that mass of moving darkness. I think he was killed," he yelled.

"Jesus, I don't know. He did sound, as if he was in terrible pain and I really thought they were just images," Rob said. Horrified, they stared at each other.

"Yeah, they were really trying to get into my mind," Benny volunteered. His voice, a husky, strained muttering sound, shook. "I could feel it like a web of coldness and then it turned hot. They really want to contact us. I wouldn't mind talking to them, if we could be assured that they wouldn't hurt us."

"We'll never understand them, their language is all grunts and high pitches," Rob said. "I didn't recognize one syllable that sounded the least bit familiar. He laughed, the sound mixed with fearful wonder, ironic, without even a touch of mirth. "No wonder we don't recognize it, it's alien." Rubbing his hands over his face, he mumbled. "We can't trust them, they're technology is beyond us. No tellin what they can do. And just meeting them scares the shit out of me. It's not dark enough yet for a trip to the Pizza Parlor. We'll have to wait awhile," he added, staring at the sky. Let's clean up and instead of just one of us going for pizza, let's all go."

Cleaning up they traipsed back to camp, introspective and quiet. Luke put three logs on the fire, and as they started to burn, stared in mesmerized silence at the spiraling black column of smoke. Sitting close, they watched the flickering flames and quietly meditating, brooded over their problems, until the sky darkened to a hazy dark grey.

"Remember," Rob stated, slinging on his jacket. "I think the best place for us to land is behind that greenish-gray building that was a pasta house. It just closed. It's a good place to appear, because it's just across the street from the Pizza Parlor. Make sure you pick the back of the building." Using their tools, they pressed buttons and gradually diminishing into dark shadows, their vanishing bodies were pulled into the night sky.

Luke landed in a garbage Dumpster. Splitting upon contact with his body, the bags of garbage, with an expulsion of whooshing air, spewed their contents over him. Sinking further into oozing bags, he raised his arm and grasping the edge of the Dumpster tried to pull himself over its rim. His hand slipped on the metal and he fell back, sinking deeper in the soft sacks as if they were a feather bed. Immersed in slimy black plastic, he desperately pushed on the bags, his hands slipping through holes torn in their sides encountered another mass of wet ooze. The stench of decaying food gagged him, and pushing with his feet, he tried to roll against the side of the Dumpster.

Rob with a solid whop landed feet first, in an empty garbage can. Listing like a schooner in full sail, he raised his arms, and in a frenzied motion, swung them around like windmills. Trying to stay upright, his body weight pulled him backward and, he toppled like an axed tree.

Whump.

Upsetting containers around him in a banging, clattering din, he fell amongst rotten food, papers and cans. Tripping over his feet in his haste to stand, he pushed the offending garbage cans angrily away from him. The can's rolled in another teeth-clenching burst of noise, and rattling and banging together, they crashed against the wall of the build-

THE DEVILS PUNCHBOWL

ing. Trying to rise, without immersing himself in the offal surrounding him, he fell again slipping in the putrid slime of decaying food.

Pepper and Benny landed in the swampy ground near Elk Creek. Landing on their feet, their boots sank six inches into soft mushy ground, and plopping backward they fell on their backs into wet black slime. The slime, smelling of rotten, fishy ocean water, stuck in large, runny, black patches to their clothes.

They cursed!

Benny's voice, a soft lament, was lyrical in his choice of German curse words. The words, spoken from a voice beautifully endowed, burst from him in a soliloquy of musical precision.

Pepper voiced his disgust the loudest, his chosen words a mixture of English, Irish dialect and Mexican.

Rob whispered his curse words in two languages. The guttural sounds of a Slavic German dialect and the softer tones of English. His enunciation was clear and concise.

Luke threw his booted foot over the edge of the Dumpster and pulled himself by sheer muscular force from the wet ooze. Wiping his hands on his pants, he felt something crawling on his face and wiping it with the sleeve of his jacket smeared rotten food over his cheek.

The stink rose around him and he gagged, his throat closing painfully. He cursed again, his voice stilted with rage. Walking to a spigot on the wall, he opened it, letting the water flow over his hands. Cupping one hand, he filled it and rubbed it over his sleeves. Kneeling, he shoved his head under the running water and vigorously rubbed his face, neck and hair. Rising to his feet, he stripped his jacket off and splashed water over it. Shaking it several times, he showered the air, with bits and pieces of pasta and rotten food.

He cursed again.

Rob wiped linguine and spaghetti from his Levi clad legs. Grimacing, he held his arms away from his body and wrinkling his face in revulsion stamped his booted feet. He whispered another string of curse words below his breath and walked to the open spigot. Crouching, he rinsed his hands vigorously, rubbing them over and over under running water. Splashing his face and head, he rose and shaking his head, sprayed water in a wide arc around him.

Pepper pushed in beside him and threw handfuls of water on his jacket. Black sludge and slime dripped off of it. He smelled like decaying fish. Benny stood next to him patiently waiting for a turn at the water spigot, his face mirrored his revulsion. Every few seconds, he whispered explicit German words.

"Hey, be grateful it isn't garbage," Rob said gently, rising to his feet. He started to laugh, as large drops of water shiny in their wetness dribbled over his face. One drop hung like a dew drop from the end of his nose, and his voice, emerging rough and muffled, vibrated in his throat. "You guys wait here, I'll scout the parking lot first and look for any familiar vehicles. Then if it looks like I don't know anyone, I'll go inside and get the pizza." Walking away, he rubbed his hands over his head and face, wiping the water off on his jacket. He waved at Luke.

"What kind did you get?" Pepper called softly, as Rob hurried to cross the street.

"I got four medium combinations," he said, stopping next to their huddled shapes. "And I got four large Pepsis, too. C'mon, let's go!" Pressing buttons, they teleported, their bodies, melting like shadows, vanished into the misty night.

Appearing on their sleeping bags, Rob balancing the stack of pizza boxes and the bag of Pepsis, fell to his knees. Climbing to his feet, he lay the boxes down on a flat rock.

"I'm going for a quick wash and then change my clothes," Luke announced, jumping to his feet. "I'm not eating with this much filth on me. Put my pizza on top of the oven so it'll stay warm." Grabbing his kit, he ran for the creek.

"I'm coming too," Rob yelled at his running figure. Setting the boxed pizzas on top of the oven, he rummaged in his backpack and pulling out his kit ran after Luke. For a few seconds Benny and Pepper stared at each other. Their clothes were smeared with black mud and Benny's hair on the back of his head was coated with it. Shrugging, they laughed and grabbing their kits followed Luke and Rob.

Stripped of his clothes, Luke walked into the creek. Rob, Benny and Pepper followed, their voices subdued and muffled. They gasped, sucking in short gulps of air when the icy water met bare bodies. The bubbling water gurgled over its rocky bed, the sound a soothing remedy for frayed nerves. Soaping vigorously, they lay back beneath the surface for a second, and jumping up ran for the shore. Toweling dry, they picked up their soiled clothes and ran for the campfire. Throwing their dirty clothes in a pile, they rummaged through their backpacks, hurrying to cover their cold bodies.

"How 'd you feel when they were trying to get into your mind?" Luke asked, picking up one of the boxes of pizza. "I felt as if something was trying to creep through my brain, and then, it turned hot. I think they were doing it with their eyes. Whew! Their eyes were weird. Compelling somehow, to the point I didn't want to look away."

"I don't want to meet them again," Benny said, stuffing the crusty end of a slice of pizza in his mouth. Chewing vigorously, he swallowed and lay back with an exhausted sigh. "They're so advanced intellectually, they probably could control us in some weird way. Never again, and I do mean, never, if one of them starts to appear, I'm going to disappear."

"Me too," Pepper said emphatically. "If there's only a glimmer, I'm gone and I mean I'm gone. And I'm not waiting for anyone. I'll just use these magic buttons on this tool and presto, be somewhere else."

"With that I'll agree," Rob said. Staring absently at the slice of pizza he held in his clenched hand, his mind wondered. "I've come to some conclusions about the aliens. They don't appear here outside the mountain, by that I mean, they appear only inside the mountain. So . . . I think the spaceship has been rigged up as some kind of way station. They just don't seem to have the power to transport themselves from their world. And I'd really like to know whether their from our future, another dimension, or time-travel from another planet. And just maybe, wherever they came from, this spaceship was forgotten over the years. Maybe, when the computers on the bridge were turned on, it somehow produced a signal they could read again." Staring at the flickering flames for a second, he glanced over at Luke.

"And, I also think the aliens in the ice cave, are being held in suspended animation, frozen in some chemical way, and then, put on the ice. Maybe, Pepper's right." Rob shrugged his shoulders negatively. "They're from our own future or maybe even from another star system. Maybe in thousands of years we conquered space flight, so we could travel to distance worlds. I think if we experimented with some of the computers on the bridge, we'd find a map of their world. All I know is, their technology is way beyond ours."

Expelling his breath in a lengthy sigh, Rob smiled anxiously and, a worried puzzled expression crossed his face as his eyes skipped over each of them. "You know I've been having the most awful thoughts, all day. If they're from our future, maybe they came back to collect human sperm and ovum to strengthen their gene pool. I've even thought, they might want to interbreed with us to make a better specimen of human beings in the future."

Luke, Pepper and Benny booed, their voices noisy with humor.

"Yeah, maybe in thousands of years, humans evolved to physically weak specimens and they lost their ability to have sex," Benny volunteered. He laughed, the sound contagious in its spontaneity.

Luke yelled, a rude sound, noisy and exuberant. He choked on a suppressed laugh. "Hey, maybe the men can't do it and, they've come here to learn from us. I haven't seen any women trying to appear. They probably can't trust their women. They're sex starved, and maybe, they'd attack us on sight, because they see us as studs, really virile specimens."

They roared, their laughter loud and uninhibited.

"I'm not kiddin guys, be serious," Rob said. Stuffing his mouth with his last bite of pizza, he wiped it with the palm of his hand. "I've thought a lot about this and hard tellin what they wanted, because we can't understand them and frankly I'm afraid." He shuttered, physically shaking.

"I found the funnel that formed behind them fascinating," Luke said. "I imagine they're using it as a passageway from their world, but why can't they come through in their bodies. They look like images to me. They somehow landed here at least once, and we know that's true,

THE DEVILS PUNCHBOWL

because we've seen their spaceship and their bodies. We can prove that. Also, if they're just images, why did the guy on the end scream like he was being killed when he stepped backward into that void? It seemed like that dark mass devoured him. I'll never forget it, it'll haunt me forever." Shuddering, he stared beyond the fire into the dark shadows surrounding their camp. "Another thing, each of them held a crystal, so I think they have to be a power source."

Luke sighed, bending over his knees. "And I think when we use the tool, it seems easier to appear if you're familiar with where you're trying to land. We'd never been behind that green building, so we couldn't really picture it. All I thought about was the back end of the building and I landed in a Dumpster. An experience I'll never forget."

"Me neither," was coursed in shouts, as they all agreed.

"From all your thinking, have any of you decided what we should do about all this? Any solutions?" Luke asked. Gesturing, he waved his hands through the air pointing at the mountains. "We've already decided that we have to keep the cavern a secret, so I guess, I'll answer my own question and say we'll do nothing. All of us need an education. What we should do is forget about the cavern, until we get our degrees."

"Amen, amen," Pepper and Benny yelled together. Laying back on their sleeping bags, they laughed. Sitting up suddenly, Pepper stared first at Luke and then Rob. "Don't forget, we still have more to explore. There's that brilliant room down near the ice cave where the aliens are entombed, and the lighted area further north, past the entrance into the cave where the tunnel into the spaceship is. Then there's the long passage that ran vertically in the space ship. The one we thought was an entrance to the engine room."

"Yeah," Benny said, interrupting Pepper. "I'd like to find a way to get outside the ship and examine its plating, it probably could tell us a lot. There has to be an exit we could go through."

"Are we going to do any of that tomorrow?" Luke asked. "I'd really like to stick just my head through the wall in the weird hall that goes nowhere. Rob's upper body went through, so I think my head should, and after what happened today, we'll, have to have lookouts for the aliens. I'm not staying either, if everything around me starts to go weird like it did this afternoon." A grimace crossed his face, his somber expression changing, enhanced by the flickering firelight dancing over it. "Or, maybe we should take one more quick look around, call it quits and go home?"

"I don't see why we have to go back in the spaceship," Pepper said. "And besides, except for looking, what could we do? And, I vote that we never go near the weird passage again. It disappeared. It formed a black hole, an opening into cold, dark, empty space. I think it was an entrance for time travel, maybe even from another star system. Maybe, it could completely swallow one of us." He trembled, shrugging his shoulders. Naked fear formed a dark shadow within the enlarged pupils of his eyes. "What if, every time we make a trip into the spaceship, those aliens appear? Anybody else thought of that?" Pepper lay back on his sleeping bag, and turning on his side, propped his head up with his hand.

"I know I have," Rob answered. "I've thought of nothing else since we left there today. Maybe if we don't enter the spaceship for a while, they'll forget us."

"Okay, I agree," Luke stated. His eyes moved restlessly and, tracking the boundaries of their camp, came back to the small area around their fire. He stared at each of them. "Raise your hand if you're in favor of leaving in the morning."

Everyone raised their hand.

Whooping, they moved into a tight circle on their sleeping bags. They whistled and clasping hands, smiled at each other.

"Okay. C'mon," Benny quipped. Laughter danced in his eyes. "I'm not crazy about this part, holding hands. The hand I usually hold is soft and small. And I'll be deliriously happy when I get to hold it again."

Looking solemnly at each other, they spoke together, their voices falling and rising in unison. Speaking precisely and solemnly, they uttered a similar oath to one they had made up in kindergarten, not in the high-pitched excitement of childish voices, but in the deep cadence of manhood.

THE DEVILS PUNCHBOWL

"I swear by everything that is holy and sacred to me, I will not divulge to anyone, the knowledge of what we found in the cavern upon the penalty of my life, so help me, God."

"Hey, we haven't decided whether we're coming back every year. Are we going to do that?" Luke asked.

"Let's leave it until next year," Pepper groaned. "This is heavy stuff, I don't even want to think about next year."

"Yeah! Forget next year," Benny said, emphatically.

Rob grinned. "Here's to next year, Bro's," he stated. Laughing, he held up his cup of Pepsi, in a toast to the ambiguous next year.

Luke looked pensively toward the lake. "I'm going to miss this place, he thought. And then smiling to himself, he whispered. "Until next time. We'll be back." Rising to his feet, he shoved another log on the fire and picking up his kit left for the creek.

"C'mon, let's brush our teeth, I'm tired," Pepper said. Picking up their kits, they followed Luke, and hurrying back to camp, climbed into the soft warmth of their down-sleeping bags and zipped them closed.

Rob was the last. He cleaned up. Crumbling pizza boxes between his massive hands, he placed them with a log on the fire. Standing quietly, he watched as the boxes burning in a green-blue blaze turned into gray ash. Yawning, he raised muscular arms over his head and stretching as far as he could in every direction, released some of the built up stress and ache in his muscles. Stripping his Levis, jacket and sweatshirt off, he stepped between Luke and Pepper and crawling into his sleeping bag, lay back with a sigh.

"Night, guys," Rob called. He wiggled, and grunted, a long chest deep, satisfied groan. Sighing, he brushed his hands several times over the baldness of his head. Thank God, he thought, his face breaking into a wide grin at his own conceit. I can finally feel some hair growing back. Misty Dawn will like that.

"Hey guys," Rob whispered, his voice as sweet and dark as melting chocolate. "Today was a real winner. I really enjoyed myself. I got to meet some God-awful aliens, fall over a bunch of cans, immerse myself in rotten food and then roll around in the rotten stuff some more. I especially enjoyed falling over a bunch of garbage cans, and wallowing in putrid rotten food. A for real doozie, a winner," he repeated. He chuckled softly and snuggled further into his bag. "Especially the putrid garbage. It made my day." He laughed, the sound thick and heavy, rolled from deep in his chest.

"Don't remind me, Rob," Luke muttered darkly. "I'll never get the stench of rotten garbage out of my nose."

"Yuk!"

"Yeah, the smell was almost as bad as some of Pepper's jokes that backfired," Benny said. "I can remember . . ."

"Oh shut up," Pepper interrupted. Rummaging down further into the warmth of his bag he pulled it over his head. Muffled by the thickness of his down-bag, he added. . . .

"Sometimes, to hear you guys' talk you'd think my jokes were just my ideas. Remember, lots of them were jokes you wanted to pull on someone and I just went along with it." He snorted an indignant rude sound. . . .

"Besides you're beginning to sound like a bunch of gabby old women."

They laughed.

Enjoying the closeness of the moment, Luke thought about his friends. "I feel wonderful," he whispered to himself. They had conquered; solved most of their problems and he felt, all of them were immensely pleased with themselves. He was! They had made the right decisions.

Watching clouds drift lazily across the face of the moon, they fell asleep, twitching and turning as they dreamed. The moon climbed higher into the sky, its light painting the rugged landscape in soft shadows. Stars appeared, and then disappeared, as layers of clouds in restless drifting clusters moved across the sky, obliterating their shine.

A pair of large blue eyes became visible in the darkness and around them, a nebulous vapor materialized into a face. Gathering in the light cast by moonlight and the dying fire, the irises, dilated and huge, glowed a fiery red from deep within the pupil. The eyes moved restlessly over the sleeping figures, and then, holding an elongated tube of crystallized

THE DEVILS PUNCHBOWL

light up high, an infinitesimal ray traveled over the sleeping boys. Satisfied, the being nodded and turning his face upward looked at the stars.

"They're learning."

Garbled English emanated from the moving vapor. The image strengthened, brightening into a soft glowing mass in the dark. Curly, white-gray hair blew around its wrinkled face and the image swept it back, annoyance showing in the stiff aggravated movement.

"It's a beginning . . ."

"Slow, but at last, a beginning . . ."

"Perhaps now they're ready to learn."

The image sighed.

Luke woke abruptly. "What?" he mumbled. Waiting for an answer, he pushed the sleeping bag away from his face and lifting himself rested on his elbow. Sleepily, he listened. Straining to see the bumps that were his sleeping friends, he frowned, and wiping a hand across his eyes, yawned.

Silence.

Dark.

Everything was quiet, weighted down and hushed. Nothing moved. Rolling to his stomach, he covered his head and went swiftly back to sleep.

A log in the fire snapped, causing a chain reaction of crackling and hissing. The blue eyes within the cloud of vapor, watched patiently, until an acute anxiety clouded their depths. A whirlpool mass of circling, twisting darkness formed around the figure, and immersed in a diminishing eddy, the bright blue of the eyes started to fade. Raising a hand almost hidden by a moving mass of darkness, he pressed the elongated brilliant crystal against his chest, and vanished within the spinning dimensions of a darker black hole.

EPILOGUE

BOYS FIND TREASURE ON FATHERS' PROPERTY

ON JUNE 23, four local high school boys found a treasure in gold on one of their father's properties near Pacific Shores. It has been determined that the gold bars weighing approximately fourteen ounces each (troy weight) are thought to have been mined during the California Gold Rush. The parents of the boys, choosing to have their names withheld, are currently looking for a buyer. The money will be used to finance the boy's education.

Both the state and federal government wanted to claim the gold, but yesterday, issued a statement that except for tax purposes they have no interest in it, as it was found on private property.

AUTHOR'S NOTE

This is a work of fiction, all events and characters portrayed are strictly fictitious. Any resemblance to persons living or dead are strictly coincidental. I have used a certain license in my portrayal of events at Del Norte High School, at Crescent City and at the Devils Punchbowl. This was done only to make the story line a little better and to give my locations more pizazz.

I hope you enjoyed getting acquainted with Luke, Pepper, Benny and Rob and could relate to everything that happened to them. And especially, I hope you enjoyed reading the book, as much as I did writing it.

M. DALBEC MILLS

The Airel Photograph on the Cover of the Devils Punchbowl, is courtesy of the Smith River National Recreation Area